BOMBMAKER

DANIEL J. DAVIES

A NOVEL

BOMBMAKER. Copyright © 2023 by Daniel J. Davies.
All rights reserved. Printed in the United States of America.

ISBN 979-8-35090-368-3

For Mumsey

"Ah! To return to life! To stare at our deformities.
And this poison, this eternally accursed embrace!"

ARTHUR RIMBAUD

"Wherever you go, whatever you do, I will be right here waiting for you."

RICHARD MARX

PART I

September 4th, 1989

SIPPING this root beer was the last pleasant feeling he would ever have.

All this sweat was something he hadn't expected. But wearing the nice suit and tie was necessary to get past all the guard posts, to look the part and use the phony security passes forged by Marcel's team. So Fadi had scooted along Windsor Street on the little Vespa, already damp with sweat despite the nice breeze, despite being beardless for the first time in ten years. The bulky helmet didn't help things either. But Marcel had said it too was necessary. "This is a special helmet, Fadi. It can stop bullets. Imagine you are zooming toward the target, zooming toward immortality, and a bullet finds your head that stops you from igniting the charge."

About a half mile before the guard post was a little corner store. Fadi had parked the Vespa on the sidewalk and popped the helmet off, then went inside to spend the single dollar in his pocket on a cold root beer. He sat on a bench out front and cracked the can open, taking a long sip of the sweet stuff. The sound and taste of the drink weren't the first sensations today that he realized he'd never feel again. He'd had this same thought the whole morning: the sting from the razor on his neck, the crisp warmth of the shower, the coffee, the choke of the tie.

Fatu had never tasted soda at the time he first met her. Later she would allow herself one tiny glass of root beer with ice in the late evening at their home. To her it was a vice, like smoking, sneaking out to the porch, even hiding the glass behind her back, the shameful smile with her face down as she closed the door behind her. *To be able to serve her a tall glass on a tray, the bottle set beside it, lots of ice.*

He held the last sip in his mouth a few seconds, swallowed, then tossed the can into a recycling bin. He threw his leg over the seat of the Vespa, latched the chin strap of the heavy helmet, clutched the front brake, turned the key, and held his breath as he pressed the ignition switch. His chest buzzed as the engine started, and he breathed out. He had spent the last few months coaching those crafty Egyptians on how to turn this little bike into a big bomb. Much of the space formerly taken up by the 150 cc engine had been filled with meaner things, adding weight that required stronger wheels and housing, keeping the moped as skinny and innocent-looking as before but with a belly full of anger.

The rest of Windsor Street was a shaded lane of Arlington's nicest homes, few cars passing. Straight as an arrow. All the extra weight also made it difficult to steer. Despite practicing for several days with a dummy weight, something about this arrangement felt different, more lopsided. He whirred down the street at max throttle, thirty-two miles per hour, and on his right a long brick wall began, which he followed for a quarter mile until he came to the front gate.

Without hesitating he pulled up to the booth, where a guard greeted him and asked him to turn off the engine. Fadi showed him the perfect credentials, including his new ID badge with the clean-shaven face he didn't even recognize in the mirror. The young man looked at it twice, smiled. Then he said, "Morning Dr. Ross."

"Morning."

"Got you working on a Saturday too, huh?"

"Yes." He smiled. "At least I can come in a bit later though. Damned if I'll wake up at seven on my Saturday."

He laughed. "Wish I could say the same for myself." Then he leaned into the station and pressed the button. The arm swung upward. "Have a good one."

"You too, thanks."

He handed Fadi the badge and papers, which he put in his coat pocket. Then he squeezed the front brake, turned the key, and pressed the ignition button. Exhaled and cranked the throttle. The Vespa pushed him forward with its high buzz, pushed him forward as the arm closed behind him. That was the easier one, Code C access, visiting employee badge, not much scrutiny at the gate. They gave those to teachers, consultants, janitors.

The Roberts compound was huge, but Fadi knew the layout so well he could have given directions to any building in the place, could have told maintenance men where each power station was, each water meter. He was scooting along at a good pace now, trying to clear his mind, to think of nothing, to pray. But suddenly Marcel's voice blared in his ear. This, he knew, was the real reason Marcel had insisted he wear a helmet: so he could be the only thing Fadi heard, a surrogate conscience, blocking out all internal persuasion contrary to the mission, keeping the plan front and center. Less a shield against bullets than against any errant, abortive thoughts that might invade his skull.

"You are doing well, my brother. You are strong and calm, you are a warrior, you are holy, you are my brother."

Even the sound of the Vespa's engine couldn't drown out Marcel's sermonic pleading. They were watching him through binoculars. There were men in the hills tracking his path, only a few places along the route obscured by a building, the corner store for example.

Marcel knew to stop talking when Fadi pulled up to the second gate, this one manned by a guard who looked nearly identical to the previous one: young, clean, very kind eyes, the brows turned up in permanent sympathy.

"Morning, sir."

"Morning to you." He handed him the papers only.

"Thank you. Got you working today?"

"Yes, though…" Suddenly he froze. He couldn't get a word out, couldn't even think of what to say. The language he'd spoken his whole life was now like a foreign tongue lodged in his throat.

The guard looked up from the papers. "You okay, sir?"

Sweat fell into his eye. He tore at the chin strap, finally removing the helmet. Drawing a huge breath despite the clamping of his chest. "Yes."

The guard disappeared into the booth. *I'm finished. He's calling for help, and they'll realize I'm not Dr. Ross. Prison.* But he returned a moment later with a thermos.

"Here you go, sir. Little Coke. It's cold at least."

He poured some of the Coke into the thermos top and handed it to Fadi, who looked at it suspiciously. "Had a man pass right out at his post the other week. Hotter than hell."

He brought it to his lips, closed his eyes. It was cold. He took that first small sip and felt the sweetness in his cheeks then followed it with a gulp that emptied the cup. What a feeling, that simple kiss between his cheeks and the sugary water. He opened his eyes.

The guard was standing arms akimbo, an unworried smile and clear eyes. He was likely from northern Virginia, the manners and the bulk of him, the straight back in his fatigues. "Does the trick, doesn't it?"

He handed the cup back. "Yes. Yes, it does. I'm embarrassed."

"Maybe one more gulp there, sir?"

"Oh, no, thank you. I sit right next to the cafeteria in Caldwell, so I'll have a nice glass of water when I get in. Just so terribly hot in this suit, this helmet. But, you know, have to dress professionally, even on a Saturday."

The guard gave him a quizzical look.

"Coke machine. I sit right next to the *Coke machine.*" He fanned himself. "Guess I'm a bit flustered is all. The cafeteria is in *Hanson*, of course, closed today in any event."

The guard nodded. "Well, get inside to the AC, sir. I won't keep you." Then he stuck his hand out. "Name's Sam Hicks, by the way. Don't believe we've met."

The white hand hung in the air. Fadi looked at it while considering if the blast would reach this far, no way. It was meant to break the bones of the building, not to blow outward. He shook the man's hand, callused skin but the hand felt kind, an almost pleading sensation. "Ross. Phillip Ross. Phil."

"Nice to meet you."

"Likewise." As he put the damned helmet back on. "Take care now."

Just as he was cranking the gas, the man said, "Hope you're not lonely today."

"Sorry?"

"Caldwell." Motioning eastward with his chin. "It's empty, figured you knew. Only second floor folks work on Saturdays, and one through three are being scraped for asbestos. Workers aren't even in yet. You must be on another floor. Otherwise, workers will kick you out when they show up later."

He froze a moment at hearing this then managed to sputter out, "I'm on four, yes." He nodded and coasted off.

Empty. Do I turn back? Empty?! Eight months of planning and they hadn't discovered some damned asbestos treatment. This was now pointless. To Marcel, anyway. He could dismantle the building, the *symbol*, as planned, but the blast, the very last spasm of his life, would not take others with it. Empty. No, he had come too far, and he was so close to his end. What was in the building made little difference. And after he was gone, no one, save for him and this man, Hicks, would know that he had knowingly continued on toward an empty target.

He traveled inward, waffled concrete buildings on either side, benches in small grass areas for government workers to take lunch breaks. Empty parking lots. The motor, the sweat.

"Good work, my brother." Marcel's voice again in his ear, trapped inside the helmet.

Fadi glanced toward the hills beyond the eastern wall.

"Do not look up!"

He buzzed forward, coming to a wood sign that read "Caldwell." Then he brought the Vespa around to the back end of the building, down a hill, where he stopped with the engine still running. The rear entrance, right under the second floor, the perfect target for a well-placed *boom*.

Empty.

"Allah is in your heart, you are a great man, you are my brother, Fedayeen." Then words in Arabic followed that Fadi had heard so many times before, but the strange syllables evaded comprehension and might as well have been raindrops on glass.

11

He flicked open the special latch next to the ignition, set the switch two clicks to the left. This had all been his design, so ingenious, he now thought, to use the bike's electrical system to ignite the charge, no wasted space, just like the invention that had made him wealthy enough to retire, to pursue his *true* calling, as he'd said to his white mother all those years ago.

"Allah's voice, Allah's servant, Allah's champion…"

He looked at his tan hand on the throttle, the thing that would propel him toward the building and set off the blast. It looked nothing like Nadat's little hand. She and her mother making bread in the kitchen. Every movement of Fatu's was mimicked by Nadat's little version of her hand. Nadat would look up at her mother, repeat whatever she was doing, the smaller clump of dough squishing in her tiny fingers. Thank God she had gotten Fatu's eyes, "The Eyes of Fatima." That was how Marcel had described his daughter's eyes, a great compliment of beauty in Egypt. For a woman to have the eyes of The Prophet's daughter, and Nadat had gotten those eyes, but they were so little, and her hands were so little.

"My brother you will live on forever, you are a great servant, you are…"

He unsnapped the helmet and threw it to the pavement with a great *clack*. Then he loosened his tie and peeled his coat off. Though he knew Marcel and the others were watching, he dug into the bag at his feet and pulled out the expensive mobile phone his brother had recently bought him. He dialed the numbers, sweaty and shaking. The mechanical ringing was chopped up and distant.

"It's me. Everything…yes, everything is fine. Listen to me. I love you so very much." Tears with sweat, stinging. "I love you so much. I'm sorry. No…goodbye." He hung up and put the phone back into the bag.

The two hundred feet in front of him he could do with his eyes closed. The practice course in Marcel's warehouse had been made to exact measurements. The only tricky part was weaving between the stone pylons, which was why the tiny bike had been chosen. But it was the only way into the tender underbelly of this evil place; the Egyptians had assured him of that. With enough power and pin-point aim, they could bring down the entire southern wing. *Empty*, that his life would break in such a way.

He twisted the handle backward, released the brake, and was brought forward between the stone blocks, fifty feet away from the back door now. Closer, his thumb hovering over the ignition, the burst that would end this knotted string of feelings and thoughts, that would bring him back to Nadat and Fatu, but he didn't know, didn't know what was in that blackness on the other side of this door, but he charged forward, ever forward, and hoped God would greet him, God existed, that his two sweet girls still existed somewhere separate and good. Allah, Allah…not moving forward but the door getting bigger and moving toward him, and the door larger and larger, the door…Allah, Allah… Al*lah*, Al*lah*…Nadat, Nadat, Fatu…Nadat.

CHAPTER 2

Emma Ripley darted awake. It was that dream again, the ghostly Layth standing over her, grinning wide, no eyes in his sockets. Was she still asleep? No, the clock said 5:54; the digital numbers were too real. Her heart was a hummingbird, sheets wet and stuck to her legs. The memory of evil fucking *Layth* stuck as well.

She peeled off the covers, took her glasses from the side table, and put them on as she navigated the cold floor, heading toward the kitchen with the lights off. The room was touched blue with young light from the window, sterile across Formica counters as the coffee sputtered into the pot.

The old apartment had been revamped before she moved in. Refaced kitchen, new pipe work, fake hardwood floor panels throughout. Not a thing hanging from the walls, a few sticks of institutional furniture left behind: a table and chairs in the kitchen, the bed and bureau, a brand-new sofa that had somehow made it all the way from the 70s without being used. All cups, crockery, cutlery, flatware, and fridge had been provided, brand new. She wondered what poor government dipshit had previously called these premises home.

But Emma made every effort to avoid making this place her own, leaving any smudge of a personal watermark. *This is not my home.* Any comfort found in these walls would be false and ill-deserved. *This is not my home.*

After a quick breakfast of cereal and toast, she showered, dried her hair, put it up in her usual salt-and-pepper bun, and gave herself a look in the mirror. No makeup to smooth the wrinkles around her eyes, no lipstick, nothing to hide the puffiness. She put one earring in, paused, then removed it. Chose one from eight pairs of flats, one of three purses.

It took the usual forty minutes to trickle along the beltway from Fairfax to Arlington. She parked in the rear lot and scanned the card key at her belt while holding her coffee and books. The door closed behind her with a metallic echo in the basement. Lights blinked on overhead as she clacked down the hall. When she'd first found this alternate entry point — one that allowed her to circumvent the employee check-in post, the metal detector, and more importantly the stew of milling co-workers — she'd been a bit taken aback by the glaring security breach, that one could access the building with an anonymous card key, with a weapon even. But because she didn't want to lose her little secret passage, she'd kept the glitch to herself.

Her office was large, located at the rear of the building on the fifteenth floor. On the far wall opposite the window hung a framed photo of Reagan left by her predecessor and nothing else. The aging wooden desk held a computer, all the various standard-issue office supplies, and Evan's school photo from first grade.

She took a bag of tobacco and the rolling machine from the drawer and set to work rolling a cigarette while waiting for the computer to boot up. She smoked and sipped her coffee. Strong, blind-broken rays shone through the window.

This morning's tasks involved little more than scanning files of Arabic writing and highlighting every occurrence of what were referred to as "flag words," or anything that might be construed, amid this stack of civilian correspondence, as hostile literature. Although not at all according to protocol, she'd taken to simply translating the typed or written documents onto her computer, on which she could then use a program to search for any of the over one thousand flag words or phrases. Like her basement-door entry point, she'd kept this work-around secret from the folks upstairs, at least until such time as she could gain a senior enough audience to ensure that she got credit for her discovery.

At noon she headed to the cafeteria for the typical Tuesday offerings of Caesar salad, half turkey and Swiss, white roll and butter, and an apple juice. She took her lunch to the back parking lot and ate alone in the sun, smoking at the end and drinking the last of the juice.

There was a staff meeting at 2:00 that took place in a dim room and featured a grueling slideshow, during which she nodded off twice. On the way back to her office she stopped for a coffee. She was standing in the middle of a very long and gray hallway, slowly dropping five nickels into the vending machine. A cup popped into the chamber, there was a pause, and after some mechanical clacking around, the syrupy stuff poured into the cup.

"Hi, Emma."

She took the cup from the dispenser, did not turn around.

"Hi, John."

"Have a second?"

"Sort of busy."

"I just wanted to talk scheduling."

"Okay."

"The 25th is your weekend. But the Orioles are playing at Yankee Stadium. And Evan has always wanted to see a game there. And with some luck I was able to get tickets to two of the games. So I was thinking he and I would stay there Friday and Saturday, catch the games, see some of the city."

"So how are you proposing we do the weekends?"

He paused. "Well, see, the other thing is that the weekend before is his team cookout, which we agreed was more my thing. So I was thinking if you were okay with it, he'd just do those two weekends in a row with me and then the next one with you and we'd go back to the original schedule."

Still staring at the machine. "Will it just be the two of you?"

"Come on, Em."

"I'm just not sure how I feel about the *three* of you sharing a hotel room in a strange city."

In the reflection she saw him tilt his head, a classic gesture, nearly impossible to counter. "Come on, please?"

"I only get him every other weekend. You see him all week." She didn't know why she'd said that, maybe her innate need to argue about any little perceived injustice. It made perfect sense for John to take Evan to New York, same with the team cookout.

"I realize that," he said. "I'm just putting it out there. It's one weekend."

She took a sip of the coffee. Too hot to taste. "Fine." And shrugged a smile as best she could.

He smiled back. "Thanks."

Then she added, "But you need to give me more notice."

"Sure." Hands fiddling with the keys in his pocket. "Everything good? Working for Thompson still good?"

Damn that terrific smile.

A quick nod, another sip as she rotated herself away from him. "Take care." She walked down the empty, reflective hallway.

Back in her office, she shut the door, plunked down at her desk, and glanced at the picture of Evan. It had been just under three years since the quick divorce and custody arrangements, but it still stung when the actual details were mentioned, that she got to see her son only every other weekend, from Friday evening to Sunday afternoon. She was the mother. She was the one who was supposed to get the bulk of custody. All the other women she knew or heard about always got full custody, ceding the odd weekend to the dead-beat husband, who was all too happy to take the two-day offer.

So whenever the subject came up — and it did often — she felt like a negligent dad, some jerk who welcomes the freedom from responsibility now that the marriage is over, the dad who calls his son "champ" and "sport" because he barely knows the kid. And of course the whole thing was constantly brought to light because she and John worked in the same building, on the same floor. Co-workers invariably asked about her weekend with Evan every other Monday. They always knew whose turn it was.

To make things worse, John happened to be a pretty good father. And to make them even worse, he'd been a fine husband. They'd met in Morocco: he in the State Department, she an interrogator. There wasn't too much he'd had to do to get her back then. One of the few American men, working a foreign post, somewhat handsome, incredibly kind, bright. And with the things she saw all day, the deception, the various webs of lies and coercion and grown broken men, John's warm eyes and military manners were more than enough to get her into bed by week two.

Though she would never admit it to anyone, with the career she had chosen and the lifestyle she was living, it had been unfair of her to bring Evan into the world. And it did more than sting when she recalled how John had resisted the idea. Every point he had brought up was valid: how they were stationed in a country too dangerous and too hostile to rear a child, how neither of them could be certain in what hemisphere they'd be waking up from month to month. The painful part wasn't even that he'd been right, but that he had been the responsible one, the one to choose parenthood and rearrange his life to accommodate for their toddler son. It was Emma who had made the wise career decision at the expense of her family. John had picked the life of a father. He'd moved to Virginia, taken the lousy office job so Evan could grow up in a good school system with the grandparents a few exits away.

When they had first come up with the arrangement, they were both filled with a naivety usually reserved for much younger couples. He had insisted that Emma take the promotion and relocate to the more volatile Tangiers. Of course, that was no place for little Evan, so John had called in a favor and gotten that hum-drum position at Defense back in Arlington. But they'd been hopeful they could maintain the family: letters, high phone bills, long plane trips whenever possible. It was temporary and good for her career, good for their family's career. She could stay there a year, maybe two, eventually get a transfer to France, even settle back stateside as an instructor, when Evan would just be starting school.

As it turned out, their marriage was not tough enough to survive being split by the Atlantic, deprived of the nutrition of physical contact; the drawn-out silences they used to joke about in person became heavy things over the expensive phone lines. Every little story John told about Evan was like a knee to the stomach: you're a bad mom. Emma would respond with jabs at John's career and whatever small victories she could share about her own, though the highly classified and often illegal nature of what she was doing allowed her rare ammunition.

It dragged on for eight months, and the phone calls became less frequent, laborious for her and, she guessed for him too, because he rarely phoned. The insults became more overt, more personal. The pressure of being a single parent, of sitting at a desk filing papers all day had begun to weigh on John too.

Within a year, the phone calls were happening only about once per month, and the letters she wrote were mostly for John to read aloud to little Evan. Another ten months. Emma often considered whether, if there had been any appropriate candidates at hand, she would have had an affair. So of course she assumed John was cheating, bringing home younger women, introducing them to Evan. It was amazing how her imagination flourished as her exposure to actual facts diminished.

When her department was shut down amid accusations of inhumane interrogation, she had stared at the phone for an hour before picking it up and dialing. Her tone was alien, a mix of feigned joy at the news and terror at the prospect of coming home to a husband and kid she no longer knew. She didn't tell him the real reason, made it sound as if she'd finally gotten the domestic post she'd been applying for this past year, though he would later find out the truth.

The homecoming was as awkward as she'd feared. The way it felt to hug him at the airport. Even picking Evan up in what was meant to be the most sincere joy had actually felt sickening. As she touched her son's tiny body and the bones in his shoulders, she felt the weight of her absence, all those years expired and irreplaceable.

They went home and she saw his room and Evan ran to show her each and every one of his toys and the crusty paintings he'd done at pre-school.

After putting him to bed, she and John sat in the kitchen drinking wine, he discussing the boring details of his job — details she could tell he found boring — she mumbling predictions about the shortcomings of her new job. The cheap red wine dry on the roof of her mouth as she glanced around at John's poor attempt at decorating, store-bought pictures, lime paint in the dining room. It felt like a first date where she'd gone home with the guy way too soon.

Hours later they were undressed and huffing around John's sparse bedroom. That first night back was filled with the muted sparks and fumbling of two strangers back from the bar. Emma thought it wonderful and exhilarating, and as they sprawled across scattered sheets afterward with romantic props like moonlight and sweat and a wine bottle, she actually felt alright. All those years ago there had been something between them. Was it absurd to think it could be regained?

John made every effort to sew things up, and Evan was already as bright and cheery as he'd prove to be in later years. But for Emma the damage done by the years away, along with her suddenly mediocre position, could not be repaired. Evan still clung to his father as they watched TV on the long sofa, and she and John were never able to replicate the hope contained in that first night back together.

They both showed an expertise at prolonging an unhappy marriage, pretending long silences were okay or not there at all, tossing the occasional subtle attack, or using Evan to make the other feel like a shitty parent. With work and commuting and all the duties a three-year-old required, there was remarkably little time for the two of them, and this they filled with idle work chat or household chores or talk about their son.

Evan turned four, then five. Emma and John went months without sex, and when they were together it was always incredible, but more the result of prolonged chastity and alcohol than any natural chemicals. And Emma was certain that John must have been thinking too that this could go on forever, this sort of daze they were living in, this blank need to keep the family intact, driven perhaps as much by John's perfect upbringing as by Emma's complete lack of a familial example.

Her affair hadn't been planned. And the short, muscly, pock-marked Marine from her hometown in north Florida wasn't as attractive as John, nor as well-bred or charming. And meeting him in that clean hotel wasn't even as tantalizing as the occasional romps she and John had. Slow months had begun to clump together: a sad job and a home life with imperfection she was helpless to point out. But it was there, nonetheless, something absent even with her perfect husband and child. The uninteresting little staff sergeant had simply shown interest, and they'd had a bit in common to talk about. But mostly it had seemed like an exit, even though Emma would need a few years before she could admit that. It had been a way out of that stupor.

Now here they were. Same building, same floor, same son, scheduling weekends with no more warmth than a stranger in an elevator pushing the button for you.

The last hours of the day were the worst. The green letters on the computer blurring and burning her eyes, the swishy Arabic characters on paper melting into each other. She did very little from three o'clock on. Chain smoked sometimes, sometimes sipped the black vending machine coffee. And she thought about her first sip of icy gin.

The sunlight shifted across her desktop, slatted and clean, the yarns of smoke all that reminded her that time persisted even in this room. In the afternoons, her memory came back at its loudest, at its most horrifying. The screams of grown men, strong, tough men who could withstand anything unable to withstand the machinations they devised, the clever breaking down of a person. Faceless shrieking echoed down empty hallways.

Alec fucking Randolph. That was all she could think as she entered her office to find a stone-faced, broad-shouldered black man sitting in the chair, twisting around to look at her, his flattop still immaculate but graying above the ears.

"Mr. Randolph." She walked in, holding a hot coffee. "What a surprise."

"Emma."

As she moved around to the other side of her desk, he rotated his torso to follow her. "Can I get you a coffee?"

He looked at the paper cup with the playing cards around the side. "Thank you, no. I hope you aren't busy."

She sat and put the cup on her desk. "Well, actually, I am. Quite."

He studied her in silence, a classic trick of his to make someone feel ill at ease. But it wouldn't work; she knew the games too well. She had to make him say the next thing without prompting.

He stood. "Mind if I close the door?"

She said nothing, and he walked over and shut the door. "There we go." Returned to his seat. "How's Evan?"

She took a sip of her coffee, nodded.

"And John? I hear he's now in Defense as well."

She nodded twice, slowly. And Randolph started with his little silence trick again, but she could tell he thought better of it. "Aren't you at all curious what I've been up to since we worked together?"

"No. And I'll assume you know damn near everything I've been up to. Keeping on top of information is what your department does, right? Tabs? Keeping tabs on all of us?"

He smiled, looking upward as he rubbed his short gray-and-brown hair. "Well, you're busy here. I'm sure very demanding work, this sorting through subversive literature is taxing and requires a lot of you. So I'll get to it. I've been sent here, as you may have guessed, because we want you back."

In an unaffected voice, "Thank you very much for thinking of me, but I must respectfully decline." She smiled.

"For something specific. Something you're well equipped for."

"I doubt that."

"Emma, this is something you could be of great service on."

"I've got that here."

"You do?" He smiled and looked down, regarded one of his fingernails. "Tell me, when's the last time you actually felt useful here? Felt as if you were being taken full advantage of, your education, experience, everything you do well? When's the last time you had that feeling? Even the least bit of praise?"

"Every day."

"I mean, you could probably go months without producing a single document, a single bit of work, with no fear of reprisal. And no praise or sense of worth when you've done well. I know this sector, Emma. I know the kind of dead-end people they get to work here. And I know you're not one of them."

"This is what is right for me."

"I also know Upstairs has become aware of what goes on here. Or, rather, what doesn't."

She paused to consider his face. Of course he would use such vaguely deceptive tactics to coax her away, little lies, little prods. It was what they worked in all those years. You lead your target just a touch off his intended path and you've got him. Get him to believe one tiny untruth. But at the same time, she could completely believe that Randolph would know such information. The high-ranking assholes he golfed with.

"That's right," he went on, "the top, oh…six floors of this building will look very different in about five months. Too much funding has been given to a department that produces approximately nothing." He studied her a few seconds then added, "But John will be fine. Your son will be fine."

It's an overseas post he wants me for. He wants to send me abroad. He's thinking I'll be concerned about Evan because I'll be away, so he wants me to feel secure that John will still have a job.

"A hardship post, I'll assume?"

A smile. "That's why we want you. Nobody *thinks* as you do."

"Spare my ass the smoke, Alec. How many before me?"

"I'm sorry?"

"Who'd you go to before me? You at least went to Benning, the pokey prick."

"Benning is dead."

A slight alarm, the awareness of which she could see reflected in his face.

"Heart attack. First tee."

"First tee?"

"I was with him actually. It wasn't a quick one. And I'll have you know that prick was my good friend of over twelve years."

"Well, I'm sorry for your loss. And for the program's loss. He'll be impossible to replace."

"We want *you* to replace him. We want you back doing what you do. And *this*…" He waved his hands around at the nearly blank walls. "… isn't it."

"I have to be near my son. I won't leave him again."

"We can arrange that you'd be near your son. This post is very nearby. In fact, your current commute from Fairfax would be decreased by two whole exits." He grinned.

She reached for the coffee cup but simply wrapped her fingers around it before moving her hand to the top drawer, pulling out the bag of tobacco, the rolling machine, and papers. She filled the chamber with moist tobacco, made a core, and then sent a paper through the machine, licking the gum. And as she stared vacantly at the dim window with the cigarette in her mouth she flicked the Zippo open. Without looking at Randolph, "You mind?"

He began to wave his hand, but Emma was already lighting the thing. She sat back, still looking toward the window. "I can't do what we did."

"This isn't what we used to do. As you know, most of the tactics formerly open to us are no longer considered viable. And besides that, being at a domestic post…"

"Bullshit. You don't want me for some cock-sucking desk clerk."

"I see the language hasn't changed."

"This is here in Washington, and you need someone with an Arabic background…"

He nodded.

"…coercion, intelligence rendering, manipulation." She could see this made him uncomfortable, so she added, "*Torture.*"

A grimace.

"Right, Alec?"

"No."

"No?"

"You know as well as I that certain public…overreactions have caused our sector to behave more discretely."

"I know that? What I know is that we've never exactly been held to any sort of scrutiny. How am I supposed to buy that there would be anyone watching your people, anyone to ensure the actions of Benning aren't repeated?"

"I don't think you realize how good a man Benning was."

"And you were never in a room with him. You don't realize how goddamn brutal and conniving and soulless he was."

"Benning was one of the best people I've ever known. I realize you've seen some things. You and he and the others had to undertake some charges that the rest of us wouldn't envy. But he understood all the while why he was doing it. We never shared any personal information, as you know. So the only concept each of you had of the other was based on how you acted in your duties. But Benning had very personal reasons for caring about national security. In making sure radical forces in that part of the world never found their way over here." He laughed and shifted in his seat. "But this isn't about him. This is about whether you want to take a crack at turning your foundering career around. Whether you want to feel useful. Whether you want to be able to go home to that empty government home of yours and at least think that you've protected Evan, even if you can't be a mother to him every day."

"I don't think like Benning anymore. There's a limit to what I will do. That fucking building of yours over there still keeps me up at night. I don't need another one here. What we did to Layth…"

She noticed her breathing was rapid, her forehead sweating. She took a drag, which sent her into a coughing fit. Randolph didn't make the slightest move, only waited until she was done. She had always liked that she wasn't treated like a woman with them, never the least bit of chivalry, no door-holding or tending to her comfort, no more than they would a man. No cliché attempts at work-place indiscretion. Just the work.

"What we're offering is the chance to continue what was left unfinished back in Africa. We're talking about the same group, the same bunch of horrific human beings who have always been poised at our front door. But they've grown bigger and more dangerous, the most dangerous to our domestic position of any group on the face of the Earth. I'm offering a chance to pick up what you left behind."

"I left that shit behind for a reason. Nothing we did made things any safer here."

"I think with this project you'll feel differently."

"I doubt that."

"This one is from right here."

She paused, looked at him, and his eyebrows lifted in that classic bit of patience.

"This one, if you will look at the file, I think will interest you immediately." He reached into a briefcase on the floor.

"No need to show me anything."

But he ignored her, setting a manila folder thick with papers across the desk from her. "Just look at the profile."

She sat upright, held her cigarette high as she crossed her other arm under her elbow. "Aren't you forgetting something? Your requisite little spiel, security, classified, et cetera?"

"Needless to say, this information is of the most classified kind. In fact, it doesn't exist."

"So you won't mind taking it off my desk then."

"I trust you not to go leaking this to anybody. You know it would do no good."

Silence. She placed the cigarette on the tray, and the smoke crept up in a hesitant wave toward the very dim sunlight. The same smoke that benchmarked the path of her days into their boring little segments, that gave her a tiny bit of comfort during the excruciation that was every other second of her day.

"You're curious, you know that. You can read this, without any harm, no commitment. At least out of curiosity. Why not read it?"

She hesitated, then reached across and took the file, sat back, and opened to the first page. Case profile. Two photos paper-clipped to the top corner. An Arabic man, likely Magreb, maybe Moroccan, one with beard, one without, very tan. No turban. She'd read these profiles hundreds of times. The first page outlined the suspect's background, place of birth, any known terrorist alignments, sometimes offered connections to actual attacks, displayed all known kin, domestic relatives. In this case, all the basic information was very typical of a suspected terrorist living in the States. The man had been schooled at The University of Massachusetts, then MIT, led a common yet exemplary life with zero inflammatory behavior before a short string of attacks. What was different from all the other dossiers was in bold letters at the bottom of the page: "**Suicide Bombing**."

But it was the Location of Target that was completely atypical of anything she'd read all those years in Morocco or Egypt. "Arlington, Virginia, United States of America."

She looked up at Randolph. "This is Caldwell."

He nodded.

She remembered the barrage of news coverage, the *Post* articles for weeks, the exposé attempting to outline what, exactly, the government was up to in the Caldwell Building. But still, why would this be some sort of classified, top-secret case. This was national news, and last she had heard it was vaguely connected to Al-Thaghr. But as in most suicide bombings, it was a case for ballistics, ascertaining the signature of the bombing style, scanning all known terrorist publications, dealing in informants and counter-terrorism. This would have nothing to do with her.

She looked up at Randolph, scrunched her brow. He seemed to read her confusion. "You're wondering what is so different about this, besides the nice little setting in our own backyard. Wondering where we fit in. Well, and this is certainly just within these walls. I don't have to tell you what happens if this leaks, do I?"

She stared at him.

"He's alive."

"Who is?"

He pointed to the folder in her hands. "Subdallah. He's alive. And he's been right here in Washington these past ten months."

CHAPTER 3

At least it was Tully today and not Wilson or MacNamara. Tully was
the only one who knew how to feed a person. He took a measured
quantity of oatmeal, slid it a little into Fadi's mouth, and made sure
none slipped down his lips. If a little happened to spill, he cleaned it
up immediately. Fadi knew the two nurses simply didn't care for him,
which was why they left food to crust around his lips, on his chin, his
neck, sometimes until it was Tully's shift and he took a nice hot towel
to clean his face.

Today it was Cheerios for breakfast, and Tully sat in a sort of stupor,
scooping five or six O's, a bit of milk. He said "Okay" each and every
time he approached Fadi's mouth with the spoon. Fadi guessed he was
a little slow, maybe the very thing that made him a good orderly, his
gummed-up mind unable to grasp how redundant this routine was or
how top-secret or high-interest the detainees were. Fadi couldn't help
but wonder: who else is in here with me, perhaps just behind this wall?
A few old friends?

It wasn't light out yet, though he guessed it was about 7:30. A dim
glow pulsed through the barred little window, and only half of the gray
ceiling lights were on.

Nurses came and went, mostly barking orders at Tully for taking
too long with the bed pan or new sheets. And Tully would simply bow
his head, nod a few times. However long Fadi had been in this place,
months, a year, Tully had become the only person he looked forward to
seeing. He was kind enough, and he sure didn't come in and ask questions for hours like the others. On the weekends, when the nurses were

on half shift, Tully would bring in checkers or Connect Four, both of which were easy enough to play with only half a hand.

Months earlier, Fadi had asked Tully to loosen the belts across his thigh. They'd been secured by MacNamara, too tightly as usual, and there was a great pain coming from below his knee. He remembered how confused Tully appeared when he'd mentioned his shin. Tully looked down at the space where his lower leg would have been then back up at Fadi. He'd smiled and gone ahead with changing the sheets.

After Tully had finished feeding him, he wiped Fadi's mouth with a wet towel, nodded, turned Fadi's bed to face the far wall, stood, and limped out of the room. He could hear the dragging of Tully's sneaker on the floor, a sound he heard throughout the day, the rubber squeak down the hallway like a clock ticking.

The early mornings were the longest part of the day. There was no means of telling time in this room, only that small window, glowing like a television set left on in the early dark. There was breakfast and then hours would go by with the little box getting brighter, and shoes down the hallway outside, never any voices, nothing on the walls. Even one of those anatomical diagrams adorning most doctors' offices would have been a welcome addition.

He'd gotten used to the itching sensation coming from his lower legs or his missing left arm. That had been the worst in the beginning, tied down, squirming this way and that, unwilling to call for help. But he'd found a way to concentrate and control the discomfort until the itch went away. What he couldn't get past was the wisp-like pain he felt in his right leg. No amount of wiggling or meditation could make that go away. It was in his mind to begin with, but during those first few months he'd still look down at where his feet should be, where his left hand should be. His brain would send the message to clench his fist, hoping that would defeat the pain. But it was only made worse.

If it was a sunny day, a little square of light from the window would fall near the fire extinguisher across the room. This was around the time the doctors would come in. Fadi called this noon. Although even when he'd finally begun speaking and had asked the doctor what time it was, he got no response. A block of true sunlight, dashed on its way to the floor by five bars in the window, and so five dark lines too moved across the floor and up the wall, made italic as the sun shifted westward.

When the square of sunlight hit the fire extinguisher, Fadi waited. Today, it took a long time for the doctors to arrive. There were a few metallic *clacks* outside the door as it unlocked, then nurse MacNamara shuffled in, her squeaky little sneakers and wide hips followed by Dr. Bauer and then by a third woman Fadi hadn't seen before. Behind them was Tully, pushing a wheelie table with a tray of lunch on it. He slid the table to the far side of Fadi's bed then stood there as if frozen. On the tray was a paper cup of tomato soup, tuna sandwich on flimsy white bread with too much mayo, a stack of baby carrots, carton of orange juice, a stale-looking shortbread cookie, and some black tea.

"Morning, Fadi." Bauer looked at the clipboard, which might as well have been affixed to his coat by chain. He always had that damned thing, doodling and scribbling notes, gazing at it whenever he addressed Fadi.

"Good morning."

Bauer looked up, smiled. "Well. You're in a good mood today." Then he turned to the nameless woman at his side. "Mr. Subdallah rarely speaks a word to me."

"How are we this morning?" Looking back at his clipboard.

What possible information could he be looking at? What has changed in my vitals or his chart over the months? Fadi said nothing in return.

"Fadi, I'd like to introduce you to Captain Fuller. She'll be visiting with you regularly. Taking Mr. England's place."

"Ah, yes, taking Mr. England's place. I see. And now that the charming Mr. England is gone, perhaps you could tell me his real name."

Bauer ignored him and looked down at his clipboard.

"Or perhaps simply tell me how you landed on such a silly alias for a man with a British accent. Why not Mr. Clapton or Mr. Python?"

Bauer turned to Emma. "Captain Fuller, you'll soon find that Mr. Subdallah has a penchant for asking slightly...asinine questions. And that..." He stopped, turned to Tully, who'd simply been standing at Fadi's bedside, smiling from person to person, uncomprehending. In a bright, kindergarten-teacher voice, "Tully, thank you."

With his mouth gaping open, Tully nodded twice quickly then set the paper bib around Fadi's neck. He took the spoon from the tray and scooped a bit of soup, placing his hand below it as he guided it toward Fadi's mouth, saying, "Okay."

Fadi reluctantly obliged. Then Bauer said, "No, Tully, it's not lunch time. Thank you, that will be all."

He stood.

"You can *go*, Tully."

He nodded and walked around the tangle of people on his way toward the door.

Emma couldn't help but feel a twinge of sympathy for the man, even at first glance. He was obviously missing some wires upstairs, and as he headed out the door she noticed how twisted his gait was, one leg dragging behind as if nearly dead. It had long been the practice of such places to hire the mentally feeble; such men were perfect for the menial jobs needed within such top-secret walls. Emma thought back to the man in Cairo who'd rinsed out the cells with a garden hose. That same look: no one home.

"So," Bauer continued, "you see, Mr. Subdallah here…"

Emma interrupted. "Why is this prisoner in such heavy restraints?"

She turned to MacNamara then to Bauer. They were silent.

"Nurse, loosen those belts across his sternum and arms, and completely remove the ones across his legs. Those are unnecessary. You can restrain his arm with leather straps. The point is to keep him here, not to cut off circulation."

The nurse hesitated, looked at Dr. Bauer, who nodded without making eye contact. So she set about adjusting the straps.

Emma slid the single chair over to the bedside, sat a few feet from Fadi, who kept his gaze fixed on the ceiling. Just as she had instructed him to do, Bauer began to read aloud from his clipboard. Even though she'd been thoroughly briefed on Fadi's circumstances, she'd told Bauer to read from his profile, in front of the patient, in order to make him believe this was her first exposure to his case, a way to make herself seem less informed.

"Amputation of left arm at the elbow upon arrival in ER, along with index and ring fingers of the right hand. Five days later, due to complications from third-degree burns, bone fragments, and infection, the patient's legs were both amputated, right leg below the knee, left leg at the thigh. Third-degree burns over the neck and right shoulder as well as across the right side of the abdomen. Eight broken ribs, shattered collar bone, twelve broken teeth, broken mandible, crushed orbital bone, shattered pelvis, detached retina in the right eye…" He added cheerily, "Only one cracked vertebra, loss of hearing in one ear." He turned the page and exhaled. "Skin tissue treatments, 1, 2, 3, 4…5 rounds of surgery to correct spinal issues and internal organ damage, unable to correct retinal damage." He looked up. "And how are your new teeth, Fadi?"

Fadi smiled at him, bright, fake-looking dentures. He chomped once.

"Prisoner was…"

Fadi interrupted. "Prisoner, patient, guest. Which is it today?"

"…was unresponsive for about the first two months, in and out of consciousness, and then when he did manage to stay awake for more than a few minutes at a time, he tended to only grunt or moan. And when he got past all that, he was completely silent for a good month. But he'll talk to Tully. Won't you, Fadi?"

No response. And then a few seconds later, he fixed his eyes on Emma. That one eye of his was still very large, with red veins, even into the iris. He jerked his head sideways, motioning Emma to come closer.

Bauer waved his clipboard. "Careful. Nurse…"

"It's fine," said Emma. "What is it?"

She held her ear close to Fadi. "He's not really a doctor. Did you know that?"

Emma looked over at Bauer, who was busy scribbling something onto his clipboard.

"He comes in every day around noon. He sits where you're sitting, and he asks me questions. Not things a doctor would want to know. He asks about my family, about my friends, about very specific friends. That clipboard, I have seen it. It's blank most days or has little drawings on it, little doodles of swords and shields."

She glanced back at Bauer. Nurse MacNamara was now standing at his side.

"Are you going to ask me the same questions? Do you want to know about my friends as well? You aren't a doctor. You are a captain. But you have come in and said you aren't a doctor, like Mr. England did. I hope you are better than he was. I told him everything I know, and yet he wasn't satisfied. He was an angry one, Mr. England. I found it funny that he would spend several hours visiting me, doing little things to make me uncomfortable, not letting me sleep, turning up the heat, putting a big duvet across my body. Do you know how hot you get without extremities? I didn't realize, but you get very hot. Anyway, after all he did to make me sweaty or tired, the nurses and poor old Tully would act like regular staff and make me comfortable again. It's like you people don't know who you are or what you're allowed to do. At least Tully has the decency to point me east twice a day."

"I didn't realize that was part of protocol."

"Mr. England always made sure to straighten me back out."

Fadi smiled again, that wide, plastic smile.

"I'm sure I'm better than Mr. England."

Fadi fixed those two different eyes on her. The damaged one lifeless but like a searchlight, while the healthy one was striking, a sort of crystalline color. She recognized it from the extensive files she'd had to pore over the previous two weeks. The school pictures of Fadi as a younger man, before the beard. They weren't allowed to shave the beard; that was a specific stricture in the new Practices brief she'd had to memorize. Had to respect the prisoner's religious beliefs, a far cry from Egypt and Morocco, even rotating his bed toward Mecca.

"Doctor Bauer. Nurse. Could you please leave us alone for a few minutes?"

Bauer stopped scribbling on the clipboard, looked over at nurse MacNamara. "I'm afraid we can't do that, Captain Fuller."

"Why not?"

He motioned for her. She stood and walked over to him. He whispered, "Protocol dictates that no fewer than two personnel attend to the subject at all times. New protocol. We can't leave an interrogator alone in here with him."

"Are you kidding?"

33

"I'm afraid I'm not. Medical staff only. Surveillance tapes go missing, no witnesses." When he saw Emma was still unsatisfied he added, "Mr. England."

She paused to study his face. A few scars down the left side, the other cheek pockmarked. Strangely, she had never been told Bauer's rank. He was certainly military, but she believed Fadi: he was no doctor. She glanced down at his notes. Childish drawings of huge medieval swords and shields. He clamped the board to his chest.

"Okay, Doctor," she said loudly. "Of course."

This was a poor introduction. She'd already displayed a lack of authority in front of Fadi, a negative when she needed to establish her ability to increase his comfort. If she seemed like an important person, he'd be more prone to believe her promises. It was rare within Arab communities for men to respect low-ranking women, though this man wasn't exactly like the Arabs she had dealt with in the Magreb. Someone like Fadi, who had been in both extreme discomfort and extreme isolation for roughly ten months, would be susceptible to both approaches, the promise of added comfort, the appeal of finally having a companion, someone he could trust. He'd obviously taken to Tully, maybe she could even use that.

She walked back to the bedside, sat down, and pulled the metal chair closer. Offering him a smile. "Looks like we can't get any privacy around here."

He was quiet.

"You can talk to me, you know. I'm not going to start in with the serious questioning today. I promise. You'll see I keep every promise. But today, you can feel free to talk to me as if we're both just regular people. I'm not looking for you to disclose any information." She leaned forward. "So, let's try again. Looks like we can't get any privacy around here."

Fadi was silent again. Then he cleared his throat, seemed to consider something. "I have enough privacy, thank you. I'm alone most of the day."

"Do you prefer to be around people? Or do you prefer privacy? When you were outside, which did you prefer?"

"People. For a few hours, anyway, the right people. Other than that, I liked to be alone. I liked to work."

"Me too."

"You too? Is that part of your method? You pretend to be just like me, we become friends, I tell you who my other friends are?"

"Yes, that's part of it. But today my method is to actually just talk with you."

"Why?"

"Your case fascinates me. No one has ever survived a suicide bombing. Later, I will read you, your visual cues and gestures, your responsiveness, figure out what it is you want."

"You will be disappointed." He turned away from her as much as possible, as much as the girds and his missing limbs would allow. "There is nothing I want." He stared toward the little window, the little box of real light to remind him this wasn't some limbo before heaven or elsewhere. "Nothing on this earth."

CHAPTER 4

Nourredine Rahman Subdallah came to America in 1948, celebrated his seventeenth birthday by praying and asking God to let him survive the long freight from Morocco, stuffed into a makeshift cabin with twelve others. It was a secret room with a lock on the outside, a small hole for a toilet, and plenty of rice, beans, and water. His only friend had secured a job for him in Somerville, Massachusetts, bussing tables at a greasy little spoon in Davis Square, working sixty-five hours a week, between that job and his job cleaning buses at night. He would later joke to his son that he was a bus boy in the morning and a bus man at night.

He shared a single room in Boston's Arab-rich South End with two other men: one his Moroccan friend, the other a Syrian with halitosis and a love for Twinkies. The one day they had off was Sunday, which was when they could adhere to a regimen of prayer in the safety of their little smoke-filled room. On the other days Nourredine at first felt incredible guilt, but there was simply no time for him to pray, and besides that he was afraid to stick out further by excusing himself for *salah*.

In this way several years passed quickly, Nourredine living and working illegally, earning a pittance, the scraps of which he still managed to hoard, sending sixty dollars each month to his parents in Beni-Mellal. "Yes, I am praying. Yes, I will return. America is beautiful."

On his day off he would gather friends together for epic soccer matches on a field below I-93, playing for hours, Nourredine able to skip around the others, the ball sticking to his foot at will, or flying on a curved string to an unsuspecting teammate's head at the goalmouth.

The games reminded him of Beni-Mellal, the neighborhood matches on dirt courts with skeleton goals and bare feet, how he used to control the pace, the flavor of the game, calmly asserting himself over frenzied, faster players. After a week of being talked down to at work, feeling like a dimwit, he needed a place over which he could still exact control. Afterward the men lied sweaty and smoked and talked about their homes or plans to move families to America.

While working a late night sweeping buses in the lot, he met a French-speaking woman from West Somerville, the daughter of Canadian professors. Lara was suspicious at first, this quiet woman, but that she spoke French seemed like a miracle to Nourredine, who after two years still struggled with English, and managed to come off as little more than a six-year-old in speech. And the only people with whom he could speak Arabic or French were the men packed tight in those smoky cafes and apartments in the South End. These men spoke of Arabian wives and tradition, knitting themselves ever more closely together with Muslim brothers. But Nourredine had other dreams.

He saw this beautiful little Francophone nymph at least twice a week as she debarked the last bus of the night from Cambridge. After noticing some of the books Lara was clutching, he went to the library and put several French poems to memory. The next week he greeted her with flourishes from Cocteau, two or three lines here and there as she walked by, and he'd smile and shrug. Lara had no idea what or who he was quoting but eventually responded to the attention and began to stay behind on the gray-lit, empty bus a few extra minutes while Nourredine picked up the newspapers and swept old cigarettes and dirt into a pan, explaining excitedly how he planned to open his own restaurant on Elm Street.

"How would it be different?" she asked.

"It will be the cleanest place in all of Somerville. I am the greatest cleaner in the state." They carried on their secret friendship for months, all alone on their own bus, free from the gaze of the local white men. Until eventually Nourredine worked up the courage (preluded by a poem) to ask her on an actual date.

Nourredine had to become a legal US citizen before he could start his own business. And after only a few dates with Lara, he decided they were ready to start a life together and late one night on the bus asked her to marry him. Her parents, though proud of their progressive airs, fought Lara in private about her plans.

"Your union will not be welcomed in this town, in this country."

"We will stay anyway."

"And your children? What about their lives? They will be neither white nor Arabic."

"They will be your grandchildren. You will love them."

"Lara, we only want you to have every chance. You have your schooling, you have this country. Why do you want to make it hard on yourself?"

"I'm in love with him, Mom. It's very simple, I'm afraid. And you will love him too, I know, and you will certainly love our children. I only wish you would skip past all this so we can get on with our lives."

It was still months before they truly accepted him, the exact moment of which Lara could recall years later, an imperceptible slump in her father's posture and countenance as Nourredine sat at their table and recounted his trip across the ocean. They began to find his odd French accent worldly rather than uneducated, his high enthusiasm downright American rather than ignorant. Nourredine seemed to sense this too, because it was later that night, as the two men drank coffee in the cold, that he had asked Mr. Peau's blessing to marry Lara. The answer was a hand on his shoulder, a squeeze with a grin.

In Somerville in the 50s, even as infectious and reassuring as Nourredine's smile was, the couple attracted unwanted eyes wherever they went. Their life together was tough at first, even with the nice little two-story place on Mass Ave paid down by Lara's parents and Nourredine's growing jar of cash. There were permits, building code violations, and above all the resistance of the old guard to a Moroccan (or, as they called him, an Egyptian) re-opening The Town Diner on the corner of Highland and Elm, right in Davis Square, competing with Shelly›s, which was a filthy place no one even went to anymore. Rocks through front windows, paint cans tossed across the slats, unresponsive police. And at first very few people responded to his want ad.

But five months after putting down cash, The New Town Diner was open for business. Although it was a slow evolution, even the gruff old Irish from Winter Hill would make their way in before work for breakfast and coffee and the free papers, and then they began bringing their families on Saturdays.

Nourredine kept his promise to Lara: his was the cleanest place in town. He instituted four rounds of deep cleaning per day: a small one first thing in the morning, another after the breakfast rush, one right before dinner, and the biggest one after closing. The place smelled like bleach and lemon, and Nourredine was right there with the staff, scrubbing grease clumps from the griddles, mopping, scraping dried ketchup and sticky spilled shakes, refilling the napkin holders, piling the garbage out back. That he worked right down in the grease endeared him to the proud and reluctant local white men on his staff.

The coffee was strong, the food nothing special but served on very clean plates, without the usual heavy taste of the griddle. And Nourredine's grin was hypnotic. New patrons would enter to find his wide smile at the door, or behind the counter, his apron white and starchy, and every now and again he'd greet a customer with a "Bienvenue," which unwittingly alleviated a lot of the locals' resistance to patronizing "an Egyptian Arab." They soon learned that he was, in fact, from Morocco, a name with which they were unfamiliar enough to, when coupled with the French, find benign.

Nourredine worked from 5:00 am to just after 9:00 pm. Lara was able to knock off from her job as a receptionist at a nearby dentist's office at around 5:00 and would walk over to the diner for fries and a shake, then take care of the register and the bookkeeping while Nourredine and the guys scrubbed the place down after closing.

In 1952, with steady money coming in and a good bit of Somerville opening up to the idea not only of Nourredine but of his marrying a white girl (although here, again, the French they spoke somehow helped convince many a local that the two of them were from some strange country they'd never heard of), their first child arrived. He was born on March 2, the very day Morocco recovered its independence from France, the news of which Nourredine would not receive for weeks, as

39

he was far too busy announcing his new son to the customers. He held up pictures of the shiny child as he went from table to table.

Georges Fadi Subdallah was a huge baby, just under eleven pounds, and nearly killed his mother at birth. He was named after Lara's father and took his middle name from his paternal grandfather.

Nourredine toyed with the idea of taking his new family and some of his savings back to Beni-Mellal. At times he did long to be with his mother and eight brothers. He'd moved to America four long years before and hadn't been back since. He put off the plan and swore to himself he would return when his family was bigger and the children old enough to make the trip, swore that he wanted Georges to be exposed to Moroccan culture, to the Arabic side of his family. He didn't realize it at the time, but he was destined never to see his home soil again. In the end, he had decided it would be best for Georges and future children to have the benefit of American schools, speaking English and French and Arabic in a monolingual country, and being near Lara's parents, who often visited to gush over their little grandson.

Georges was a happy baby, always cooing and crowding his fat cheeks with a big smile. His skin was the color of tea with milk, his eyes a deep hazel hue borrowed from mom. Like Nourredine in his initial American years, Georges would spend the first part of his life convincing people that he wasn't black, in spite of his hair, his skin. To this purpose, Nourredine and his wife decided early on that it was best to have Lara take him to school whenever possible and pick him up afterward to mill around long enough for people to get the picture, to hear her French accent as she held Georges's hand.

At the age of six, Georges was enrolled in The Brown School on Willow Ave, where he would mingle with the children of machinists, freight loaders, road workers, and factory men. Irish and Italian. No black kids, no one with anywhere near the complexion Georges showed up with on his first day. Neither of his parents ever realized just how tough it was for him those first years. The kids called him "commi" and whatever cocktail of racial barbs were at hand. His hair, like his father's, was tight to the scalp, coarse, like a black man's, though many black kids of the day were straightening their hair like James Brown. Georges's skin was here and there starred with dark spots, which proved strong ammunition for kids on the playground. His younger brother and sister would be fashioned more closely after their mother, with light hair and eyes, skin able to pass for some sort of Mediterranean background, Greek or Armenian.

That he wasn't athletic at baseball and basketball didn't help either. And just as he was beginning to gain friends in elementary school, as the kids were beginning to accept him as a regular part of the class, it was time for middle school and a new bunch of Irish construction workers' sons to contend with. On his very first day he sat alone at lunch, comforted by the brown bag lunch his mother had made him, a tender little reminder amid all the name calling earlier that day. But he opened the bag to find an old clump of dog shit right on top of his sandwich.

Most subjects came very easily to Georges, particularly the more logical maths and sciences, the focus on rote knowledge and even some practical applications, about which Georges was never shy to ask his teachers, much to their consternation ("But why would anyone ever want to use this method to deflate a balloon? Why do we need to know that oil doesn't mix with water?"). This seriousness in the classroom, coupled with his ability to throw a baseball exactly like a girl, made the kids lash out at him even more. When one of the two Callahans in his homeroom pointed out to the class that Georges should be better at sports because he's "colored," Georges turned sharply in his chair, a great scowl on his face, and said, "I'm not colored. I'm Moroccan." The entire class laughed, and the students took instantly to calling him "Maraca," a name that stuck to him that year and into high school. It wasn't long before he came to like this name, even introducing himself as Maraca. It quickly took on a friendly connotation, and even his teachers began to employ it (before a new school year began, Georges was sure to gain an audience with his new teachers, imploring them to address him as Maraca).

At home, Nourredine practiced a deliberate sort of Islam, one he was still ironing out as Georges was a child. It was important to him, in particular, that the kids were exposed to the humility found in the

Koran. Whenever one of the children would let slip the slightest hint of pride over another kid, he would immediately remind them of their place, citing the text as if a rulebook. He constantly sought ways in which the basic teachings of Islam would mesh with the American way of life. But this included very little of the actual rituals. He was loose on his enforcement of *Salah*, at first making the children pray in the morning and at night only. He was careful about just how much of this was allowed to seep out into Somerville life, especially when it came to his diner. The kids' clothes would be exactly like those of their classmates, even little Alia, the spelling of whose name he'd decided to Anglicize slightly. He warned Georges early about keeping his prayers secret from his classmates. The little guy wondered as he walked to school with his backpack, *Why should something so important as talking to God be kept hidden outside of home?* So his prayers began to seem like a special secret only he knew, and often during the day he would glance at classmates and wish he could let them know how easy it was to talk to God.

When Georges would come home from school sullen-looking and pout for hours before revealing the cause of his pain, Nourredine would put him on his knee, bounce him a few times, and whisper "inshallah." God's will, which at first made Georges angry with God. He saw Allah as yet another parent, a grandfather of some sort. *If it is His will that causes my classmates to insult my skin, to push me on the playground, then I hate Him.*

But as he grew older and small successes came, when the measure of absolute worth that was the grading system seemed to favor him, this God's will began to give him comfort. When something terrible happened, he'd remind himself that it was also God's will that he should get the highest grades in the class, and it was God's will that he was given his sweet mother. Inshallah.

In how people succeeded or failed, gained friends or were bullied, he soon began to see a basic underlying system. Georges apprehended the world as having its own will too, that if you worked hard, did some good, and were friendly to every single person, eventually you would find small rewards, which would turn into larger ones. The worst bully in middle school had teased him mercilessly for weeks, but Georges then saw him being picked up by his father after school. The man was dressed like a homeless person and slapped the kid on the back of the head, something Nourredine would never have done. Georges nodded and told himself he had been rewarded with a kind father for being diligent in his studies, not teasing the other kids even when he thought of something clever. If you are good, life will be good. Inshallah.

The children had no idea how much their mother suffered during these first years. A dark baby led around by a beautiful French woman in old Somerville, the concerned eyes of her co-workers when she brought her little son in after school. A perfect mini being, the little man who'd changed her life, but the women gave him phony hellos and condescending slow talk. Even worse were the few nights when she and her husband could enjoy a meal out together, or a movie, or even a show downtown. The glares from homogenous couples or loud whispers from across the street.

But never did an ounce of the confusion or fear make its way down to Georges, or Yusef, or Alia. To the kids, their mother had a proudly raised chin and perfectly spun curls and a handbag to match each dress as she walked them the two blocks to school. She was the looming figure who, around the corner from the schoolhouse, knelt and suddenly became visible, if only to wipe some smudge from their cheeks or forearms, a knotted brow as she worked, one which would then release and reverse itself for the last few seconds as she bent to kiss each on the tops of their heads. *Mes chatons, mes chatons.* Good day, my little kittens.

CHAPTER 5

"Subdallah cannot be treated like any other prisoner you've interrogated."

"Okay," she said, snuffing her cigarette instead of shrugging.

"I mean it. He's been here nearly a year, and we've managed to pull exactly shit from him."

"Well, if *Mr. England* is who I think the fuck he is, I'm not at all surprised. He was all fear and control. Other antiquated hogshit from his silly KUBIK handbook."

Alec took a long drink from the unlabeled bottle of beer, turned toward her, and leaned on the railing. He'd always been a good-looking man, and was aging well and, she could tell, deliberately into his upper-class life here. He was the only black man Emma really knew stateside, after so many years in the Maghreb. The last seven years had given him much, this old brownstone in Georgetown with the small deck shaded by oaks, the new hardwood and leather and marble they'd passed through on their way to the porch. It gave Emma pleasure, somehow, to think of herself in her little government-issued housing in Fairfax, the plain surfaces, crumby drywall, so little of herself invested in where she called home. It made it easier to think every day of moving somewhere else, less nailed to the shitty circumstance she'd found herself in.

He exhaled. "Some respect, if you would. The man's barely dead two months. Anyway, like I said, the rules have changed since your time with him. We're allowed to use fewer tools."

"Right." Emma's hair was smoothed away from her face, tied back. She wore jeans and a man's shirt. She put another cigarette in her mouth and looked around for her lighter. "Tell me something here, once and for all." She lit the cigarette. "Why?"

He paused a second. "There are very few of you left. You'd be surprised. Very few. I mean people who have any experience in this at all. In fact, even all those years ago there weren't many people who had actual domestic interrogation experience, along with the language, the culture."

"I've been filed away in that fucking department for years, Alec. Now I'm suddenly useful?"

"Benning was our first choice, yes. But can you blame me? The way you left the program? I was sure you'd never agree to another position. That much makes sense, doesn't it?"

"And now there's just no one left."

"Not exactly true. But like I said, this is like nothing we've had experience with. All these angles coming together. He's an American citizen who Arabicized himself in college, it's a domestic target, and the biggest thing of all of course is a suicide bomber who's survived. The questionable status he must have held, the mental state he was...he is in. There's no precedent here. And you're right about Benning, probably. He wasn't the right tactic. *You* very well may be. Benning had the... well, what was needed in that different time, that place. But you were always the best at improvising. You were better at lulling, at promising. A suicide bomber, he's already resigned himself to whatever peace he thinks is awaiting him on the other side, sitting next to Allah, virgins, whatever else."

"It doesn't make sense. What *made* him the bomber? He was too valuable."

"When his wife and daughter died. He must have become less valuable, mentally. His...*brother* works in very odd ways and is very known for his ability to smell even the slightest decrease in faith. He once hanged fifteen members, publicly, for no real trespass, only a perceived waning in loyalty."

He shrugged.

"I don't know that you're the best. But I really think you could get something from him. After nearly a year of this guy. The thing is, he's not one of the targets we'd work on overseas. He truly is American. No translator needed. He'll be able to read your cues as well as anyone. Like a criminal you used to tune up stateside, but one who has tried to make himself as much a Muslim extremist as possible. You have the background for both."

"You're not telling me something."

"I'm not. You're right."

She squinted at him, tilted her head as if regarding a sculpture for meaning. "Urgency. Something's happened recently. I'm guessing Subdallah has become a higher interest subject. He was nobody, now he's somebody."

"Of course there is a reason."

"Some part of a chain that's recently surfaced."

"Of course."

"But you can't say."

"I can tell you that new intelligence has come to light, which we need urgently to counter. And this man is the only good link we have our hands on. Needless to say, the implications of this are potentially dire."

"So I'm going to be in the fucking dark again, is that it?"

"You can be briefed only insofar as it's necessary for retrieving intelligence from the detainee, as always. You will be assigned an analyst. Reg Olsen, he's good. He'll brief you on the information we're trying to draw from the subject, you will dig it out of him. It will be similar in nature to your work in Morocco, in that it will help us move upward in the hierarchy, eventually leading to the discovery of the man in charge of this American cell. Among the things we have going against us is the fact that Subdallah has been in confinement for so long and cut off from contact with, or knowledge about, the doings of his higher-ups. He was the bombmaker and the bomb, the technical brains behind every strike from Thaghr. He helped plan things years out. He was...*is*... perhaps the most famous bombmaker."

"I've never heard of him."

"Among the men who deal in signatures, he's a celebrity, if a despised one. You should hear them talk about his devices, his *brilliant* design.

And he can still play a pivotal role, which is why we've kept him. Not to mention he was Marcel Karim's best friend, his mentor, in some ways."

"Some friend."

"That might be the best thing about him."

Emma took a long draw and held the smoke in. "Alright, tell me about his family. I need to know what assets we have available to us."

"His father is dead. Mother has been out of the picture a while. She's white, seems to have become a point of embarrassment in his adult life. Brother and sister in greater Boston. Again, he stopped speaking to them. Two incendiary forces seem to be the death of his wife and daughter. Both were killed in a botched CIA raid in Egypt, shot by Americans. Subdallah likely sees the death of his wife and girl as the fault of the US military. But he was radicalized even before that. The timing of their deaths coincides very closely with what seems like the inception of the Caldwell plan. The attack occurred about eight months later."

He looked down, crinkled his brow.

"They were so close, and yet Karim sends him in. It doesn't make sense. He was a genius with mechanics, electronics. And with the Egyptian engineers, they knew exactly where to hit Caldwell, the perfect place to crumble the three floors they found most offensive, the perfect amount of charge, even on that little bike."

"Not quite perfect."

"How do you mean?"

"Subdallah is still alive."

"That is a small miracle."

"So what family do we have on him? What people does he care about?"

"No one. We've found no one. Siblings he's been alienated from for years, some cousins outside Beni-Mellal. You remember that shithole, I'm sure. He cut himself off in his late twenties, forged his own family, wife, daughter. Traveled around North Africa, the Middle East."

She held the cigarette high and tucked her hand under the elbow in a common pose. "In the desert we'd spend a few weeks interrogating, a month tops. If he didn't spill by then he went off to whatever version of prison was available. Or to whatever version of execution. Why's this dickhole made it so long?"

"Domestic stage changes things. He's an American, his target was in America. He was barely alive for months, and not much better for months after that. He did have a lawyer at one point, if you can believe it. If you can believe that still nothing leaked. With the pain he's gone through we even had a shrink suggest he'd lost his mind; I think she was trying to get leniency, suggest he was unfit for prison. Major thing that's allowed us to get around usual red tape is the severity of the target. As you can imagine, most of Washington had some family member or friend working near Caldwell. Even though there were no victims, it still shook the shit out of a lot of us."

"This guy's already made his peace. Hard to say what we can use on him. Might as well be speaking another language to someone who's already dead."

Alec let out a long sigh, leaned on the rail, and shook his head. "I can't say what cards we have left to play with this guy. A human being who decides his own life is secondary to the cause."

She said sing-songingly, "I'd rather bribe a man who has everything than a man who has nothing."

"Who said that, Charlie? Hell, you know better than I that a lot of these Arabs, even the ones with huge families, ten kids, wives, money, even they're willing to sacrifice for what they think is on the other side. It was much simpler back when we thought the only people sent on suicide missions were mental cases, the dirt poor, or otherwise fucked up. Subdallah was bright, rich, once a family man. Principled, even. He's pretty damned American, started his own business, played college ball."

Emma again thought of her apartment, the emptiness, so little of herself there. She saw her son roughly fifty days per year, no husband, no man in her life, graying hair. A perfect candidate to strap a bomb to, but nowhere for her to aim at, nothing she felt heated enough to want to destroy except maybe herself. *A guy who tried to blow himself up has more to live for than I do.*

"So how do we reach him?" she asked.

"He's lasted through some of the most excruciating surgeries, burns, loss of limbs, pain, from what I'm told, great enough to make someone insane. Benning wanted to waterboard him. He lasted longer than anyone we've ever seen, well past the point of allowance. Took over eighteen sessions before it was kiboshed."

She shook her head. "Fear won't work. We can't squeeze anything from a suicide based on fear of adverse circumstance, that's basic. But we can't exactly make promises protecting something in this world, a place he felt quite at ease leaving behind." She snuffed out her cigarette. "Shit, Alec. Might as well try to press a ghost at this point, go to the morgue and press a damn corpse. I'll need time. I'll need a lot of time with this guy. He'll need to get to know me…develop a rapport…"

"We don't have time."

"Why?"

"They're right at our doorstep." He turned to face his little yard again. "Since you left, Al-Thaghr has become the most immediate threat to our country. It's like a corporation, all these Arabs who claim to hate western ways. But they have built a company. It has hierarchy, as you know better than anyone, and it has in-fighting and favoritism, coups, promotions, *terminations*. And Thaghr's role has become the wing aimed at America. From everything we can tell, their sole purpose is to do damage to the US, whether here or abroad. The funding is incredible. Subdallah was a rich man, but what he contributed financially was a spec compared to the investment from some of Saudi's top families, a few Iranians, Egyptians. That sort of funding makes them strong, mobile, welcome in many countries, and very good recruiters. Other cells focus on that goddamn Qutbism, overthrowing leaders not deemed Islamist enough, lending support to the Afghans against the Soviets or the Iranis. But Karim's cell, Subdallah's cell, was all about the US. Caldwell was their second on our soil, first major one, but they've been holding their cards a while. Now we can expect more. As this decade has unfolded, the Islamists have slowly taken the place of the Soviets on the international stage. At least as far as we're concerned."

"Who are we trying to get?"

"You ever hear Marcel Karim's name before last month?"

She shook her head.

"Or Ali Al-Jeddah?"

"Nope."

"Marcel Karim took the place of Thaghr's old leader. This guy became an imam when he was very young, gained tremendous power. And Subdallah and Al-Jeddah were pretty much his number twos. Karim is a calm man, thoughtful, the kind everybody likes right away, even some European journalists made him a celebrity for a time. He picks up followers like dust. He'll talk in a room or a mosque, have ten youngsters dying to sign up. And he nurtures that, woos them for a few weeks. Funny thing is, those grunts never see him again, not really. Thaghr is its own cell, and even within it there is a perfect amount of exclusion and segregation. The grunts are easy to catch, like we always say. But these guys don't know shit. Maybe their lieutenants do."

"So I can see why Subdallah was such a huge find. What I can't see is why he was sent on this mission. If he was so high up, why would they be okay with him dying?"

"I don't know."

"And Al-Jeddah?"

"Subdallah and Karim, they're principled, decent even. They seem to be able to show compassion. Al-Jeddah is nothing of the sort. He is the most vicious of anyone you would have come across in the Magreb. He throws off his family, his country, he has a sadistic streak the size of my..."

Don't say it.

"Chimney. A truly sick man. We think he and Marcel Karim are still in the States. We know they were here planning Caldwell."

"There's something you're leaving out."

Alec's wife began to open the sliding door, but he waved her away with a smile. "You're right." He shifted in his chair, crossed and uncrossed his legs. "There is another reason we need you for this. The chain goes back very far. It goes back to your work in Egypt, to Al-Thaghr." Then he added, "But it's all been leading to something. And we don't really have time, Emma."

"Why?"

He actually looked around before speaking, "We have it in fairly good confidence..." Exhaled, a long breath. "...his cell, they're planning

50

something else, something soon, bigger than Caldwell. Their grand plan has always been for three hits. Three attacks in a small window. It's an old IRA tactic, builds the terror level exponentially. They will get bigger, and they will be soon. Al-Thaghr is peaking right now, size, funds, sophistication, leadership. This will be the biggest attack ever on US soil."

CHAPTER 6

When Georges was just three, Nourredine bought his son a tiny stuffed soccer ball, which he'd throw down the hall for Georges to scurry after, kicking it off the walls with delight until he returned it to his father, who would again toss it down the hallway. This game went on for hours. Georges slept with the ball, and at the age of six it was replaced with his first real soccer ball.

Father and son would tap the ball back and forth for hours at night after school and work were finished. Georges's feet seemed to be infected with the same magnetism as his father's, the ball clinging there as if by a good bit of magic. He played on youth soccer teams, charged up the field with the ball, stopping to search for trailing teammates, who would catch up, only to be served a delicate, perfect pass they hadn't the coordination to receive. And little Georges would stand in the mirror before games, in shin guards and shorts and team shirt, and say, "I am a soccer player." *Inshallah, I have been given this.*

But a strange thing happened after fifth grade, something for which Nourredine could find no reason: suddenly soccer had become a fringe sport. It seemed all the parents signed their kids up for soccer during the younger years, but at around the age of ten, the teams became sparse, only a few youth leagues to join. The kids took to baseball, basketball, and other more American sports for which Georges had no talent and Nourredine no comprehension.

So when Georges was twelve, his dad presented him with his first football, which the boy held and pondered for several minutes. He dropped it on the ground, and watched as it bounced neurotically. The oblong corners and stitches seemed part of a cruel joke his father was playing. He had tried to throw one of these on the playground, an act met with immediate chuckles.

"My son, this is American football. This is what your friends play, what will make you into a true American."

"But what do I do with it?"

They had no television, nothing to model or practice from, so they spent an afternoon punting the ball, held lengthwise, back and forth, chasing it as it skittered about. Eventually, Nourredine borrowed a book about the sport, scrounging for any similarities that must allow football to share a name with the game he loved. He scoured the papers for stories, seeded his customers with questions. He even went to The Paddock to drink Cokes and watch the Sunday games. But the sport seemed without any fluidity to him, stopping and starting, men using their hands and fouling constantly. He saw only two instances in which a player even put his foot to the ball and decided that his son could serve that purpose just as well as any American boy.

Sunday at Trum Field. "Georges, most young players today you will see throwing the ball back and forth to each other, like this." An end-over-end toss. "You see them play games, run back and forth, tackle each other. This is not for you. Men get injured, lose teeth, break bones. We are smarter, tactical, and we have true foot power on our side. You, my son, will be a kicker."

Nourredine explained to his son how no one in America concentrated on football's kicking game. How, if Georges would simply practice his punting, placekicking, and drop-kicking an hour each day, more on the weekends, he would enter high school with a mile of advantage over anyone else who would try out for the position. And as Nourredine began to plan for his son's education, the staggering tuition fees also put the idea into his head that Georges could head to college on a scholarship, almost as a loophole. Punter, the position no one focused on, but a vital linchpin, nonetheless. "You will be a football player."

He went home that night with his new ball, walked around with it the way he used to do with the soccer ball. This one had simply been reshaped, a slant on his previous self-image. In the mirror he stood and looked at himself holding the ball. "I am a football player."

So Georges dutifully practiced his punting into a net for an hour each day after school. He and his father would go to the field on weekends and kick back and forth. At the end, Georges would attempt ten field goals, with Nourredine simulating pressure by tossing handfuls of grass at the boy's face. Nourredine would measure and chart the progress each week. It wasn't long before the boy was launching the ball twenty-five yards, thirty by the summer after eighth grade.

By the time he matriculated to Somerville High School, his self-confidence was surging. His body finally filled out, his frame extending to over six feet, and the lively and serious eyes of his mother mixed with exotic skin tone made even the conservative local girls take notice, though he wouldn't have his first kiss until college.

It was here, in a first-year history class, that he first learned of Benjamin Franklin, which was the beginning of a life-long infatuation. Something about the way Franklin methodically approached his obstacles, spelled out solutions, mapped his progress by charting daily goals and creating checklists. It all rang true in his head, fit into his own worldview, his own internal map and approaches to school, to kicking, to friends. It was an extension of what his father always taught him: doing this will equal that. It was a measure of Allah's promise. He adopted Franklin's daily ledgers, marking to what degree he'd progressed in industry, friendships, social standing, frugality, studies, kicking, and a dozen other fields. Over his work desk hung a small poster of old Ben, in the coonskin cap he wore during his later trips to France.

When he went out for the team his first year, the coach didn't understand what he meant by a punter and kicker. Kids didn't just play punter on his team. He was suited up in full gear, run through the same paces as the others. He kept up on the agility and speed drills, but everything involving touching the ball or physical contact made him seem like a true foreigner, in the end mostly unfamiliar with the rudiments of the game, even running backward on one occasion.

But after the 2nd week of practice, when the coaches invited any interested players to stay after and try some kicks, Georges seemed like a grown man by comparison, spiraling his punts as if from a rifled cannon, his form by now powerful and ballet-like. And his placekicking was sharp and similarly hulkish, booting each one through the uprights, never missed within thirty yards. The coaches gave him the smaller pads, the light helmet with a single bar. He would continue to participate in agility drills and calisthenics, but during contact drills would go off with one of the injured players to work on his kicks and punts.

Even with a growing group of friends and much wider acceptance, each day at high school was a battle. He applied the same trick his parents had used: speaking French whenever possible to confound the ignorant locals into thinking he was from some unknown place, one that at least spoke a white tongue, just so long as he distinguished himself from the local coloreds. And his nickname, which he always made known right off the bat, disarmed a lot of the potential ire, made him come off as playful, self-deprecating and, though he wasn't exactly a funny guy, made people think he was the class clown, always smiling or looking down bashfully.

He'd work at the diner after school and on weekends, so whenever classmates came in, particularly with their parents, he'd be sure to introduce his beautiful white mother to them, perhaps speak a bit of French within earshot, and offer a coffee on the house.

Although all the Subdallah children picked up Arabic, Georges had begun to fight the use of it in high school, wanting nothing but to be integrated, to do the opposite of sticking out. He spoke it with ease early in life, but it lay dormant for years before he would use the language again.

There were very few Arab or Muslim students at Somerville High. On the first week of classes, he noticed a girl shoving books into her locker. She stood there, head wrapped, wearing a burka and backpack, only her face exposed. He made friends with her immediately, though it was some time before he would allow himself to walk down the halls with her.

He took to walking Ollani home most days; her house was right on his way down Highland Ave. She was smart but always reserved, looking downward on their walks from school even after they'd become good friends. She spoke of how demanding her family was, how important it was that she get nothing but A's. But he still felt as if there were some missing thread between the two of them — the strict up-bringing and adherence to Islamic laws, the two foreign parents where he had only one, the complete lack of striving to Americanize herself. Georges took pride in considering himself Arab, but when walking next to Ollani he felt anything but Arab.

One morning he went to meet her before first period. Spray painted on her locker was "Jew." She never came back to school, and for months Georges wondered what had happened to her, marveled at the fact that an alternative to high school existed, her parents obviously had a fall-back plan, she'd been sent *somewhere*. A few years later he saw her in Porter Square from across the street. He tried to yell but the passing cars were too loud and the light was red. He took one step but changed his mind.

Though he was part of a team, being the kicker in some ways served to separate him further from his typical classmates. They took a liking to him, called him Maraca, joked around in the locker room, but never treated him as truly equal. It was still a new phenomenon to have a player, a high school kid, who wanted to do nothing more than punt and kick. During freshman year he was used mostly to punt and follow-up the occasional touchdown with a point after. The first game of his second year he was presented with a field goal attempt from thirty-eight yards out, at the time a school record. He cleared the cross bar by several feet, and in the final minutes beat the record with a forty yarder. Due in part to his team's inability to score, the coaches used him more and more, opting for field goal tries as often as possible, some games ending 12-7, all points owing to Georges's foot.

As much as the field goals gave him a good rush of adrenaline and that temporary swarm and smacks on the back from teammates, it was the punting that excited him, especially punts from around the other team's forty yard line. Georges would even start to hope that his teammates would be forced into fourth down — too far out for him to try a field goal but close enough that he could boot a good, high punt, chipped just right to land at around the five, where his teammates would be waiting to down the ball. He even began to map out, to the faster kids on the team, exactly where the ball could be expected to land. This gave him an even bigger thrill than some long kick at game's end for the win.

And though high schools hadn't yet begun to keep track of punt statistics, Nourredine attended every game, scribbling distances in a notebook, tracking his son's progress. He wanted hard numbers to present to any college coaches.

Family practice never stopped. Even into senior year, Georges's father would shag footballs for him well into dusk. As the boy grew taller, his yardage increased, that long leg swinging like a pendulum below, smooth and perfect. That Somerville's coach began to rely more and more on field goals and team defense became a popular subject in the local papers, and even *The Globe* wrote a small blurb about it. They were winning games with scores of 9-7 and 15-0. Other teams began to focus on their special teams, plugging up Georges's view, hopping around like mad, but Georges and Nourredine simply responded with deliberate practice, and it was his father's idea to start working on his foot *speed*, as a kicker, shaving off nearly a full second, ensuring that no rushes had a chance of reaching the ball before it was booted.

His senior year the state records all fell, were reset, and broken again, the year capped by a loss in the state championship game (21-9, all points on field goals). Nourredine had taken an interest in college statistics, gauging his son by their standards, writing letters to assistant coaches, full of numbers, comparing his kid's foot to those of college players. Each one included a stats package, by year, with averages, longest punts and field goals, touchbacks, total points, big pressure wins. Each coach received a player profile packet: a small photo of his son, paper-clipped to the front, along with stats and newspaper clippings.

I am a football player.

Several letters came back to Nourredine from schools as far west as Stanford, or small division III programs in upstate New York. But most were unable to offer football scholarships or simply didn't have funds available to pay for a kicker. Columbia and Cornell expressed great interest, especially upon hearing that Georges was making straight A's, but both made very clear that it was against Ivy League policy to offer scholarships.

Georges, Nourredine, and Lara spent night after night weeding through schools, looking at rankings, financial packages, loans, grants. When the dust had settled, UMass-Amherst seemed the place Georges would matriculate to in the fall. The coach was a kind man, who'd actually visited the diner to speak with Nourredine and Lara, seemed to accord a greater respect to the kicker and punter positions than most coaches. And when the financial packages and numbers came in, a combination of smaller academic grants and state aid wound up being the deciding factor.

So after graduating somewhere near the top of his class, spending hundreds of hours honing his foot, making cold road trips to stand on the sidelines while he waited to be called in to punt or kick from the thirty-five, Georges was able to attend The University of Massachusetts at Amherst on a bit of a scholarship, heading two hours west, away from his family for the first time, where he knew he would have to perform that pacifying song and dance yet again, speaking French, introducing himself as Maraca, smiling widely, playing down the ease with which he cruised through his subjects.

Amherst lay in a valley of flood plains cupped by a ring of mountains. The loping hills and patchwork farmland were like nothing Georges had seen before, and the way he gazed out, open-mouthed, upon the landscape outside the bus window was exactly the way the valley locals gazed at him when he walked along downtown. It was the way the other kids in his dorm sized him up as well, for about the first two weeks anyway, before he put on his show, that weeks-long flagellation filled with French, allusions to his working-class upbringing, and the barrage of self-deprecation. The artfulness in how he'd diffuse all the assumptions before the kids had a chance to vocalize them. "The camel I rode here is outside refilling." Big smile, slumped shoulders.

Georges had landed in Central in the early 70s, the hippie section of campus. The free and radical ways so many of the students spoke and acted was disturbing at first, coming from conservative East Somerville, wrapped in the dug-in white old guard. He'd ventured to Cambridge a few times, even into Boston, and his grandparents were free thinkers, but Somerville was very much his home, and his friends were all within a few blocks, so many older brothers being paraded off to Vietnam, their parents veterans of Korea and Nixon campaigns.

Georges spent his first year in the Van Meter dormitory, never directly smoking pot but certainly inhaling a few trunkfuls in all those late night rooms, the kids with long hair and bare feet spouting off about the war yet again, Nixon yet again. It felt dangerous, as many new things did simply because they were unknown. But soon Georges joined in the discussions, chiming in with whatever Moroccan history he could and even eventually a bit of the prejudices he'd faced growing up.

During a late night, after he'd showered and was alone in the bathroom, he'd gaze into the foggy mirror, stare at his face, and more and more he would see Maraca. Not the prodigious kicker, not the A student, but simply Maraca, that cartoon smile wider than his face, shoulders hung low under feigned gravity.

CHAPTER 7

It was Friday night, just after nine, when Emma finally pulled into the parking garage after a long day of briefing with the analysts, watching tape of prior interrogations of Subdallah. She flicked on the ceiling light to her apartment, even that sound echoing around the unpadded place. Threw her keys on the counter. She cracked two ice cubes into a glass, filled it with so-so gin and soda water, squeezed a lime over it, and dropped the wedge in. Then she kicked her shoes off and settled into the institutional couch, the right angles and coarse fabric uninviting.

With the cigarette and cool booze and the dim lighting, exhaustion seeped into her. But when she closed her eyes, just as she'd feared, images from the interrogation tapes played behind her eyelids. She'd had to study hours of film from her predecessor. Men shivered and cowered, slumped in chairs like noodles, sobbing in Arabic for their mothers.

Benning ("Mr. England") had used his typical methods, short of the physical bruising and shaking he'd relied on in Morocco. The Old Stuff. The basic principle was to assert control, superiority, fear, to "own" the subject, as Benning had been so fond of saying. Over in Morocco and later in Egypt and Tangiers, Benning had fed on it. Most of their detainees called him Mr. Benning and were petrified of him but gave up very little. Back then, the place had been split in two: those who used the old methods and those who had been taught the new ones.

As a criminal interrogator stateside, Emma had been brought up with greater limits on her methods. She wasn't authorized to offer fake bribes or use comfort deprivation, many of the tricks allowed in war time, so she'd had to learn more subtle manipulations: *rapport*, pitting prisoners against each other. In criminal investigations and, as she had learned, in interviews with Arab terrorists, discovering motives was the key to making someone spill. It was shocking at first to find out how many of these so-called radical terrorists had joined the movement solely to escape poverty or support their families. Many of them had little stake in the actual cause. Cash and family, even thousands of miles across ocean and desert, tended to make a man tick.

The grainy black-and-white tape of Mr. England pounding on a table brought those old memories back. The shrieking, the sleep-starved, black-hooded men shoved into blank rooms, shoulders slumped, spirits broken but still silent. Back then interrogators had found ways for certain interviews to go unrecorded, which allowed men like Benning to use the full menu of persuasion. Men who hadn't slept for several days became like the insane, flinching at shadows, cowering, eyes recording shapes and figures that simply weren't there. Men would admit to killing little children in countries they'd never been to; they'd confess to strangling dogs in their cells or burning fictitious secret files and flushing them down the toilet. The place became like an asylum.

And Al-Thaghr. Back then it had become an obsession, on the edge of every other thought she had, day and night. They were all chasing the same men, asking the same questions, tracking down ghosts, near mythical names as if from children's rhymes. No matter how much they would squeeze the underlings, no one gave up anything to help catch the three or four top drivers of the Magreb cell. More bombings, more civilian murders, more signs vaguely pointing to a domestic plan. The small group would spend sixteen hours some days, pouring over reports, intel, conflicting statements of insane prisoners, all trying to piece together fragments that might lead them upward.

The end had been abrupt, as simple and final as a period. Suddenly, the very core of all meaning in her life had vanished. She had spent so many years – every hour of every day – thinking about Al-Thaghr, what they were planning, how they were organized, each new detainee and his wants and drives. That story had been cut from her life so long ago. Now it was back. Subdallah was just the next part. He was Layth and he was every other poor fanatical soul she had crushed in those filthy chambers.

She never understood what truly caused the department's demise. Randolph had placed a sheet of yellow paper on her desk one night, sat across from her without a word. He'd wept, she remembered that. *Our country no longer fears Al-Thaghr, they are no longer a threat, people say. They forget, they all forget.* He borrowed a cigarette, simply walked out with it unlit, the last she'd seen of him until he walked into her office two weeks ago. Back home accusations surfaced in some of the papers: inhumane practices, squandered funds, *torture.* They loved that last one. With the fall of her program came an aimlessness; even with a perfect little boy back home there was an empty place, something unresolved always in the darker corners of her brain.

Emma slid a second cigarette from the pack, made another drink with fresh ice, sat at the desk in the corner. And as she peered around the sparse room, all she could think of were more ways to simplify, ways to *own* less, get rid of anything that might suck her back to this place or any place. It wasn't just empty space; it was the government's empty space. It was replaceable; she was replaceable. She thought about the last visit to John's house, how he'd filled the place with knickknacks, a new Magnavox, lawn furniture, bathroom tiles, Evan's toys scattered around the backyard. The time spent in the Middle East hadn't had the same effect on him, and maybe that was part of why they'd split. Emma had come back without that hunger for ownership, for collection, for luxury or ease. Overseas, she had nurtured a silent envy for the women she saw walking the streets, buying single loaves of bread for large families, exact rules of dress and décor. They didn't return home to stereos and new sofas, or piles of records arranged just so.

To take her mind off the tapes and the day's worth of debriefing, she sliced open the large manila envelope from Beltway Connections, the dating service she'd applied to a few weeks ago. She'd had to fill out a profile, send a photo, describe her dream man. Twenty-five bucks. In return they'd sent her about a dozen similar profiles of men. Each sheet had a small photo of the guy, along with all his stats, hobbies, career type, interests, a paragraph about what he was looking for in a woman. She flipped through the first half based solely on the little photo. Lots of older men, men with beady eyes or big necks, several photos obviously taken years ago. She'd put her desired age range as 30-55, which she now thought was a mistake; only older men would match up to her, a 38-year-old mother.

Her mind immediately began to size these guys up. Based on what they do, their photo, their little paragraph, she gave them all motives: this one wanted a few weeks of sex with an easy woman, this one a mother and cook, this one was simpering and feeble.

She was surprised when, at the end, she found a copy of her own profile. The photo she'd sent in was one of the few she had around the apartment. It had been taken when she was thirty and living overseas. She looked young, her hair longer and pulled back, smiling but not too much. It was a lie, the picture, her age, the smiling. As interests she'd included reading, wine, films, racquetball, hiking. *Divorced, one child,* that would send them running.

"I'm an outgoing, active woman, still twenty-four at heart. I like to get out into nature on the weekends for kayaking, biking, or hiking on the C&O. But I'm also looking for someone to rent a good video with on Tuesday night for curling up on the sofa and sharing a good bottle. Good on the phone is a plus."

My God, that is terrible. She looked at the photo, imagined a man seeing her face, reading the profile, reading between the lines, looking closely at that smile, seeing how phony it was, how far off that time was.

She set her cigarette in the ashtray, took a long drink, and went back through the set of men, this time turning off her scrutiny and landing on six candidates. She slid the paperwork back into an envelope, licked the gum, sealed it, and even though it was late Friday night went straight to the mail box and posted it.

"I'm so sorry, buddy."

"That's okay, Mom."

He said this as he looked out the passenger window. He made the seat look huge, cleats resting on the dashboard in some new posture she'd not seen before. She wondered where he'd learned it.

"So which one, Mom?"

Emma paused, both hands on the wheel of the old Volvo wagon, facing forward. "Hmm?"

"Subway or Pizza Hut?"

"Oh." She turned left down Chain Bridge and hit a red light. "I like Subway, don't you?" She faced him. He was still staring out the open window, head resting on his fist.

"Sure."

Evan never got to eat fast food or go to movies with his father, so Emma made sure he did both on their weekends.

The light turned green. She drove south toward Braddock Field. It was sunny out and had been warm upon waking this morning. Sweat and a thumping heart, though she couldn't remember her dream. There was panic as she'd groped for the lamp, and the clutch of pressure on her chest. The consecutive days and nights spent in interrogation with Fadi and the others had brought with them a resurgence in her nightmares of Layth and darker figures.

It was all she could do not to load a tumbler or two with gin before picking up Evan. But of course she hadn't, no, this was her weekend. *This is my life. Harrison is not my life.*

And she'd taken it easy on the cigarettes too after last visit when Evan had thrown the half carton of smokes in the trash. *Thanks, buddy.*

"Who's the kid on the team again? The goal-scorer?"

"Robbie. But he's not....never mind."

"What?"

"Nothing."

"What is it, buddy? Isn't he your friend?"

"Yes, but..." He turned to face her now. "I score goals too."

Rolling the wheel slowly as she turned onto Clemson. "I know. I know, buddy. I think you're the best on the team. That's not what I was saying. I'm so proud of you. I think you're so good out there."

"You didn't see my last game. I had *three* goals." He now turned back toward the window, hung his arm halfway out. "And I stopped a goal. Robbie only had two."

"I'm so proud of my little soccer player."

"And the game before, against the Bluejays, I had three goals then."

"You told me on the phone. You were so excited. I remember. I told everyone at work."

There was a long pause, and she could see Evan floating his hand in the breeze.

"Mom, what do you do?"

"Well, hon, I protect us from bad guys. I told you that."

"That's not what Vivien told me."

"What the hell did *Vivien* tell you?"

He was silent.

"I'm sorry, buddy." She laughed, if only partially. "It's just…do you see her a lot?"

He shrugged.

"Well, I catch bad guys. We're very safe. Your daddy and I both catch bad guys and keep them away. And we do a great job, and there's no chance they'll ever get here."

"Do they ever get here? I mean, have they been here before?"

"No, honey. Never."

"Because of you and Dad." He nodded as he said this.

When they pulled up to the field, all the other kids with the maroon shirts were already scampering around tall cones, booting balls back and forth as best they could, chasing the regular errant shot. Evan hurried to join them, and Emma surveyed the place for the other parents, most of whom she had a hard time remembering. There were lots of couples set up on the small bleachers at center field.

Just as she was taking an empty seat among the parents, it was time for opening kick-off, followed by a mayhem of little bodies like shaken soda cans. She locked her gaze on Evan and never looked elsewhere, just hoping he'd once glance up to find her. Minutes went by, and he chased the ball and even made a good pass, but he was focused on the game. More minutes, and Emma's lips started moving. *Come on, come on. Look up here, just once.*

There was a whistle and a throw-in. As Evan scurried to cover his man, he studied the bleachers to find his mom. Emma waved emphatically, her eyebrows raised. As soon as he'd made eye contact, he looked back at the kid throwing the ball in.

The game carried on – two twenty-minute halves – with few scoring chances. And Emma did her best to center on her little guy as he ran tirelessly up and back, up and back. Eventually, her mind began to wander, beyond her control, toward the men who sat in that gray building only a few miles away. There were cinderblock walls and bars and glass between them and Evan. She structured them in a neat ladder, Karim's face at the very top, Fadi and Ali just below, dark and light, anger and intelligence.

When the whistle blew, signaling a goal, she was shaken from these thoughts, saw all the maroon kids gathering and slapping high fives to each other. They seemed to be crowding around Evan. Then a hand was placed on her shoulder, one of the moms. Emma flinched and turned toward her. The mom, a bit fearful looking, removed her hand and simply gave her a thumbs up.

Then Emma found Evan again. He was grinning, jogging back to midfield, but he looked up at her and smiled. And Emma smiled back.

After the game, the custom was for all the kids to gather along with their parents and drink Gatorade from white paper cups. The kids got sillier with each minute, and the parents slowly clustered into subgroups. Emma did her best just to stick near the one mom she could surely identify.

It was well past noon when they got back in the Volvo, Evan's sweet stinkiness and cleat mud filling the car.

"I thought that was such a good goal, Evan. You're different from all the kids out there. You just look like a better player. You pass."

"Thanks, Mom."

They stopped at the Subway on Route 123. It was crowded, and the smell of bread was thick as they stepped up to order. At the register, the man asked if they'd like to add chips and a drink. She looked at Evan.

He seemed unsure. "Can I get a Coke, please?"

"Sure."

"And cookies?"

"*A* cookie."

They sat. Evan spread his wrapper across the table, set his cookie out on the wrapper, and took long sucks from the straw.

"Does Dad let you get Coke?"

He was mid-bite into a sandwich that looked gargantuan in his hands. He shrugged. Then he sat chewing a while, out of breath between bites.

"Mom?"

He strained to swallow.

"Yup?" Emma broke off a small piece of his cookie.

"Hey!"

"What? Can I have a bite?"

He shrugged and took another pull from his Coke.

"What do you do at home?"

"What do you mean, bud?"

"I mean, like between our weekends?"

"I work and I think about you and I see my friends. And I sleep in my big bed."

"Are you lonely at your house?"

She paused, chewing the morsel of cookie. "Maybe sometimes. I miss you, for sure. And I'm thinking about you. But I'm not sad."

He nodded. "Maybe you could come over more to my house."

"Maybe, bud."

"And I could come over more. Like on weeknights."

"Of course, honey. I'd like that."

Emma watched him dig into the big sub, and she thought back to when he had to climb up just to sit in a normal chair for dinner. And in his very skin she could see the passing of time, as if the difference between then and now had been clarified in his bones and cheeks and in the little hairs on his arms, and even this scene she couldn't quite enjoy because she saw it too as past…already the past, and what had she done to help make this little man, to seed in those bones something good?

CHAPTER 8

Also living in Van Meter was the freshman backup quarterback, a heavily recruited lefty from Ohio, who carried hopes of the starting position after the senior QB graduated. Stan Ingrid was tall and skinny, with long hair and a strange ability to rocket the ball with his bony arm even farther than Georges could punt it. He was made fun of for his hair, at first, before given due for his play. Stan was also quite a pothead coming into college, which was why he'd chosen to live in Van Meter. When he learned Georges was from Morocco, he launched into a speech lauding the great fashions and hash dens in that country, how Brian Jones and Keith had taken a trip there, asked if Georges could secure any shirts for him.

That first year there was very little competitive draw to the game of football for Georges, and he was even more isolated from the team. Games had become more a mental trick to him than anything else, standing there with cold hands, wearing a coat over his cardboard pads, no indication of when he'd be needed, or whether it would be to punt the ball, thread an angled kick through the uprights, or blast the breath out of the thing on a kick-off. The Minutemen were fairing no better at scoring touchdowns than had Somerville High, so Georges would often be called on for three or four field goals per game, half a dozen punts, and a handful of kick-offs. During a gray and freezing game up in Maine, he'd counted himself in twenty-six plays, between field goals, kick-offs, punts, and a single extra point.

He and Stan would walk to and from the practice field together, which was on the opposite side of campus, and Georges was content to listen as Stan talked about the finer points of the passing game, something coach Lester apparently didn't grasp. The guy had a wispy way about him, never angry, always happy to see Georges after class. A group would often trek back into the woods to smoke a few joints, Georges joining them for the trip but never partaking. The kids in Van Meter seemed to accept him, patted him on the back, stopped by his room to get him on their way to dinner.

Though he came to find this openness refreshing, he never veered off the course he and his father had set. No drinking, smoking only cigarettes (a habit intentionally started his first day away from home), and he studied and practiced at an even more frantic pace. At Somerville High he'd been able to stay ahead of the group with relative ease, but the electrical engineering department at UMass comprised a much brighter lot, which also included a good helping of Asians and Arabs and Indians. The field was expanding, the supply of jobs ever increasing, and UMass had recently sunk a load of state funding into a force of professors and tall cement buildings. He had been sure that some sort of applied science was for him, but it was his hero's love of electricity that made the decision for him, following Dr. Franklin's lead.

He began with a double major in electrical engineering and history, which would later become his minor. He nurtured his love of Mr. Franklin, loading up on every book about him in the school's library, learned of his focus on the formation of civic and social clubs, and his insistence on including a pragmatic element with whatever theoretical idea he came up with. His checklists grew, and the notebook quickly filled with daily details attempting to capture the exact success of his life. There were pages upon pages of hours studied, sums of practice kicks, social cultivation, even a few recent pages about romantic efforts.

Strong competition in his major brought Georges's work ethic to the level of infatuation. He awoke two hours before his first class, snuck into the grad lounge, and pored over his notes with coffee and a cigarette. After dinner most nights he would spend hours in the library, breaking only to smoke out front with a Turkish student who somehow went by the name Eric.

On one such night during second semester, with two big midterms coming up, he found himself in his usual seat on the 23rd floor, the usual student working the reserve desk, a pale, skinny kid with short hair who always wore a sneer, spoke in slow sentences to him. Earlier that night, even after Georges put on his big smile and responded in perfect English, the guy handed him the book with instructions fit for a five-year-old. "Now, listen carefully. This-book-needs-to-come-back. Okay? Right *here.*" As Georges walked away, he heard mumbling, could catch only the word "turban."

He sat for hours at a table by the window, new snow visible under far-off lamps, this remote floor likewise spotted with the odd light. His books and papers were arranged neatly across a long table, the nearby desks abandoned so late on a Thursday. He'd snuck in a thermos of coffee, and on his first sip the cap came loose, spilling the stuff—now lukewarm—down his chest. So he took a long breath and went to find Eric for a smoke break.

They stood in the December air just outside the library's front door, smoked a cigarette each and then started on another. Eric talked as usual about his home in the South End, the large family that pooled its money to support his studies, the pressure to find a job beyond cabby or grocer. No loans without repayment, he said.

Georges had passed by the reserve desk on his way to the elevator, and now as they stood outside the same guy walked by as he left the building, turning his head slightly at Eric, hands in his pockets. His work boots crunched on the salted sidewalk. Georges explained about the guy, and Eric, whose complexion was a few shades darker, said they'd had a heated exchange at the beginning of the semester brought on by the guy's refusal to loan out a book; he'd said his friend had already reserved it.

Later, when Georges would recall this night, he remembered not being at all shocked when the crew-cut, stark-white kid came back, this time flanked by two bigger men. It was quiet, except for the sound of soles crunching on rock salt, no words. One of the bigger men simply removed both hands from his pockets, Georges saw a quick tinge of light on the man's fisted fingers. The three stood before them, and one

70

let out a long foggy breath. Again the flash of light as the bigger man swung his fist suddenly. The blow he delivered to Eric's head was muted and dropped him like a wet newspaper to the pavement, where he lied motionless.

The kid from the counter then turned to Georges. "And this fuckin' towel head too, always up in the reserve, ain't you? All these fuckin' niggers do is read books. All's they study is shit like engineering, can't speak English but they all speak calculator." He laughed.

Georges now saw what was in the big man's hand. It was a combination lock, the latch looped across his knuckle. The guy noticed Georges's gaze, wrapped his hand tightly around the lock, the little sickening click sound.

"Commi Egyptian fucks, alla yous."

He grabbed Georges by the shirt and pushed him hard. As his head bashed into the plate glass behind him, there was a bright light, and when he opened his eyes stars moved through the sky. It was now as if the three men had grown and the night had gotten darker, little comets shooting here and there.

Georges put his hands up, said calmly, "I was born in Somerville Hospital in 1952."

The kid holding his shirt grinned sideways.

Then he repeated, more quickly, "I was born in Somerville Hospital in 1952."

"Shut the fuck up." The kid slapped him across the face.

"I'm from Somerville." This time his voice came out a whimper.

"Ain't from shit."

Georges muttered something, tried to form the same sentence, but only a squeak came from his lips. He started to form the word God in his head, and as the guy pushed him against the glass, the word leaked from his mouth.

"What's that? You praying, you fucking queer?" He turned. "You hear that?"

The man to his left sunk a low hook into his ribs, knocking the wind from him, a tight ache now in his side. He couldn't breathe, and the panic rushed into him, his brain trying to force air back into his lungs, telling himself to perform that most fundamental action, but nothing came. And as his head began to go faint, the word God came to him again, this time as Allah. For the first time in many years Georges closed his eyes and prayed to Allah. He asked for nothing, but simply repeated the name over and over in his head with his eyes shut. The same white light flooded his brain and even hurt his eyes, like sunlight, and the stars moved across his inner eye.

"Hey!" A voice came from far away.

He opened his eyes.

A man shouted, "Hey! What the fuck?"

He squinted to see in the distance a group of people hurrying toward them. As they got closer, he recognized several of them as his hall mates from Van Meter, along with about a dozen others, all tripped out in patched pants and army jackets, long hair.

"Maraca?" It was Stan.

But Georges could only nod.

"Hey, fuck off, you broads."

Now the group was surrounding the three men. Two of the women knelt by Eric, turned him over. He moaned.

The guy slammed Georges once more against the window, let go of his shirt. "What you gonna do, huh? What?"

"There's more of us than you," said Stan, followed by a chorus of mumbles.

The three men turned now on the crowd, puffed their chests a few times, looked down at Eric. "Fuck 'em. Fuckin' commis all run together."

Then the kid from the reserve desk turned to Georges. "We'll see you around, towel boy. Don't even think of telling nobody. Got six of my family on the force. I know where you live too. Got your name, Georges, got everything."

Then the three men bumped through the crowd, shoving a few of the hippies sideways.

An ambulance was called but would take what seemed like hours to arrive. Georges could do nothing but slump down on his haunches and sulk into his hands as the group gathered around him. He felt innumerable hands on his head, his shoulders, even the white girls touched his thigh, held his hand. All was dark in his mind as he sat in the cold, and the hands were indistinguishable as single hands but rather felt like the heat of a blanket. A great tremor overtook him, as if the offered warmth shorted his system. He shook and it drew a few gentle coos from the girls. "Oh God." All went white in his mind, and he swore he heard a whisper, not formed as a word, but a simple, calming breath. Then nothing, not a single thought.

CHAPTER 9

Goddamn Alec.

Emma drew the shades, letting in more of that mid-afternoon sunlight Fadi used to tell time. No one had opened the shade before, not even Tully. It put into relief the dust on the table, the window sill, even the metal footboard.

Why did you poison my mind right before an interview?

"Better?" she asked.

"Thank you."

"And how do you feel without the restraints? Are you more comfortable?"

He turned his head toward her, laughed. "Oh yes. In fact, the light is so nice, and my limbs feel so much better, let me tell you all about my friends and where they live, what their plans are."

She laughed.

This pressure. Why can't they understand? Pressure doesn't help. Not me, not our subjects. Especially not someone like Fadi. But Alec had barged into her office, first thing, to make sure Emma felt it. We need something, and fast. He was a fist of stress, and Emma had to decompress herself before meeting with Fadi. She could not betray even a hint of desperation.

Emma dragged a seat across the floor to the side of the bed. "I understand. How about if I promise not to try to get anything from you again today? Didn't I keep my promise?"

He looked toward the ceiling, a numb smile on his lips. Then in a spasm he drew a quick breath, winced.

"Are you okay?"

"Yes. Just a bit of a cramp. I'm fine."

"Is it strange? Your legs?"

"No, it's normal, feels like normal having no legs." He squirmed with a grimace on his face, a bit of sweat on his forehead.

She snorted. "So you're from Somerville, right? I went to Tufts."

"Yes, did Mr. England tell you that?"

"I used to work with Mr. England. In Morocco. Egypt for a bit."

He smiled. "Is this why you're here? Because I'm Moroccan? Because you can relate to me?"

"How are you Moroccan if you're from Somerville? I'd say you're American. If you were truly Moroccan you'd be in rather less pleasant circumstances right now. You certainly wouldn't be in such a nice room."

"My father was born in Beni-Mellal. My mother was a white French Canadian. How does that make me American?"

"Because you were born here. There is no way around that. That's what American is, nothing in particular.»

He laughed. "It's the Statue of Liberty. Is that your direction? I was as good a citizen as anyone. My father was the perfect example of what an immigrant is supposed to be, supposed to act like. He worked eighty hours each week, started at the bottom and ran his own business until the very day he died. He married a white woman to further cloud his race and make his family closer to white. He did everything right. Imagine him crossing the ocean all those years ago, *illegal*, arrives with nothing, works disgusting jobs. He's thinking all the while how he'll evolve, progress toward a life of comfort, of providing. Money. So he works himself to the bone for the next thirty-five years, scrubbing, managing, pouring coffee, scrimping through the tough times when people wouldn't come in. His head down all the while, still aimed at that thoughtless end: to be successful in America."

"And I imagine Somerville wasn't an easy place. Especially east. I lived on Broadway for a while. You know Ball Square?"

"Yes, I know Ball Square." He laughed then winced in pain.

"What?"

"If only you were sincere with your questions." He looked at the ceiling, smiling. "That area was terrific. I wish I could talk to someone about it."

75

"Why not me?"

"You are an interrogator. A 'gator' as you like to be called."

"I don't like that name. And like I said, I'm not trying to get anything from you today. That was a special area to me also. For less time."

He rolled his one good eye. "You were a student, not a local. Somerville is very different."

"Do you remember The Paddock? Paddy's? They had the best pizza."

"Quite brave of you to go there. A Tufts student, a woman. And your southern accent, I bet it was even thicker back then, which Boston people love. I imagine the locals were very nice to you."

"After a few weeks, yes. I got to know the bartenders." She paused. "You have an ear for accents."

He turned his head and squinted at the sunlight, seemed to consider something. "UMass. That is where eastern Mass went, those who had any brain and at least a little money. That was where you met the true chowderheads, the grit. Not Harvard or Tufts or MIT."

"You went to MIT too, didn't you?"

"You know I did. Can you please stop asking me questions to which you already know the answer?" He laughed. "For both our sakes?"

"Was it tough?"

"Yes."

"But you graduated early."

"I spent my summers there. I wasn't as smart as the others, but I worked harder than anyone. I worked in the dining hall kitchen and drove a delivery van for a caterer."

"MIT is where you learned about electricity."

"No. UMass. That's where I learned the very basics and a little above the basics. That's all you need. The high theory and engineering, that's if you want to become a professor or to work at a big corporation, maybe one right near MIT. Look at Franklin. He read a few elementary books on current, leyden jars, very basic things, the rest was in doing. You learn by looking at things the way they are, studying what is, not what might be."

"That's how you came to invent the...what do you call your system?"

"Conservator is what it was called eventually. But it is simply a self-assignment system for elevators. You see..."

76

"I read your file. I know the gist of it."

He grinned. "Yes, I don't want to bore you."

"But your patent allowed you to retire, didn't it? Like Franklin, though even younger."

He regarded her.

"I'm a bit of a Franklin nut myself. Funny, he earned enough money to retire so he could pursue his electrical studies. You earned enough money to retire *because* of your electrical advances."

"The money from that was largely inconsequential."

She snorted again. "I beg to differ. A lot of people would find consequence in that kind of money."

"Any American."

"So then you would. Because you're American."

He ignored her. "The patent allowed me time to focus on more important goals. I was freed from my father's fate. I wouldn't have to work myself to death. I would have time for my family, for pursuits I saw as noble. Although, starting my company did still consume some of my time."

"And did your brother help free up your time? Yusef?"

"I gave Yusef a gift. Heading the company was perfect for him. He had a bureaucratic mind for it, the paperwork, jumping through all the proper hoops."

"He also made more money for you, right?"

"Again, inconsequential. And the money came easily with the patent, along with several others. You see, it was my idea to package the Conservator with our other, less original hardware. That way, we were able to sell multiple systems to all these new buildings springing up, we did all their elevator work. And with the Conservator saving them so much money on power, we had no problem finding clients." His voice sank a register, almost to a snarl. "So, you ask if Yusef helped me make money. No, he didn't. I helped *him*. I allowed his large family to grow larger. I paid for him to move to Belmont so he could try to sneak himself in with America's picket-fencers. His kids, now that they were diluted further by their Irish mother, would pass for European. My invention allowed all this."

"Did he have a share of the company?"

He looked incredulous. "Yes, he had control. I gave him control. I never had any interest in being a company man, which Yusef was so good at. I continued to receive my due for founding the company. But by the time I was thirty I had almost nothing to do with its running. Then one day I get a piece of company mail, a statement. And on the top of the letter is written Joseph Subdallah, President. *Joseph*. He would have changed his last name too, if he could."

"When did you last speak with him?"

Fadi turned his head toward her, paused. Then a huge smile spread across his face. Emma was disoriented by it. He looked handsome briefly, or at least that smile of his, for a few seconds, made him look human. Fadi laughed and said, "My God."

"What?"

"You have quite a style, don't you? Sitting there with your posture, question after question. Look how serious you are?"

"How serious *I* am?"

"Yes, you. You're less an interrogator and more like a blind date, you know that? These questions, when was the last date you had? Are you married?" He looked at her hand.

She smiled, re-crossed her legs. "Well, I told you, I'm not trying to squeeze you today. I'm just talking."

"More like I'm doing the talking here. Anyway, where were we? Yes. I haven't spoken with Yusef in probably five years. I sent him gifts and his children gifts. I'm still their uncle, even though they have everything. They celebrate Christmas. Can you believe that?"

"Didn't you? With your mother?"

He shifted. "Not really, no. We would have gifts during that time, but not Christmas. My poor father wanted so badly to be a part of this country. He did everything he could think of. It had nothing to do with my mother."

"When was the last time you spoke to her?"

"Are you gathering a list of possible incentives? Someone whose safety you can use as leverage for information?"

"Just talking. I know, roughly, how long it's been. Maybe four years?

Is that about right?"

"June 24th, 1986. Her birthday. That was the last time. I sent her a gift each year, but we never spoke. She disapproved of my moving overseas, taking her granddaughter. She never liked Fatu, either, our marriage.»

"Did you ever want Nadat to go to school here? Isn't it safer?"

"I wanted her to see the world when she was young, the Arab world. I wanted her to learn Arabic first, to grow up with her own people and family there." Fadi's voice faltered. "Shit."

A tear ran down one side of his face. It was surprising to Emma that his right arm tried to reach for his face, given that he'd been without a hand and lashed to the bed for so long.

"Please, allow me," she said as she reached for a cloth.

"No." He wiggled to his left, smeared his face along the pillow, sniffed wetly. "You see? Your job will be most difficult." He squirmed under the restraints, like a turtle on its back. "You might be excited to finally see what means something to me, what you might use to get me to talk."

When he turned, the sunlight shown on his face, the crevices torn by self-infliction, torn in attempted exit from this place, but still Emma saw the scars trying to seal themselves back together against their master's wish.

Finally he settled and fixed both of those eyes on her, the one dead and icy, the other very much alive. "But all that is gone. Fatu is dead. My Nadat is dead."

Dinner was late that night. Fadi was wheeled into a room adjacent to the kitchen, another small, undecorated concrete place, where he was positioned sitting upright, his limbs unfettered.

Pouring rain outside, just like that night. The place got so quiet after dark, and the only sound was the constant rush of raindrops. And it was the same room they'd put him in all those months ago too when he was first starting to gain a mental grip on his surroundings, after those black months of coma. That night replayed in his brain over and over, the letters, the words. Back on that night it wasn't Tully, but rather some quiet young nurse with a frying-pan face, someone he'd never seen before or since. She slid the hospital table through the door and placed it across his lap then left the room without a word. Several minutes went by, no sign of Tully, then several more. Fadi was starving and eager to see what nameless mess awaited him, so he grabbed the cover between his two fingers and lifted it away.

It was that dull pink ham, two slices on a plate. But what Fadi saw next caused him to lose his grip on the metal cover, which went smashing to the floor. He reared back, his heart pounding, lungs sucking for air. He sat frozen for what seemed like an hour before finally swiping his right nub across the plate, erasing what was there just seconds before Tully arrived, dragging his bad leg behind him. But the image stuck in his head. Scrawled across the plate and the slices of ham, in bright yellow mustard, were the words: "TALK SHE DIE."

CHAPTER 10

There was sobbing and strange prayers in a language Georges half understood. Eric's family — those who lived in the US — gathered around his hospital bed like mourners. Without exception, all the men were enraged, all the women in tears. They kissed Georges on the cheek and mumbled a few words and offered gestures of peace to him. They must have assumed he and Eric were great friends.

Georges found himself stunned, speechless, and unable to move. He imagined his body absorbing the emotions as they churned about the room. How loved Eric was, how insulted and angered were his cousins and uncles, how heart-broken his aunts. And he thought of the girls who'd crowded around him that night outside the library, their hands on his cheeks and his neck.

That afternoon he went to the library, up to the reserve desk on the 21st floor, and in his most tranquil, innocent voice, inquired about the kid who worked Thursday nights, said he thought he'd gone to high school with him, just wanted to know his name. The girl behind the counter paused to study him — Georges was certain she knew the kid was in trouble, the police had surely come by to question the staff. But she told him his name was Tim Dunn.

Though he was tempted to ask where he lived, he held his tongue, instead thumbing through the campus directory, hoping that Dunn was listed, that his dorm address was current. It turned out he lived in the Southwest towers, not forty feet from Eric's dorm, and across campus from Georges's. He sat in his room with the booklet open, looking every few minutes at Dunn's name, his address, hoping it was this year's address, but between every few thoughts came a lilting, almost cowardly voice in his head, muttering a quick, dim prayer for the address to be old, for Dunn to be lost, for him to quit school.

After dinner time, his roommate returned, followed soon thereafter by a line of the usual hippies. And of course the place filled with smoke, despite the open windows. They asked after Eric, a few of them having been there two nights prior or at least having heard the news. In the short while he'd lived among the potheads of Van Meter, Georges had come to understand that their distaste for any show of aggression or violence trumped pretty much any other ethos. Even with Georges being a Muslim, with his darker skin and coarse hair, to them Dunn and his buddies were the true others.

But their presence tonight served only to irritate Georges's ticking mind. He struggled to fully convince himself that a reaction was necessary, that giving way to this white, blinding rage was the only way to get rid of it. And to do that he needed to be assured of the impossibility of ever assimilating to this place. He needed to be reminded of all the times he'd been called commi or towelhead. The pats on the back each of the kids had given him, the echoes of camaraderie and assurances of protection confused him. All he sought was a single-mindedness, to know one thing for sure and to do it. All his life the greatest thing he lacked was an exact direction, an all-knowing finger pointing him toward the right decision: soccer or football, Georges or Maraca. Such a voice could be crystallized if only these people would not be so damn friendly.

He had to get out of that tightly packed and smoked-in room, so he shoved a few things into his backpack and left the dorm, heading down the hill to campus with no destination in mind. He wanted sanctuary, a quiet space. He was tempted to call home, to speak with his mother, who he had always turned to for her calming influence, the coolness of her voice. But how could she truly give him advice? She had never faced violence directed at her very being, aggression toward nothing more than the fact of her existence. And his father would, as always, simply regale him with tales of the 50s, back when integration was unheard of, back before he could have any hopes of attending university or forging any white friendships. His father would dismiss whatever assertions Georges made about prejudice or bigotry still existing.

So he walked to the center of campus, circled the pond as his mind announced thoughts alternately of rage and temerity, the near crippling anger, the balancing peace. He sat for a while on a bench near the water but was bothered by a group of students behind him sitting on the grass in a circle, breaking into laughter every few minutes. At the Campus Center he sat with a cup of coffee, watching the kids go by with backpacks, the same clothes, the same smiles. Two linemen from the team walked right by him.

As the sky grew dark, he headed down the central walkway, past Bartlett Hall and Herter, then onto Stockbridge road, where he stood at a bus stop, not even sure where the route would take him. After twenty minutes he changed his mind, found himself smoking outside the Catholic Newman Center, in front of which stood a sign, "Offer Kindness to All With Good Will." Figuring the place would be empty on a Saturday evening, he walked through the front doors, followed the sound of organ music, and came into the chapel. Inside the small place a man was seated below the great organ pipes, booming slow and deep notes. Georges sat in the last pew, studied the depictions in stained glass of St. Stephen, St. Mark, Paul, St. Justin of Palestine.

Going to the very back corner, which was dark and where the dark wood was padded by red carpet, he removed the musallah from his backpack, unrolled it on the floor, facing toward the front of the chapel, slightly skewed. He placed it just to the side of the soft carpet, directly on the wood. The old rug had been given to him by his uncle on his eighteenth birthday. Georges had been uncomfortable then by the man's admonitions, "Do not lose your way." But as he knelt now the cushion on his knees instantly calmed him. It had been years since his last salah, and he'd forgotten the positions, was tempted to use the nearby holy water to cleanse his face for ablution but thought better of it.

As he brought his forehead and hands to the floor, a single tear ran along his nose and dripped to the rug. Flashes from that night came into his head but from what now seemed a great distance, and he saw himself from far away and was calmed. It could have been seconds or ten minutes that brought him to this place, this stillness of mind, but the organ music was all he heard, and the wet tears were all he felt, flowing in a definite route over which he had no control, and this too soothed him. Is this praying? Am I praying now?

The next moment he was aware of a hand on his shoulder. He had fallen asleep, prostrate, hands and knees and toes and palms on the floor.

"Pardon me."

Georges pulled back with a start, jumped to his feet. Before him crouched a man, chubby, mid-thirties perhaps, black trousers and white buttoned shirt.

"I didn't mean to startle you, young man."

"I'm sorry. I..." But he didn't finish the sentence, instead rolling the rug and stuffing it back in the bag.

"It's okay. You are welcome to pray here. I should just advise you that a service is set to begin in fifteen minutes, which might be distracting. Please stay."

"Thank you, no. I'm fine."

Georges brushed past the man, saying thank you twice more as he exited.

Standing at the foot of the gigantic towers in the southwest corner of campus, fixing his eyes on what he thought was the 19th floor, imagining the lighted window was Dunn's. His pack was heavier now. Rolled inside the prayer rug sat a piece of metal pipe, what he'd found on his long walk here, in addition to a few sticks he'd decided against. Room 1902, 19th floor. Timothy Dunn.

Getting past the student security post was no problem. He simply told her he was visiting, flashed his campus ID as he hurried past. She didn't even record him as a guest. His ears popped, and the elevator doors opened with a chime on 19. The hallway was a square loop, with doors leading to rooms along the outside. Already music pulsed from behind the doors, a group of students squeezed by him with several six packs. A door opened, the volume rose, closed again.

Georges was frozen against the wall, his backpack across his chest now as he felt the tip of the pipe through canvas. What if Dunn emerged from one of these rooms? What if he was with the two ogres? He went to the men's room, which was empty, and sat on one of the toilets with the stall door closed. He sat for what might have been an hour as that dim voice whispered to him hopes that the address was wrong, that Dunn was nowhere near here, that Dunn was the one sitting on a toilet somewhere shivering, scared of the cops, scared of the retribution that was surely his due.

People came and went, used the urinals, the stalls, showered and shaved and washed their faces, all laughing and bright white skin with dark chest hair and Boston accents. He knew if he came out of the stall how their eyes would track him in the mirror. Soon the place was empty, so he unlocked the door, and it creaked with the first inch as he opened it. Then the bathroom door swung open. He gently shut the stall door, put his eye to the crack. The guy used the urinal, flushed, and went to the mirror. Dunn's reflection. He recognized the squirrelly face, the tight hair, the few pimples on his chin. He was running a little black comb through his hair, whistling, in a clean shirt, going out no doubt.

Georges unzipped the bag slowly, put his hand in and felt inside the rug for the pipe. Watching Dunn smooth that hair back while Eric wriggled in pain on that hospital bed, while Georges wandered across campus on a Saturday with the white kids roaming in packs and hoards of friends and the music boomed through the walls. He let the bag fall to the floor, unlocked the door. The voice that had assured him over and over that Dunn wasn't here, that he was cowering in some dark corner, now tried to whisper something to him but came out as a faint mumble. Then he heard his own voice squealing, "I was born in Somerville Hospital." Over and over.

The door squeaked again on that first few inches, and Georges froze, though Dunn didn't seem to hear it over his own whistling. Georges took two steps across the floor, the pipe behind his back, then slid two more steps until he was at Dunn's shoulder. He stood and saw his own face in the mirror, placid, nearly lifeless, his eyebrows arched in what looked like pity. Then he focused on Dunn, who was mid whistle. He brought the comb down by his side then put both hands up to chest level. But Georges had already started the pipe in its arc, swung over and down to the back of Dunn's head.

The kid's body flopped to the floor, though his hands came out just in time to pad his fall. Georges stood over him with the muffled bark of the music. Dunn moved a little, then brought his hands to his head, moaning. *I was born in Somerville Hospital.* His arm traced another blow onto Dunn's shin, then another. The kid let out a howl, and blood rushed from a crack at the back of his head, which sent Georges running out the door. He shoved the pipe down the front of his pants and pushed the button for the elevator, waited. After a few seconds he rushed to the stairwell and ran down nineteen flights of stairs. At the very bottom he checked the pipe for blood, none, and tossed it to the concrete floor, hurried out of the building.

It didn't occur to him that he'd left his bag behind until he was halfway back to Van Meter. He realized it contained nothing that could lead back to him, but his uncle's prayer rug would be discovered. He thought about the absolute comfort the coarse old fabric had offered his knees, the way he had fallen asleep there, the peace he had found that was now unfurled. He saw someone tearing the rug to shreds.

When he got back to his room, a few kids were still there, including Stan, playing some bootlegged live Zeppelin record, the scent of pot clinging to the place. "Hey, Maraca."

And Georges collapsed at his desk chair, let out a long breath. He stared at his right hand, which trembled a few seconds, but he watched and saw it calm itself, and his breathing was level, and his mind was clear at last. As he removed the shoes from his aching feet and rubbed his knee, he replied toward the ceiling, "Call me Georges. Okay?"

CHAPTER 11

Just a few pecks at a glass of gin and tonic, that was all, to loosen herself up. After all, this was her first date, essentially ever. She needed to relax, not think about work, not think about Evan or John. Arriving home from Friday rush hour, she'd decided to pour herself a little drink, smoke a cigarette, dislodge work from her brain.

So, in that squared-off government sofa from the 70s, she'd plopped down with a rattle from the ice in her glass, lit a cigarette, and begun to study, for a third time, the little dossier sent to her by Beltway Connections.

Taking a drag, "Ryan Schank." Exhaling. "Who are you?"

No matter how many times she scrutinized his profile, no real sense of the man in the little passport photo came through. His description was as much bullshit as hers. "Mature (but not *too* mature) professional, looking for that perfect woman to explore the world and grow old with. Movies and wine are a good place to start."

Thirty-five, never married, no kids. Industry: restaurant.

As the sun sank west and dimmed the living room, Emma flicked on the lamp on the side table, gulped the last of the gin, and headed back to the kitchen. She swished the glass in the sink then began to picture the scene at dinner: sitting across from him, questions about each other's jobs, will the rain ever let up, a joke or two from Mr. Schank that she'd have to laugh at. Not only that, but she'd have to be *convincing*. So she decided another quick drink would do the trick, make that laugh easier. A few ice cubes, splash of gin and then another splash, that fizzy tonic. Before leaving she glanced around the living room then straightened up the pillows on the couch and swept crumbs from the coffee table.

The Thai place in Arlington would have been tough to find in daylight and without that second drink (or the third little gulp right before leaving). When she finally pulled up, there were no spots left, so she had to park a ways down the street and then clack along the sidewalk in those flimsy old heels. Her original plan had been to get a cut and color the night before, maybe even a manicure, but the night's interrogations and post-briefs had wandered on too late.

So this was her best effort, arriving late, frazzled, several drinks deep. She wore a conservative periwinkle dress and sort of matching purse, unevenly worn heels, her hair blown dry, three minutes worth of make-up, nails painted in some color called "coy blush," and the silver earrings she'd gotten in Egypt.

She saw him right away, in promised white shirt and blue sport coat, standing by the bar with a glass in his hand. He waved and smiled, took a few steps toward her.

"Hi, very nice to meet you."

They shook hands.

"Nice to meet you too," she said.

That hand went right into his pocket. Emma had neither pockets nor a drink to occupy herself. They stood a few seconds, and Emma's eyes scanned the room. The place was busy, each barstool taken, several couples and nicely dressed co-workers standing with beer bottles or wine glasses.

"We have a reservation, but I think we have time for a drink here. Can I get you something?"

"Bombay and tonic." The words left a bit too quickly.

"Sure."

They stood next to a group of younger professionals while Ryan flagged down the bartender, ordered her drink, paid, and handed it to her.

"To Beltway Connections," raising his glass.

"Cheers."

"This your first date?"

"What? No."

"No, I mean, through Beltway?"

"Oh. Yes. You?"

"My second."

I wonder what happened on the first.

They talked for several minutes, Ryan framing questions to Emma, she at best sending them right back his way. Within a few minutes, she had finished the gin and tonic, which she thought was light on the Bombay. Ryan suggested they get another and bring it to their table.

The dining room was loud and packed and dimly lighted, with intricate wood carvings of elephants under the glass tabletops. Most of the guests sat at regular seats, but in the center of the room were six low tables with only cushions to sit on. Ryan had specially reserved a small table in the middle. So here they sat, crossed legged on the floor, no back support, the booze washing over Emma, who now wished they'd sat in the smoking section, something she typically found vulgar.

She thought of her dark little apartment, of regular Friday nights, a few drinks, a cigarette, clicking around the few TV channels, then early to bed. "So," she said, "what do you do?"

"I own a few restaurants in Fairfax, over off Braddock. Sort of German, family-style."

"That sounds interesting."

"You'll have to come by some night. The food's almost edible." He paused and then smiled.

On queue Emma's face lit up and she laughed, leaned forward over the table.

When she'd stopped, he asked, "And you work for the government?"

"Yes, I…"

A waiter appeared and took their orders. Ryan suggested they split a bottle of chardonnay, to which Emma nodded, and also pointed to the empty glass in her hand, "Bombay and tonic, please."

"So what sort of work with the government?"

"Yes. The goverm…nment." Nodding. "Mostly defense."

"So would that be somewhere around here?"

"Somewhere, yes."

"And you mentioned Egypt earlier. When were you there?"

"About ten years ago. Interrogations." She said this last word slowly, with mock gravity.

Shaking his head, "See, that's *fascinating* to me. You get to travel the world, see exotic places, do work that actually helps people. Me, I'm pouring over accounts on a Sunday, trying to keep my books from going up in smoke."

She laughed again, and only because of his face did she realize it wasn't supposed to be *that* funny.

The waiter came back with a green bottle and bucket of ice, showed its label to Ryan. Emma stood, mumbling "excuse me," and headed toward the bathroom. After using the toilet she stood in front of the mirror, looking into her own eyes, trying to ignore the darkness just below or the wrinkles to either side. *What are you doing? You're blowing it on purpose. How drunk are you? Easy on the Bombay. How are you so good with questions and yet so bad with them? You know nothing about this guy, aren't you interested, don't you* want *to be happy? If you're going to sabotage, then admit it. Don't pretend like you want this date to work.*

A toilet flushed and a stall door swung open. Emma began to wash her hands. A young, pretty girl in a dress that was too short stood at the sink beside her and opened a compact, dabbed her cheeks, then glanced at Emma. "Oh my God, I *love* those earrings."

Touching both ears. "Oh, thank you." And a little smile.

When she'd returned from the bathroom, their food was waiting, two red curry dishes with a mound of molded rice. They both tried chopsticks before giving up and going with knife and fork. The bottle of wine emptied quickly, Ryan now gulping at it and refilling both their glasses. The gin and tonic sat untouched throughout the meal, but once the wine was gone Emma needed something to sip on.

The check arrived, and Ryan reached for it, but Emma intercepted him, insisting they split it. After a good deal of argument, Ryan relented, and Emma put a few twenties on the table. They stood and moved back to the bar.

She could tell Ryan was a little drunk when he waved his hand dreamily at the bartender. He handed her another drink and moved closer, leaning in a bit.

They walked through the front door and into her apartment. "We've got gin and we've got tonic."

"Great."

She poured two drinks with a single ice cube each, because she'd forgotten to refill the trays, and brought them into the living room. She sat next to him. Ryan was drunk and nervous and turned the glass on his palm. Very suddenly he moved in and planted a wet kiss on her neck then moved to her lips. Emma edged back and smiled at him, then looked at her drink before taking a sip.

Ryan took a sip too and smiled, and they sat in silence a while.

Pointing to a small picture of the Aswan dam that stood leaning against a wall, he said, "So…yeah, Egypt. That's *fascinating*."

"It's another world."

"You're interrogating…*who* is it?"

"Bad guys. All bad guys."

"You're getting intel from them? Something we can use to catch other bad guys?"

"That's pretty much it, Ryan."

"What a great feeling that must have been. To know you're doing something to save other people."

She looked into her drink. "Yes."

"So, it was a while ago. I'm sure you're allowed to talk about it. I mean, I don't want to get you in trouble or anything. But…what a neat thing."

"It was something else." Swishing the ice cube around.

"What's one of the best ones?"

"Sorry?"

"A really big case. I mean, there must have been some very bad guys, Arabs. Someone you helped catch."

"Well, Ryan, it's funny. You ever hear of Al-Thaghr?"

He made a face as if deep in thought before finally shaking his head.

"Of course you haven't. Bad guys. *Real* bad guys. We caught this crop of young students, from Egypt, Saudi, Algeria, you name it, caught them buying up a lot of *plastique*. We had them in our little building, in the basement, put them through the paces, really uncomfy times for these youngsters, if you get my meaning. But one of them, Layth, he was different. He was kind, patient, and even seemed a little contrite, you know? Big brown eyes, always wide open. Anyway, Layth and I, we became friends. As much as possible, given the circumstances. I did a lot for him, made things better for him there, made it so the worst of the interrogators would never deal with him. I pulled strings, because Layth was giving me some juicy, juicy intel. Weapons caches, plans. But even bigger, he was giving up his boss."

A wave of nausea passed through Emma's stomach.

"The weird thing is that I began to *trust* the kid. I was a kid myself back then. But Ryan, you know what happened?"

He shook his head, eyes focused on her.

"Well, I cooked up a deal to give Layth leniency. In exchange for his big, big boss's whereabouts. We made a deal, and I backed him. I went to *my* boss and told him, 'this guy is different. He's telling the truth. I'd put my reputation on it'. So, Layth gives us a few names, some locations, we set up a really beautiful sting." She leaned toward him. "And do we get him?"

He shrugged, his eyes hazy.

"We *do*, Mr. Schank," hitting his shoulder. "Can you believe it? We actually get the bastard. And I look like a damn hero. I get up on my horse, of course…of course and start preaching that this is the way we have to operate. No more torture…oops, I'm sorry," patting Ryan's arm, "I'm not supposed to say that…*ssshhhh*. We're *nice* to people. Well, we let Layth go. After all, he helped us. Some time goes on, we think we're really getting somewhere. A month passes, then two. Then my boss calls me into his office, says he has an update on my boyfriend, Layth."

Emma looked over at the picture of the dam.

"You see, Layth was not a good man. He went back to his buddies, back to Al-Thaghr, pretty much immediately after we let him go. And he schemed, and he schemed, and he and his brothers built a pretty cool little vest, which he then wore into a market in Cairo, and he pushed a little button. And then…" She made a cartoonish explosion sound while moving her cupped hands apart slowly. "Kids, a few babies, women, men. Bye-bye."

Ryan reared back. "Oh my God."

"So, yeah, it was cool work."

"How could you have known?"

"I'm *supposed* to know. All I was there for was to know. You see, Ryan, I can really read people. We read people and get whatever we want out of them, and that stops them from doing bad stuff. Except when it doesn't." She put her glass down. "Where's the bartender?"

"Can we maybe take a break?"

Emma crossed her arms and looked down at her feet, nodded slowly with a little sway from side to side. Still looking down, "I'm a bad date, huh?"

"I've had a fine time." Ryan placed his glass on the table.

"But you're going."

"I think I should."

She placed her hand on his neck and scooted closer to him and put her lips to his and focused her mind on kissing him, on what the movements of her lips should be.

He pulled his head away and gently took her hand from his neck and held it. "It's okay, it's okay."

She didn't realize what he meant until she felt the first bit of wetness along her cheek.

Reg Olsen was a patient man and a competent analyst, a fact Emma found at first perturbing. She was used to being at odds with any analyst she might be paired with. They were typically civilian and never actually in any rooms, never exposed to the very human eyes of their subjects. This created a clear division line between them and interrogators. That, and the fact that analysts often knew more intel than their partners, a broader set of facts, connections, possibilities. *Macros*. All of this was intentionally controlled by men like Randolph in order to avoid too much information inhabiting any single interrogator's mind. Particularly, the true repercussions, plans, and gravity of any single *guest* were often made opaque to Emma and her colleagues.

So it was annoying when Emma began to like Reg's company. Though this morning a grand headache made Reg's propriety irritating.

He was in his mid-fifties, gray, single, and very kind right off. Smart, too, the sort that made her think he had some experience in domestic criminal work, if behind the scenes. Reg, like everyone else, referred to their subjects as Visitors or Guests, almost as if these men, who stayed up for days in a row and had to be transported from room to room in black hoods, were simply passing through their hotel for a few days. Emma thought perhaps the joke helped everyone retain a cognitive distance. But Harrison was also a strange place; what else would you call these men: prisoners, detainees, subjects? They were nothing, really, fleeting occupants of the sparse rooms, not put through the legal system, usually not extradited to their home countries (who just as often rejected them), and certainly not protected by much.

Fadi's was a rare case, owing partly to his US citizenship, partly to his public death. So he was detained in this halfway house for an indeterminate amount of time, sitting in his room for hours alone, not yet put into the proper justice system, the men Upstairs still holding out hope that he'd be the one to break this thing open, to give them that elusive nugget about the head of Al-Thaghr and his magnum opus.

Emma and Reg sat across from each other in a bland interview room, at the plain folding table, on two folding chairs, sorting through stacks of papers Reg had prepared the night prior. Like all analysts, Reg had purview into a more macro level here, though not as broadly as Alec Randolph. He collected intel across multiple guests and interviews, making ties, corroborating intel as best he could, and wading through a sewer of lies, hearsay, and misinformation, later to be doled out to the 'gators.

Always walking around with that manila folder...

Alec knocked and opened the door at the same time, greeted them both, then called Reg over to him.

Emma pretended to be making notes to the transcript of yesterday's Fadi chat but was really listening, as best she could, to their conversation, rare as it was for the two of them to speak in her presence. With her eyes on the table, she could scarcely make out a word they were saying, but from their tone she guessed Alec was stressed, that he'd just been given a dose of pressure from his superiors. Urgency was one of the main driving forces here. And though she couldn't hear their words, this conversation was full of it.

When they'd finished speaking, Reg returned to his seat, betraying none of the gravity of their talk. And Alec took a seat beside Emma.

"How many sessions with Subdallah so far?"

"Just a handful," she said, making a tick next to some random line of script.

"It looks as if he's opening up."

Emma turned to face him, but without eye contact, pretended to be thinking, but really she wanted to remind Alec that he was no interrogator.

"Do you think you still remember how to tell when a guest is ripe?" He tried to say this as a joke. "After all this time?"

She looked back down at the paper, circled the word "question" for no reason. "He's still a green banana, Alec."

"Not there yet."

"Suicide bomber, sir. We talked about this."

Alec glanced at Reg, whose eyes were buried in that manila folder.

"How many…" Alec paused here, and they both knew he was going to ask something you just didn't ask.

"How many more until he cracks?" Emma suggested.

Alec was silent.

"Probably one."

Here Reg looked up from his work.

"Or as many as a dozen." She grinned. "Baker's dozen."

"Goddamn it. I'm glad you're able to take this lightly."

"I'm not. That's the range. Maybe if you'd tell me more details it would go quicker. Give me something I can *use*."

"I've told you all I can." Alec stood quickly and walked toward the window, hand on hip. "How about if I told you to hurry the fuck up!"

He removed his sport coat, and Emma could see the patch of sweat at his lower back.

"A new motivation technique, sir?"

"I'm glad this is a chuckle. You don't see Reg laughing, do you?"

"I've never seen him laugh at anything."

"Alright," he said, putting his coat right back on and heading toward the door. "I don't have time for this shit. Reg, please tell *Miss* Ripley where we're at."

He left and the door clanged shut a second later.

Reg did not make eye contact, eyes fixed on that folder.

"So where are we, Reggie?" She shrugged.

"Well, we have a few new flag words to try with him. I have one or two lukewarm locations we could use him to triangulate…"

"We're talking about Fadi, here? The dead guy, guy who's been cooped up in this turd farm for a year?" She smiled. "Locations, from him?"

Reg took a long breath in, seemed frustrated for the first time Emma could recall.

After a few minutes, he said, "Think I'll use the head." He stood.

Emma leaned back in her chair, stretched her arms behind her, yawned. "I could use a coffee. Might join you." She stood, kicked her chair back. "Need one?"

"No, thank you."

They both paused at the table a few seconds, Emma making a point to gaze toward the drawn window, while from the corner of her eye she could see Reg rap his fingertips on the folder twice. Now it would be awkward for him to take the folder with him. And he knew the coffee machine was two floors down, while the men's room was straight down the hall.

She took one step just as Reg did, and they both walked toward the door. Reg opened it and held it for her. She stepped into the hallway, Reg right behind her.

"Sure?"

"No, thanks." He patted his belly.

The coffee vending machine was in the opposite direction of the men's room, so she at first took a step with him, then turned on her heel. She headed the other way, turned the corner, and paused for two beats. Then she crept back around to watch as Reg headed down the long hallway, footfalls echoing. She slid along the wall and grabbed the doorknob, turning it gently, all the while eyeing the older man as he walked.

She slipped inside and eased the door closed.

Once inside, she dashed over to the table and cracked open the folder. In it were a few dozen typed papers, interview transcripts, along with guest profiles and a master timeline Emma had seen a dozen times. She flipped through the pages, glancing toward the door, back and forth, scanning – some of the 4x4 photos she recognized; others were new.

"Fuck."

Her fingers slowed. The transcripts were all similes of one another: that same language; denials; any quotes with names, dates, or locations highlighted in pea green. But nothing macro, nothing about Karim or Al-Thaghr's plan. Any corroborated dates or locations were marked in red, of which there was only one: Caldwell. Lot of use that was. Subdallah, Musif, Sahdim, Maples…all men she was more than familiar with.

Emma was beginning to lose hope and get more nervous that Reg would be back any second now. Then the last bundle of five or so pages, stapled together, the cover of which was a profile. Name: Ali Al-Somali Al-Jeddah. The photo of sunken eyes, dark and as if from a great distance, looking fatigued by the world they beheld. *This was him.* It was a face she knew, but only from old photos, grainy, often from a distance.

Capture Date: 9/29/89

"Those fucks!"

They have him. They've had him for two weeks.

"Thanks for telling *me*!"

She glanced up at the door, her heart now fluttering. Excited, she was excited, they had an entire level now: Fadi and Ali. But they hadn't told her! *Easy, don't let them know you know, data asymmetry, flip it on the bastards. Use it.*

Following his profile page were a brief transcript (Bauer had gotten impressively little from the man) and two pages of connection briefing: confirmed facts or locations or schemes directly connected to this guest. Then his cycle: sleep deprivation, prolonged standing, prolonged sitting, low rations: the typical introduction. But it seemed as if Ali was holding up well.

Her mind now racing, Emma could barely set her eyes to focus, but she skimmed until she noticed a number: 4,500. Projected civilian impact: 3,000 to *4,500* dead. Next was a paragraph, pecked out by old Reg on a typewriter, a synopsis of plausible intel, as it was called, outlining no details of the actual planned attack – sea, land, air – only that it was, as they'd suspected, in the U.S., and aimed to eliminate 4,500 civilians.

There was a final page, the very last, thick with Reg's prose, but she didn't chance it. Emma stood, gripping the last leaf of paper, sweat now on her forehead. She quickly replaced the sheet, stacked the papers neatly, and slid them back into the folder, arranging it carefully on the table.

Then she flopped into her seat, took a pack from her breast pocket, tapped a single cigarette from it, lit and drew long and deep, exhaled. "Shit."

When the door opened she took up her pen and set it to paper, just as Reg was rounding the table. Cigarette in left hand, pen in right. The folder seemed to glow across from her. Reg took his seat and was silent a while, didn't touch the folder or any of the papers before him.

Again, he tapped his fingers across the folder, and Emma found herself unable to look up, simply ticking and circling random words on her script.

Finally, Reg puffed a long breath and said, "No coffee?"

CHAPTER 12

Georges spent the rest of the year checking over his shoulder as he walked across campus and took to wearing a new Sox cap wherever he went. He could find no report of an attack in John Quincy Adams tower, never saw Dunn at the Reserve desk again. Eric was released from the hospital after a few days, refusing to press charges, so the three men were never apprehended, though of course the story spread; the hippies from Van Meter had helped make sure of that. But just as Georges had feared, the mutation of fact as the tale went from lips to lips left it very different from its real form. Now, the two Muslim students had antagonized the three men, shouted at them, they were drunk, armed.

It was four weeks before the cops found him, likely through the reserve desk. As Georges sat studying in his room, two dark-blue men materialized in his doorway. They entered, confirmed his name, stumbled over his surname. "Where were you? Were you one of the men attacked that night at the library?" Georges was surprised at the calmness in his own voice as they questioned him.

He asked, "No charges were ever pressed against the kid who beat up Eric, were they?"

The two cops looked at each other. "No."

"Just wondering how you knew it was Dunn who did it."

"No charges were pressed."

After a few more minutes of questions, the men seemed satisfied. They stood to leave, then the red-haired man produced a rug from his bag, Georges's prayer rug. "Do you recognize this?"

He stared at it, perhaps for too long, but then he simply shrugged and pursed his lips. In perfect English he said, "I am not Muslim."

A few days later, as Georges sat quietly in the front row before class one morning, a girl explained to her friend how the two Muslim students had had some sort of metal lock or something around their knuckles. *Why else would someone in the hospital not press charges? If you're innocent, you would want the guys arrested, but he didn't do anything. He's hiding something.*

Stan came to visit Georges in his room often. He would plunk down — with or without a joint — on the old couch with the green cushions, around the same time each night: after practice, dinner, shower. Sometimes he would prattle on about Coach Lester's offense or the dining hall food. Georges usually spun around in his chair, listening with that patented smile. But in the past weeks he stayed focused on his books and his notes, grunting here and there.

Lighting half a joint. "How's your friend, by the way?"

"Eric." Nodding down at his papers. "Eric is good. He's a strong guy, already mostly healed up."

A little puff. "I guess you've got to be stronger than just a normal person."

"We're just normal too, not any stronger." Looking at the pencil in his hand. "A certain thing will hurt everyone the same."

Though Georges would always feel a bond with Eric — born probably from seeing the kid unconscious and murmuring — the two would drift apart over the next few years. At the hospital, Georges had shared with Eric his idea for some sort of club for minority students, to which Eric had simply shrugged. He expressed hesitancy about drawing attention to the fact that they were Muslim, and when Georges had his club Eric would later refuse the invitation to tell his story to a full auditorium.

At the first meeting of The Five Pillars he booked a huge room in the campus center, at the front of which stood a large blackboard where he wrote the night's agenda. Thinking specifically of Franklin's example for civic clubs, he wrote out very direct, actionable items, including coming up with a way to get the university to pay for a shuttle to the mosque in Springfield, listing the estimated price and frequency. The last item, as would be the case over the many subsequent years, was to open the floor for suggestions, all of which would be listed and then voted on, the top three making the final. These agenda items would then become the focus of the next meeting, each member charged to come up with workable solutions for next week. This helped steer and control the content of the meetings, and all the while he gave the impression that the club had been around for quite some time. Some members suggested prayer at the end of each meeting, which Georges said was a great idea but insisted that it be made optional, and he even booked an adjacent room for that purpose.

Fifteen students arrived at the first meeting, but the number slowly grew as spring approached, until at the last meeting of the school year, over fifty members showed up to write down their names and contact information. By mid-semester the next year Georges had garnered nearly two hundred members. What power he felt in standing before the crowd, controlling the meetings, the topics, calling on the raised hands. But he felt equally powerful when sitting quietly at the back of the long van on the way to Springfield, knowing his fellow members saw him as the leader of this great club, knowing he needn't even display his control. But for each time this feeling washed over him he reminded himself of what had happened that night with Eric, of his own weakness, and he prayed to remain humble.

He still created and paid for the printing of hundreds of flyers each week, assigning one member from each living area to post them, ensuring steady coverage across campus. The mid-70s saw much publicized turmoil in the Middle East, and only slightly less paranoia was focused on the Egyptians than their Russian allies. So on several occasions Georges saw derisive scrawls covering his flyers, or even opposing flyers placed on several billboards and trees, some more racist than others.

Public hate for their club, in its many forms, was growing and manifesting in more aggressive ways. At a meeting, two of the assigned members, in two different living areas, reported having been physically accosted while posting flyers. One even had her stack of papers taken from her. So as the last item of the day, Georges opened the floor to suggestions for how to combat this opposition. Dozens of members offered ideas, ranging from more passive ideas, like petitions, assigning night patrols, going to the administration; to more radical ones, like waiting in ambush in the more dangerous living areas and attacking the offenders with sticks, showing that the Muslim community was strong in numbers, suggesting that single cowardly bigots would never venture out in fear of such reprisal.

Each option was put to a vote, which drew the meeting well past midnight. The list was whittled down to the most popular three, which were petitions, administration, and a third—Georges's favorite—an open invitation to all students on campus to attend a club meeting.

Georges began work on a special flyer, written in English only, announcing an open forum discussion at The Five Pillars's next meeting. The heading read, "Two Female Students Maliciously Attacked," followed by an outline of the club's purpose and some of the recent aggressions toward members and the Arab community as a whole. He even convinced the two women to file reports with the campus police, though neither could provide a description of her assailant. He made triple the usual number of posters, assigned twelve members to flyer duty, and he used the influence of two members who worked for The Daily Collegian to get a blurb written in Monday's paper.

The larger room he booked in the Campus Center couldn't accommodate the huge turnout, which included students and faculty, a Collegian reporter and photographer, and even someone from the Hampshire Gazette. The Women's Rights Caucus was well represented, the reason Georges had intentionally called out the victims' sex.

Georges sat calmly in his chair behind the podium as the din grew louder, next to a few members he'd designated as sergeant at arms, secretary, and lieutenant. He did everything to give the appearance of a regular meeting, so on the board behind him was the agenda, including the three main items voted upon last week, one of which happened to be, "The attack on two female club members." He checked his watch twice, waiting until it was ten past the hour, then stood at the podium. All rows were packed with people, and others stood at the very back, the place growing silent as he stood. He waited a few more minutes, not saying a thing but letting the crowd grow aware of his presence.

The Five Pillars, that's who you are. You are the leader of The Five Pillars.

He said, "Two women were attacked last week. Your fellow students, here at UMass, classmates. Women. Perhaps two women who you've passed on campus. They were physically assaulted. One outside Hampshire in Southwest, another in Northeast. For doing nothing more than posting regular notice of a meeting, something we have done every week for quite some time. Men assaulted them, stole their belongings, printouts that had cost over fifteen dollars. But worse were the words they used, the verbal threats based on nothing but their clothing, their culture. These women have brothers who will have to hear this news. Imagine hearing this about your own sister, hundreds of miles away. Imagine how powerless you would feel.

"Maybe some of you don't have that twinge of emotion that I do in hearing this. Maybe you don't listen to this news and feel the fear that I do, or the anger. But you see, I've been in their shoes before. I too was assaulted, right here on campus, last winter. I watched a good friend of mine beaten unconscious by three grown men who held combination locks in their hands."

Here, he took a black and silver lock from the podium and held it up in the air. A flash and a snap from the camera.

"'I was born in Somerville,' I told them as they turned on me, aiming to do the same they'd done to my friend. All I could think to do was repeat that, 'I was born in Somerville.' I suppose out of the belief that I, as an American, would be exempt from their attack. But it did nothing. They grabbed me, slammed me against a wall, struck me in the ribcage."

He grasped the podium, looked down.

"I suppose I was trying to tell them that I was just like them. I was born on this soil. I've lived in this state my whole life, played football my whole life. But yes, my skin is darker, my hair isn't straight or fine. And as you look at my friends up here with me, you'll notice that they don't look quite like everyone else. But as much as I thought..."

Then a voice from the very back of the room, "TOWEL HEAD!"

All heads turned toward the noise, and there was a shifting of bodies back there. Several students from the club were standing and ran out of the room toward the person who'd yelled. Georges was silent, though the microphone did tempt him to speak and exhibit his power over the club members, to show those in attendance that his group was against violence, despite the violence heaped upon them. But he was quiet. He stood and waited, his chin up, hands on the podium, a stony look on his face.

He cleared his throat and went on, not mentioning the interruption, resisting the temptation to point this out as illustration. Instead he calmly recalled what had happened to Eric, how they had been saved, how good will toward them did truly exist at this school, but how violence persisted. He described the two women who had been accosted while posting flyers — where they came from, their families, their hobbies — but was vague about the actual details of their assault.

He had grown to relish the calm that soaked over him when he spoke before the club, and in this larger, more serious venue, the quiet gave him a good chill, made his skin crackle with life. Only the odd cough or the clicking of the camera, and his voice through the PA, filling the place, filling the ears of white students, faculty, strangers, his friends. On the podium was a simple piece of paper, scribbled with about a dozen words (Layla, Aba, attack, Somerville) to help guide him. It made him feel more sincere, more conversational to speak without a script. He paused, let silence rush in, then boomed back with heavy words.

"In a typical meeting of our club, we would announce this shared issue and, as a group, decide on the best course of action, democratically. Tonight is certainly a bit atypical. Tonight is itself the course of action. As a group we decided that too much violence has occurred, that we have found ourselves far too isolated from the community into which we hope to integrate ourselves, or at the very least to live peacefully with. Which is why we have opened up these doors. Our solution is to show ourselves, to show our fellow students that we are striving to be a part of this country and to allow this country to be part of ourselves. I hope you can realize the temptation we have to shut ourselves in, away from this violence, away from these feelings of alienation. We want to strengthen ourselves in numbers, to fight. But as great as that temptation is, the draw to truly become part of this school, this community — and I think I can speak for my brothers and sisters — is much greater.

"All are welcome to become members. After each meeting, we pass around a clipboard and sign-up sheet. Please, join our club, learn about who we are, how we are different, how we are similar. I'll say it again: everyone is welcome in our club."

After a brief pause, Georges continued with the other two items on the agenda: locating an alternative mosque to travel to, and pressing for greater accommodation for dining and schooling during Ramadan. As he transitioned abruptly to these fairly banal points, Georges could hear and feel the crowd stirring, restless in their seats. People along the very back wall shifted out of the room. When the meeting came to a close and the sheet was passed around, Georges handed the floor to Mahzar, the sergeant at arms, for announcements.

The two reporters approached Georges afterward, as the crowd filed out, the man from the Gazette noticeably irritated at having to wait for the student reporter to ask his questions. The Gazette was interested, apparently, in more incendiary quotes from Georges, prodding him in a certain direction, toward anger, though Georges did little more than reassert much of what he'd said in his speech. He smiled. A few photos, some pats on the back, some older professors from Smith giving him a pleasant yet condescending grin and introduction.

The sheet came back filled with names, numbers, addresses. Many of these would turn out to be fake, and quite a few were from people who would attend only one meeting. Well-intentioned white students showed up the first week, listened, watched. But so much of what was discussed had nothing to do with them: mosque visits, a potential Haj to the Middle East, the occasional religious rant by one of the more conservative members.

Within a month of Georges's speech, the club deflated to its previous size, and the meetings returned to normal. There was a nice piece written in The Collegian, but the Gazette never ended up publishing a story. When Georges finally got a hold of the reporter, the man insisted that he'd pushed to get it printed, but that in the end the editor couldn't find a place for it amid many other socially important pieces.

It was late one night after a heated club meeting, the small crowd gathering their things. Georges stood waiting for the sheet to be returned, though he figured there were no new sign-ups anyway, not this late in the year, not with such a small group. But when the room had cleared out, a lanky student approached him with the sheet. He had a few days' growth on his face, very dark hair, medium-hued skin, big eyes. He handed him the sheet, said that he was the only one who'd written his contact information.

The man had a tranquil voice, soft but somehow very powerful. Georges asked him where he was from, was he going to see his family over break, how was he finding school so far, was he having any problems with teachers, with classmates, with work. He answered Georges in French, but to Georges the accent was very strange. He was a freshman, almost done with his first semester. He came from Egypt, and when asked about returning home, about his family, he looked down and shook his head, with the slightest shade of sorrow, but with rage right on the edges.

Something about the thinness of the man but also the muted confidence, perhaps the comfort of speaking his mother's language, drew Georges to invite the guy to a coffee upstairs in the Campus Center. They sat, and though Georges asked most of the questions, the man answered clearly and seemed relaxed, his gaze periodically following the white girls who passed by. After an hour of talking about Egypt, about strides Georges thought the club was making, things they had yet to accomplish, whether their big meeting with the reporters had been a success or not, they took their empty cups back to the counter, stood, shook hands. The man turned to head down the concourse, but Georges called him back. He invited the kid to spend a few nights back at his parents' place in Somerville over break. He said they could take the bus together, better than being alone the entire winter.

The man smiled, considered the offer a moment, his eyes once again briefly distracted by a passing woman. Then he nodded and reached out to shake Georges's hand again, said thank you in French then in Arabic. As he walked away, Georges was struck suddenly by his own odd behavior, having invited this stranger to his home, to meet his parents and brother and sister. But the way the guy seemed so lost, unsteered by any sense of purpose or even hope, it made Georges feel older, mature, like a brother. He watched Marcel Mahzar Karim leave through the front doors, his dark jacket and hair against the white snow, bright under the lamps, bright and untouched as this tall Egyptian Algerian lumbered through the thick cover. Georges blinked and did not see his future in this boy, could not, any more than the snow on Marcel's shoulder realized where it had just fallen.

PART II

OVER the previous weeks, Emma had become sole gator for Fadi, at her own insistence. For hours each day she had done little more than listen to his stories about back home, his discourses on Western imperialism, slowly adding in tidbits about her own life, methodically at first, but as she opened up more — about Evan, John (if only with pseudonyms), the course her life was on. She'd actually started to feel better. And the meetings she had with Fadi became a nice break in her day, something she looked forward to. Each week they seemed to grow more at ease, Fadi lowering his shield by millimeters, and Emma too slipping from her usual decorum. There was something magnetic about him, disarming even, especially during those rare smiles of his.

Sometimes, she could even separate his face from the monstrous one it was often paired with: Ali. A man whose name had edged dangerously toward the tip of her tongue during conversations. But she kept that secret from everyone.

She had begun telling him, at length, about her son, how she saw him only every other weekend. At hearing this Fadi had flinched, and seconds later brushed a tear with his nub. That she had a son nearby, he said, and was unable to hold him each day and put him under the covers, was a crime.

Today was the first time they'd met in an actual interview chamber, instead of Fadi's room. It was a dim, low-ceilinged room in the old basement, cinderblock walls, copper pipes running overhead, and the smell of damp. Emma sat across the table from Fadi, resting her forehead in a hand that also held the nub of a cigarette. Fadi sat tall in his wheelchair, studying her for several minutes as she rubbed her temples. This was an early interview, just after 6:30 on a Friday morning, which was the reason both for the atypical room assignment and for Emma's pounding headache.

The headache owed, also, to the string of gins she'd soaked up at home last night, not too many hours ago, the astringent taste still on her tongue. She'd sat on her sofa with glass after glass of martinis on the rocks, which by night's end contained only whispers of vermouth. At that same time Fadi had lied on his left side in bed, turned to face Tully and the game of Connect Four, wordless for an hour while the rain fell.

With head still in hand, Emma squinted her eyes at the guard standing in the corner. "Sergeant, uh, Cupczeck...er...Gorman is it?"

"Grover, ma'am."

"Right, sorry. Any chance you could get us a couple coffees?"

"Ma'am?"

"For my friend and me." Motioning to Fadi with a wink.

Fadi cut in, "No coffee for me, thanks."

"Then some tea. Cup of coffee, cup of tea."

Gorman hesitated, then stepped toward the door, asking, "Cream?"

Emma looked at Fadi, who said, "Milk, please."

"Same here. Thanks, Grover."

He left and the door clanked shut behind him. Emma fixed Fadi with an incredulous look. "I can't believe that worked." Shaking her head with a smile. "He's not supposed to leave the room."

Now finally sitting back in her chair, taking the last puff from her cigarette.

"You look well today," he said.

"Fuck off." A breath of smoke. "Not feeling quite a hundred percent here."

"Me neither," he said, lifting what was left of his arm, a little Maraca smile.

Emma paused at first. His limbs had always horrified her. But over the months and nearly hundred hours they'd spent together, she realized his condition had now mostly disappeared in her eyes. She laughed with a huge smile, and Fadi smiled too with those fake teeth.

"How'd that date go the other night, by the way? You never told me."

"Oh, it went okay."

"Second date?"

A guffaw. "Not waiting by the phone." A strong thump inside her temples.

"That's too bad. And how was Ben's game? Did you make it in time?"

"I did. Lots of little tikes kicking the ball as hard as they can, then chasing after it. It's barely soccer." She grinned. "But the guy likes his new shin guards. Those long socks too."

"I used to love those games. It's too bad soccer doesn't stay popular. He'll be finding another sport in a few years. Baseball perhaps. Tell me, when you go to those games, is your husband there?"

"Depends on the day."

"Do you stand together?"

She reared back. "Of course we do." Taking the pack of Camels in her hand.

"Is he seeing someone?"

"Hey, *hey*. Who's the interrogator here?"

He shrugged.

"That's right. *Me*." Sifting a cigarette from the pack, then into her mouth.

"You know, there isn't great ventilation down here."

"Well, I'm sorry. I don't get to pick the rooms."

"One of our walks would have been nice."

"I forgot to ask, ok?" She snapped the Zippo open and lit the cigarette. "Wow, you're Mr. Questions today, aren't you?"

They sat in silence with only the smoke moving in the little room, and Emma tucked her hand under the elbow of her other arm. "Garcon?" Tapping the table, looking behind her, then smiling timidly. She dragged and exhaled. "Ok, we don't."

"You don't what?"

"We don't stand together at the games."

"You and Jason."

"No, we don't."

"Why not?"

"I tried. A few times. I'd try to talk to him about Ben. He'd move a few steps to talk to one of the other moms, some woman he knew. They had history, all those parents. I couldn't join in. I'd try to move next to him, start a conversation about anything at all. He'd go quiet. He just doesn't want me there. That's the thing. He doesn't want me invading the nice little world he has. *His* son, *his* soccer mom buddies."

"I don't believe that."

"I can perceive things, you know? I can tell when someone doesn't want me there, little cues."

"Are you picking anything up now?"

A quick middle finger, then back to her regular posture. "I can tell."

They both smiled widely. A bit of Emma's hair fell over her face. She smoothed it back behind her ear, and the room once again fell silent a while.

Then Fadi said, "Fatu and I were glued together. Especially those first years, before Nadat. Then the three of us were glued. In a different way." He looked at the dingy corner of the room, black water stain from the ceiling down the wall. "What was I thinking about the other day? An argument we had. It was about school. It was one of those silly fights I guess all couples have, about plans for the future, their child, things way off." His eyes narrowed in thought. "We must have still been in America. Fatu wasn't even pregnant yet. For some reason, right from the start, we always assumed we'd have a girl. We talked about where to send her to school. Fatu said an American education was best, something conservative, maybe a private girls' school, but she insisted our daughter be unlike her, that she have the exact same education as any boy."

"And you didn't agree with that?"

"No, I did. But I suggested we couldn't plan for everything to be perfect, we couldn't assume we'd still be in the states in ten, fifteen years. And that if she had to go to a traditional Arab school in Morocco or Egypt or somewhere else, that might be just as well. I remember she started to cry. That was the first time I think she realized she might not be staying in America for the rest of her life, having this safe life. That broke my heart."

"Taking her away from the US?"

"Not just that. It was something else. It was talking about our future. Fatu had such a clear vision of what she wanted, because she had such a clear vision of what she *didn't* want, because of the life she'd had. But not me. I tried to imagine the future and couldn't see one. I looked ahead, at where my life was going, and I couldn't see anything, not a perfect life with kids, a wife."

"Why?"

"I don't know."

"Why do you *think* then?"

He looked down. "I really don't know."

Emma leaned both elbows on the table, not feeling a single throb from her forehead. "When you tried to imagine your future, what did you see?"

Shaking his head, looking at the table. "Nothing."

"How could you not dream a little? Everyone does that. Even I did."

"I saw nothing." He looked up slowly, met her eyes. A thin coat of liquid turned his crystalline blue eyes a morning color. "I knew."

"You knew what?"

"My path. That it wouldn't allow for these dreams Fatu had. Good dreams, the kind everyone has. The reason I started yelling at her, it wasn't her. I was mad at myself. At my selfishness. Because I saw that what I was doing to my life, it was now affecting the future of the poor woman I loved and my children.

"What I did..." Shaking his head. "...the decisions, the stubbornness, self-righteousness, it killed the two people I loved most. And that was all I ever wanted as I was growing up. Those two girls. I had them, but I still wanted to go down that path. I insisted."

Now the tears came, and Fadi's good hand wiped them from his cheeks before they could reach the floor they rolled toward. He took one long, wet breath through his nose and set his eyes on Emma, who was still leaning toward him, cigarette in hand. The phony eye in his living socket seemed to look either very far into the past or the future, and the live one shivered and seemed to beg questions from the present, from Emma.

A hollow smile. "I killed them. They are dead because of me. And not just my actions but because of who I am, who I truly am. I loved myself, my ideas, too much, and I followed them. I brought my girls to Egypt, where they were to die. I had everything for them here, and I had my mom and Alia, and my dad. My whole life has been a mistake, one that has killed many people. I don't believe in God anymore, but I pray to him to punish me for what I have done."

He put the elbow of his right arm on the table and held his weight there. Once again, his eyes fell to Emma, whose face glistened with tears even in the low lights of this place. He made a motion to the cigarette in her hand and her arm lowered to the table, hand halfway between them.

"When I first woke from my coma, I was in a place of peace. My mind had not yet gripped the world I was in. I didn't realize I'd come back to life. Then in a flood my memories returned, what I had done, my daughter, my wife. I wanted so badly to escape this place. I begged, let me die. I wanted only to join them again, saw a place where my deeds were erased. I cannot tell you the horror that washed over me when I learned I was still alive."

She was quiet, and his hand reached across the table to meet hers, and as his fingertips swept out to take the cigarette they brushed the top of her wrist.

"Emma. Why did I survive the explosion?"

CHAPTER 14

Membership in the club stayed flat over the next semester, as it would throughout the rest of Georges's time. Incoming freshman were always eager to join, to feel part of something in a school that seemed so big at first. But sophomores and juniors eventually found themselves more or less at home on campus, stopped praying so often, became uninterested in holy days, and ceased to attend meetings. So for Georges meetings became a matter of inspiring the uninspired, giving comfort to the scared new students, and inventing incentive to keep disenchanted upper classmen in the club. And though Georges would not have uttered this aloud, the constant threat of racism had begun to evaporate.

But Marcel, quiet little Marcel, was different from everyone. He was scared, in his own way, especially the first months, and shy. He arrived at meetings early and immediately sat in the back, moved only to raise his hand for a vote, rarely spoke during sessions. Afterward he would wait his turn to approach Georges, speak to him in French, which Georges could see he found comforting. Marcel had said very few words during their trip out to Somerville over winter break, had been very pleasant to both parents, speaking French with Lara and Arabic with Nourredine. It was on the long bus ride back, as they crept along the pike in heavy snow, that Marcel had begun to speak more openly.

He was born of an Algerian mother and an Egyptian father, given a strict religious upbringing, first in Algeria and later in Egypt. As a child in Algiers, he was made to study the Koran for hours each day, given a private tutor to guide his recitation, to shape his tajweed into beautifully intoned music. Though hesitant at first to describe his early

Koranic reading competitions, Marcel eventually told Georges all the details. At eight years old, he had been the youngest of all competitors, frightened during his trip to Cairo, although accompanied by his teacher, facing children as old as eighteen and from as far away as the Maldives and Indonesia. Sitting before great men, he was read a few words and would then have to continue the passage by heart, his eyes closed, until told to stop. Even at that young age he overwhelmed the judges with his recitation, his voice, his perfect memory. He recounted the way grown, bearded men wept and sought to meet him and touch him in the great halls after he had won the competition. And sadly he recalled how such success and pressure had spoiled The Word for him as a child, how he lost his love for prayer for many years.

Late into the trip, as the bus rolled into the valley at night, Marcel told of how both his sisters had been raped as teenagers, their attackers never brought to justice, now left unweddable to live as spinsters in their father's house. Marcel had searched for the men, had apparently discovered they were from the wealthiest family in a coastal province near Alexandria. His face alighted as he recounted the nights spent standing outside their lavish home, just beyond the walls, staring into the house for any movement. Full nights without sleep, roiling, watching them. "I was terribly ashamed, though I was just sixteen, that I could not bring them to justice, or perhaps show them my own justice. You see, in Egypt, my sisters are now to be unmarried forever. It was one night that did this, two men, for a moment of weakness, a very, very short period of Godless action has damned my sisters. Why is that right?"

After weeks of surveillance without any action, Marcel would wander the streets, sobbing. He said he visited several dark alleys where he knew bad men to live, hoping the few coins he carried with him would hire a killer. But again he was a coward, unable to approach the dark faces and stinky huts, unable to coerce even these criminals to his purpose. He wandered away from home for days, found himself on a bus going east. Its last stop was in a small town in the northeast. He told Georges how he'd stumbled hungry into a Mosque, hoping to find scraps. How he heard a booming voice, followed by cheers. At the back of the temple was a tall man, head wrapped in a turban, his hands peacefully joined before him. The imam was calling for an end to the military presence in their small town. He spoke softly, yet forcefully, the crowd reacting with cheers and yelling.

That night, Marcel watched as the one main dusty thoroughfare of the town was packed with protestors, the screaming, chanting, torches, signs. The small outfit of guards there was overpowered easily, driven out of town. One of them was positioned not twenty feet from Marcel, and he saw the man run over by the mob, stepped on, spat on; then the butt ends of signs fashioned from hoes were driven into the man's guts. He lay there bleeding and lifeless, his open eyes looking right into Marcel's where he crouched.

His face was placid as he recounted this story for Georges, now a world away on a snowy bus, speaking in French and surrounded by loose Boston accents. Georges listened, his muscles tensed, and he thought he could smell the road and the dust and hear the boom of beautiful prayer off stone walls. He saw Marcel's gaze fix on something a million miles away, something in the future. "That was when I saw my true calling." He turned to Georges. "I was to be a man of God. I began to study the very next day. I became pious once again. I prayed. As a child, you spend all of your time trying to sort the world out, to find how all the pieces fit and how the gears work. And there is a moment when the world stops spinning long enough for you to look in its belly. There is a great silence, and a calm in your mind. That is God, my friend. But I never forgot my sisters' criminals. I asked God for justice every day. I submitted myself to God, but I did this by choice for a reason. And I expected God to know this reason."

"Why did you come to America?"

He looked down, then off in the distance, paused a moment. "My community elected me to. My village is paying my way here. As the brightest student I am expected to succeed, to learn English so that I can lift us from poverty." He smiled, tilted his head back.

"Your village must have done much to come up with the tuition, the plane ticket."

Marcel looked forward, at that same place far off. "Mainly the money came from the wealthiest family in Alexandria."

It was not long before Marcel became comfortable with English. He began to ask questions at discussion and even offer ideas for classmates' issues, so sophomore year Georges chose him to replace the old sergeant at arms. He would now join him at the front of the room at group meetings. And eventually he asked Marcel to try his voice at the occasional speech, then at a few campus-wide events, also manning the table during UMass Club Day.

Though of a tall, lanky stature his soft and full baritone held a strange power over people, and his lack of crafty English vocabulary lent a frankness not found in typical rhetoric containing all the weapons of high wording. Georges was at first ashamed of the fear and envy he felt as Marcel began to demand so much respect, but Marcel's humility put him back at ease, as it did with the others. It was impossible to find a hint of ego in this plank of a man. Georges pictured the imam from the village who had mesmerized Marcel as a boy: the calm voice, the muted physical movement, the boom. Where did that power come from? It wasn't a palpable thing, not the words or even the eyes or his voice, but the way he had of emitting that inner calm. It was disarming, drawing Georges in along with the others.

He and Georges became inseparable over the next years, as Georges went into his junior then senior year. Every few months a report of some graffiti or slur or crime against an Arab student would make its way to their meetings. Georges and Marcel would counsel the more distraught members, Marcel using his hands and his voice to work what seemed like magic, and Georges had by that time become a master at using all available channels to make the grievance known, the perpetrator hated. Marcel naturally became the emotional center of the group, with Georges acting as its chief officer and tactician.

It was never a question as to who would take over as president after Georges graduated. Marcel showed great deference in asking him what his plans were, to which Georges simply put his hand on his friend's shoulder and fixed him with a brotherly smile.

Even after Georges had moved back to the eastern part of the state, he would make regular trips to Amherst for club meetings, sitting benignly in the back of the room as Marcel spoke, standing when introduced as an elder statesman. He still wrote to Georges for advice but more and more was making his own decisions, choices slightly less dependent on using the system to his advantage than Georges had employed. The club still crowded the SGA with as many representatives as possible and made sure to insert good writers on the Collegian staff early, but Marcel's means become increasingly more incendiary: rallies, protests, physical demonstrations outside the campus center.

On one of Georges's visits to campus, Marcel invited him to view their latest demonstration, in reaction to the United States' support of Israel during the Suez canal crisis. In the grass at the center of campus lied a dozen students from the club, strewn about, covered in phony blood, all wearing burkas and turbans, motionless. Stuck in the crowd was a large poster with a map of the Suez Canal, to the west labeled Egypt, to the east the US and Israel. The actual canal was drawn in gruesome, bloody red, below which, written in the same red, "US Out."

As close as they had grown over the last four years, Georges was hesitant to confront Marcel about his new methods. He could see that something had changed in him this last year, though he wouldn't discover what it was for quite some time. The club's power, established by Georges, was now being directed less at protecting and integrating its members and more toward exhibition, outrage, and isolation.

He walked beside Marcel, through campus, by some piece of construction that seemed to have been there for years. Marcel had grown a few inches over the previous summer and walked much more upright, his hands calmly clasped behind his back.

"Do you think the club has changed?"

"It has continued its growth. The growth you initiated."

"This is a bit more overt than what we used to do."

"We've evolved along with the climate."

"You are the president now. It is your club."

Marcel stopped, turned to him. "It will always be yours. And I will never forget what you have done for me, my friend."

Georges smiled. They continued along the outskirts of the construction site, a bulldozer, a tall mound of dirt sprouting wild grass.

"I have told you about my studies back home."

"Some."

"Many Arab boys grow up with little Western education. Instead, we are put into classes early on in which we do little more than memorize the Koran. These classes are, of course, of utmost importance. But they must be supplemented. Anyway, I took such classes as a boy but was fortunate enough to also attend fine schools, ones with a broader curriculum. In fact, one school in Lebanon was attended by as many white students as Arab. Some Christians and Jews."

"How progressive."

Without a pause. "But at this school there were also opportunities for Muslim boys to expand their study of the Koran. After classes, certain teachers offered for the boys to play soccer. It might surprise you, but I loved soccer growing up. Absolutely loved it, as did my best friend, Ahmet. About eight of us showed up for that first meeting. The teacher was an Egyptian man who had been dismissed by the Nasser regime for speaking out against the state. But he gathered us in the school's tiny gym and told us that each day we'd have an hour of Koranic discussion followed by free time to play soccer. About half the boys returned the second day. But I grew to love this teacher. He opened my eyes to many things, including just how imminent the danger is."

"Danger of what?"

"Encroachment. Western and secular ideals threatening to blunt the beauty of Islam. But within a few months of having met this man, he was again thrown out of the school for what they saw as subversive writings. Thrown out by Western trustees, of course."

"You were a teenager. That was years ago."

"After this man left my life, of course his teachings stayed with me, but my life still began to wander, and I found few to speak with on the same matters, few who understood. But by God's will I was reunited with this man last summer. I saw that he was leading a Koranic study group in Islamabad. I arranged to spend the summer there, working and studying. I want to tell you a story he told me and the nine others in the class.

"There was a boy who prayed to God five times every day, followed His word very closely, loved God, and felt God's love guiding his every step. And he knew from a very young age that he was being led by God and protected by His love. His life had direction and purpose. At a later age, this boy set his prayer rug out and stood upon it under God's watchful eye, and he submitted himself to God and repeated his un-ending service. But the boy's father pulled the rug out from under him. So the boy set the rug out again, and once again began to pray."

Marcel put his hand on Georges's arm as they walked.

"But his father took the rug from below his feet, interrupting his prayer. This carried on for many months. Until the boy sought out a fellow believer and bought a gun from him. He bought a dull-looking revolver and five bullets. He loaded each bullet into the gun, one by one, counting as he placed them and saying a small prayer with each. And he spun the chamber and snapped it into place. He then set his prayer rug out as usual, holding all the while the gun secretly below his robe. And as he felt his father's presence behind him, he turned and fired the gun. He put all five bullets into his father's chest. Finally, he stood upon his rug, and offered his hands up to God. This time God heard him and accepted his hands and saw what he had done to His service. And the boy was blessed. He was blessed with the word of God that is His Whisper and His Breath."

CHAPTER 15

The place was still buzzing from yesterday's announcement. Ali Al-Jeddah was now a known guest.

A ceiling of clouds made it dark in the early afternoon, rain flooding the courtyard outside. In the halls, orderlies and guards set out mop buckets to catch leaks. Emma sat at her desk in the closest thing she had to an office in this building. It was little more than a long wood-veneered table circa 1961, a few chairs, a broken computer, and a metal-grated window that looked onto the courtyard. She'd spent the previous night there after a long session with the "new" guest, rolled a cot into her office late at night. It was all she could do not to let Randolph know that she already *knew* they had Ali and had for some several weeks. And to rub Alec's nose in the fact that Bauer had gotten zero intel from him. Now they had turned to her.

This morning she'd awakened before her alarm and then gone for a long jog around the perimeter, used the women's shower. Living the way she did in an undecorated government apartment, it was no inconvenience to stay the night at the office. Her hair was still wet, pulled back in a ponytail, Tufts Diving sweatshirt, which she would have to change out for her plain, white button-down before interrogations began.

Reg had brought two black coffees, which now sat on the table steaming, next to Emma's cigarette in the ashtray. Across the table were strewn case files for several of the visitors with possible connections to the US Al-Thaghr Cell. They now met twice each day, and Reg would digest any intel Emma and the others were able to pull, make every attempt to verify it, and brief them before each session on what they needed to pull from each visitor, the concrete stuff: locations, plans, dates, associates, some greater understanding of the exact hierarchy. That was often the most elusive info, some map as to the order of things, mostly because cell members, themselves, had very little idea about who was running the show, perhaps exposed to just a single boss, a few cohorts, whispers of names or vague ideas of leadership. And through it all – as Reg outlined the initial briefing of Ali's profile – he never once alluded to 4,500, or any specifics of an attack at all.

The news of Ali had been the biggest to date, after Fadi's capture — or rather his resuscitation. According to yesterday's briefing, they had brought in Ali Al-Jeddah, recently obtained by the feds — a handful of detainees had all placed him as a regular at an IHOP off the Beltway in Falls Church. The news set the place abuzz. The system had worked perfectly in discovering his whereabouts: interrogators had pressed and squeezed some Syrian grunt for days until, finally, he coughed up a few key locations, which were then surveilled for two days. Al-Jeddah was found walking into the back entrance, where he was taken into custody and eventually brought here to Harrison. The amazing part was that he had been taken without any witnesses, no leak as to his fate or location. It would take longer for his comrades to become spooked or mistrustful, or to assume Ali was giving anything up. Data asymmetry: they had an intel source the other side didn't even know was in their hands.

"Walking up the stairs" it was called. Each member of a cell was a single step to be used to climb up the hierarchy, the upper reaches tougher and tougher, fewer steps up there, fewer men. And to many of the gators at Harrison, it had seemed as if they'd spent all their time questioning the lower stairs of the American cell. But finally they'd gotten two of the top: Subdallah and Al-Jeddah.

Reg split open one of the manila folders. "Born in Somalia to wealthy Saudi parents, schooled in London, then kicked out of Harvard for some sort of sexual no-no, brought on as both a financier and, we think, strategist behind a half-dozen international bombings. After Subdallah, Ali Al-Jeddah is the most important guest these walls have ever seen. He can do the most harm and the most good.

"This one is simple, Emma. We need to know where he meets Karim.

We know he's in the country and had a direct hand in the Caldwell bombing. We think he hasn't left US soil since then. All the low-level grunts don't really count for anything unless we can get Ali to talk.

"Al-Jeddah is smart, at least his shell is. He's slipped only a few times. His parents were billionaire bankers. After the big construction family in Saudi, they were the closest friends of the Saud family. He was raised a bit in Somalia, boarding schools in Lebanon, London, then college in the states, at least for two years.

"Second oldest of thirty-five siblings. As a son of his father's favorite wife, he inherited somewhere in the range of forty-four million, mostly tied up in oil and land holdings, a few European hotels. Hasn't worked a day on any of his business affairs in many years. He's sourced a lot of the money, but not all of it.

"He's cultured, sometimes Western, sometimes insanely fundamentalist. He's backed rebels in Iran, backed both Yemen and the Saudis in the same battle. He's connected to Iraq, Iran. We think he might even be involved in this latest Afghan tussle with the Russians."

"Which side?"

He smiled and shuffled through those stacks of papers, the same futile attempt to outline an entire person in writing.

"Loves airplanes, has owned half a dozen. Father did too, crashed a plane and died in the fifties. He has a boatload of kids, doesn't seem to really give a shit about any of them, hasn't seen his wives in years. They all live in Saudi in a compound, and the wives are like sisters. Something happened though, something big. He fragmented. He was one of the biggest people in Saudi Arabia, non-royal anyway. He had a prosperous family, all under his wing. He still held *damahs*, like in the old days. The sons would gather round him like a sultan, kiss his hand, ask for allowances. He'd marry off his daughters to curry business favors.

But suddenly he broke off. He wasn't ever really all that religious. I mean, he was as Muslim as your typical Saudi in the 70s, but he wasn't becoming a mullah any time soon. Then, *poof*, a nut."

"What did it?"

He leaned back, let out a long breath. "I have no idea. Even one of our better rats, a guy who squealed on his own brother, knows a good deal about AT, he doesn't know. Something with his family. Like, something not okay even within the progressive Saudi set. He left the country, spent years jetting around, flying planes, visiting a growing number of friends from the Muslim Brotherhood, especially in Egypt. But we have no idea how he became a part of AT, how he met Karim, Subdallah, any of them.

"He doesn't know that Subdallah is alive, so maybe now's the time to use him to give up something on Ali, something huge, something we can then use to get Ali to disclose the golden ticket. We've got the middle domino in place, time to start working on the first one."

Her left eyebrow raised as if by static.

Reg then added, "Oh, and you're going to like this. We have a *wedge*."

"A wedge?"

"A wedge." He smiled and shook his head. "Subdallah hates him. Fucking *hates* him. We know this for sure, got it from the Egyptian. And I mean hates the son of a bitch. They fought like two high school girls."

Now Emma smiled too. Fadi wasn't supposed to have a wedge — that wonderful means of prying a subject into disclosure. He was a ghost, a shade, no needs or desires left. But hatred, now that was a different story. Over her years in Africa and the Mideast she'd seen hatred guide men just as strongly as love or religion or greed. It was almost too exciting as the possibilities swarmed into her mind. Perhaps she could inject Fadi with a bit of earthly emotion yet.

Fucking manila folders on the table. Spread like playing cards, offering about the same luck. Ali had won again last night. He rose from his chair when she walked in, waited for her to sit. He was fresh looking, without the heavy dark circles under his eyes the others carried. He was an elfish little man with ghoulish sunken cheeks and bony fingers. His English was superb and held accented tinges from his schooling in England.

She knew it might take a few more days worth of low sleep, a windowless room perhaps. To crack him would be the toughest task she's had. He was richer than the rest combined, seemed to believe in the supposed cause of Thaghr, had three wives and twenty-one children living comfortably in Saudi. He wouldn't be lured by offers of money, safety for his family, probably couldn't be bribed to save his own tail. Funny that these things made him very similar to Subdallah — a man who had tried to blow himself up.

He'd been very quiet, evasive as any man on his first night, though he'd been here for weeks. It was bad strategy to press them right off, then they knew what you wanted from them, let them plan. So she'd spent no more than twenty minutes in very light questioning with Ali those first evenings, much to the dismay of Alec Randolph.

And now with about two hours before her next session, as she sat at her desk, her mind set about structuring this man's internal framework: his wants, his needs, the very basic and most powerful incentives in his life. Finding what made him open his eyes each morning was the key to what made him strap bombs to humans. Whatever made him tick made him destroy.

The room was quiet, little rain sounds through the window. As she lifted the cigarette to her lips, she thought briefly about the stack of profiles from Beltway Connections on her table at home, the photos clipped to dossiers, probably less truth than the ones she dealt with here at Harrison.

What the hell made these men open their eyes each morning?

On a piece of yellow notebook paper she'd sketched one of her many attempts at a hierarchy outline, like a family tree. At the top sat Marcel Karim. Below him, connected by lines, were Ali and Fadi, side by side. From their pictures trickled a river delta to the many grunts who'd passed through these walls. Emma tapped her pencil's eraser back and forth between the two, back and forth. He and Ali were the only two men who occupied this level, just beneath the supreme leader. The eraser tapped twice on Fadi's face and then stopped.

CHAPTER 16

After MIT, Georges foundered for months, two diplomas on the bedroom wall of his childhood home. He worked Saturday shifts at the diner, looked after Alia, now fourteen years old. There were few jobs befitting a man of his terrible learning. Friends' parents or neighbors would offer interviews at engineering firms or finance houses downtown, and he'd put on his only suit and interview well with the vice president or lead tech. Every job was wanting or imperfect in some way or else too permanent.

On a Saturday, Alia fell violently ill with pneumonia, and Georges spent every possible hour with her, praying and listening to his parents worry about how they would pay the bills — the diner had had a string of light months recently. Alia recovered fully, but Georges was still left with images of his family wasting away, parents unable to work, unable to clothe their daughter. One of his classmates — briefly a member of the MIT chapter of the Five Pillars — had offered to set him up repairing elevators around Boston. Georges called him from the phone on his parents' kitchen wall. The pay was fair, and he could use the odd bit of knowledge absorbed over the last six years, but mostly he toted heavy boxes of assorted tools, set up blockades in office building lobbies, and followed around the grizzled old veterans, none of whom had endured a lick of college. Despite his friend's assurances, much of the work had very little to do with electricity, the bulk of elevators in the early 70s following hydraulic models. So Georges had to learn menial tasks from scratch, doing the occasional circuit rebuild or simply replacing one of the feed wires in the engine room at the bottom of a shaft.

After several months of watching other men do their jobs, Georges's brain – almost passively – had begun working out optimizations to some of the more common issues with most elevator systems, particularly around efficiency in how elevators in a multi-shaft system were hailed.

He would wake up early each morning to read the papers and whatever books he and Marcel were discussing. He'd then drive to his assignment, do his work, and wrap up for the day at around three. It was during this time that he often found himself driving aimlessly around Boston or Cambridge as the season turned cold and dark. So many years of studying, of practicing his game. There had always been something to move toward, something to get better at. Empty hours in the past had felt frivolous, so easily converted into progress. A blank hour at day's end could be spent going over lab work or last night's reading. But now they were barren. Even after spending an hour or so of free time sketching out the rudiments for his eventual patents, he'd be left with empty space.

What have I done today? His Franklinian journal now terrified him, and he stopped recording entries for the first time since high school.

It was around this time that he tasted his first drink. A sip of cold beer. He'd gone to a pub in Central Square with a few of the guys after work, a long day of staring at electrical cords in dark elevator shafts. Doing nothing useful the past eight months, nothing that made him feel his place on Earth was the left side of some equation.

So he'd decided to have a beer, which tasted horrible. Then a second one before going home. Over the coming months he bought his first six pack, drank it in silence by himself, slowly working six beers, then ten, into his nightly routine. The dark nights and pointless days did not mix well with his first bouts of drunkenness, and he mostly cried at night, sometimes prayed, scribbled letters to Marcel that would never be sent. The entire winter went on like this until his mother found him one night, sitting on their front steps, crying into his hands, stinking of booze. She tucked him into bed as he sobbed and apologized, and she sat there with him until he'd fallen asleep, singing a song in French he'd not heard since he was eight. She stroked his hair as he went off to sleep, repeated to him that everything would be fine, that he'd find his way, that he'd done his work his whole life, and that soon God would send proof that he'd done the right thing.

His letters to Marcel – now in his senior year at UMass – had grown fat with lamentations. Marcel responded with his calming French, telling him to be patient, and of course pointing out that Georges himself was hoping for a patent of his system in order to make money. To which Georges replied he was simply looking to be in a place where he didn't have to rely on money. That the only way to transcend the materialist, financial bent of life was to *defeat* it. Marcel asked him if the best way to defeat hunger was to eat a hamburger.

At the end of the school year Georges drove the two hours west to see Marcel graduate. The ceremony took place in the low bowl of a football stadium, packed with thousands of anonymized, black-draped seniors. Individual students were not called up to the stage to receive their diplomas; instead, the president announced that all were graduated, which was when the crowd stood and threw their silly flat hats into the air. Georges met Marcel outside the stadium under an oak tree as kids oozed out with parents on either side. Marcel sauntered out alone, smoking a cigarette, a new habit. Still very skinny, but long and ghostly in his dark robes, beard thicker than ever. He leaned forward so Georges could see the top of his cap, on which he'd drawn five straight sticks with chalk, the symbol for the Five Pillars Club.

He smiled when he saw Georges. "Are you proud, Papa?"

"Yes, my son. Although your symbol looks like you're counting days in prison."

They embraced and Georges looked into Marcel's eyes, which were dark. "I got you something," Georges said, revealing a soft package wrapped in newspapers.

"You are quite the wrapper."

He opened the gift, a gray t-shirt with the word UMass on it, below that a picture of five Doric pillars.

A smile. "Thank you, my friend." They hugged again.

"And I have something for you."

"What?"

"A graduation present."

"I don't think you understand how these things work, my foreign friend."

He handed him an unwrapped book with an envelope folder in its pages. The front cover was in Arabic, a word Georges didn't recognize.

"Signposts. By Qutb."

"Your hero?"

"It is a book that will change things for us. This…" Tapping on the cover. "…is where we are going."

Georges smiled, though with a look of confusion as he tore open the paper. Inside was a simple note, "Souviens" along with a check for $5,000. Georges stared at the piece of paper. It was written on one of Marcel's own checks, from Western Bank, the handwriting taut and neat.

"What is this?"

"An investment."

"Marcel, where did you get this money?"

"No need to worry about that. It is important to me that you are able to take advantage of your invention. I know you have applied for a patent, but I foresee someone from this country stealing what is yours because you don't have money. You will pay me back when you are a rich man."

"You know I don't want to be a rich man. And I can't take this money. This would feed a hundred people from your village, and I wish you would tell me where you got it. This worries me."

"Don't worry, Georges. It is legal money, mine legally. But it is dirty. I can't spend it on myself. I can't buy things with it, because those things would carry the same dirt. But I am giving it to you so the money is now clean."

"What in God's name are you talking about?"

"My brother, you took me in during a time that I was lost. I have always been happy that you are my friend, so I'm showing it. This is a tradition where I come from."

"$5,000 is not a tradition where you come from."

He smiled again in a way Georges couldn't recall having seen when they were at college together, even a bit condescending. "Another tradition is accepting all offers of kindness. You cannot refuse this." His face went serious. "It is a gift, my brother. I want to help you get your adult life going."

Georges said nothing, just looked at the check once more, began to speak, but Marcel hushed him. So he put the check in his pocket, and they walked side by side toward the parking lot across near the Southwest towers. Georges looked up at John Quincy Adams dorm, thought back to that night where he'd clubbed Tim Dunn in the bathroom, and he glanced at Marcel, who carried with him an air of surety Georges couldn't remember having himself, as if UMass had been a small root in his path, something to be acknowledged only long enough to be stepped over.

As they walked, Marcel held the cigarette in his mouth and unzipped his graduation robes, then pulled the new gray sweatshirt over his head, slung the gown across his shoulder.

Here was a boy from the lowest rung of an impoverished country, sent to America under the financial steam of his entire village. A boy who'd worn the same thin parka every winter since being at UMass, maybe a few pairs of khakis, those ratty old shoes. He would never agree to go into town to get food, always deferring instead, even on Saturday nights, to eat at the putrid dining hall, often alone, each time secreting little bits of bread and fruit to eat between meals. Where had this boy gotten $5,000 to give to Georges, by most Middle Eastern standards from a well-to-do family.

"And you said I will repay you. Won't my repayment carry with it the same taint this money had for you to begin with?"

"You won't have to pay me in money. It will be something clean, and good." He held the pack of cigarettes up for Georges and removed another for himself. "Come, let's go to the dining hall." Offering a flame to Georges then lighting his own. "My treat."

CHAPTER 17

"Once you had the invention completed and ready, how did you go about getting it in place?"

Emma pushed Fadi in a wheelchair along the single walk of the small atrium. The rain had stopped, a well-drawn fall afternoon for Northern Virginia, somehow a few leaves on the ground in the treeless yard. When she'd heard that Fadi hadn't been outside in nearly a year, except for transports, she pulled some quick strings with Alec to allow them this half-hour stroll, said it would do wonders in getting Subdallah to trust her. That Fadi was immobile and the inner yard inescapable also helped. When she delivered the news, even the stony-faced prisoner couldn't hide the little squint of joy in his eyes. Neither the dreariness of the day nor the institutional facades or sparse landscaping could damper Fadi's excitement at the blast of fresh air, the crisp wet smell.

Of course, a guard had to accompany them, and Fadi's one good arm was in restraints to avoid any possibility of communicating through signals. They also put him in a cap and glasses to hide his face.

"It was a single favor, really. I mean, once I had enough money for a true prototype, it was a favor done for me that got me a meeting with Hudson Elevators. I simply presented the basic concept, along with a chart..." He laughed. "One drawn by hand and colored in by my mother. I showed this to a man named Ficks at the company. I remember he paused behind his desk, looking up toward the ceiling. I swear he sat there for twenty minutes without saying a word. Then he asked what I wanted for it, and I told him it would need to always have my company's name on it, that we would need money for production, based on the number he required, that we would deliver the product, along with a few men trained on its installation and so forth. He hesitated at this, and I had to convince him that I was capable of delivering. But Ficks was a good man; I would work with him for years, and he was always fair and honest, even with bad news. We shook hands then and there, and I was promised a few dozen pre-orders, a large payment very soon. I was happy. I remember being happy, as if my life were changing dramatically. But it was nearly a year before I saw the first dollar. The red tape, the expenses, the safety checks. That's what sucked up the most time. Anything involving elevators has to pass multiple rounds of scrutiny. But once that was over we were in business, and things were amazingly easy.

"I was working maybe fourteen hours each day. Paperwork, training, hiring, banking, everything at first. That was around the time I enlisted my brother, Yusef. He was just coming out of Bentley. He had a mind for all the paperwork and loopholes, something I never had. But it was a good idea not to let Hudson buy out the technology, because it allowed us to also sell to Otis, which gave us enough business to last a lifetime. Even longer."

"So after this thing was invented, all the technical details were ironed out, it was just business? No need for you as an engineer?"

"No," he snapped. "There is always a need, always a need for someone who truly knows the way things work. And Yusef said we needed to diversify, said we needed more. So I spent quite a lot of time and money on a few ideas, for escalators, to try to decrease the incredible maintenance they require, along with an emergency response system for large office buildings, which never got off the ground. But yes, I've learned that in business, whatever business you begin, it's usually from something you're skilled at, or something you have a passion for. In my case, it was probably both. But once you have your product, food, gadgets, whatever, all business becomes very similar." Then he added, "So I lost interest in it."

"What were you interested in?"

He turned slightly to let her see the profile of his smile.

"No, seriously. I'm just imagining, you were driven, you would admit that what you were doing was typically American. Aspirational. You worked hard, earning money, building a business. I'm trying to imagine what it was that fueled this, if you were in fact not interested in money. How could you resist?"

He turned forward, looked up. "It felt programmed. I saw my father scrubbing dried grease every day as I grew up, sweating, sweeping change off dirty tables. It was generational momentum, as if I were carrying all the potential he'd built up and worked to create and brought over on the boat with him. Even after I'd begun thinking outside of that, in college, something much deeper was still driving me toward that goal. The very cells of my body were conspiring to keep Nourredine's desire alive. Which was a handicap I fought against each day."

"Well, my father was a garbage man down in North Florida. He barely even drank yet still managed to beat the Christ out of my sister and me." She laughed. "So I'm having a hard time feeling bad that your father was a good man, a hard worker."

"But you can't deny that who your father was somehow inspired you or pushed you a certain way in your life. Whether by example or whatever the opposite of an example is."

"Maybe."

They came to the end of the courtyard, where there stood a tall, heavy door, beyond which there were only four more to pass in order to reach true fresh air, outside the walls of this place. Emma turned Georges around. The sun winked a second from behind the clouds before being muffled again.

"You know, it's been over two months. We've met nearly every day. Why not work with me, why not tell me more? You might get a favorable transfer." She paused before adding. "Visitation rights."

"I'm afraid your understanding of the balance of incentive is very much askew."

She laughed. "What the fuck does that mean?"

"I mean you know exactly who I used to work with. These are men ten times as cruel and merciless as all these tough Virginian football players you have working here, more brutal than the worst days with one of your phony English interrogators. And as far as comfort, promises of good things, I'm afraid those times are behind me." As they wheeled away from that great door, the sun played again along the edges of a cloud, soaking the courtyard gray and then brightly shadowed and gray again. Fadi's lopped and emaciated thigh wriggled once like a baby then twitched upward.

CHAPTER 18

Saturdays, he still worked at the diner. Just like in high school or on college breaks. Now, as a twenty-seven year old, still walking through that bell-chimed door at six in the morning, still tying on that stiff and starch-white apron. Even after his own company had begun to take off, to demand long days, Georges worked from six to three each Saturday, alongside his parents and Alia. Yusef's two toddlers had retired him from diner work, though the family often stopped by to eat on weekends.

The breakfast shift was rough today, nonstop rotating customers at the counter. Lara worked the register and the door, magically corralling new entrants into some sort of order only she knew. And Nourredine still had the energy from thirty years earlier, scraping eggs and home fries off the griddle with Hamid, or greeting the regulars at their table with a fresh pot of coffee and sports scores, or else squatting at kids' level to teach them a single French word.

Now the rush had dissipated, only a few students in sweatshirts hovering over coffee cups in Alia's booths. Nourredine whistled some made-up aria in the back as he shoved old bread into the oven for croutons, while Lara chopped tomatoes under the old A&W sign. This time reminded him of high school, the little piece of quiet between charges, when he'd stuff in math problems or a chapter or two of reading. He watched Alia sweep some change into her hand then go on wiping her tables.

Georges spritzed a bit of Scrub, bleach and water, onto the countertop, wiped every inch, then set out fresh placemats. The bell chimed; he and his sister looked up. Two men in long white thobes drifted into the place, whispered something to each other, then headed for the counter.

"Hello."

"Hi," said the smaller man.

"See some menus?"

They turned to each other, and the smaller man said, "Coffee, please. For both." His accent was heavy and English-sounding.

Georges flipped two mugs over and filled them with fresh coffee. Each man bowed his head slightly. He turned his back and starting drying the glasses with a cloth and as he did so could hear the two of them speaking some strain of Arabic that offered only the odd decipherable word or phrase.

From the kitchen, Nourredine was doing his normal prodding of Hamid, reminding him about each tiny task he'd been doing perfectly for the last ten years. The flourishes of Arabic commands flew out every few seconds.

"Is this your father?" asked the man.

Georges turned. "Yes. He is the owner."

"You look like him. You are Arab?"

Georges nodded.

"From where?"

"Morocco."

"Ah." Nodding. Then he mumbled something to the other in Arabic. It seemed the larger man knew no English. "It was an important day for your father last week."

Georges's mind went back a few days, tried to consider what had happened, aside from his thirtieth birthday, celebrated right here at the diner. "Yes." He smiled. "Morocco's anniversary."

"I trust your father celebrated."

"We both did."

The smaller man once again translated, which cued Georges to return to his duties. He finished drying the last of the water glasses, refreshed the condiments. He then took the morning's garbage out to the back lot and tossed the bags into the dumpster, which was brimming. Then he slipped into the kitchen, washed his hands, and headed back out to the lot. A long window box sat along the back wall. From here he began to pluck bits of mint, until he had enough for the rest of the day's tea.

By the time he returned to his counter, the larger man had finished his cup, so Georges refilled it. The smaller man was now reading a folded English newspaper.

"What do you think of this?" he asked Georges, indicating a picture of a tanker on fire.

"I think it is a shame."

The man cocked his head. "Oh? Do you support Hussein?"

With a shrug. "It is a shame for men to bicker like that. At least two shipments have been attacked, shipments going to Arab people. Children, families. A few men argue over power, and such ego jams a wedge into Arab unity." He turned to the kitchen quickly. "It is such in-fighting that is perhaps most dangerous to the Arabian cause. These lines drawn only during modern times. Sects of Islam killing each other. And what do the Western oil companies do?" He shrugged again as if helpless. "They sit back and play each side against the other. It's a classic strategy, to support the enemy of your enemy. That's the only reason the US gives weapons to Saddam or arms the mujahedeen in Afghanistan."

"So you are not political then."

"Iran and Iraq are not political. They are selfish. They are men attempting to impose ego in the guise of principal. Do you realize how important population is going to be in the coming decades? Millions are dying or in poverty. Iran and Saudi Arabia will have to import more and more workers, and the Middle East will begin to look like America, stuffed with more filler than natives. Then what? And meanwhile Arabs are wiping each other out left and right."

"You are passionate about this." But before Georges could answer, he began to translate to the other man, who listened with a tight brow, considered a moment, then nodded.

Georges added, "I think certain things about the Imam's rise are virtuous. But when a man rises, no matter his ideology, he becomes in danger of falling."

"Who said that?"

"It is just something I know to be true."

The man nodded, sipped his coffee, and then Nourredine yelled from the kitchen.

Georges put up a finger. "Excuse me."

As now happened about once per week, the igniter on the new pizza oven had ceased to work, so Georges was sent around to the rear of the big thing to adjust the wiring. After only a few minutes he gave the signal to Nourredine to test the start again, and the oven was working.

He hurried back to the counters in time to see the two men standing, the small one holding the bill. He held out his hand. "My name is Nazim."

"Very nice to meet you. Fadi."

"Hello, Fadi, and this is Faruz."

He ripped a tiny corner of the bill and began to write on it. "I'll tell you, I like what you have said here today. Some of us enjoy gathering to speak of such things." He handed him the paper. "But it is also just a group of men who enjoy each other's company. We meet Tuesdays and Saturdays at this address, after afternoon prayers. There's a green door at that corner."

Looking down at the address. "Thank you. I would be interested."

"I hope to see you. Otherwise, thank you for the coffee and the discussion."

The men went to Lara at the register with sullen looks on their faces. And though Lara smiled, even more than usual — perhaps upon seeing the men engage with her son — the men remained stony-faced and simply collected their change before walking out of the diner.

CHAPTER 19

"May I ask you something?"

He half turned, lifted an eyebrow for her to see. "Are you serious?"

A brief pause while she turned his chair around and went back down the courtyard path. "I believe that a lot of what you've done in your life, your clubs, your plans, even some of the more violent things, have been with the aim of helping people. Is that fair?"

"That is simplifying. Again, you don't seem to realize that principle..."

She laughed. "Yes, principle. But at the very root of many of your group's actions, you're thinking that the world should be changed, yes? That something you are doing will lead, ultimately, to a better life for Nadat, for Fatima."

"I am not trying to make it worse for others."

"Nor am I. You might think we are enemies, on opposite sides, but what we aim to do is set things right, the way we see 'right' as being."

"In light of our nice day, I won't speak the many arguments that come to mind."

"Well, no, let me ask you then, is there something about Muslims, about Arabs, that makes them the only ones you would protect, you would fight for? If you saw two young girls, very young, about to be gunned down, one white, one Arab, would you save one over the other? And would you feel no regret over the death of the other?"

"You simplify things, and you use a ridiculous riddle, but it again shows that you don't understand. But yes, as callous as you might consider me to be, I would feel regret, and I always do. But my regret, for any such action, is of the fact that they are *necessary*. In your scenario, perhaps I murder the man with a gun to the two small girls, yes? He dies so that I may save lives and, more important, a *way* of life that would want to protect innocence. What I would regret is the very fact, the very *truth*, that put that man in a place that would have me need to shoot him. So, my regret, in your silly scenario, would be that the shooter exists." Then he added quietly, "and that I was in a position to do something."

"I'm sure we would both like a world without unnatural death, without rape, without suffering."

"Yes, and free balloons."

She slapped his shoulder. "But can you agree that what drives me to do my work is striving toward this?"

He hesitated. "Yes."

"Then what I have to ask, you will believe, is with this singular goal in mind."

He jerked his head sideways. "Stop."

The guard, who had been walking a few paces ahead, also halted.

"Come here."

She leaned to place her ear near his mouth.

"The guard, he's too close."

Emma held her head near his a few seconds, and when she pulled away, Fadi's beard grazed her cheek.

"Corporal, if you would walk ten paces ahead."

"Can't do that, ma'am."

"Corporal, the detainee wishes to exercise a religious rite of exemption, as allowed for in Section 12 of the handbook. You can check it yourself, and in which case there is to be one sole chaperone, of his choosing."

The young man hesitated then took several steps forward. They continued wheeling along the courtyard.

"Emma. Tell me what you know about my family. My family that still lives."

"I don't understand."

"Tell me what you know about them."

"Just what I've told you. Yusef is in semi-retirement, still on the board, lives in Belmont, Massachusetts. Alia lives in Brockton with her husband, who I believe is a watchmaker or something. Your mother has been in Somerville for nearly forty years now. That's about all I know."

Fadi studied every word for traces of deception, or any hint that Emma knew the truth about Alia, considered if she could be connected to the threat written on his food all those months ago. *Talk She Die.* He was asked questions regularly, by Bauer, by others, any of whom could have been the culprit, sent there to see if he would talk, to see if they needed to make good on their promise to liquidate his family, if they knew that he had, in fact, remained secretly close to his mother all these years, and even more so to Alia. But he knew Emma was not the one. Even stronger than this feeling was his growing need to release himself, somehow, from this weight, to damn the men who had put him here.

"What is your question?"

"Ali Al-Jeddah."

He was quiet.

"You know him."

"Yes."

"What kind of man is he?"

"I'd imagine your books are correct. He's as bad as they say. A murderer, a rapist, sick with power."

"But where is he weak?"

"In each of those places."

"Money?"

"No. He has too much of it. But he has always craved power. Have you seen pictures?"

Emma nearly told him that she'd met him the previous night. "A few."

"But you have not smelled him."

"Pardon?"

"His scent. It is the first thing people notice about him. Long ago he became obsessed with perfumes, colognes. He spent quite a lot of money manufacturing his very own scent, claiming that he had discovered something unlike any other. He always travels with it. And his secret is that he will often dab a bit onto his palm before meeting someone, so that his scent then stays with the person after they shake hands, long after he has left the room. That smell used to clog whatever room he was in. You never get used to it. Rose and lemon."

"Charming."

"He was born with a rare nutrition deficit. His body could not absorb nutrients. He was tiny, nearly left for dead by his father in So- malia. But his mother saved him, and he came up very small, was picked on his whole life. It perverted him, made him hate any part of humanity that wasn't disadvantaged. Although he has done horrible things too to those weaker than he. He disdains beauty, and ease, and good fortune."

"He has many children, many wives."

"Then you know he killed two of his children. And nearly killed his first wife."

"Not exactly a man sensitive to loss."

"Stop."

The guard walked on a few feet before he noticed and paused him- self, his back to them.

"Come here."

Emma put her head close to his.

"You are a good woman, I know. And I trust you. But you must never tell anyone that I have told you what I am about to say. It can't be known, even within these walls, even with people you trust most of all, that Fadi Subdallah has spoken out."

"I give my word."

"There was a gem in his life. I don't know if she still exists, or if this was all a lie. But he had a mistress."

"We know her. Lana."

"No. No, this mistress was his oldest daughter. He loved her, the only one of his children he loved. You see, she was the only one of his many children stricken with his same deformity. She was a wisp of a thing, so sick as a baby that he even took her to a US hospital. I met her once. Even as a teenager, with all the riches and treatment, she couldn't have been more than ninety pounds, well under five feet. With eyes sunk back into her head. But he lavished her with gifts, brought her everywhere. She moved like an old woman. There was talk among some of us, rumors."

"Of what?"

"My God." He breathed in. "That she was his lover. His own daughter. This sickly thing, he'd somehow fallen in love with a girl that had suffered as he had, though hers was much worse, and prolonged. He knew she would never fetch a husband, would never live a normal life, and for all he sought to destroy, for all his hatred of success and beauty and genetic fortune, when it came to this poor girl, he wrapped his world around her. He did anything for her."

Emma stood straight. "Jesus."

"Let's keep moving."

She pushed on, as did the guard.

"But that is your key to him. Nobody knows it, but even a man as truly evil as Ali, he has a very weak spot for his own daughter. Whatever mutated, horrible form of love he knows, it is for her."

CHAPTER 20

What usually gave him joy — those first hints of spring breaking through the tips of tree branches — now made him feel jittery. He was walking from a Sunday family lunch in Somerville, toward Cambridge, down Mass Ave. A route he had done hundreds of times in the past, that heavy casserole his mother had perfected working its way down his belly as he walked. These walks had grown longer with time, in the few years his business had begun to grow, to automate, to become boring.

Now Yusef did so much of the operational and day-to-day, so there was less and less reason for Georges to spend time in the office, where staff had grown to twenty full-time employees, in addition to the army of contractors and sub-contractors out installing their new system across Boston.

In the distance Georges noticed – as he always did – the tallest buildings in Boston's skyline, spread long across the Charles. The Hancock and Prudential towers, two places he saw as his last great conquests, the largest and most lucrative contracts on Yusef's list.

The sun was out, shadows drawn long from the cars and bikes that passed. The sidewalk was drying from this morning's rain, which would no doubt incite even more budding among the tree limbs. A half hour to Harvard Square, then on toward Central, his feet retracing the exact same steps. When he finally arrived at the front of the old building that housed their offices, he stood and spun his keychain around his fingers, looked farther down Mass Ave., and decided to keep walking.

He'd kept every letter of Marcel's over the last four years, tracking his progress, which had brought him back to Egypt for a long spell there. Those letters, posted in beautiful script, smelled as if from antiquity. Marcel had spent the years in religious pursuit, finally made understudy to the most revered Imam in a village north of Cairo. He wrote of the many changes that had occurred in his home village during his years away. Cars parked outside the wealthy homes on the outskirts for all to see. The clothing children wore was perhaps the most striking. Athletic warm-up suits, American team gear, English football jerseys.

Outside money had begun to "rip through the village like a storm," mostly in the form of clothing, but also the odd hotel, and even the dozens of government jobs available a short bus ride away. It put surplus money into the villagers' pockets, which paid for the farmers' stores, and the shepherds' wool, the bootleg clothing sold from car trunks. Visions of Morocco and Egypt flooded his mind, colors never seen before, fabric, spices, oceans of sand, strange dialects of Arabic.

Georges crossed into Boston, walked a few blocks through elegant Back Bay, the row houses and fine stoops abrasive to his thoughts of far away. So he rushed with his head down along Mass Ave., past lavish Newbury Street, the Berklee School of Music, The Symphony, and Christian Science Church.

He was now in the South End, decrepit row houses once like those in Back Bay, but from a bygone era of prosperity, from where the rich had long since been bled out. Beautiful brick facades remained but were like abandoned shells, plywood patching, long grass pursing cracks in stoops and sidewalks.

As he turned left onto Shawmut, the neighborhood changed another shade. There was a Syrian café jammed into a small corner unit, and next door a smoky halal restaurant, the smell of spice and burned meat. When they were kids, Nourredine would drive the family by the tiny apartment building he'd lived in during those first years in the States, pointing out the second-floor room where he and his friends would meet and drink pots of plain tea and talk of their families back home.

A Middle Eastern grocery, words in Arabic that probably meant spices, cigarettes, rugs, fabric. His father had described a hookah café where job listings were posted. The Arabs living in the South End were a big family in that way, whenever a man heard tell of some job opening up — bus boy, cab driver, janitor — he would post it on a communal wall, which was swarmed daily by the unemployed. He told of what those cafes were like during work days, for the men without jobs, either with families across an ocean, or freezing in a shared hovel nearby, or else lost altogether. The jobless were skinny and had eyes missing some tinge of color. "Far away looking," as Nourredine told his kids. It had always stuck with Georges, like limbo, a place to be feared. And he wondered if his father had purposely fixed him with that image.

The old café of his father's days, corner of Shawmut and Union Park, had long since shut down. But he carried on down Shawmut, came to Waltham Street. There was a single door at street level, paint peeling, no sign or address. He walked past then turned around, saw a man in a tunic simply open the door and walk in, closing it behind him. So he came back to the place, steeled himself a moment, then twisted the knob.

After closing the door behind him, he could feel the eyes. The room was larger than he'd expected, and marvelous. At the front was a counter, backed with assorted colorful boxes and small bags for sale. There was a single long table, along which ran a bench on one side and a mishmash of plastic chairs on the other. One wall was filled with books, another with paintings of pots.

In order to avoid standing there for too long, Georges stepped over to the counter, where a man met him. Without a word, he made a sweeping motion with his hands, bowed slightly, as if presenting his wares.

He looked around again. At the far table were two groups of men smoking hookah. So Georges turned to the vendor and said, in Arabic, "Hookah, please," with an accent odd enough to give the man pause, to squint his eyes before turning his back, taking a tall, octopine pipe system and setting it on the counter.

Then the man said in English, "Would you like a flavor?"

"How many?" In Arabic.

In English, "Strawberry, chocolate, blueberry, mint, vanilla, cinnamon…"

"Mint. Please."

So the man set a small block of aluminum on the counter. Georges paused, waited for the price, but the man said nothing, only put both hands out with palms up. Georges took the hookah and block, studied the room once more. Toward the back the place opened up to a section with large cushions on the floor and low tables. There was a group of four men lounging among the cushions, sharing a hookah. Georges went to the back, set himself up in the corner with the hookah on the table. All were obviously watching him.

He unwrapped the block and set it on the nest at the top of the hookah. After removing his jacket, he used the tongs to place the coals in position, put the mouthpiece of one of the pipes between his lips, and sucked through the hose, just as he had learned during those nights in Van Meter. Water bubbled at the base, and the small brick glowed as smoke gathered in the glass vase. Georges took a long gulp, held it in a few seconds until there was a burn, and his lungs pushed the smoke out in a coughing fit. As much as he tried to stifle it, the coughing continued.

The men in the group near him laughed. Georges tried to smile but had to deal with the remaining itch in his throat. His head became light. After a few minutes, he tried another puff on the hookah, this one smaller, and more pleasant, like a huge whiff from a cigarette, but cleaner, fuller, and with a minty heat at the end. A calm washed over him, and he leaned back in the cushions, studied the room once more. Low-hanging lights with grated metal gave the room its glow. The windows were all covered, and there were woven rugs along the concrete floor.

The man behind the counter walked over to the group, whispered something, then went to the far wall, which contained shelves with books and a small supply of records. He walked his fingers along the LPs, stopped and pulled one from the row, held it a second before taking the vinyl from its sleeve and setting it on a small turntable. Scratching sounds began, followed by a lone male voice, singing long notes, words Georges couldn't recognize, but placed in such vulnerable exhortation that their meaning didn't matter. The man was asking for something. The last note was held, pitched up and back down again. Then some percussive instrument began, and two voices melted into the original.

The music played at a low volume, and from just that single small speaker, but as Georges took another puff, the percussion snapped with life, and the rhythm was slow and wavelike.

Georges set the pipe down a while, put his head back. Later, the vendor came over to his table, hands folded at his waist. "Some tea?"

"Yes, please."

He returned with a ceramic pot and set a single cup on the table before Georges, poured a light colored tea into the cup, and set the pot down. The tea was bitter, but the liquid felt good on his throat. When he finished the first cup he lifted the pot, and as he poured he heard a voice from his left.

In a strange Arabic, "How are you?"

He sat up and squinted his eyes at the looming figure who now stood across the table from him. He recognized him as the man from the diner all those months ago.

After a pause. "Nazim is my name. And you were...Fadi, yes?"

"Yes." He stood, offered his hand.

"If you would care to join us, you are welcome."

He glanced at the other men, who were not looking over. "Yes, please."

Georges stood and bent to take up his hookah.

"Please, share ours."

"Thank you."

So he brought his cup and tea pot with him, and the men shifted over to open a spot of cushion.

"You remember Faruz. And this is Ali and Jesper."

"My name is Georges...Fadi. But I go by Fadi, please."

"Fadi. Hello." The man sat. Nazim was probably around the same age as Georges but with a beard half an inch long, and he wore a bandana to hold his long hair from his face. They all wore thobes, loose and airy and, Georges thought, very fitting in this dim room with plush cushions. Each of the other three made a gesture of touching their foreheads and saying something Georges couldn't understand.

Ali, who was sitting nearest to Georges, lifted one of the pipes and offered the mouthpiece to him. He asked a question, which Georges interpreted as, "Do you take this?" To which Georges simply responded, "Yes."

So he held the pipe to his lips and pulled a strong cloud of smoke into the chamber. The flavor was strong and unrecognizable. His head went light and his lungs wanted to clear themselves, though he resisted by taking a sip of tea.

The four men continued a previous conversation, which seemed to be about labor regulations in the States. Georges had to concentrate on what they were saying in order to understand, and portions were too fast, the dialect too muddy to follow. At one point, it became heated between Nazim — obviously the leader of the group — and Ali. Faruz made a calming gesture to both by putting two hands out, palms up. And all four were silent a while, each taking a puff from the hookah, a sip of tea. And then Nazim and Ali apologized to each other.

"Tell me, Fadi, where are your parents from?"

"My father is from a small village outside Beni-Mellal, in Morocco."

Nazim nodded with lifted eyebrows.

"And my mother...she is the same."

The sentence seemed to have formed beyond his making.

"Morocco can be a great country. They have fought hard to free themselves from the rule of the French and the Spanish. I do not agree with their chosen Malik." Then he turned to Jesper and smiled. "But nobody is perfect."

Georges smiled too and nodded. "So how do the four of you know each other?"

Jesper and Faruz looked down, and Ali began to say something but was interrupted by Nazim. "It is easy to know a friend in this town. There is but a small community. We are members of a...family we have built here. It is a place for Arabs to come together, to pray, to..." Some verb Georges didn't know. "...the battlefield of America. In many, we are stronger." He smiled. "And of course it allows us also to visit the Turk's." Motioning toward the man behind the counter. "Many of our meetings take place here. But they are not on Sundays. Today is usually for lighter discussion."

Georges reached again for the pipe, gesturing for permission, to which Nazim nodded.

"Perhaps such a group doesn't make sense to you. Your English is good, you are a citizen."

Not yet taking a drag. "I understand well. At the University of Massachusetts, I created such a club. I called it the Five Pillars." He looked around, the men each facing him. "It was an honest club, small at first. It began about ten years ago and continues to this day."

"That is very impressive, Fadi. What made you build this club?"

"I was once attacked for being Arab, for being Muslim." Georges could see the men flinch at this word. "My friend and I were beaten for nothing more than that. And I was angry, though he was forgiving. It was made from that, a confusion I felt, between how I was supposed to react, with anger, with intelligence, with compassion, I didn't know."

Ali spoke, "Was there…" But Georges didn't know the last word.

So Nazim said in French, "Justice?"

"Yes, there was justice. Not from the police though. It had to come from me."

Each man nodded, and Nazim made a grave face, crinkled his brow. "Of course, my friend. Though such justice is not easy, and it is not something we want to do, sometimes we still have to do it. Isn't that right?"

There was silence, into which the light, droning music now seeped. After a while the four men began conversing in fast and cloudy Arabic. Ali argued the need for justice (the new word for George) to be impactful, *as bright, blinding, dangerous, and nurturing as the sun*. Georges recognized this quote from somewhere.

Ali took up the worn, metal tea pot and filled Georges's cup then slid it toward him, slowly across the rough wood tabletop. So Georges drank. Their tea was much better, smoother, with a hint of spice. And the smell was rich wet earth from another place…

CHAPTER 21

The sun made it difficult to see during her drive along the beltway into Arlington. Emma's old Volvo wagon chugging along the open road, not a lick of traffic this late. She'd taken Evan to the doctor's this morning, picked him up from John's. She could feel him inspecting her clothes, trying to figure out her new job, dressed down as she was. Emma had told him it was in Defense but dodged all other questions. He probably knew it was somewhere on her old turf, something classified, maybe a little illegal. She wondered if he resented her, given the boring job he'd taken to do what was best for the family.

She'd been tense with fear sitting in the sterile office, not dissimilar to Fadi's room but with more decoration. The little guy was hot as a coal, his eyelids feathering open and shut. Waiting to hear the doctor's assessment, she swore she'd give up her job, replace her obsession for catching bad guys with an obsession for her tiny son. As panic set in, she even wondered about getting back together with John, started drawing pictures in her head of summer days on porches, lemonade and footballs, lots of green grass, she holding hands with her husband while the boy bounced across the lawn.

It was a simple fever, likely brought on by food poisoning. Have him take these, stay home, liquids, monitor. Relief. A hug too tight at first drew a groan from Evan. She had to call John at work, let him know the news, ask that he come home and tend to Evan for the day. "It's easier for you to take time off. Today is a big one for me." A sting as soon as the words left her lips.

"I'm sorry, John." Dropping him off at his father's. "I'm sorry."

Then the clean drive to Arlington along the unclogged beltway. She killed the engine, sat a few minutes as she studied the building, out there padded by woods, unassuming, the men behind these walls, dangerous on both sides, true terrorists, military killers. She sat in her mommy car in the sun, wanting to delay the transformation that always occurred crossing through those doors. Through the doors she was nothing but a construct, a patchwork of half-truths, a tangled invention. Except with Fadi. But of course it wasn't him she was meeting today.

He rose to shake her hand, smiled. The few weeks of depravation — "clock-shaking" as they called the sleepless, windowless treatment — had done very little to Ali's disposition. He was regal, charming, and well mannered. He still had that damn smell on him, the one that had clung to her hand for hours after their first meeting, even when she'd gotten home. It was a chemical version of lemon and rose.

"Your hair is changed. Very nice." In that Arabic British.

"Thank you."

The typical room, one guard, camera, few chairs, blank as can be. She set a lighter on the table between them, slightly closer to him. Then she took a pack of cigarettes from her back pocket, tamped one out, set it in her lips. Ali hated smoke, from every report she'd read, couldn't stand to be near cigarettes, had nearly killed a cohort over it.

His hand shot toward the lighter. "Allow me."

"Oh." Her best little southern belle voice. "Why, thank you." She even tried to make herself blush a bit.

She was wearing a blank, gray sweatshirt and jeans, hair pulled back, no makeup. "How was your night?"

He smiled, leaning back with legs crossed. "Very bad. I am weak, ready to talk."

She grinned and took a long drag. "Oh." Looking around the table. "There is no ashtray." Turned to the guard. "Ericson, would you mind terribly? I believe there's a spare one in 6F."

He paused a few seconds then left the room. Emma ashed on the floor.

"This is a big day."

152

"And why is that?"

"This is the last time they will allow me to talk to you."

"Very sad."

She said with a goofy teenage smile, "And I am the only person who knows a certain something. No one else here has any idea."

"Oh yes?"

"About your family."

"Ah. You realize one of your chums has tried this route. Protection for my family, etcetera. Do you not speak with each other?"

"This is not a bribe. Not exactly. Because I will tell you this information whether you are quiet or not. It is news, more than anything. And I'm telling you only because I too am a parent."

A placid grin seeped across his face, guessing her next move. "Please, not my children." He laughed. "I'll talk, I'll talk."

"No, no, they're fine. They are fine."

"I just have news." Raised eyebrows. "Good news."

"Okay."

"Your daughter is to be married."

He nodded.

"Baraka. She is to be married."

His lips parted just a bit. "Baraka?" Then he shook his head. "Impossible."

"Nope, one of our little spies confirmed it. Even checked with your son, Rahman, who is overseeing the arrangement."

"You have chosen the wrong gambit here. The wrong daughter."

She pursed her lips. "No...no, it's Baraka." Then she said, "She's the little one, right?"

Still not breaking his countenance. "Who could she possibly be marrying?"

Emma looked puzzled. "Some local man. I can't remember his first name, but his family's name is...Haddad? Does that seem right? Rahman has some business deal with their family, something about financing a new airport in South Saudi."

He rose to his feet, pounded the table. "Haddad!? She is not marrying Haddad! My little locust is better than Haddad. No, no. This *cannot* be. I must be put in touch with her at once. I demand it. Put me in touch with Rahman!"

This man, who'd reacted like a stranger to all news about his three wives, his slew of children, who'd been callus in his dismissal of his son's death.

"Ali. Please, sit. We don't have much time. That buzz cut will be back here any minute, and like I said I'm not supposed to be telling you this. We're not supposed to supply family information. Sort of counteracts all this isolation stuff." She leaned back. "I thought you'd be pleased."

He sat. Eyebrows now scrunched in worry. "Pleased? Would you be pleased if your most beautiful daughter was marrying a playboy? Someone given everything in his life, built disgustingly perfect? *Haddad.* He has earned no part of his life."

"Do you not care for their family?"

"Care for them? I would care to explode their entire household." He leaned in, his yellowish face. "I would crush each one like a beetle, you understand? You think what happened at Caldwell was devastating, you let me out for twenty-four hours, you will see a family *truly* devastated." His breathing was heavier. "My little locust." Then some mumbling in Arabic. His eyes were darting about the room. "There was no courtship, and I am her father. And she loves no other man. Rahman has no authority..."

"When were you last in touch with her?"

Five weeks ago, a phone call.

"I don't know."

"Well, you've been apart a while. And now suddenly your huge family is without a patriarch. You went missing. I'm sure they fear the worst. Again, that's why it's so strict to keep you isolated, free from contact. It makes it easier to get information from you."

He stood again, the elfish frame. Pacing about the room, pushing fist into palm. This was not allowed, not in the least, one interrogator, no guard, subject standing, unfettered. But Emma let him simmer, let him pace a while as gears and tumblers arranged in his brain. Men used to asserting their will with ease, now locked up and power starved, not a single word escaping to those they control.

Finally he turned to her. "You must let me contact her."

"What?"

"Yes." Leaning with hands on the table corners. "You must. There must be a loophole, something."

Emma shook her head as she tapped ash on the floor. "Ali, like I said, I'm not even supposed to have told you this. You have to be isolated until we get something from you. Then you become like any other prisoner in the US, full rights and all." Then she added, "Or even extradited. Not my wish, you understand, because I know that once you're sent back home, you'll never see the walls of a jail."

"Please." His face was now close to hers. He looked at the door. "We don't have much time, as you said."

"I just…I don't get it. I really thought this was good news. I mean, like I said, this is my last day they'll let me talk to you. I'm being moved off. And no one else is to know about this. We're certainly not authorized to be telling you this information. But it's harmless, I thought. I have a daughter around her age."

"Yes, of course it is. Harmless. And a letter to my child would be harmless as well. Surely, there must be laws in America."

"But everything that enters or leaves this room has to be authorized. I can't sneak a sheet of paper out of here. If I get caught passing a letter…"

"What about a trade?" He backed away, said something in Arabic.

"For what?"

His eyes were darting around again, that lovely sweat at his forehead.

"There's nothing you can give us. You're a low-level grunt. We wanted a boss or two, a cell leader, something like that. But based on our intel you wouldn't be able to provide anything."

"I can give something." He paced again. "Give me a cigarette. Please."

She did.

He lit and inhaled, then coughed. "Fucking smoke."

"Ol' Private Chip Steak will be back in no time."

"Okay."

She slid paper and pencil on the table. "There are two sheets there. One for me, one for you."

He sat, the cigarette in one hand, pencil in the other, those brittle hands like two separate minds trying to best each other. She could almost see that internal struggle, the tumult inside this man.

"I need you to give me locations. I need Karim."

At this he looked up.

"And we'll verify it too. Won't take long. But you need to give me something I can use. A letter is a big request, so I need a big present from you." She tapped the table. "Names, three locations, good ones. It has to be Karim. We know he's nearby. We already have several people who have given locations. Likely, yours will just corroborate, but it will show good will on your part. They have to match what we have, or your letter will not be mailed."

Those hands, shaking, battling. The cigarette, the pencil.

"Don't worry. No one will know. You will be able to write to Baraka, your 'little white one'."

He looked up, likely surprised Emma knew what the name meant.

"This will do no harm. We already have it. Draw your picture. If it matches ours, you can write to her."

His head slumped, and there was a great silence in the room, broken by stifled sobs from Ali as his hand began to scribble on the paper. Line after line, names, addresses. A few tears smacked against the paper. He wrote for minutes and finished just as the guard returned with the ashtray, set it down. Emma snubbed her cigarette.

Ali slid the paper over to her as he explained the connection. He met Marcel every Wednesday and Saturday behind one of his variety stores in Arlington. She asked what it was they planned on those nights, what was coming up. But he shrugged, couldn't say a word.

He hung his head, no longer sobbing. "You will get this letter to my little girl?"

Emma stood, folded the paper. "You have done well, Ali. This will help. And I promise you I will get a letter to your daughter."

"She is just a tiny thing, too frail. I'm the only one who can understand her, you see, who can take care of her." He looked up, those ghastly eyes and emaciated cheekbones. The eyes searching for help, a look she hadn't seen since those years in Africa. She turned her back, wondering now where his daughter really was, what she was doing.

Perhaps thinking of her perverted dad, trying to call him without answer, unaware that he would never touch her again.

She motioned to the old guard. "All done."

She let the door close behind her and walked down the hall with the man. "Well, Reg." Handing him Ali's letter. "Here's another for your sick fucking collection, you dirty bastard."

The old man smiled and slid the blank envelope into his breast pocket.

CHAPTER 22

Nazim responded in slow Arabic. "Your idea is good and comes from a good place. But the outcome of good remains fundamental, whatever your outcome might be, one cannot become distracted by the tactic. And sometimes when a tactic involves anger or vengeance for vengeance only, a man becomes drunk with it, and he forgets what end he is after, becomes lost in anger and vengeance, which after all offer sustenance to an *individual* only, and for a short time only. They do not offer sustenance to the principle."

Ali, whose elbows were on the table by this point, paused, then slowly leaned back into the cushion, staring calmly at Nazim. He looked over at Jesper. "So," he said, "does young Fadi's case fit?"

"You will have to ask Fadi this." He turned. "When you met this Tim Dunn..."

He nodded.

"Was this to fulfill something within you, or was it to put right a situation?"

"I suppose it was both. I wanted to put right a situation that was..." he thought of the word. "...*crooked*, but putting it right satisfied something within me as well." Then he added, "If only for a little while."

"There you have it. Perhaps the true measure of an action is whether it provides lasting sustenance or leaves you hollow after a time. Fadi, after you confronted this Dunn, did you then create your community? Your club?"

"Yes."

"And this was done because?"

Georges thought a moment and was happy to realize he had the answer. "Because I needed something…lasting. I wanted to build something that would help my brothers, my friends, a stranger coming to the school or America for the first time."

"So, Ali, I would say that Fadi's second course does *fit*, as you put it."

Ali said, "I will bet that Dunn did not attack another Arab, and will not, as long as he lives. A man who does such a thing is a coward. He is afraid. You need only meet him with the slightest strength, and he will bow."

Georges could see that Nazim was displeased by this remark. He turned, "And Fadi, you say this club still exists?"

"Yes. I still visit a few times each year." A bit of sadness in his voice.

Then Ali asked, "And who else has been the leader of this club?"

"My friend was president after me. He was also the strongest. Then others."

He glanced across the table to Nazim. "And your friend's name?"

Georges felt his throat clench, and he paused the tea cup below his mouth, then lowered it, looked from Ali to Nazim, who said, "It's okay, it's okay." With that same calming smile. "We just think we may know him."

"Forgive me, but where did you gentlemen say you were from?"

"We are from all over. Egypt, Somalia by way of Arabia. Yemen."

Georges studied them, and here his mind wandered, until the words seeped out. "Marcel. Karim."

Nazim smiled, and Georges could see the others nodding.

"Your friend has been quite busy in his home of Egypt, hasn't he?"

"I don't know."

"Aren't you in touch with him?"

"A little. I know he went home to look after his mother and his sisters."

"Yes, his sisters especially, I would imagine. Come…" He handed the pipe to Georges once again.

He smoked, his throat still tight and now he might have been sweating too. So he drank some tea. His head was light, and the music filled his mind when no one spoke, and he thought of and felt only those things from this very instant.

"Tell us, Georges, what do you do?"

"I have an elevator company."

"You have your own company?"

"Yes."

"Is this your father's company?"

"No."

Ali cut in, "Do white men work for you?"

"Yes." He looked down, paused before adding, "We have over thirty employees now."

There was a pause, then Jesper chimed in, "Faruz and I both drive cabs at night and work as custodians during the day. We attended university in Cairo as biologists, but came to this country five years ago."

"Is there no work for biologists here?"

Nazim leaned back, seemed to consider something a moment, before asking, "And tell me, Fadi, because you are able to obtain success in technology, and make money, do you feel as if you have risen high here?"

"Not at all. That's not what I meant."

"That is good. You see, the problem with Western thought is simply that it corrupts whatever culture it infests. The true terror is its ability to (in English) *hypnotize* others into believing that the goals of Western culture are actually *your* goals as well." He gestured to Ali. "That is what the West has done so well. In Africa, now in Arab culture. It's not a simple question of might, wealth, military, or numbers. It is cultural hypnosis."

"Hypnosis." Georges said it in Arabic, and Nazim nodded. Marcel had begun to use the exact same word in his letters, describing the way small children in his village wore American team jerseys, begged for blue jeans and sneakers. The way Marcel lamented that these kids would soon be the leaders of Egypt, wear western suits and ties, and fill their homes with electronics.

"Tell me, Georges Fadi, why do you not yet have a family?"

"I have not had time. I have been deep in studies, or else starting my business. I have no time for anything else."

"You see? No time to pray…"

"I did not say that."

"…no time to find a wife, to have kids. Hypnosis, seeking Western goals, it clouds your ability to seek a true path, it takes over and leaves no room for contemplation."

Nazim took a long pull from the pipe, the water bubbling as Georges sat speechless. And then the eyes of Nazim flashed a moment with anger or something deeper. Then his face went benign again.

"But you are a good man, Fadi. You are strong, no doubt. You have men who will follow you because you are their boss, and if they do not they do not eat and neither does their family. But as just a young man you had many more men who would follow you for your ideas and likely for your courage. I suppose you must think of the difference."

Just then the music stopped, the phone buzzed loudly. The Turk walked over to the counter, answered in Arabic, then set the receiver down and made his way to Nazim, leaned and whispered in his ear.

Nazim nodded, looked at Ali. Then he stood, each man joining him. "Well, sadly we must go."

When Ali rose, Georges was struck by how short he was. Behind the draped tunic his arms were bony, his cheeks sunken.

Georges stood.

"But I think it was fate that you have met us here, Georges Fadi."

The others walked toward the door, leaving only Ali and Nazim.

"And I would like to again invite you to pray with us. On Saturday we meet next door, at 48, the green door. I hope you will come and meet our brothers and talk and sit with us a while. We want our community to be strong, especially with men like you."

He offered his hand, which Georges shook.

"What time?"

Nazim smiled. "Whenever you can come."

Ali put his hand out as well, and they shook.

He walked back along Shawmut and then down Clarendon, toward the T stop. His mind was at once frantic but unable to grip single thoughts, only the vague idea that he had somehow endangered Marcel. He needed to let his friend know. Were these men attached to the family from Alexandria? Had he now leaked information that would get his friend killed?

161

It was at this time that Georges noticed a smell that would not leave. It seemed to be without origin, not from flowers or mimicking anything natural. Many blocks later, he discovered the source. The scent of fake lemon and rose clung like nettles to the palm of his right hand.

CHAPTER 23

"Pull!"

The spinning clay frisbee rose toward the sky and shattered with a *boom-crack*, shards falling earthward, and a wash of particles that seemed to continue their assent before disappearing. Emma knelt on the dirt road and wiped her forehead on her shoulder. She snapped the spent shell from the barrel, flipped the gun belly up, and put her hand out to Alec for another bunch of shells.

"That's the last of the box. More in the truck."

Still crouching, she took the gallon jug of water, now quite warm, and tossed her head back to take a good gulp. A splash made its way to her neck and chest, which was already wet from the heat. She wondered if Alec had glanced at her arms or chest or elsewhere when she'd peeled off her t-shirt to reveal a white tank top. No, certainly not. Not Alec Randolph, the most proper man she'd ever worked under, abroad or elsewhere. Now he was her boss again, though she still had only a vague sense of what his actual rank or position was, or what sector their little group fell under.

"Weren't kidding about the heat."

Alec nodded and ran his shirtsleeve across his face. He was standing in stiff posture, light-blue button-down shirt, khakis. Like Emma, he'd begun sweating seconds after they'd gotten out of his Jeep. He was also right about this spot: it was perfect for trap shooting. The two-hour drive along 66 into West Virginia was worth it. The old farmland had been in his family a handful of generations and now sat mostly dormant and overgrown, but certainly remote enough to blast a case full of shells on a Sunday. The road from which they shot used to run to the laborers' quarters and now had a mohawk of tall grass down its middle and looked out on a vast field of weeds, corralled by an old wall of stacked rocks. On a rise farther out was the old barn with a coffin-sized hole in its roof.

Alec went to the Jeep for the last few boxes of shells, of which they had far less than they had clays. Emma had worn sneakers and long shorts to hide the lines of blue and the bruises that spotted her thighs so easily and mysteriously these days. When Alec had asked her along, she'd teed up a nice refusal in her head but then pictured only the shooting, which she'd loved since she was a girl, and had somehow found herself mouthing the word *terrific* to her boss. Reg had cancelled last minute, leaving just the two of them to meet early this Sunday at Alec's house, to ride west in near silence with shitty little gas station coffees in the cup holders.

When he returned, she handed him the weapon with the barrel facing downward. "Yours."

She took a stack of clays from the box and set one in the pocket of the trap, which Alec had built and tended to stick every few launches. She queued her foot on the switch.

"Let's see one."

She stepped and set the spring loose, flinging the wobbly little disk on its escape route toward the barn. Alec liked to wait until the clay started the downside of its arc before firing. He stood steady until the thing reached the tree line before taking his shot. It burst into two large pieces, which plopped into the bushes. "Damn." He gave the weapon one angry pump and set an empty shell fleeing from the ejection port. Alec had wasted no time in telling Emma about the great pedigree of trap and skeet shooters from which he'd descended. Apparently, his grandfather, Vic, held quite a bit of esteem among the shooting community. It had taken a bit of resistance to get Alec to forego much of the etiquette and vernacular he was used to. But he was a damn fine shot, at that, even better than Emma.

She loaded another clay into the trap, pulled the spring. "I suppose I should just tell you the news now."

Alec, the shotgun already tucked tight to his shoulder and his eye locked down the barrel, at first looked perturbed, then seemed to relax a bit, perhaps realizing he'd not be getting in a proper day's shoot. "I suppose." Then said, with much less gusto, "*Pull*."

A mechanical *clack*, a few seconds of silence, and a perfect disintegration of the pigeon.

"You know we made our biggest breakthrough on Friday."

"I'd heard, yes." Snapping the pump down and back. "Ostensibly."

"What's that supposed to mean?"

"Sorry."

"No, really, what does that mean?"

He turned toward her, lowered the barrel. "I'm surprised at you. You know better than I that intel is only as good as it proves to be in the field. Ali gave up some juice, but will it cash in?"

"Second highest ranking member of AT we've had in captivity."

"Don't tell *him* that."

"We get him to cough up some juice on the *leader* of the cell."

"Ostensibly."

"Well, up to now, you and your team had *ostensibly* jack…"

He held up a hand then knelt on the other half of the dirt road, the seam of tall grass running between them. "I'm not saying that you and Reg haven't done an incredible job. With Ali. Especially Subdallah. But think about how many times we got a guy to cough out in Egypt, then we run the intel up the flagpole and find out it's bogus."

"I'm hesitantly optimistic."

"As am I." He lowered the weapon to a downward angle, gazed out toward the high weeds of the field and the broken barn. A long breath. "It's taken too long."

"I'm sorry."

"I realize it couldn't be going any more quickly. But we're running out of time."

"You mean your superiors are paranoid."

"All I can say is there's real reason for them to be paranoid."

"This is bullshit. Reg and I need to know. It might give us something we can use."

"It's classified."

"I don't believe this section of the government works on those terms."

He turned to her and set a grave look on his face. "You can guess as to its nature anyway, can't you?"

"Yeah, I suppose I can. But if we knew more details, maybe Reg could confirm or deny that what we're hearing from our guys matches up."

"Reg has his orders."

She paused to study his face a few seconds. "Hell." And though the heat made it unappealing she pulled a cigarette from her pack and lit it. They both faced the field and the lumpy hill where the barn sat, and both wiped a forearm across their faces at the same time. Emma took a drag and then a good draught of water from the jug, then another drag, and as she exhaled, "I want to be there."

Alec had started shaking his head before the words were complete.

"Why the fuck not?"

"You realize I'm your superior."

"*You* realize I'm the most qualified person you've got."

"That's a stretch. And you're about as close to a spring chicken as I am."

"I've got more domestic experience than most of the team you'd be bringing in."

"You don't know that."

"I can sure handle a firearm better than any of those meaty bitches at the bureau."

He smiled. "You might be right about that. But this isn't some raid, anyway. Won't be a shot fired. It's surveillance only, for the feds and whoever else they want to throw in to futz it up."

"And Arabic? Shit, Alec, do I need to type up my resume for you?"

"You're perfect. Doesn't my hiring you prove that I think that? But you can't do everything. Doesn't make sense to have you along on this. We'll have teams at each of those three locations, might be waiting for days, weeks. Nothing will come of it."

"But you know one location is prime. And we know when Karim meets Ali there. All I'm asking is to come along. You forget I was a cop a while. A long while."

"I don't forget that. But right now you're an interrogation special-
ist. You and Reg have done well in informing this investigation. That's
huge. I don't see why you need to be on the stakeout."

"I want to see that fucker's eyes."

"You don't trust that we'd bring him back to Harrison."

She turned to face the forest, took a long swig of water. Alec stood,
took two shells from his shirt pocket, held the shotgun under one arm,
and clicked the shells into its belly. Then he took two more steps to the
edge of the road, began to ready the weapon until it was snug, the barrel
angled slightly downward. Emma held the cigarette in her mouth as
she slid the next disc into the trap and slid the spring back, clicked the
arm into place. Alec aimed toward the barn, then said, "Let's see one."

Click, silence, *boom*, dust.

He pumped the shotgun as Emma reloaded the trap. This time, Alec
waited until the clay was just a few feet from the ground before evap-
orating it. Then he walked through the weeds and leaned back on that
stone wall, lowered the barrel.

They were both sweating, but something about seeing Alec, his forehead near pouring with the stuff, emboldened her.

"Thanks for putting me on Ali." She said flatly.

"Of course. You were the natural choice."

"I appreciate that. I never assume I am, but thanks. Putting me right
on him, letting me be the first…that meant a lot to me. And the timing…whoa, how it synced up with my work on Fadi." She crossed one
arm below her elbow as she held the cigarette and squinted. "That I was
able to get in on Ali, and ramp up my squeeze on Fadi." Shaking her
head. "Damn. Beautiful. Anyway, thanks again."

He regarded the silky black of the gun barrel. Then they were both
silent and birds started chirping or else always had been.

Emma waited just a while longer, then said, "How about maybe?"

"I'm good with maybe."

Emma went to the wall a few feet down and sat on a flatter part.
She reached her hand out to Alec, who passed the shotgun over to her.
With the cigarette in her mouth, she pumped it once, sending the spent
shell into the weeds forever. Alec looked embarrassed.

"I guess this isn't your weekend with Evan."

"Right."

"What's the little guy up to?"

"Up to being big these days."

"I know what you mean. Anna…well, seemed like she was only that cute little girl a few days. Then she's a woman, one who hates her mother, hitched and having kids herself."

"I didn't realize you were a grandpa."

He winced. "Mind if I ask you something?"

She looked at him, sun and sweat pinching one eye shut. Then she laughed. "Same approach I used with Ali."

"How long's it been? You and John?"

"Good five years."

"You seeing anybody?"

She reared back. "Jesus Christ, sir."

"No really. I wondered that when I was looking you up again, why you haven't remarried."

"It's not that easy is why."

"Any suitors?"

Emma put another cigarette between her lips. "Yeah, plenty of suitors. Look at me." She lit the cigarette and faced forward, shaking her head. "No. I don't want suitors. I move around, once again have a job I can't talk about, have a little boy. I've got severely dyed hair, pack-a-day, I've got nothing but mama clothes. None are knocking, and I don't want them to."

"Shit, sorry for asking."

"Thank you for saying that."

"Well. I suppose while I'm at it, I might as well go for broke."

"You'd make a terrible interrogator, Alec."

"I've always wondered, what ended it for you and John?"

"I did." She tucked one hand under her elbow and held her cigarette up in the air. "With the help of an airborne fresh out of Fort Bragg." Her hand slowly descending like a plane.

"I'm sorry."

She shrugged. "It was for the best."

"Not easy on the kid."

"I'm working on that."

A sound pricked her left ear, something hidden in the weeds. She stood and walked to Alec, dug into the pocket on that silly shirt of his, found two shells. With only a nub of a cigarette getting smoke in her eyes, she stood behind the wall, flipped the shotgun upside down, fed it ammo. Emma could sense Alec walking over to the trap, could hear him feeding a pigeon into slot. She lowered the weapon, took a small rock from atop the wall, tossed it into the weeds where the sound had come from. As the stone landed, two small birds — one black, one baby blue — set out in a weave pattern off toward the tree line. She locked the blue one in her sights and fired. Both birds fluttered wildly toward the woods and disappeared in shadow. Emma turned the shotgun back toward the barn, steadied the stock at her shoulder, and mumbled through the side of her mouth, "Let's see one."

CHAPTER 24

My Elder Brother Georges,

I hope you and your family are blessed and that Allah smiles upon you.

Your letter brings me sorrow, because I know you must have been worrying these many days. I sensed the great alarm in your words at having met these strange men in a strange room. Do not fear. You and your family are safe.

I know of the men you mentioned. Upon receiving your letter, I asked men in my mosque about those who you met. N- and A- both belong to a common group, one I will not mention here, and I leave their full names from this letter for fear that it will be intercepted. But rest assured, these men mean you no harm. On the contrary, I cannot recommend strongly enough that you begin a friendship with them and that you visit their group. They need your guidance.

Over the many years that we have written to each other, I know I have seen in you a great confusion and aimlessness, one which I think we could even trace back to the end of your time with the Five Pillars. And though I have tried to restrain my advice, for fear of sounding like a parent, I do believe that this great emptiness you have described can be fulfilled only through service to a cause greater than yourself, a service to your God, to your brothers.

In meeting with this group, you will be forging a bond between us, one that reaches across the ocean. These men also need your leadership, I feel, the same spark that blinked inside you all those years ago in Amherst.

I hope you will take this great step and that you will write to me whenever you need my help.

Your loving brother,
M

The next Saturday Georges took the same walk across the Charles, through Back Bay, and into the South End. It was midmorning, and a light dew covered the grass and the leaves in the city. By the time he showed up at that green door he was layered in a membrane of part sweat and part dew.

He knocked. No answer at first, so he knocked harder.

One of the men from the Turk's opened the door, dark skin and beard. "Yes?"

Georges gave him a look. "I met you at the Turk's."

"Oh, yes. Okay, come in."

Inside was a street-level apartment, windowless like a basement, with low ceilings and several posts in the middle of the room. The place stretched back a long ways, and the walls were painted a fresh white, with sparse adornment, save for a circuit box on one wall. Very little furniture as well, simply a large carpeted area, at the back of which were stacked some folding chairs.

Georges could smell incense burning, and as he walked in and his eyes adjusted, he found that about a dozen men were standing near the back, rolling up or holding prayer rugs. Georges now realized he had come right after Salah, and that the man from the Turk's had purposely invited him after prayers.

He stood and waited in the middle of the room, until from a darkened corner Ali appeared. "Hello." Reaching his hand out. "Georges, yes?"

"Fadi. Hello."

"We were expecting you several weeks ago."

"I apologize and meant no disrespect."

"Fadi." It was Nazim, wearing a long tunic with no shoes. "How are you, my friend?"

171

They shook hands. "I am well, thank you. I apologize for my rudeness in not coming the other week."

"Not at all. We were expecting you sooner."

"Yes. Busy with family affairs."

"That is important."

Georges simply nodded, and there was a silence in the place as they stood a while. Then Nazim said, "Come, help us set up."

A few of them set about unfolding and arranging the chairs in a loose circle while the other men stood and chatted. When they were all set up, Nazim sat down, in a way that made Georges think he had a bad back, bracing with his hands on his knees. He motioned to the seat beside him, so Georges sat. Within seconds the others found chairs themselves and were silent. Nazim spoke in that intentionally slow Arabic. "My friends, I introduce our friend Fadi to you."

He looked around and offered a very Maraca-like smile, but no one responded.

"Fadi has accomplished much in his young life. He created a strong organization of faithful brothers and sisters, ten years ago, which is still alive. It has used many ingenious methods, both peaceful and heated, to achieve attention and the insistence upon our legitimate place in the world. A world in America where a Muslim can be free to worship and live without compromise."

Georges looked around again but still found a sea of unmoved faces, dark beards, and stern glares.

"This community, this was the place that a very great young man first felt at home, an Arab in America not six months, a man who was lost, by his own account. Fadi took him in, as a brother, and became a friend and comrade with him. This man received control from Fadi after he left school. And after that this man went back to his home in Egypt, where he has built a powerful following."

Some men in the circle seemed to loosen their posture, nearly imperceptible shifts in facial gestures. A gruff man with a reddish beard lit a cigarette and leaned an elbow on his thigh. At this, Ali rose and turned on a box fan in the corner.

"So let us welcome our brother, Fadi."

The men, in staggered unison, mumbled some words Georges didn't recognize.

Georges once again felt uncomfortable in his clothes, simply because of the loose garments the others wore. He crossed his legs, and in as smooth a motion as he could muster, slid a cigarette from the pack and into his lips, lit it with a *click*. He felt Ali gazing a hole into his side, so turned and offered the pack to him. He shook his head.

"We have much to discuss today."

A man interrupted. "What about the vandalism in Lowell?"

This was followed by a string of rumbling from the others. Nazim acted as mediator, motioning gently with his hands, which finally got an organized conversation started. As the man continually restated the horror he felt in someone defacing a new mosque, Nazim steered the conversation back to solutions, steps to be taken by their group.

The meeting went on like this for over an hour. Subjects would be raised, and the more vocal of the group would always chime in, simultaneously, until Nazim brought the conversation to order. Georges said nothing, simply watching and listening as best he could to the various dialects. He found the flow of the meeting inefficient, thinking back even to the earliest days of the Five Pillars, during which meeting subjects were always written on the blackboard, votes as to what would be discussed the following week. The crowds were much larger, but even they were more controlled than this group of headstrong men. He was tempted at a few points to remind the group of the initial topic. The place had been so peaceful when he'd arrived, but these men each acted like a leader, and Georges thought they must all be important, well educated. His mind immediately set about ordering this group into segments, factions, mapping out alliances. The men were obviously friends, and always ended in deferential positions, but the place pulsed with anger, with conviction. Egos like the cigarette smoke.

Nazim shot his hand out to glance at his watch, and the men were silent. By now the place was thick with haze, and many of the men were leaning forward, each having engaged in some heated talk or other over the last hour. Ali stood and walked over to the door, wedged it open with the box fan. Light crept into the place, and Georges could see that some of the men were unhappy about this.

Afterward, the men lingered outside the door and smoked or squatted on their hams and joked with each other, as if crossing outside the threshold allowed it. After a few minutes, most of them made their way around the corner to the Turk's. Georges stood, uncertain if he should join.

Then Nazim put a hand on his shoulder. "Come, Fadi. Let's get some cigarettes from Ahdi."

As they crossed Shawmut, Georges could feel Ali's eyes at his back. They walked a few blocks west, stopping at the same shop Georges had entered before. But this time the grocer greeted Nazim with a bright smile and a kiss to both cheeks. They chatted, and the man gave Nazim a pack of Pall Malls without charging.

They sat on a nearby stoop. Nazim held a match for Georges. With a distorted British accent, "And this man, your friend Marcel Karim, you have been in touch with him lately?"

"We have written letters quite a lot since graduating, since he moved back to Egypt. He was my best friend in college, and the best friend I have ever known."

"So you know what he has undertaken back in Egypt?"

"Yes."

"And what do you think?"

"It doesn't surprise me in the least. He has been talking about becoming an Imam since the first night we met, and I have watched him find his voice, and I know the reformation of life in his village, in his country, has been heavy on him for quite some time."

Nazim paused and looked at Georges. "He has done much, very much for such a young man. We are great admirers of his. He has more work to do. And a good deal of his goals would be better served if he were to come back to the States."

Georges looked at him, his eyebrow cocked up. "Have you suggested this? Are you in touch with him?"

"Yes. And yes. He would be most welcome, and we even have ways of delivering him safely, funding his work here. He would be well taken care of."

He dabbed out his cigarette, though held onto the butt. Then Nazim stood. "Will you come have some tea with us?"

Georges stood. "Thank you. I think I will pass this time."

Nazim held out his hand for Georges to shake, something he could tell the man was not accustomed to. Then Nazim was off, still holding the cigarette butt as he crossed the street.

All those late nights smoking cigarettes with Marcel, when the problems of the university would roll off his tongue so easily. So much was ahead of him then, and he remembered being overwhelmed by how vast the world used to be. A vastness now pinched over the years, like an eye closing.

Georges attended every meeting over the next three months. Each Tuesday night and Saturday afternoon, he would make the long walk across the Charles to the South End, rap on that old door, and enter the dim, smoky room. They prayed together, flopping rugs out across the dingy floor, rising and submitting in synched rhythm. Then the rugs were rolled up and stored away, folding chairs placed in a half circle, oriented toward Nazim. Georges made a point not to always sit near him, to assuage the others' growing mistrust.

The thought of having Marcel here at once excited and terrified him. Bringing back an artifact from a more inspired time in his life, to be sure, perhaps giving him the shot he needed to right his path. But Marcel also seemed ill-fitted to this phase of his life. It was shame, this hesitance, shame at how Marcel would view the turns he had taken. From Five Pillars leader and mentor to generic business man, fretting about margins and bottom lines, hiring, firing. Commerce.

After meetings, they always headed to the Turk's for tea and shisha, where things took a more light-hearted tone, the jokers of the bunch showing themselves, talk of women, Americanisms, football.

It was here that Georges first felt comfortable speaking, which later bled into group meetings. At first, he chimed in with questions meant to remind the men of what their original issue had been. "Mahmed, so do you think that one must join this blind race for money in order to be happy here in America, or can abstaining from this mindset actually give a man an advantage?"

It carried on for many meetings like this, with Georges asking rhetorical, Socratic questions. Until men began posing questions back at Georges, wondering about his opinion. "You are successful. Are you happier now that you have raised your own company?" And when Georges began to speak more regularly, he was shocked by the attention they accorded him, no interruptions, no impatience waiting for him to finish. All seemed to be truly interested in what he had to say.

On a rainy day at the Turk's, after a particularly heated meeting, Jesper asked, "Fadi, you are a strong man, and I respect your accomplishments. But how can you say you are in the same position as we are? You have not come to this country, you have not given up your family, you are not applying for work at a grocer with an engineering degree in your pocket."

"Sometimes you see inequities, very clearly, because they confront you every day. They are hard to miss, in this case. Other times, you see inequities for themselves, whether or not they happen to be imposed on you that very day. To fight an injustice only because it affects you personally is not a righteous path."

The men were silent, uncharacteristic of these meetings. Nazim nodded assent, and others then joined him. That was the last time his business success was ever brought up as a negative, and Georges noticed a marked change in their attitude toward him too. Men began looking to him as they looked to Nazim. And Georges was instinctively moved to put on his Maraca smile, to humble himself, deprecate his stature. He had to battle the urge he had fashioned since he was ten years old: to lower himself in order to fit in.

After one meeting he stopped by the grocer's on Shawmut to purchase a few garments. He bought a loose-fitting tunic, one very similar to what Ali wore most days. He would make the walk from Cambridge in jeans and a t-shirt then stop at the library to change in the bathroom, jamming his clothes into a backpack.

CHAPTER 25

John's lawn was perfect. The grass was freshly cut and edged, three is-
lands dark with mulch and puffy with mums in the early spring, two
oak saplings he'd planted seven years before now with thick adolescent
trunks. Emma parked the Volvo at the curb, sat in the car a while. In
the passenger seat was her pack of Camels, just sitting there in the sun.
She shook her head and laughed nervously. "Oh no, you're not coming."
With hands on the steering wheel she just sat and watched the place,
the shut shades and pretty flowers and invited driveway. She waited
then shook her head again before plopping the pack into the glove box
and finally getting out of the car.

"Hi, Emma."

"John."

"Come on in. Soccer ran over, pizza and bullshit after. He stunk to
high heck, so made him take a shower before seeing you. Just on the
back porch listening to the O's. Something to drink?"

"Sure."

"Milk or ice tea?"

"Either of them sweetened?"

"Tea."

She nodded. John set some cubes in a glass and poured sweet tea
from a plastic pitcher into it. He'd hated sweet tea when they'd first met,
until Emma had started making her mom's blend out in Egypt. Not too
sweet, bit of mint.

They sat in plastic Adirondack chairs on the back porch, which looked out at grass and dark woods. It was shaded, the back lawn taller and spotted with various toys: big plastic bat, whiffle balls, some sort of propeller blade, toy machine gun. The hose was unraveled and strewn wildly across the grass.

"Sleepover last night."

"Looks like she had fun."

John gave her a glance he'd done often when they were married. It was something short of anger but a warning just the same.

"Do you miss coming to work at Morganson?"

"Not a bit."

"Your commute is substantially better."

"Yes."

"What are your days like there?"

She shrugged, looked off toward the woods. "Boring. How *is* Morganson? I'll bet the middle floors look a lot different, don't they?"

"They did some cleaning of house, just like you predicted. But most of the good ones are still there, some of the bad." He looked at his hands. "Gotten a bit more exciting, I suppose. Some of the internal security heads that came in have brought some fresh ideas. Anyone at your new office I'd know? Defense guys?"

"No."

"So, is it a big space? It's in Arlington, right?"

"Thereabouts."

"And…so, who do you report to?"

"You know, same old structure of bosses."

"Mmhm."

Emma took a sip of tea, which was just right. She set it on the arm rest. "You definitely happy there?"

"Sure."

"And you feel like it's secure?"

He let out a long breath. "Much as a job like this can be. And you?"

She ignored him. "Is she staying over here? I mean, does she spend the night?"

"Come on, Em."

"I'm just asking. I didn't mean for it to sound like that."

"I'd be happy for you if you met someone. Really, I would. I think I've gotten there. Want you to be happy."

"Not me." Shaking her head. "I want you to be miserable, alone."

John gave one of his long laughs that started with a few staccato chuckles and one sustained note. "You're not seeing anyone then?"

"Maybe here and there."

"You should."

"Work, you know?"

"Yeah."

She pictured the pack of cigarettes roasting in the glove compartment, felt a little sorry for them. She turned to looked into the kitchen. "Where is that little jerk?"

"Really into combing his hair now."

"What?"

"He and his friends, they wear mousse now, plaster it all over their hair, part it sideways or spike it."

"Sounds ridiculous."

"Well, it is."

She faced forward. "Little guy's changing, huh?"

"Real fast."

She looked around the backyard at the gas grill, little brick patio, the toys, thought of the shitty little government apartment poor Evan had to suffer through every other weekend. The right-angled furniture and pointless art that had come with the place, drab colors, barely used Nintendo Entertainment System with the just-released Super Mario Bros. 3 tucked under the TV. Soon enough, it would occur to him that there was nothing of his mother there, no knickknacks or personal items from which to get a sense of who she really was. If it wasn't already the case, he'd start to dread visiting her, each weekend actually obscuring his perception of her as a real, living being.

Tears had slipped down her cheeks without her knowing, and she tried to wipe her cheek with her shoulder, but John noticed.

"What is it?" He sat forward. "What's wrong?"

"The little bastard." A long breath. "My God, look at me." She smiled and laughed as even more tears came. "I'm fine. I'm exhausted."

He stood and disappeared through the glass door, came back a few seconds later with a handful of tissues.

"Thanks. I'm sorry. Nothing was wrong, really. The hair thing...the combing." She dabbed her eyes and patted her pocket for cigarettes. "I just wish I still lived here. I'm sorry. I want to live here again."

"Emma..."

"No, no, I know. I just really fucked up. All the decisions. I'm not sure I told you how sorry I am for what I did to you guys. Not just the one thing. I don't know why I stayed out there. I should have come home to be with you guys, my two guys. I didn't realize it. But I'm in hell now. I don't know who I am half the time. That damn place."

"Work."

"And home. They're the same." She took a long breath, which seemed to catch a few times. "Ok. Oh, fuck, I'm sorry, John. I wasn't expecting this. Nothing was wrong. I guess it's the quitting smoking thing."

"I didn't realize you had."

She looked at her watch. "Yeah, two and a half hours."

They both laughed and sat facing each other a few moments. Emma took a long pull of iced tea. "This is good."

"Em..."

"Let's forget this. Can we forget it?"

"How can you say that?"

There was a knock on the glass doors behind them. On the other side stood Evan, clean and skinny.

Emma rose and waved with her best smile.

Her son waved back and pointed excitedly at his new soccer jersey, a t-shirt with a picture of a lightning bolt on its front. Then he turned and pointed to his back. Number 33, her favorite number. He spun back around to face them, soundless on the other side, beaming at her. His hair was still dark and wet-looking, packed down with mousse and combed neatly to the side.

CHAPTER 26

The group began to resemble a family. For some men, it was the only family they had, having either lost theirs to violence or left wives and children overseas indefinitely. But mostly it was like a family because each man filled a certain space, a specific role. Nazim sat at the head, the patriarch. Respect, both forced and organic, washed over him from the others, just like a father. Other men were like uncles, the younger ones children to Nazim. And Ali played the part of irate eldest brother to a T, bringing fury and immediacy to whatever problems presented themselves, projecting his point of view over others'.

Even after six months of biweekly meetings, Georges was still searching for his role, though it was becoming part father and part mother. He calmed men down, brought agendas into perspective, and was often needed to be the voice of reason when Nazim was unable, or when Ali was out of control. It carried on in this way for many months, into the first hints of winter and as the sidewalks were stuffed with snow.

Late one afternoon, at the Turk's, when most of the others had left, Nazim, Ali, Faruz, Georges, and Jesper sat at a table smoking. Georges could feel the silent signals being sent among the four of them, obviously deciding whether or not to let Georges in on something.

"Fadi," Ali finally said, "when you were at college, you have spoken of many great practices the Five Pillars Club undertook. Mosques, voting, defending the honor of Muslim women."

"As much as we could."

"But I wonder, was it ever necessary for you to use other methods?"

Georges knew exactly what he meant. "What do you mean?"

"Methods needed when an establishment is not reacting properly to your wishes."

He thought of that first year he'd returned to UMass, after Marcel had taken the helm. He did not know why, but he said, "We staged protests, yes. Very graphic protests. For example, for the US to keep their hands out of the Egyptian concern, or out of the Israeli concern. We used real oil, fake blood. There was quite a lot of heat around this too."

"That is something. Protests." Here Nazim put a hand to his chin. "And this man, Tim Dunn, the one who attacked you. Did you do more things like that?"

"There was never a need."

"But that type of method, of course, still availed itself."

"Yes."

"You see, I ask because we are taking a special trip to Washington in about two weeks' time. We could use your help down there."

"What is your plan?"

"Well, we are joining a few loyalists to protest a certain bill about to be passed in Congress. You know the one?"

"Concerning OPEC, yes?"

"Yes. Though we can't seem to make our Arab friends back home see that their deal with the West is a deal with evil, we think perhaps we can put some sense into the white Americans in DC, or at least begin to make trouble for them. We have spoken much about how oil and its wealth have stained a select few in the Arab world, made them Western, greedy, at the expense of true Arabs. All the wealth does not belong at such a small top. But now that Arab royalty has tasted cars and airplanes, they are beyond correction."

Georges smiled. "You sound like a Marxist."

Ali cut in. "Well, recent times have shown that a revolution, whatever its root grievance, is easily understood by all of the oppressed." He took a long breath, clenched his fist, "You see, the greed of a..."

Nazim interrupted. "Fadi, will you come with us?"

Georges did not hesitate. "Yes."

They got two rooms at a Holiday Inn near Adams Morgan, Georges sleeping on a cot in a room with Jesper and Faruz. For much of the time, there seemed to be no plan. They prayed regularly, ate very little, sat at a coffee shop nearby and drank tea with dry toast. Ali and Nazim would disappear for a few hours at a time, during which the three others would walk along the mall or visit the strange historical monuments, huge and intricate, Georges translating the grand language carved into stone there. It struck Georges how interested Faruz and Jesper were in the writings, how much they smiled at the revolutionary ideals, the focus on men's souls, on freedom from tyranny. They smiled and nodded seriously.

Finally, on the third night, Ali and Nazim called Georges into their room. They sat him on a bed. Ali's scent filled the place. The TV blinked mute in the background, night traffic swirled by outside the window. A single overhead lamp hung from a chain. Both men looked nervous. Nazim began to speak but then made a motion toward Ali. "Fadi, there is another reason we have come here to Washington. And why we wanted to bring you here as well. We know you are a true man and believe in what we are doing, which is the only reason we feel we can share this with you. We trust you. We also see you as a future leader of our cause."

Georges lit a cigarette, which seemed to irritate Ali.

"There is a company, which is headquartered near here, in Northern Virginia. It is called McHallan. Do you know it?"

Georges shook his head.

"Well, it does as much harm to the Arab way of life, like the entire US government. It creates contracts for the exportation of oil from Saudi Arabia, Iraq, Jordan, Kuwait, and others. It used to do so for Iran as well. This company works hand in hand with the US, and in fact has paid much in political contributions to many senators and lawmakers. So, you can imagine how laws, contracts, and policies tend to be made in direct support of this company's interests."

He drew a long breath and clenched his jaw.

"You see, this situation has gone unchecked for years and years. A few of the Saudis, Jordanians, Kuwaitis, they have become sick with oil. And they have forged great bonds with the US, because the US is the biggest drinker of oil in the world. Of course, America wants to prolong this relationship, or else they risk being cut off, which would put a stranglehold on its own economy. And more important, its imperialist hunger. So much of these deals are undertaken by supposed private companies, like McHallan. These companies might as well be government sections, and the US government might as well call itself a private company."

"What can we do about McHallan?" He laughed. "Do you propose we spray paint their office building? Are we here to protest outside Congress?"

"That time is over. These are not men who react to principle. They are cowards, and so far they have been unchecked and have acted however best suited them. Adbas has been taking peaceful routes against them for a year now. Nothing. So we have been authorized to do something more. One smell of danger, and these men will be filled with fear."

"OK." A long pull from the cigarette. "How are we going to do this?"

Ali glanced at Nazim. Then he stood and walked over to a small gym bag on the bedside table. He unzipped it and removed a single dark sphere about the size of a pool ball. "With this?"

He leaned into the light, and Georges could see that he was holding a grenade. It looked like a toy. Georges had never even seen a gun before, let alone this comical weapon tossed around in movies like water balloons.

Ali made a move to throw the grenade to Georges, who flinched, set to catch it, though he held his cigarette. Ali laughed and sat in the chair, holding the thing lightly in his fingers.

Georges took a long breath and a drag as he tried to calm himself. "What are you going to do with that?"

"We have two more, that's what. This is something I have been planning for several months. It is easy and virtually without risk. We have a man who works in the building. He has been there for years without knowing what the company really does. He has daughters in Iran."

Nazim cut in. "Look, Fadi, you don't have to do anything. Nothing. But the times are calling for a greater sense of urgency and action. We will always try peaceful means and will continue to, but this travesty, what's occurring between the US and our perverted Arab brothers, is beyond that now. Bills are being passed, laws are being made to solidify this disgusting bond. We could have every Arab American vote against such policies, but the government is corrupt here, and the Arab world is filled with despots and monarchs. How can we change such men with debate, with solidarity?

"Such things have been successful with other cells in our greater organization. We don't speak much of it, but because you have risen to a voice of respect here, you should know that those who we are connected to fully support this action, and many of our experienced soldiers have advised us."

Ali rolled his eyes.

"We have ensured that this plan is perfect, that no innocent people will be hurt, and none of our brothers will be in any danger."

"Why do you need me?"

"We don't," Ali said quickly.

"We need you because we want to bring you forward into more important things with us. This has long been a part of what our group uses to achieve our ends. And in you we see a young, important gear in our machine. To have you participate in this is both useful and a symbol of your growth, of our growth, as brothers fighting for the same cause."

Long smoke ticked upward into the hanging light. He thought of the dark bowel of an elevator shaft — they were all the same — slaving away on a company that did no more than allow men to climb to their tiny jobs. He saw himself in that little office of his, as an old man, childless, smoking in the dark late into the night, fretting about bottom lines and new hires. And he couldn't help but think of Tim Dunn, such a little troublemaker. How the evil of Dunn's existence had directly shaped his life, but also how other evils must exist, beyond his knowing, how the world cried for repair.

"I am interested." Dabbing out his cigarette and crossing his legs. "And I am very grateful for your gesture."

The McHallan-Walters Building had sprung up amid the urban spill into Northern Virginia, just outside Vienna. Its seven stories sat isolated from Chain Bridge Road, several hundred feet from any nearby structure, the fact of which Nazim had assured Georges. The previous Thursday, Georges had been sent to buy a used car from some kid in Fairfax, five-hundred in cash, no paperwork, Georges looking mostly downward as they shook hands. He'd driven the car back to their hotel, parked it right next to the van Jesper had somehow procured. Then they waited two days, during which time Georges poured over a set of street maps, schematics, and contingency plans.

Early on Saturday, Ali, Jesper, Faruz, and Georges packed into the tiny Datsun, leaving Nazim in the van about three stoplights down a back road. The four of them drove toward the McHallan Building in complete silence, Georges at the wheel, having studied and memorized every twist and turn in the area. As they sat at a red light, he wondered how he'd gotten here, holding this decrepit steering wheel in this torn-up little car, with three men dressed now in jeans and t-shirts and full beards, having crossed an ocean to get *here*, to this generic office building, actual grenades secreted in their dark hands.

He thought back to the day his mother and Alia had truly realized how successful he'd become. The fact of which had never been mentioned, of course, but he could see it in his mother's eyes that day, when they had come to visit, saw the troop of people under his command, noticed the nice furniture, the respect each employee showed him. He knew it was probably the slow string of gifts that had finally told them — the microwave, the shopping trip on Newbury for Alia, the new rug or offer to pay rent on a new place nearer to school for his little sister.

It felt as if they could see him now, as if the sun staring right into his face as the stoplight was actually them. They saw with great confusion their son and brother jammed into this Datsun with the strange men, could see the grenades, could see their intentions. For a moment, his mind searched for a way out, an excuse.

The light turned green, and as he drove on he also imagined the shock, the sense of justice achieved by putting a dent in this structure. The cost or damage wouldn't really matter, but almost miraculously the five of them could make a larger mark in the security these giants took for granted, the unjust actions they put forth without an ounce of fear of reprisal. And this thought pushed him forward, through the green light, and into the empty parking garage.

There was no AC in the old car, and Georges had begun to sweat immediately. He wiped his forehead as he pulled the car to the B1 elevator banks, the layout perfectly familiar from the two days spent studying schematics. The engine clucked in the empty garage like a dying animal.

The three got out of the car and shut their doors, and Ali leaned into the passenger-side window, checked his watch, showed it to Georges. "Two minutes."

Georges nodded.

"Two minutes."

They opened the door to the elevator banks. The janitor had done his task, putting electrical tape across the knob latch, vertically, not sideways. This would avoid suspicion if detected, a common practice among custodians to avoid having to constantly unlock doors.

Georges watched them a few seconds as they headed toward the stairwell, then he put the car into drive and made a wide U-turn, heading out of the garage and around to the far side of the vast parking lot. One minute to go. He pulled the car just outside the main doors, facing outward, engine angry, windows open but sweat still stinging his eyes. He thought a second about what Yusef and Alia were doing on this spring Saturday. How much they looked up to him, his success in business, all the money he had, the shower of respect from his employees. And here he sat, scorching in Virginia, sitting in some high school kid's dirty blue Datsun, waiting to pick up his friends for a getaway after they'd blown a good hole in the bottom floor of an empty building. Like children chucking bad eggs at passing cars and running off. He shifted the rearview mirror, looked into his own eyes, the one thing about him that had never really changed. *What are you now? A terrorist? A guinea pig?* The time Tim Dunn had looked at him and…

A rumble in his gut first, then a loud blast like a *whoosh* of air, another rumble, then another. A few windows shattering like busted teeth, but the building stood firm. The main glass doors buckled in large plates and smashed to the ground. It was through this hole the three men came running, down the main walk, then darting across the grass and over a short hedge. Georges opened the passenger door. All three men jumped in, and Georges sent the car into drive, jamming the gas. But the engine stalled.

"You idiot, come on!"

He turned the ignition to start the car again, this time easing the accelerator, and off they went. He took the perfect route through a small neighborhood of old houses, then a right on Alexandria Lane, a left on Row Street, where the gray van waited with its engine on next to some woods. The men got out of the car, and Georges, Jesper, and Faruz ran to the van. Ali took a squirt gun from his bag and began to spray the back seats and front dash with it before throwing a Zippo into the car, standing a moment as tall flames rose and fell. Then he too ran toward the van.

Adbas steered them down the lane and toward Chain Bridge Road, by which time they were safely chugging toward the beltway.

"Well?" he said.

"Perfect. Two minutes, that's all it took."

"And all charges went off?"

Faruz said, "I think so."

"We're not sure."

Then Georges said, "I counted three blasts. All three went off."

There was silence. Then Ali said, "We needed more explosives though. Three grenades will cause a little distress to the contractors but will not put a strong hole in the foundation."

"We agreed this method was easier, and safer, and that the message would be the same. We know what McHallan is doing, and we are willing to take strong actions if they continue. Men with families will reconsider, their wives will beg them to change jobs, will question why their husband has been targeted with so much heat."

"Still, it would have been better to completely demolish the building. Wipe it from existence, just like the men who work there." The van was quiet after the remark. Then Ali added, "And Amid did his job. We were able to access the building."

"Good."

"He kept up his end, so I guess we will have to keep up ours." The van zoomed along the beltway without further word or music or any break in the rhythm Nazim had set for them. A terrific electricity still needled through Georges's blood, as if the girds of his very life had been shaken with that blast. Perhaps Ali was right, perhaps more force was needed. Ali turned to Georges, a look in his eyes so distant, so fulfilled, then he turned forward and laughed. He laughed as mad as the rumble at McHallan, mad as the flames he set to consume that car.

CHAPTER 27

It was odd to think of planning around rush hour for a stakeout. But it was necessary, so the three-car group had hit the beltway at fourteen-hundred hours, sharp, followed the outer loop a dozen miles before taking their exit. They arrived at Ali's convenience store about three hours before the advised time. Already stationed at the edge of the shopping plaza was a minivan that held the surveillance team.

Emma knew these poor fuckers had been stationed there for the last fifteen hours, just in case. She knew the real target window was between eighteen and twenty-hundred hours tonight. That was when Marcel Karim met his buddy and now first in command, Ali Al-Jeddah. According to Ali, they met at the rear door of his convenience store, MacLean Market, spoke for no more than thirty minutes, and Marcel disappeared without further communication for the next two days. Then it all repeated. Not a word before or after these meetings.

Emma had accompanied agents Woolcroft and Hetch, two older feds who had spent a lifetime sitting in cars and watching buildings. The other deployment would be arriving any minute now but would have no direct contact with them. Alec had finally buckled and allowed her to take part, but only from the surveillance car. Just the same, she had been outfitted with Kevlar, offered a standard issue piece by Agent Woolcroft, a .22, which she'd deferred in favor of her own snub nose, which had fired thousands of rounds at the range and exactly zero in the field.

MacLean Market sat snugly in the middle of a large shopping plaza, shared by a Wheeler's Grocery, Kim's French Cleaners, Burger King,

McDonald's, Patriot's Bar and Grille, and a little shoe repair shop. The agents had chosen the ideal spot, next to two decoy vehicles along the side of the parking lot, allowing them a good view of the back door without drawing suspicion, along with a straight route to either the front or back lot. The narrow drive that lead behind the row of stores was backed by a thick forest, which led down to a creek and small neighborhood beyond.

The agents hardly spoke and used their binoculars the way people use reading glasses, stuck to their faces from the first minute after parking. At regular intervals a status check would come over the walkie, preceded by a crunch of static. All clear.

Then quiet, no birds, no people coming or going. As eighteen-hundred hours approached, Emma could feel her throat clench. All that work she and Reg had done, the intricate mapping of hierarchy and lies, befriending Fadi to get that weapon to use against Ali: his favorite daughter. All for this bit of intel, the fact that he met a man, at this place, at this time, so the feds and that other group from whatever department she now worked in could line up outside a bit of suburban-sprawl plaza on a Thursday afternoon. She couldn't help but feel like a fortune teller, knew a man would show up at that very door, at this time, the most valuable target the CIA had locked onto in many years. All because of her.

She took out her pack of cigarettes and held it on her lap, removing a single smoke and sliding it back into the soft pack. It was now eighteen hundred, six o'clock to the normal people driving back home along the beltway, home to garages and din-din and family TV, perhaps even stopping in to Patriot's Bar and Grille for fries and a beer after a hard day. Not Emma though. She was sitting in the back seat of an old Bronco, staring at a graffitied manila door along the backside of a convenience store.

Twenty minutes passed. The twins up front didn't lower their binocs even once, no comments. The walkie scratched a few cryptic messages, probably meaning *all clear*. Nothing. Emma noticed her foot tapping on the floor, shaking uncontrollably. *This is it*, was all she could think now. She would catch the greatest threat to the American way of life that no one knew about. But soon maybe people would know, and she would keep Evan safe and all these commuting assholes too.

Nineteen-hundred hours. The sun was drawing long shadows across the concrete and dumpsters. Emma heard one of the other two units mention that no one had been sighted going in or out of the front door, though the store was open. The foot tapping persisted, and even though the temperature had gone down she'd begun to sweat, so she cranked her window down just a crack, could see Agent Hetch's ear twitch. And it twitched again with the flick of the flint on her lighter. She got one drag in before Agent Woolcroft finally lowered his specs and shot her a glance.

"Are you crazy?"

She flicked the cigarette out the window.

Nineteen-thirty, visibility now left to a dull gray as the sun tucked behind the woods. Emma's mind began to wander, thinking now of Evan, now of Fadi. The entire day her mind had been fixed on Karim, just as it had been inhabited by thoughts of Fadi for so long. Each minute that passed without contact made it less likely that Marcel would actually show up. It was frightening when suddenly thoughts of her son would make their way into this crowded space. She could allow herself to be absorbed by Fadi, Ali, or Marcel, but not her own kid. The odd weekend wasn't enough. Each month, each year that passed like this, she was losing him, or perhaps even doing damage to the little guy, growing up without a mom there. Eventually, he would adapt, get used to her absence, and it would be too late…

A beige pinto pulled right in front of their position, creeping slowly. The agents lowered their glasses, sat upright, waited as the vehicle slid past them and alongside the back of the plaza, past the row of dumpsters and stacked trash, crawling as if on fumes. Emma's eyes locked onto the shape in the driver's seat, the outline of the head and shoulders like a shooting target. The car stopped a few feet from the back door of the market, but its brake lights remained aglow for several seconds before finally dimming. Some fuzz from the walkie. She couldn't make it out, but it was certainly interrogative.

Agent Hetch picked up the walkie and clicked a button. "Negative."

They sat without movement or sound, just watching the back of the car.

"What are we doing? That's him. That's *him*!"

Hetch raised a hand. "Quiet."

"Goddamn it, that's him."

A static question from the walkie, then a pause, followed by another question. The man in the beige car sat still, and the light around them seemed to be dying with every moment that passed.

Emma collapsed back into her seat. "This is fucked. Why not? This is the window. It's him! He's sitting there. He's probably watching us in the mirror." She took her pistol from its holster, flipped open the cylinder and closed it with a loud *click*.

"Will you shut up? We've got every route blocked. We can't just spring. And in any case, you're staying here. Put that away."

For the first time that day, Hetch had actually turned to face the back seat. He fixed a cold gaze on her, obviously attempting to subordinate her. Emma took a long breath while she met his eyes, with no plans of submitting. Suddenly Woolcroft said, "The lights!"

Emma could see the car's rear lights glow red. A voice came through the walkie again, this time saying very clearly the word *Apple Pie*. Three men dressed in dark green fatigues and vests sprung from the woods and within seconds had the car's path blocked, sidearms trained on the driver through the windshield. Within a few moments, four others had materialized, followed by a Dodge Charger sprinting around from the far end of the plaza, further blocking the path. The two agents in front of the car barked orders calmly, then waited. After about a minute Emma could see the taillights shut off, then the door swung open. Her breath held in her throat. One foot dropped out, then another.

What she saw made that breath fall to the bottom of her gut. Two sneakered feet, blue jeans, a polo shirt. Even from the back, that closely-cropped dark hair. It was some young kid, his hands raised above his head, visibly shaking. Two of the men grabbed his hands and proceeded to jam him against the wall and cuff him while the others searched the car, popped the trunk, the hood, tossed bags and trash from his backseat onto the pavement.

DANIEL J. DAVIES

A blurry voice from the walkie. Agent Hetch turned to look at Emma, but said nothing to her, instead speaking into the walkie, "Affirmative."

He held his glance on her again, which was met by a gaze that said she could do this until the end of time. He jerked his head sideways. "Come on."

The three of them got out, and Hetch tried to lead her over to the group, but she ran around him. The kid looked even younger as she neared. Maybe nineteen, twenty. He was mumbling something in quick Arabic, only bits of which could Emma decipher.

"Ma'am, are you the translator?"

"Sure."

She stared at the man. In Arabic, "Calm down. Calm down. Speak slowly."

"Why am I being held?"

"I don't know. I'm just a translator."

"Well, tell these men I am innocent."

"What's he saying?" Hetch ask.

"That he didn't do anything."

"Ask him if we can expect any of his friends. If he tells us, we'll help him."

"Are you here to meet Ali Al-Jeddah?"

"No."

"What is your name?"

The man looked away. His arms were pulled tightly behind his back by two agents. Emma saw now how young the man really was, clean shaven, with crystal-blue eyes, certainly shaking with fear.

In a very calm voice, "What is your name, my friend?"

"What's he saying?"

She turned to Hetch and fought the urge to shout at him — that would be a bad show of disorganization, a cardinal foul now that the interrogation had begun. So, with a smile she said to him, "Christ, Hetch, calm the fuck down, would you? I'll get something from him if you'll let me talk for more than a second without interrupting."

"We need to know if he's alone."

Emma turned back to the man. "Hey." Waiting until he finally met her glance. "Listen. I'm the nicest person you're going to meet. It will get worse from here. I can help you, but you have got to let me know if my men are awaiting an ambush here. Are you alone?"

He nodded, his eyes now toward the ground.

"What is your name?"

"Hamal."

She turned to Hetch and Woolcroft. "He's alone."

"Are you sure?" His weapon was still drawn, and he looked toward the woods.

"I need five minutes with him. You can leave him cuffed, but it needs to be alone."

"Absolutely not. We have protocol here. It's not whatever screwy department you're from. This is the United States."

"I'm from Defense. We have protocol as well. Have you searched for ID?"

"Nothing on him."

"I doubt he's a civilian, doesn't speak a lick of English. Do you want to mirandize him?"

Hetch ignored her question. "He could be faking, and we go by the book on this one."

"I'm saying five minutes in the back room there. Take the clerk into custody and replace him with this son of a bitch here," pointing to the Italian-looking man in plainclothes. "I can find out where he's from, what he's doing here, if he expects Karim to show. And, by the way, if he does, we need to clear out of here, A-fucking-SAP so we don't spook him further."

The lead fed, who had been watching from a remotely posted vehicle toward the corner of the plaza, had walked to their position. "I am in charge here. I believe you are just a translator."

"Yes, sir. I am also incredibly familiar with this group's organization. And all I'm asking is that I be allowed to," turning to Hetch, "*translate*," now back to the lead fed, "in private, and have this lot cleared out in case Karim is still on his way. We're wasting time."

The head, a chubby gray-haired man in suit with no coat, looked at his men, then at the captive before turning to Emma. "You've got five. Agents Hetch and Goddard will accompany you. Agent Trujillo will engage the clerk, don't need him getting spooked. I'd rather get in and out of here without anyone knowing."

"Ok."

"Five minutes." He made a circle motion with his hand, which sent the five other men to quickly clean up the scene, removing the three cars. Next thing Emma knew, it was just the four of them and the back lot had returned to normal.

The agents lead Hamal through the door and into the back storage room, where the four of them squatted in the freezer among boxes of orange juice cartons and quarts of milk. Emma handed the man a can of 7UP, which he cracked open and gulped from.

She fixed a stony glare on him. "We have no time, Hamal, so it is very, very important that you tell me the truth and that you do so quickly, so I *know* it is the truth. You are not a citizen, are you?"

He shook his head.

"You will not have any rights, do you understand?"

He nodded, obviously on the verge of tears.

"Do you like my accent?"

"Pardon?"

"My accent, is it good?"

He nodded.

"I learned Arabic in Egypt, as a student. I am sympathetic to the Arab way of life, especially the way you are treated here. But I will be gone soon, replaced by military men. Not nice ones. Once we leave here you will be put into a pit that is beyond any law."

"Ok."

"Now, can we expect Marcel to come through that door later?"

He hesitated a moment.

"Don't *think*, just speak. I'll know if you're thinking."

Hamal shook his head, steamy breath escaping his mouth.

"Are you sure?"

"I am sure. That is why I am here."

"What do you mean?"

"Mr. Al-Jeddah was to meet a man here, a great man whose name I do not know, but I was sent instead."

"Why?"

"I don't know."

"You lie."

Shaking his head, nearly in tears now.

"I know you lie. How did Marcel know to send you? What do you know about Mr. Al-Jeddah?"

"Nothing."

"You know something." She said this at nearly a growl as she moved her face just inches from his. "I'm telling you they're going to get everything from you, and they won't be courteous about it. If you help me right now, I'll tell them everything. I'll even make some good things up. Why were you sent? What were you told?"

Now sweat glistened on the man's forehead, despite the cold. "I was told to come here, to wait, that I would be met by a man, a short man who would tell me two sentences, which I was to memorize exactly."

"And who were you to tell that information to?"

"My brother."

At this Emma reared back, glanced at both agents. She could tell they were dying with anticipation.

"Hamal. Listen to me. As I have said, I am a sympathizer with the Muslim heart, and I would never ask you to betray your brother."

His eyes were now big as a baby's.

"But I need something. Something changed, didn't it? You were not originally meant to come here. You were given this plan recently."

He was now sitting cross-legged with hands behind his back and steam rising from his slumped shoulders. He nodded.

"Somebody knew." She repeated this in English as the realization came over her, a typically damning action, but Hamal wouldn't hear her. Then she raised the soda can to his lips again, put a hand on his neck briefly. "How did they know?"

"I do not know. I swear."

"I believe you. You have been used. Your friends sent you here, knowing we would be waiting."

He spat on the floor then shook his head and shot a defiant glance at each of them.

"It is true, my friend. We obviously knew to wait here, did we not? And your friends knew not to send this *great man* here, as planned. They sent you. How did they know to send you?"

Hamal was quiet and looked at the freezer floor, at the spit. Emma was silent and simply watched his face. Even from an indirect angle, she could see the little moment at which the ideas formed themselves in his mind, the realization that would break his defenses like wet paper.

She said softly, "Hamal. You can tell me."

"It is only rumor."

"I like rumors."

"Something I have heard spoken, but it is the sort of thing men tell in private, but I have never believed." Now he looked up into Emma's eyes. "Al Mudhlim."

"What is that?"

"A man from your country. Someone who has worked for us. He knows unknowable secrets. He tells us things. I do not believe in him. But I have heard we became aware of something, something very dark to our cause. And it was too great a risk for our leader to come here, so I came. My God, forgive me for what I am saying."

Now Hamal's head slumped, and he began to mumble. Emma stood and regarded the two agents, forgetting a moment that they understood not a single word of what Hamal had just confessed. Then Agent Hetch stood, pulled Hamal to his feet, looked at his watch. "That's five. Let's go."

As they led the kid out of the freezer and through the storeroom, Emma walked behind, met by the warm air and cardboard-box smell. This new man, slipping information to her counters, working in the same medium she worked but in opposite color. Everything she entered her day assuming was now poisoned. As the three men opened the door into the back lot, something held Emma in the room, a smell she could not at first place, but which she soon recognized as the plastic, mechanical odor of lemon and rose.

CHAPTER 28

It was the middle of a hot spell in summer. Georges sat at his old wooden desk in the office, sweaty with sleeves rolled up. Yusef and some of the accounting staff were there on this Saturday as well. The air conditioning was down, despite assertions by several of the elevator techs that they could fix the system. A few metal fans tossed cigarette smoke out the window.

At noon Yusef stood in front of Georges's desk. Rolling up his sleeves. "Alright, I'm going to get some shwarma at Richardson's. You want anything?"

Georges looked up, saw that Yusef too had removed his tie. He smiled, and Yusef looked worried a second before a grin spread his lips.

"Sure, please. A kebab would be nice, lamb, with everything."

"Okay." He finished rolling his sleeve. "Oh, mail there. And the *Globe* you asked for." Pointing to the corner of the desk. Then he left.

He creaked back in his chair with the *Globe*, flipped through its first pages. Pictures from Iran on the front page, a smoking, abandoned tank in the desert. Next, a few paranoid stories from China, a few blurbs about house bills. Then, on nearly the last page, there it was, three days late, but they'd picked it up. Somehow disappointing to see it in the mere Nation section, as opposed to the World. But satisfying just the same. When they'd first gathered to read it in an issue of *The Washington Post*, Georges's throat had been tight as a vine until he read, aloud, the line: "No one was in the building." What relief had rolled up through him at that. Though Ali made a sort of evil cackle, followed by some mumbling. As in the *Post*, here there was no real mention of what McHallan might have done to provoke the attack, only conjecture by the reporter. At the story's second half he mentioned a few recent sets of layoffs by the company, shipping jobs overseas, some sour business deals, not a lick about their oil contracts or supposed hand in gifting arms to a group of Kurdish rebels in Iraq. Ali had insisted that Georges make a call to the *Globe*, claiming responsibility. Nazim said no. And the *Globe* article was nothing new, really, and in fact seemed to be mostly lifted from the original story. It mentioned investigations, witnesses, the burned-out blue car, but little else. A combination of ease and frustration at the seemingly ineffectual stunt they'd pulled. No one was hurt, and they would get away with it, but the connection to their cause seemed to have been lost.

Georges leaned back and took a new cigarette from the lip of the ashtray, lit it as he stretched his arms. He shuffled through the stack of mail. An application for the new business development position, a book of coupons, and a UMass alumni newsletter about a post-football event near BC. Last in the pile was a thick, brown envelope, with the address written in bad script, odd stamps across the top. It was from Marcel.

My brother,
I hope this letter finds you and your family well. I write to you from my beautiful home country, which is much changed, I realize, as I sit here outside my parents' home. Some has to do with the work we have been graced to perform, cleaning and redirecting the morals of many town people, who have long since lost their relationship with God.
Even my dear mother could be counted among them. Though it can be forgiven, as she has been through much, with my sisters and their deviance, my father's idleness.
But the mosque has once again been placed on its rightful platform in the center of town, and in the center of peoples' lives. My mentor, a very wise yet peaceful man, has been kind enough to step down and allow me a full voice. And my brother, I have not forgotten the man who taught me what my true voice is, all those years ago. I find myself nostalgic for those times. Do you?

Though I think I know the answer to that question. Because it seems you heeded my advice and have found companionship with other great men. Men who must seem a cool drink of water in that wretched city desert. I imagine you are surprised that I have heard this, but do not be. You will find, as I have, that it is a very small family of true followers, and the thousands of miles between Alexandria and Boston are just a few feet, that the translation between Arabic and English and French is done with the ease of tuning a radio.

And much is happening, here and across the world in America. That is why I have been in close touch with our mutual friend, who praises you deeply, already, which does not surprise me. He has long been suggesting my presence is needed back across the ocean, but I have demurred in favor of leading my homeland back into righteousness. But now I believe there is room for me to travel, and a greater means.

So, my oldest brother, I write this letter to inform you that we will again be in one another's presence, to inhabit that strange land (which label I can place on your home, because I know you feel the same).

For reasons I cannot go into now, I will be arriving with my sister, who you know of. She has become a burden to my mother and father and listens to no one but me. I will be leaving Egypt in two months' time, arriving at Logan Airport on September 9th, about 2:15, Air France flight 2112. I have arrangements for my stay, so all that I ask is that you greet me at the gate, and that you welcome me with a true embrace.

Your Brother,
M

Weeks tumbled by quickly, and sleep was hard to find. He paced the apartment at night, or sat up late in his office chair, scrounging for work to do. When he did sleep, strange dreams flashed around in his mind, filled with explosions, or else dark characters, tall and phantasmal. All shook him from sleep after only a few minutes, and he lied soaked in sweat, eyes opened to darkness.

Alia was valedictorian that summer at graduation. Georges and Yusef wore the same suits they used during client trips, and even Nourredine dressed up. Lara allowed her boys to take her shopping for a nice dress and a new pair of shoes. It was sunny at graduation, and Alia was beautiful. Those eyes, even in cap and gown. Afterward they went into Boston, paid a fortune to park under the Prudential, and the family set out down Newbury Street, which was swarming with loaded window shoppers on an early summer evening. But that's where Alia had wanted to go. *Let's go anywhere. Yusef and I are paying.*

Georges was struck by how much they felt like a family that night. They gathered to eat together most Sundays at home, when Lara would cook up one of her standard chicken dinners. But being out as a group offered a new feeling, safe and secure, even among the Boston elite on Newbury, and Lara beaming in her new dress, there with her three men and newly adult daughter. They commented on the atrocious couture in the windows, the silly costumes the wealthy walked the streets in. Alia had chosen a new French restaurant at the corner of Exeter, and the kids could tell how much pleasure it gave their parents to converse with the waiter and owner in that easy tongue.

The next morning Georges drove up to the Kidder Avenue duplex he'd grown up in, parked the shiny new Volkswagen at the curb out front. He stood next to the car, reached in the window to honk the horn a few times. A neighbor yelled. Alia rushed out the front door, hurried down the steps.

"When did you get this?"

He said nothing.

She scooted down the sidewalk, smoothed hair behind her ears. "When did you get this?"

"*You* got this today."

Those tears. Hands cupping her mouth just like their mother did. Georges would look back on that moment and remember how the tears had burst and rushed down her face, as if faster than even gravity insisted.

By August the heat remained, and without rain. So lawns went un-watered, and street corners and gutters where permanent puddles had always formed now sat gray and scummy. Georges borrowed his little sister's car and drove to Logan Airport. He got lost on the way, and then got lost again at the actual airport, weaving around its many slip-shod drives and overpasses. He rushed to the gate, by this time covered in sweat, and fifteen minutes late, which he knew Marcel hated.

It had been nearly ten years since he'd last seen the skinny Egyptian back at graduation, and much had changed in the man waiting for him at the gate. He was tall, and looming, the youthful eyes and baby's skin replaced by dark beard and a serious and sunken glare. A handsome turban and loose tunic.

Marcel at first shot him a perturbed look, replaced by a smile, the same one he'd used all those years ago. The one that made you feel like the sole human on earth. The arms spread to his sides like wings, making his body seem like a huge tarpaulin. They hugged in silence, the smell of him, the same scent as the letters. Musty, as if from centuries before.

In that wispy French. "Let me look at you." He placed a hand on Georges's cheek. "You have aged well. You look comfortable."

"You…" Shaking his head.

"Changed a bit, yes?"

"What, did you start growing this as soon as I turned my back on you?" Tugging his beard.

"Yes. I did."

A few more seconds to take in the years of difference between them. Georges clean in his jeans and sweaty t-shirt, tennis shoes, well-trimmed hair. Marcel a large drape of a man, dark, with spherical head. Georges could feel the eyes of those walking by.

Marcel turned. "Georges Fadi Subdallah, please meet my sister, Fatima. Fatu, come here."

From the background a mousy woman emerged, in full burka, her eyes toward the carpet. Georges had had very little exposure to traditional Islamic women, let alone the sister of his friend, the imam. He mumbled something in Arabic, hesitated before finally offering his hand. Fatima too seemed unsure of what to do, even glanced at her brother a moment before shaking Georges's hand. Then her eyes set on his. They were a very strange crystalline color, shocking, but then tender. Georges was left smiling, nodding, had to force himself to look away. He wiped his forehead on his sleeve.

Marcel smiled again, a warm nod, and hugged Georges. "It is good to see you, my old friend."

"You too."

"It would be nice to get away from this airport."

"Right, yes. Did you check bags?"

"No. We just have these."

A small canvas bag for Marcel, a slightly larger one for Fatima.

"Here, let me get this." Taking her bag.

Marcel let Fatima sit in the front and commented on how luxurious the car was, the air conditioner in particular. Mentioned that the heat back in Egypt made this feel like winter.

Georges was still sweating. "It's my sister's."

While waiting at the tolls he glanced back to see that Marcel was looking out the window, so he snuck a peek down at Fatima's hands, folded small and nice on her dark lap, the nails chewed down.

Despite his friend's insistence on having secured a place to stay, Georges had rented rooms for Marcel and Fatima in his building. The apartment was previously storage space for the market downstairs, recently remodeled and put up for rent, with new fixtures, brand new bathroom and kitchen, and two full bedrooms. It was two doors down from Georges's own apartment in a hallway with only three other occupants.

Their first days in the country were spent settling them into the new surroundings, buying all the necessary supplies for the house, a long trip to the Hallal market in Central Square for Fatima to purchase meat and bread and spices. Marcel had also made a slight allowance in the way that she dressed, replacing the burka, which covered all but her hands and eyes, with a more relaxed *hijab*, revealing her entire face, along with an *abaya*.

Georges had walked with them to the Muslim clothing store off Mass Ave., offered Marcel money for the purchase, which he'd refused. He also insisted that Georges not join them in the store, for modesty's sake. So he got a sandwich next door and sat at the café window until they returned, Fatu carrying two large bags.

When they met on the sidewalk, Georges saw her face for the first time, those eyes still beaming and deep, a smooth chin and delicate nose, full and untrimmed eyebrows. Again he was taken aback, and both averted their eyes in nearly comical unison. Marcel laughed. Georges took her bags, and the three set out down the sidewalk, back to their building, where Fatu made them a strong tea she had brought from home.

Georges awoke nervous on the day he and Marcel were meant to make their first trip to group meetings and prayer. Up to that point, Marcel had been very pleasant, despite his obvious feelings of separateness from this place he'd left so many years earlier. The comfortable apartment with modern fixings, the busy streets packed with merchants and company logos, summer women in full display on the sidewalks of Mass Ave., cars honking into the night. He had shown manners, sitting most of the day quietly reading in his apartment, praying, reading, tea, taking the odd long walk.

On a few occasions, Georges had been ready to tell Marcel of what had happened in Vienna, he even brought the old paper with him during one visit, but hadn't the nerve to reference it, didn't know how Marcel would react, having been apart for so many years. Perhaps he had grown peaceful, reflective, a holy man, and such kids' pranks would seem only barbaric.

Georges had no idea what to expect when they met with Nazim and the others. Still no exact idea as to why or how Marcel had been summoned across the Atlantic, with an apparently open ticket, no visa paperwork, very little luggage or any sign of his existence or origin at all. He had a sinking feeling that it was but a matter of time before the gulf between Marcel and him truly showed itself. A few feet from where Marcel prayed in the morning was a desk Georges had bourn a groove into with his elbows during long years of dollar crunching.

Just before 11 am, Georges walked down the hall and knocked on their door. Instead of changing clothes near the South End, Georges had put on full thobe this morning for the walk over. After a minute, Fatu opened the door, her eyes down but a nice smile on her face as she bowed. When she saw his tunic, she blushed, actually showed her teeth in a grin.

"Morning, Fatu."

"Good morning. Please."

Marcel was sitting at the lone and sparse table, in full robes, writing something with a pencil.

"Shall we walk?"

"Yes, it's very nice out."

"We can take the route I usually walk across the river into Boston."

Marcel took his small canvas bag, and the two men left the room. Georges put on his Maraca smile as he passed Fatu on the way out. In English, "Goodbye."

"Goodbye."

They took a long tea at Al-Malik, and Marcel ate plain lavash bread in silence. As they walked along Mass Ave., across the Charles, Marcel seemed very relaxed, hands clasped behind his back. He asked Georges many questions, about his parents, Alia and Yusef, even his business. But Georges was reticent to discuss work with Marcel and aimed the subject away, using the old deprecation to play down his successes, to insult any interest he might have had in commerce.

As they crossed into Back Bay, the eyes of college students and wealthy row-house residents followed them.

"Why did Fara not make the trip with you and Fatu?"

"I'm afraid she is very lost, my sister. And has been a great burden to my dear mother. Fatu is still hopeful, despite her past, despite her position. I think she can still find herself to be of use to our cause, to her family. And she has always been much smarter than her sister."

At Clarendon Street they crossed over Newbury Street, the lavish, high-collared outfits of decorated housewives and rich college girls. Even Georges couldn't help turning his head in their direction at times, but Marcel's eyes remained forward. "But, Georges, please, we were discussing your work. You were saying that you at first were unable to get into any buildings, to have the managers accept your invention?"

"Right. Well, it took quite a while. But once we were in one building, it began to take off, because we could reference that client. Then owners and management companies began to actually call us. Almost all of them. Not this one though." As they came to the Hancock tower, that looming, mirrored obelisk, poking higher than all around it. "Tallest building in Boston. This and the Prudential. And those are really the only two significant ones we're not in."

"It's beautiful, really."

It surprised Georges to hear this.

Reflected in the brand-new windows of the Hancock was old Trinity Church. "But this is quite gorgeous, really. And the disparity." He turned to Georges. "Do most make that connection? The tiny old church next to the tall…Hancock, is it?"

"It's in a lot of pictures."

"So, your company would take control of the elevator inside this building?"

Georges laughed. "Something like that. There are actually ten in the Hancock."

"Really?"

"And they need to service all floors. Right now, typical buildings don't efficiently assign their elevators. It's like if you are a taxi dispatcher." He looked at Marcel. "If you've got a call way over here in this neighborhood, you want to always send your closest man. You save on fuel, on time."

"And your creation allows this with elevators."

"Yes. It's like a brain, really. The elevator system is the spinal cord, if you like, and is in charge of sending workers to their floors. Our system is a tweak of the brain, just allows for delivery of the blood, or nerves, or whatever you would call it."

Marcel was gazing straight up now.

"You are bored."

"What? This is fascinating."

"Ridiculous problems of America, yes?"

Looking back up. "No. Just fascinating. And I'm proud of you."

They walked on a few more blocks. Just after noon, they came to that faded green door in the South End. Georges knocked then quickly turned. "Marcel. They know me here as Fadi." He looked down, embarrassed by the childish name change he'd made. "It's just, I met these men…"

"I understand, my friend. I will call you Georges only in private."

Faruz opened the door, smiled and kissed both of Georges's cheeks. He put his hand out. "You must be Marcel."

Marcel paused before shaking his hand, bowing. They entered the room, dark after the sunny walk over, and kept cool by a new air conditioner, to which Marcel's eyes went directly. He moved gracefully across the floor, those flowing robes, and the men who had gathered in groups became silent as they watched him.

In Arabic. "This is Marcel Karim."

There were mumbles, and then Nazim appeared from the back corner, a warm grin on his face. He put his hands out, and he and Marcel embraced. "Hello, my friend. Good to see you again. I trust your trip was a safe one."

"Yes."

"And your sister is comfortable in the apartment?"

"She is. And we are near my friend."

"We are so happy to have you with us. I hope you will forgive our humble space."

"This is a very luxurious version of humble."

"I know you are our guest today, but I was hoping you might lead us in prayer."

"I am just a visitor. I will not intrude but would like to simply take part in whatever your regular course is."

"Please."

In silence the men retrieved their prayer rugs and gently rolled them across the floor and stood. Marcel did likewise, standing to the right of Georges. Ali offered water to each man for ablution. The men wiped their foreheads and hands with the water. Georges peered sideways more than once during his prayers.

After the meeting, some of the men headed to the Turk's, though it was a smaller crowd than normal. Nazim and Ali stayed behind with Marcel and Georges while the others went next door. The four men then headed over and took seats near the back, where a cloud of smoke already hung over the men there. Marcel stood until all were seated then took a spot next to Georges, toward the outside of the group. He put an arm around Georges a minute, squeezed his shoulder, then reached for the tea in front of him.

Several hours passed with laughter, several pots of tea, then some of the men cleared out, each smiling and making a gesture of reverence toward Marcel as they left. Soon it was just the four of them. The Turk was on the phone across the room, and the record ended, leaving light, rough sounds as the needle ran on.

Nazim began, "We have had a good piece of success recently."

"I know."

Nazim at first looked surprised, then his face sank. "You have heard."

"Yes."

He was silent, apparently hoping for some sort of compliment for the attack that had taken his group so long to plan.

But Marcel paused a while before finally speaking. "It was a good choice of target, McHallan. They have certainly pushed their noses too far where they don't belong. And they, as much as our Arab brothers with whom they do business, are responsible for the perversion of Islamic culture in oil-rich countries."

Nazim nodded.

"But I wonder, if I may, whether such an action will have positive effects. The desired effects. Did anyone claim responsibility for the attacks?"

"No."

"And from what I have read, the papers seem to be cooking up quite a lot of conjecture around why the explosion took place. And none of it includes the true reason."

"Well, should we have put our names on it?"

"No, not for such a small attack. We have been building our reputation based on our willingness to act in huge ways, completely eradicating unwelcome structures, casting complete fear into the unfaithful. We have built our name upon things like the event in France, showing that our soldiers are ready to take their own lives. It is a statement. We did this not only to destroy a piece of foreign intrusion, but to tell the world we are ready to die for what we know is right, what we know is God's will."

"France was very powerful, a very powerful message."

"And I'm afraid tying our name to this McHallan business would be a step backward."

Georges glanced over to see Nazim with his mouth agape, stunned, and Ali brimming with anger. Both men were quiet a few seconds, then Ali blurted, "I told them a hundred times we needed more explosives. We needed to turn that building to rubble."

"Perhaps. That would have been a start, a larger statement. More news coverage. The complete destruction of a corporate building is national news, even global. Whereas, a few photos of some blown-out windows and black smoke stains seems more like a…forgive me…an angry teenager's outburst."

Here Georges spoke for the first time. "And your thoughts on the target, itself? Not the physical building, but McHallan, as an entity?"

Marcel raised a bent finger to his chin — something he'd often done back in college — and looked at the floor. "McHallan was something we decided on, a few of the leaders. I think sending a message, broadly, to would-be commercial enterprisers about their involvement in Arab matters is an important one."

Ali leaned in. "How are we to get our hands on more power?"

"Don't worry, my friend. Your investment will not be lost."

At this Ali sat straight, a slight crinkle at his brow, glanced at Georges.

"We will be able to offer a much louder message this time."

"But we need someone with more expertise than the group here has. When we move to greater force, we'll need greater skill."

Marcel leaned back in his chair, took a pack of Georges's Dunhill's from the table, glanced at Georges with lifted brow for permission. Georges nodded. So Marcel put a cigarette in his mouth and with the slightest flourish of hands lit and dragged.

"You have with you the perfect man for creating detonators, remote devices, anything you need. A genius in this field. He has been under your nose all this time."

Both men seemed confused a moment, until, with the slightest gesture, Marcel directed an upturned palm toward Georges.

By the time they left the Turk's, the sun was going down. It was still a nice summer's night, and the air felt pure and healthy. After seeing the deference and respect all those grown men accorded Marcel, Georges felt uneasy walking back with him. And this first meeting, he knew already, was just a small taste of the power and position he'd gained over the years.

But after a few blocks of silence, Marcel put his arm around Georges and set that rare smile on his face, and he was reminded of those years of friendship at school and since. He was reminded of why he and Marcel had been so close. It was perhaps the same reason he'd gained so much influence back home.

They spoke in French, which relaxed Georges.

"You knew about McHallan."

"I did."

"But you didn't say anything."

"Neither did you."

"I guess you're surprised. To hear that I would have taken part in such a thing."

"I was surprised, yes. By the fact that they asked you, so early, and more so that you accepted."

"Quite a far cry from my little tactics at UMass."

"Your little tactics were brilliant. And there are things I learned that I still have deployed in Egypt to this day. Those are more lasting, more palatable. Though sometimes a thing like McHallan is necessary."

"You think it should have been bigger."

"Yes, I do. The type of wrong that exists is too big and padded by too much surrounding corruption to be put right by voting or peaceful force." He raised a finger. "That these men did not call on your expertise is very telling."

They walked in silence a bit, along Shawmut and into the projects.

"I know this is not easy for you, my friend."

"I'm not sure what you mean."

"My coming over here. How our paths have diverged."

"Your letter was the best news I've received in years. I cannot say how happy I am to have you here."

"I know. But you have told me the story of how you came to discover this place, these men. Does it not seem like a very large coincidence?"

"It does."

"And do you know who creates very large coincidences?"

Georges smiled, and Marcel gave him a squeeze before removing his arm.

"You know, we have taken very different paths since school. Different places, different aims. But I believe it has been for a reason. There is a reason I have been chosen to become imam, just as there is a reason you have been chosen to build a base here in America, to build a company. We have rejoined. It is like two points diverging outward." He traced his fingers out before him. "Then rejoining like this. At first it seems the points are separating, but they are actually creating a circle. And that's what this is, our living together once more, the creation of a circle, the most harmonious shape one's life can take.

"You are my closest family, Georges. I have not forgotten what you did for me. You took me into your home after knowing me only a short time. I was lost and afraid and aimless. And the club we built was a refuge, and the start of my true path. My sisters, my mother, my father, they don't really know me, don't know what I was put here for. But you do. The things we have struggled through together will bond us for all time."

"But I feel my life has been corrupted. As much as I detest the business, and can get no fulfillment from making money, I have built that life for myself."

"There is a reason for that. There is a use. You will see."

CHAPTER 29

"We are being fucked by a squirrel."

Randolph's eyes bulged at hearing this.

Then Emma added, "Sir."

Seated at the large square table with its peeling veneer were Reg, Alec, Randolph, Emma, and Bauer, who raised his chin at the news. It was after midnight and most of the staff had gone home, save for a few orderlies, guards, and the night security. They'd spent the afternoon, dinner, and late evening crammed into a makeshift briefing room with seven analysts, four interrogators, Bauer, Randolph, and a finicky slide projector.

"What's a squirrel?"

"It's something that gets into places it shouldn't get into, learns things it shouldn't know."

Randolph still looked confused. So she added, "It's a rat, sir. With a puffy tail. But a rat. We've got one."

"That is impossible," said Bauer.

"Funny, because I'd say it's a certainty."

"Why wasn't this brought up in our meeting?"

Emma simply looked at him while struggling not to make a condescending face.

He added. "How do you know this?"

"Interrogation."

Bauer made a farting sound with his lips.

"Hey, sorry, Doctor Bauer, that your facility is infested. And thank you for poisoning my stream. The interrogation environment has to be

213

pristine, and you've allowed in…" She showed her top front teeth and made a chewing noise.

Bauer turned to Randolph with a long, exasperated breath. "Sir, this woman's etiquette and lack of professionalism have become a major problem."

"Major problem?" Emma cut in. "Whose intelligence was it that caught Hamal? And, oh, I'm sorry, where did that start? Oh yes, with Subdallah, the guy you doinks have had in here a year and gotten nothing out of."

He flipped a hand at her dismissively.

"Don't be jealous, Bauer."

Reg let out a thin, fake cough, which then transitioned into a real one, deep in his throat. Emma patted his back while still keeping her eyes on Bauer.

"Alec, we need an internal investigation, *stat*. We need to find the squirrel and figure out who he's fucked and who he hasn't."

"Could be your boyfriend, Fadi, for all we know."

"Could be." She shrugged. "But if he's been breached, it's not my fault."

Randolph put up both hands. "Okay, okay, you two. Like a pair of siblings. Please…enough. We've got a more immediate problem."

"What's that?"

"Al-Jeddah's intel hasn't really landed us very much."

"What about Maclean?"

"Yes, we got Hamal, a lower-level grunt than Al-Jeddah. Way lower."

"And from him we learned that we've been fed misinformation. And the other side doesn't know that *we know*. Huge, Alec."

"That may be so. But Ali is not a citizen. We can't hold him for very long here. He'll be moved to the island, or else extradited."

"Extradited? You can't let that happen. He'll be free within the day if he's sent back to Saudi Arabia."

"Our hands are tied. Subdallah, some of these others, they're citizens or else come from treaty states, so we have some leeway. Ali Al-Jeddah does not."

Bauer raised his eyebrows. "Don't you read the papers?"

"No, do you?"

"You would have noticed a recent public outcry in the press about interrogation techniques."

She mimicked Bauer's earlier farting sound with her lips. "That happens a few times a decade. It wears out."

"Not this time," Alec said.

"But we've stopped physical coercion here. Mr. England and his meatheads are gone. No waterboarding…anymore."

"That is beside the point. Suddenly a light has been shone on our affairs. That is all that matters." He shook his head. "Paperwork needs to surface, people looking over our shoulders."

"So what are you saying?"

"I'm saying we start from scratch. The basics. We nail the grunts we have here, we squeeze them harder, whatever it takes. We work Subdallah…"

"He's given us all he has."

"I don't believe that."

Alec glanced over at Reg, lifted his eyebrows. That they had a signal together deflated Emma a bit, reminded her of back in Egypt, when even those on her side played their little mind games with each other.

Reg opened the manila folder, which was swollen with papers of every color.

"I think your Mr. Fadi knows much more than he even understands. Reg has gone through some very interesting new bits of juice we picked up from our recent Egyptian. Seems Al-Jeddah and Subdallah have been privy to a plot for some time. A local plan. A big plan."

CHAPTER 30

When Georges described his weeknight routine to Fatu — late at the office, quick Hallal at the corner, followed by the evening papers alone in his apartment — she insisted he join them for dinner. The occasion began uncomfortably enough, Georges unsure of what to wear, how much respect or disregard to pay Fatu in Marcel's presence.

She was a wholly other woman when cooking: confident, focused, driven, barking orders at Marcel, even as the two men sat in the living room with cigarettes and their mint water. Georges could not help but steal an odd glance at the pretty, busy woman in the next room. Whenever Marcel looked away, a quick peek at those eyes, the fine nose, and dark brows. She slid from counter to cooktop, sizzles and tinny sounds, a fabulous sweet smell wafting in.

At first she served them and sat herself in the kitchen to eat, but Georges dared to suggest she join them. Marcel paused, then said, "Of course, when in America…"

They ate in silence, Fatu not looking up from her food even once. It was a simple, tender lamb dish, plopped in the middle, which they all tugged at with their hands or using the fresh lavash bread. It tasted of cumin and a few other spices. But the smell and the feel of the meat in his fingers brought Georges to another place, more so than the Turk's or Al-Malik, or any afternoon prayer with the men. The simplicity, the sharing, the bare fingers, the coarseness of pulling meat from bone.

After supper, Fatu cleared the plates, though Georges tried to help. She served them tea in the sitting room.

"Will you join us?"

"I will have mine in the kitchen."

As he and Marcel sat quietly waiting for the tea to cool, Georges could hear a can being popped open, despite an obvious attempt to cough over the sound. Then liquid over ice.

He and Marcel sipped their tea a while, Marcel sitting back with a cigarette, contented looking. A few minutes and Georges took their cups to the kitchen. Fatu flinched when she saw him, quickly turned her back to the counter, hiding something behind her.

"Excuse me, won't you? Just putting these away."

"Don't worry, please." A panic in her voice.

He forced the cups past her onto the counter, and though she still tried to conceal it, he saw a can of A&W next to half a glass of ice and root beer. He smiled, but she was breathing heavy and looked nervous, her eyes flitting and fixed on the floor.

Georges's smile sank a bit. "It's okay." He put his hand on her arm, which drew a quick spasm from Fatu, and she squeezed her elbows tight to her side.

"It'll be our little secret. Okay?"

"Okay." A fake smile as she emptied the glass and the remainder of the can into the sink, then busied her hands at wiping the counter. He watched a moment, then reached for her arm again. His touch stopped her hands, though her chest still heaved.

"Fatu." In Arabic. "It is OK."

Yusef voiced his shock once at George's lighter office schedule, but Fatu served dinner each night at seven, which left a little time to wash up, change, and walk down the hall to share a pot of tea and smoke with Marcel beforehand. This went on for months, Georges often packing up his things with Yusef still hard at work under the last light of the day, and later lamplight as fall came. He had supper with Marcel and Fatu most nights, except when they had a group meeting, on which nights they'd stop downstairs for a quick Hallal before heading to the South End. And the Saturday meeting grew longer each week: discussions with Marcel during their walks, then prayer with the group, sitting in that smoky room first, then over to the Turk's for tea.

It was not long before Marcel gained control — albeit a tacit one — over the group. Nazim and Georges also held a major portion of deference and respect from the men, speaking in turn to an attentive audience. Along with Ali, the only ones Marcel seemed to listen to. The others had crept imperceptibly into submission, now nodding, now asking respectful questions of the other four. Georges felt the occasional temptation of ego when greeted with such reverence from these men, older men with money and wives and children and degrees.

No mention was made of McHallan over the following months. Georges was satisfied that no investigation would ever lead to their cell, or to him. Although he couldn't find a way to bring up their trip to the others, he was still surprised that none of the men happened to make mention of it. A part of him had hoped for some immediate change resulting from the attack, an expose on McHallan, a halt in dealings between the company and its Saudi partners, something bigger than the silence he now found in the papers and on television.

He and Marcel dined together most nights, whether downstairs or prepared by Fatu, and Marcel gave Georges time and space to speak, a nod before introducing his own thoughts. Georges was struck by how much he knew about events in the Middle East: Yemen and Saudi Arabia, Palestine, Egypt and Russia, Egypt and the rest of the Arab world, Iran and Iraq. But even more impressive were the little personal ties he'd throw in, connections to a royal here or a minister there. Boys he'd grown up with having died in Yemen or leading a secret construction operation in South Saudi to combat the rebels edging northward.

It was only a few nights after that first meal before Georges once again heard the faintly cloaked cracking of a soda can in the kitchen after supper. The very sound made him smile, and Marcel seemed to either not hear or not have a second thought about it.

With Marcel's permission, Georges gave Fatu a tour of their offices, the accountants and secretaries gawking at the covered woman as she nodded at the slow English sentences, Georges describing what certain machines were for, flicking the printer on and demonstrating the fax machine, which Fatu regarded with incredulity.

It was the first time he'd truly been around Fatu without Marcel.

She was much more relaxed, her shoulders slumped, her face lighting up without restraint.

She took up his name plate and laughed. "Why do you need a label? Do they not know you here?" Then proceeded to cover up certain letters and read aloud the resulting nonsensical names, demonstrating the progress of her studies. She laughed so much that her face turned red, and the others glanced over at the man they'd seen work so tirelessly at that very desk.

"And this is my brother, Yusef."

Yusef rose, shook Fatu's hand.

"Fadi has told me that you are the intelligence in this office and that this place would fall without you."

A glance from Yusef to Georges, then a quick smile. "Well...*Fadi* is very humble."

After finishing the tour, Georges stood with Fatu outside the office door. "How about we go down to Al-Malik for a root beer?"

Her face suddenly went placid. "But my brother."

"He is still out. Here it is customary for a woman to be escorted. Marcel and I are brothers. It's right downstairs."

It was early on a Wednesday, fall sun through the big windows not reaching the back table where they sat. Georges had a cigarette and tea while Fatu sipped at her glass of ice and root beer.

He felt like an idiot because each time she looked up with those eyes under those dark brows his breath caught. He tried to order her a second drink, but she insisted against it.

"Are you happy to be here?"

"In this restaurant?"

"In America."

"Yes."

"Were you happy at home?"

"At times. With my mother."

"What was your family like? Close?"

"Just as Marcel has told you."

"He said your mother has had a difficult time."

"When our father divorced her, it became difficult."

"I didn't realize you had separate mothers."

"Though it is taught that when a man divorces a woman he must ensure for her well-being, my family and siblings have not been taken care of well. There is little money. Marcel has provided for us more than our father."

"Forgive me. I did not know the situation. Not all of it."

She looked around the room. "Things here are so easy. Food, sweet drinks. It is more than I imagined, even."

"Your brother is kind to have brought you. And lucky to have you."

She looked out the window, moved the glass of ice.

As Georges lit another cigarette, she asked, "Do you have wives here?"

He coughed a cloud of smoke, laughed.

"What?" Tapped the cigarette. "No. No, I do not. We cannot marry more than once at a time here."

"No wife at all?"

"My business has taken all my time."

"But men here marry for business, do they not?"

"I guess you can, yes. But my goal is to marry once. Not for business reasons."

As winter crept over Cambridge, the sky in late evening was a bulb on a dying generator, and the air was cold. The wind jogging down the streets at night shooed away the few malingerers on the sidewalks of Mass Ave.

On this Monday night Fadi was dressed in a new thobe, a simple white cloth, unadorned. As he walked down the hall from his apartment to Marcel and Fatu's, he noticed there wasn't the usual sweet smell coming from their end of the floor. After knocking, it was quite a long time before Fatu answered the door.

"Marcel is not here right now," she said with her eyes to the floor.

Georges took a step in. Fatu raised her hand. "Perhaps you don't mind waiting until my brother returns."

"I will wait in the sitting room."

He walked into the apartment, sat immediately in one of the odd chairs.

"Can I offer you some tea?"

"Yes, please."

She busied herself in the kitchen. A few minutes later the kettle chirped, then a few ceramic *ting*ings. Fatu emerged with her tray. Tea pot and single cup, sugar cubes. She set it on the table.

"Please, join me."

"I am behind on preparing dinner."

"I insist. While we wait for Marcel."

She brought a cup from the kitchen and sat across from Georges. He filled her cup then his own. They both held their tea a while as it cooled, not saying a word. Fatu's eyes were unusually stern this evening and held downward as if some answer lied there.

"What is it?"

She shook her head.

"Fatu."

She shook her head again. A single tear ran from her eye then disappeared behind her Abaya.

"Fatu, tell me what's wrong."

"I suppose I am lonely. I stay in this house all day. I can't speak with my mother or my sisters, except in letters. My brother..." She paused.

"Fatu, shh. It's okay."

He reached his hand over and set it on top of hers. He rubbed the skin, which was soft and seemed so private, to be touching this woman, whose skin was only hinted at under that black cloth. He saw another tear run down her cheek and into blackness. She hesitated a moment then set her tea cup on the table and put her other hand on top of his. They sat for several minutes like this, an amazing warmth encompassing his hand, where he'd pushed into her tiny atmosphere at last, that part of her uncloaked and all the more tender.

The front door opened and Marcel walked in, tall with robes flowing. He closed the door behind him and stood, regarding the two of them. Fatu quickly moved her hands and began to collect the cups and tea pot. She said nothing as she headed toward the kitchen with her tray.

Georges rose as Marcel was spreading his arms in greeting. They kissed cheeks and stood a few moments.

"I need cigarettes. Care to take a walk down to the corner?"

"Of course."

They headed down the hallway together, both in traditional robes but still worlds apart in appearance. Down the two flights of stairs, onto the empty sidewalk. Silence as they made their way to 7-Eleven. A chime as the door opened, then muzak. Marcel headed to the counter.

"Dunhill's."

The dark little man back there paused a second before turning and retrieving the pack, setting it on the counter. Marcel mumbled something to the man in Arabic as he handed him a five. He took the bill and began to make change.

"So you intend to marry my sister."

The man froze with the register drawer open, and Georges was unable to respond.

"Marcel, I meant no disrespect by arriving at your apartment with just Fatu there..."

"I took no disrespect from it."

"Fatu was upset, feeling alone these days."

"But you would like to marry her, would you not?"

Georges thought a moment about it while the cashier handed Marcel his change and closed the drawer, obviously awaiting Georges's answer. "I care about your family very much. I think of them as my own. It seems early." His voice trailed off.

"You understand, of course, my sister's history." He stopped, regarded the man, then motioned for Georges to join him near the coffee station. "I've told you about this. No man would marry her in Egypt. She is my sister, and I love her very much. And you are my brother. I do not want you to feel as if you are receiving a tarnished woman."

"I don't see Fatu that way."

"Good."

"But I don't intend to marry multiple wives."

Marcel paused, a half grin drew up one side of his face. "You are letting this American way of life make your decisions for you, eh?"

"It is only written that a man *may* take more than one wife and not more than four. It is not proscribed that he must. Besides, wouldn't you feel as if your sister is being better taken care of if her husband's attention was not divided?"

"Whatever the case, I would have no reservations that you would not care for my sister as if she were your own."

Georges laughed.

Not a flinch from Marcel's face, save for the usual squinted eyes with which he usually met Georges's humor. "It's settled then."

"I know things are different in Egypt, but I don't feel right speaking about Fatu as if she has no choice in the matter. She does. I won't marry her unless she actually wants to marry me as well. I will want to discuss this with her."

Marcel reared back, his eyebrows raised. "I already have."

CHAPTER 31

"But he still said 'I do.' Sort of."

Emma laughed and actually blushed as she recounted her courtship with John. They sat in their usual spots, Fadi's bed elevated, Emma in a metal chair at his bedside. How far they'd come in these two months: no straps on Fadi's thighs, no pretense, a single guard inside the door (for regulation's sake), and best of all, to Emma's mind, Fadi no longer looked past her with that single, vibrant eye of his. It was alive enough to more than compensate for its dead partner.

They both laughed and smiled at the string of blunders and miscues of which her wedding ceremony had been composed. A small tear of laughter ran down Fadi's right cheek. Then there was silence.

"Were you and Fatu married here?"

He nodded.

"Fairly traditional, I would imagine."

"It was overseen by her brother." He paused. "My friend."

"How long had you known each other?"

"A few months, if that. Our courting period, that there even was one, was certainly uncommon. In her country she would have been promised away to one of her father's banking partners for the sake of business, never having met the man, to live in a compound with his other wives." Then he paused. "Although, that wouldn't have been possible for her."

Emma's lips parted then stopped.

"It was a plain ceremony, and humble. I did not know Fatu well at the time. But that ceremony was perfect for her. No attention, no pomp. Simply God and us under Him. It was at a Mosque outside Boston.

You know Watertown. My family was there, but I didn't invite many friends."

Here he hesitated.

"I suppose I kept it secret because I'd lied to my friends about my family. Many of them thought I had two Moroccan parents. I was hiding my poor mother from them. And perhaps even Alia and Yusef. I know now that my mother loved Fatu, from the beginning, without question. She had always trusted me so much with my decisions, she would never have taken a moment to question whether Fatu was right for me. She hugged her when they first met."

He raised a hand to his mouth, rubbed his beard. To Emma the only hint of his mother was that eye, just that single eye, the oceanic murk to it.

"But I was cruel to her, still. I was still trying to push away every ounce of white from my life, as if a blemish. We rarely visited my parents after the wedding. Our Sunday dinners were all but over. I know Alia still went, and Yusef had begun to bring his growing family. But I insisted on cutting myself away from them. Anger. It was anger at how perfect that family was, as I was digging myself more and more into what was imperfect. I thought so much about what needed fixing in the world, that I began to hate even those things that were good."

"You had happy times though. With Fatu. She moved in with you, you were a married couple. And Marcel?"

"Yes, we were a very happy couple. Although at first we were still getting to know each other. It was odd, to me, having her in my home at first. This was a place I'd hardly taken the time to decorate, not suitable to a woman's tastes. And on top of that here was this lovely woman, who I barely knew, living in the same quarters, making dinner for me each night, falling asleep in the bed next to me. I was lucky, I think. We were lucky. We did end up being very compatible, but it took a little time."

"I married John after a few months. Funny, I don't think I really knew him at first either. But I sort of grew to know him." She leaned back and crossed her legs. "It's easy, with someone like him, because there are so many fine things, decency, and talents, and that he was instantly a good father. I think it was me, the way I am, that stopped us. And distance. That was impossible."

"Why did there need to be distance?"

"Why did I stay overseas?"

He shrugged and nodded.

"At the time, if you had asked, I'd say it was because of work." She smiled a second. "Because I had this incredible job and was offered a post I couldn't refuse."

"But Evan and your husband. They couldn't come with you."

"Oh no. No place for a kid to be raised." Then she put her hand up. "I'm sorry, I didn't mean that. I don't know what I meant."

"It's okay."

"But the choice was simple, sure. Take the post in Egypt, move up in my career, but do so without my little son and my good husband there with me. It was a choice, and I made it, but I tried to have it both ways. We thought we could survive and then gather up two years later what we'd had. No dice. I guess that doesn't make sense to you, that I'd make that choice. You were such a family man."

"It makes sense to me. Although I don't see why it didn't work. You moved back here. You were still married."

"It was destroyed before then. That I'd made that choice, that John was so good and I was not. We couldn't match back up, even with our little guy there."

"So you ended it."

She took a cigarette from the pack but then slid it back in. "With the help of another man, yes."

Fadi's eyes closed gently, and a nauseated wave passed over his face.

"Yes," she said.

They sat for several minutes in silence, Emma flipping the cigarette pack around on the table, Fadi squirming. Then he finally said, "But I don't understand."

"What?"

"Your husband…and Evan. They are nearby and always have been. How can you not see your boy? Or John, perhaps." His eyebrows lifted and he turned his body. "It's not too late."

Georges and Fatu had been married and roommates nearly a month by now, but their manners persisted. Both thoughtful and reserved. It was several minutes of psyching himself up to hold her hand as they sat with their evening tea, which made Fatu smile and blush, but it terrified him to think of taking her into the bedroom. His first thought was of the nightmare she'd faced back home, which must have destroyed any desire she had to be with a man, even her own husband. But he was also petrified, having never known a woman. All these years his friends, employees, every man he saw on the street, they went home to wives, went to bed with them. But he was like a teenager.

Nourredine had never broached the subject, nor had their mother. Not even Yusef, who was likely too humble to speak of it anyway. He found himself wishing he and Fatu could share a drink together, if even just one, to somehow break down this wall.

Months went by, a full Boston winter with dark days and long nights, filthy snow puffed up along the sidewalks, narrow pathways for single-file traverse, terrible slush and cold that kept them indoors. Georges had certainly fallen in love with Fatu within a few months of their marriage, and she too had opened up to him. They would sit in the same position each evening in their sparse living room. Tea on the table, small TV set scraping out news reports. Georges on the couch, with Fatu on the floor before him, arm hugging his thigh.

Only recently had she started to walk their apartment without a head covering. Shiny black hair, dark as licorice, and smooth and long after she showered with it falling to her back. Tonight they sat and watched stories of local criminals and heroes, him petting her head gently as she rested her arm on his knee. He leaned in to kiss her neck. She laughed. Snow fell in the lamp light outside their window, snow at once aimless and completely directed on its path. A woman at his feet so lovely and so kind, having removed her cover and so intimately availed to him. He steeled himself and put a hand under each of her arms, hefting her to her feet.

"Where are we going?" As she gripped his hand.

"Just trust me."

Their life together carried on in the sort of continuous, looping manner that allowed years to spill forth without easy marking. Often, Georges would forget his own age, and Fatu — as was the case in many Arabian families, especially girls — didn't know her exact birthday or even year. So Georges had given her a day in mid-May to celebrate. He said it was nothing more than a time to reflect on the start of her path, that it had begun at all, God willing, and lead her to him. It was the first time she'd tasted cake, which she loved and washed down with a cold root beer, of course.

Over the first few years, they spent many nights together, Fatu hopeful that a baby would come to them after only a few weeks. She did get pregnant after several months, but carried the child only to the second trimester before it was lost. And after much consolation from Georges, they began to try again.

When the second child slipped away only slightly further toward term, Fatu dropped into a severe depression. Georges blamed himself, scheduled visits with doctors all over Boston, none of whom could find a deficiency in either of them. On some dark nights Fatu would insist that it had been brought on by the rape she'd suffered, and that it was God saying she did not deserve to be married, did not deserve a child or a life.

"It doesn't work that way, my little mouse. It doesn't work that way. That we have been brought together is the strongest sign of His will. But His will requires hardship, and a bit of our own will too. It was not easy for you to get here to me, but you did, and now we're together. It will not be easy to have a child, but it will happen."

She turned from her seat on the carpet, faced him with her elbows on his lap. Smiled up with eyes like wet paint. In her child's English, "You are right." Wiped her cheek. "You are always right."

That night they went to bed together. It had been a long day filled with constant snow as if white blood cells rushing to the ground, packing broken walks and potholes. The world outside was calm for once, without cars or voices, nothing but night and snow and them, as Georges held Fatu afterward, naked under the sheet as if out of her shell.

They spoke in Arabic.

"Why do the men call you Fadi?"

He waited. "Because to them I am Fadi."

"I don't understand."

"My name was Maraca for quite some time. As a kid, even as an adult. That wasn't me."

"To me you are Georges." She kissed him.

"Yes, that is my name for you. And you are my mouse. My little desert mouse. Who crawled across the ocean. Do you think about the things that were in place for us to finally come together?"

"Yes. And I thank God for allowing it."

"Your brother, the smartest one in your poor little village. And the village sending him to school across the Atlantic to America, to a crummy state school in cold Massachusetts. And the fact that I started a club was even luck. Much had to happen for me to start that club, to meet Marcel, to meet you. One day I will tell you everything."

A few seconds' hesitation, then a soft, "Yes."

"That is amazing to me. I am lucky to have such a friend, in many ways."

She was quiet, laying her head across his chest and rubbing his belly with soft fingers. "You are my husband."

"If not, we went through a long ceremony for nothing."

"We are supposed to share everything, right? In America, the husband and wife share everything. You told me that once."

"Yes." His throat clenched, and his mind flashed back to McHallan, the booming and crunching glass.

"My brother has told you that he has come from a small village in Egypt, very poor, that the village sent him away to college."

"And this wealthy family. These *slugs*. These…"

She patted his stomach once.

"But there is more. It is not that simple. We lived in a poor village, yes. But we did not grow up there. You see, Marcel and I have the same father, but of course I was born to a different mother. Our father was incredibly wealthy, one of the wealthiest men in Saudi Arabia. He had many wives, many children. Marcel was his second son, to his second wife, his favorite wife. He grew up very nicely. Did he tell you that?

Well, he studied Koran at a young age, like most. But he was also given a Western education, which was becoming a trend with the recent oil wealth. Our father came from Yemen to Jeddah as a boy, penniless, worked as a digger and anything else. He was the one who climbed our family out of poverty, climbed along with the royal family, latched onto them.

"He traveled much for business. He loved planes, and he owned dozens of them, was friends with a few other Saudi men who loved planes and were wealthy and who drank and smoked and married white women. His best friend was another money man. They were the two biggest. They flew together, traveled together, and they worked with the largest construction company to rebuild in Mecca, Medina, Jerusalem, even into Egypt. And Iran.

"My father lived in Egypt for half the year. He married the daughters of two of his business partners. It was something that was done. He was about forty when he married my mother, who was still a teenager. She was the daughter of a contractor. With her he had three children, all girls, before losing interest. And like I said, he followed the law that a man cannot have more than four wives. So when he wanted to marry again, he divorced my mother. But it was also considered right that a man should see that his ex-wife is well attended to. So he even arranged for my mother to marry a man of modest means. After that, he never spoke to us or saw us again. I received a yearly payment, about half as much as one would need to survive."

"I don't understand. How did you ever see Marcel? How did he come to Egypt?"

"Marcel was different from his brothers. They all clung more and more to Western ideas. They drank, they gambled, they spent summers in Switzerland. Their sisters would even go uncovered in Europe. They all eventually sought either finance degrees or engineering degrees in American or European schools so that they might continue the family business. Marcel went to the same boarding schools, new ones in Lebanon. He was tempted there, I know. But something happened to him. Something he has never told me about.

"One time he comes back to his family's home in Jeddah, and he is thin, and when a woman is nearby he averts his eyes. He is quiet but has somehow gained confidence. Everyone sees it. He used to be so restless and worried, but suddenly he is very calm on the inside and would often seem to realize something, something that would make one side of his mouth grin. He refuses to drive in cars, to let himself hear music. He used to watch TV, just the news, and even when a bit of this typical news music came on, he would have his younger sisters stand next to the television to turn the volume down. Something had changed him.

"And here we were, in Egypt, my stepfather lost his job and moved us to his tiny home village in the desert, and we are cut off from the family. My sisters and I scrounge off the pittance sent by our father. But Marcel and I had always written to each other. He was the one who taught me to write, actually. And he wrote me often about his travels. Until one day, he writes to tell me he will be moving to live with us. He must have been about sixteen at the time. He wrote often about how sick the "Western wind" made him, how modern things threatened to cloud his mind, how he needed to simplify, live humbly. He came from the best schools to ours, fifteen miles' ride each way. And he became very close with the imam and was very, very strict with his prayers and eating. He and I grew close too. He looked after my sisters and me as if he were our father. And he made us read the Koran every day, and memorize it, but also made us write and do math. He talked often of how much he hated the Western schools he had come from, yet he insisted on teaching us their ways. As if preparing for something only he could see on the horizon.

"He became obsessed with living just as the prophet had lived, which even in our humble town made him force discomforts on our family. He was not so hard on my mother, but my sisters and I were made to wear full cover when outside our home, and we ate very poorly. The only exceptions were his lessons, which would be considered more liberal than any woman around us was treated. He lived with us for over two years before he headed overseas for school. To meet you."

She rubbed his arm. "Which I am so thankful for."

Georges's mind set about putting all of these facts and times in order, where Marcel had been and when. The stories he had told back in college, what parts of his life had been tweaked or wholly fabricated.

Which was when he fell upon the fact of his sisters, what Marcel had told him all those years ago about the family in Tanta, the brothers who had ruined his sisters and the subsequent payments for his schooling and, indirectly, as seed money for Georges's own business. To this point Georges had felt a growing guilt within his belly over the fact that this huge and lucrative business had been founded on sour money. Money that even Marcel said he could not use, due to its tainted source. And as he'd begun to fall in love with Fatu that guilt gestated more each day, the apartment, the clothes, the food, the trips to Nova Scotia and Montreal, all funded by money paid out by this family in exchange for poor Fatu's innocence, or soul, or whatever good thing they'd torn from her.

"What about this family?"

She was quiet a few seconds. "What family?"

"The one Marcel told me about. The wealthiest in Tanta. The builders. The ones…"

"He has not told you about them then."

"He has, yes, but what has he told me?"

"I will assume he has not told you who they are." She sat up. Just a bit of light from the street made its way past the snow and onto her naked shoulder. "As I have said, there were three families that were bonded together. Our father was a banker, one of the two most successful in the Saudi kingdom. His good friend was the other banker, and his other good friends were the largest construction family in the kingdom. They became inseparable, these three families, each currying favor from the royal family, building, financing, forging ties with outside contractors and financiers. Their circle grew quickly. The oil money filled their pockets. Other Arabian countries were discovering oil too, though they were years behind Saudi in terms of construction and finance infrastructure. So they turned to us.

"This construction family, the patriarch had many wives, including one in Egypt, who he moved to a small village outside Tanta, built her a lavish compound on the sea, where she gave him eight children, all sons. This is considered a blessing, and she fast became his favorite wife. At first, this family knew nothing of their connection to ours. They lived in the modern part of the territory, near the port, and we way out in nowhere. But as Marcel moved, our father made it known that these two segments of our families lived so near to each other, and he even hinted at arranging a marriage between some of us, which my mother and her husband liked, as it would have meant a comfortable life for them. He hadn't spoken to us in years.

"But we met some of the older boys, when we were all still very young. We visited their home, which was like a castle, with modern electronics and drinkable water, and five cars. Marcel came too and was perhaps more disgusted by their life than anyone else. And the boys were indulgent, and they drank, and even had a few white women in the home, somehow.

"We all hated them, and the visit was uncomfortable. We sat covered and quiet as our hosts ate and drank and got louder and louder. And one even began to play a guitar, to sing with this terrible high-pitched, feminine voice. Mahzar was his name, the oldest son. It was this that made Marcel finally stand and excuse us all. They were angry at first, but as Marcel does so well, he calmed them, and they even had one of their servants drive us home. My first ride in a car.

"But Mahzar and his brothers called on us again. They arrived at our home one day, unannounced, drove up in three cars, quite a spectacle in our village. And this time they were very humble and even apologized to Marcel. They invited us to the wedding of their youngest sister, which would take place near the ocean. Marcel, though only seventeen at the time, was the male voice of our family. He hesitated but was charmed by Mahzar, who knew what buttons to push on Marcel, even on Marcel. He described the great ceremony, the tradition, the great imam who would be overseeing it all.

"Marcel consented. I remember it very well. His eyes closed, and his head sort of just slumped a bit as he turned up his palm. We would be their guests. Marcel, my two sisters, and I. But when we arrived, my sisters and I were the only women who were fully covered, and there was western music, and modern tables with place settings, women wearing dresses, men in tuxedos. And there was certainly alcohol, hidden but present. Mahzar and his brothers were even worse than that first night. They grabbed women and pulled them close to dance. They swore, were even disrespectful to the groom. 'You are the most grateful man in the room, because you are allowed to join our family.' And Mahzar put his hand out until the man kissed it.

"But as it became very late, we had no way of getting home. They had driven us in their cars, which was the only way back. Marcel fell asleep in his chair, and we simply sat at our table and drank warm water as the party grew louder and more decadent into the night. Then Mahzar and his quiet brother, Cyd, sat next to us. The smell was terrible, like perfume, I remember, but sour. They led us, my one sister and I, over to the balcony, promising the best view of the ocean we have ever seen. And we went. I don't know why, and I don't know why Marcel didn't awaken.

"Their hands soon fell upon us. We were just thirteen and fourteen years old, and these were men, and we didn't even know how to scream or who would listen to our screams, so their hands kept going, kept going. And Mahzar grabbed my wrist hard and pulled me down to the beach, and Cyd took my sister there too. I remember how much quieter it was down there, no music, not even any ocean sounds. And it was here that they'd turned even darker, just two black figures, animals. I was thrown to the ground, to hard sand with shells. He pulled at my clothing. Even as I whimpered and resisted and said 'No,' he pulled at me as if starving. And I remember his weight, like total blackness, that rancid smell and breath, and as if twenty evil hands clutched at me, searching for something I knew was just mine and something I could never keep safe. And the weight. That stink…"

"Okay. Okay. My God. That's all over now, mouse." He pulled her close. "That's all over. You're here now. If you need any proof that we are meant to be together, just look back at all that had to happen to get you here."

He scooped her head into his lap, brushed hair behind her ear. Her eyes stayed open a few seconds, staring out the window. A tear fled just before her eyes shut.

"There are terrible things on this earth. Some too gnarled to make sense of, but others are far too wonderful to make sense of. These are the things we cannot question, put here not for us to understand but simply for us to experience, to realize how great a thing there is that lies beyond our ability to comprehend. But I know the very beautiful things come only to the deserving."

"What about the bad?"

"I don't know, love."

She sat up, rubbed her cheek on his pajamas. Looking at him. "I'm glad to have found my way here. Whatever the way is, it was worth it."

He bent to kiss the top of her head then stood and began to clear the nightstand of cups and saucers. He brought them to the kitchen sink then returned to the bedroom. Fatu had turned on a single lamp and was now looking out the window at the snow.

CHAPTER 32

With late fall the nights at the Harrison Complex turned sour. Gray lights, some flickering, cast fake shadows from the orderlies and guards who skulked its halls or shuffled in to feed or move Fadi. Even the square-jaws slouched as if deflated. A week's worth of rain and gloom steeped the dim place, and Fadi's little window, that hole in the wall like a projector slot, offered not even a hint of light.

Emma had not been in to see him in several days, and Fadi nearly asked Bauer about her but thought better of it. In fact, not a single interrogation had transpired in the last week. Dinner was late, must have been nearly eight o'clock before old Tully knocked on the door, as usual, then came in pushing that table. His limp seemed especially bad this night, and there was just the sound of wheels rolling, then Tully's gait: rubbery squeak of his shoe, dead drag of his bum leg behind. He swung the table to the far side of the bed as Fadi straightened himself upright. Then he lifted the metal cover to reveal tonight's fare: portobello mushroom with some strange sauce, a few green beans, and cheese-less potatoes au gratin. There was also a small plate with plain roll on it, a Styrofoam cup of water, and a box of apple juice.

"Hello, Tully. How's your leg?"

He nodded, smiled, and then set to work preparing. He poked a hole in the juice box and cut the mushroom into manageable slivers, handed the fork to Fadi with another nod. Then he sat back in his chair. In the months since Emma had arranged for Fadi to no longer have his arm strapped, Tully's duties during meals had thinned out to little more than a few preparations, after which he simply sat in his chair, smiled sometimes, or looked down, waiting until Fadi was done so he could clear the table and set up their game of Connect Four.

Tonight the meal was especially putrid, and cold by the time it reached Fadi's mouth. He sat over the plate, fork resting on its edge with a meaty piece of mushroom skewered on it. He knew it had been a full year, more than that, with the change of season. He couldn't help but wonder what these cold months held for him. These days he thought often of what tricks Ali had pulled on Emma, if this place had been able to pry anything from that evil little elf. And tonight, as every night at dinner, the mere sight of the metal cover over his food made him think of the note he'd been served all those months ago. *Talk She Die.* So he thought about Alia and the last time he'd spoken to her, on that mobile phone, just before crashing himself into oblivion.

This place was finally buckling him. The ashy gray lights, the hard walls. Seasons had always felt like progress to him, a mark that the future was, truly, on its way. But the knocking of winter now felt like nothing more than a return to some place on a circle.

As he stared at his plate, he felt Tully watching him. The man's skin seemed even blacker, and his eyes, peering up, bright with thought, studied him. His jaw hung open. It was a look Tully had given him a hundred times, the empty, child-like gaze, but his eyes were different now, steadier, controlled. That gaping mouth and those bad teeth slowly tightened into an undead grin.

Then a chuckle, a long, droning laugh.

"Tully?"

He began nodding. "You were so *good*. For so long."

Fadi sat up, his breath stuck at the floor of his stomach. Tully's posture straightened from his usual slouch, his shoulders back and chin raised.

"You woke up. We never thought that would happen. Promise you won't be mad, but I tried to kill you. When you first got here. I failed." His eyes lit up. "But I was doing it for you, in any case. I thought you would want it. This place was just a hospital, at first, a private one, of course. But you were put here without any hope that you'd actually wake up. And I was placed here only to make sure you remained dead.

Then we noticed this hole…" Looking around the room. "…filling with many of our friends. This place became interesting, so I stayed. Then… you woke up."

"I never talked."

"You're right. For a while, anyway. But something happened, didn't it?" He looked away as he raised his hand and flapped it open and shut like a mouth. "We were doing so well. We trusted you."

He looked at the metal food cover. "It was you. The note."

"So you *did* read it? We weren't so sure, you know, because of all the talking. Either that or you don't really care about her life."

Thoughts banged around in his head, growing louder and more scattered. To breathe, to speak. Tim Dunn. He steadied his eye, even willed the dead one to burn into Tully. "I swear to God, I will have you crying like a baby in torment before I kill you if you touch my sister. I will rip the fucking meat from your bones."

Shaking his head, *tsk*ing with his tongue. "Now, now. That's not you."

"How the fuck did you get in here?"

"It was easy." He shrugged, and as Fadi peered into his eyes it was as if a light had gone on. "I'm an American, like you. My name is normal, my *American* name, anyway. I've been an orderly in DC for twenty-five years. And I've been subjugated by the white West since before I was born." He grinned. "But I've been a good boy, yes, I have, I promise. I've been patient and I've studied the Word since I became a man. It has freed me. And I knew if I was good and patient I would be called. After that, it took only a little shuffling of papers by one of our friends in the system, a few payments here and there, and my file was on top, just a black dummy, perfect for this job. The hard part was acting so *stupid* around those white idiots for so long. I thought you would never wake up, but I prayed to God that you would open your eyes, and you did. Finally, my purpose was clear. And word was sent to me that all my work, all my years, had been for a *reason*."

"I haven't told anyone anything."

"Oh, you've talked. You've gossiped your fair share with Ms. Emma. We know that already. And I know you know who else is in here with you."

"Ali."

"Your old friend. But sadly, I haven't been able to speak to him. You see, an orderly is needed only when a patient has a…handicap. Which you have more than enough of."

"Ali won't budge. You know that as well as I do."

"Maybe you're right. But maybe you've also helped our little whore friend find out his buttons. Which you knew so well."

"You know I haven't talked to her. You were here, you've been in the room."

"And what about your private little walks out in the garden? Before she arrived it was so easy, all the talking was done in your room, where I could observe. I can't think of the last prisoner allowed such casual strolls."

"I have her wrapped around my finger. The only reason those ended was because of Bauer."

"And to get such privileges, one must be giving some tat."

"We're friendly. But nothing would make me sacrifice my sister's safety. Marcel knows that."

"We know. And I have good news for you. Nothing will happen to your family. Because you have become useful once again. Not for your silence. But because of your pretty new friend, Ms. Emma. Did you know that she was one of the top skull-crushers back home, in the very early days of our struggle? She has a long, long history of squeezing people like you, like me. And she knows exactly what she knows. And she trusts you. That I believe. And now you will find out from her exactly what this forsaken country's people really know about us. This is what you will do for us."

Fadi was silent a moment. "Of course. I know something already."

Tully ignored him. "And we will give you little gems to feed her, to throw them further off our trail."

"Absolutely." He took a long breath. "But I need to know that my family is safe."

At this, Tully leaned back in his chair. A creak. Then complete silence, gray as the gray lights and dark as everything beyond the window. A huge smile cast sidelong on Tully's black face.

"I begged him." Shook his head. "I begged him to let me tell you. Much earlier, you know. I want you to know that."

"Tell me what?"

"You remember, those years ago, how lost you were? Your wife, your sweet daughter, killed tragically. You had nothing to live for, so you were willing to die. Bravo, by the way. It made you a perfect weapon. What a miracle that you survived. Don't you think?" He leaned in, clasped his hands together, bright white eyes and dull teeth. "But I get to tell you now. When I wrote you that little word of advice on your dinner. Yes, it was me." Nodding at the plate. "Your family is bigger than you think."

"What do you mean? Not Yusef?"

"No, my brother. No. Your sweet little kitten." He leaned back, another creak of the chair. "Nadat. She lives. She lives with her kind uncle. She has been his, since the day you thought she died."

PART III

THE HEAT he had not expected, nor gotten used to over the past six months. And in the afternoon, when the wind shifted pitch and blew west from the Nile, the air was still and showed its true fire. Sweat and dirt. The ceiling fan made not a whisper and worked to remind them of time's passing and little else.

Fadi sat writing at the sparse table, pen and paper and glass of warm water. Fatu in her usual chair by the window, rocking and sewing. He'd joked earlier about them both spending the same two hours each day in practice, he in script and she with her needle and thread. But Fatu had caught on very quickly, and progress in her craft quickly exceeded his.

He glanced across the room at his wife, her head uncovered, the smooth black hair with its same temper and luster. More alive than anything else in the room. The few sticks of unpadded furniture, two tapestries with quick prayers in their fabric, gifts from Marcel when they'd moved in. The tough stone floor.

And as Fadi allowed himself to drift into thought, as his pen froze and he considered buying a second box fan, the silence was broken by little coos from the next room. Fatu rose and left, returned a few moments later with the tiny bundle, sat in her rocking chair and settled the baby into the cradle of her arm.

"I suppose practice is over for today."

Fatu smiled up at him. He moved over to the wooden couch, put his feet on the table, shifted his robe up to his knees as he breathed in the hot air.

"Is her room too warm?"

"It's just her first summer. She is fine."

When Fadi had first come to Cairo to arrange for an apartment, he'd been of a singular mind to replace every comfort they'd enjoyed in America with a simple, humble version of itself. Appliances became the most obvious riddance. And furniture was not a problem, because most of what they used had come with the place, formerly owned by a visiting professor from Jordan, all cheap and hard.

But a few days before he expected his wife and daughter to arrive he'd begun to worry for the baby's safety, and had, one by one, added a few modern conveniences: the new fan in Nadat's room, the small refrigerator for formula, with a freezer for Fatu's ice. With each purchase he'd felt himself veering off course, sucked lightly westward. He swore each trespass was done only for the sake of his two girls.

The heat this summer was so bad he was nearly certain he'd find himself buying one of those new AC units he'd seen downtown, sold for over one-hundred American dollars. If the baby's crying persisted, he'd buy one tomorrow.

"And how is mother?" Reaching over to stroke her head. "How is her first summer?"

"Oh, everything is fine."

"What will you do today?"

"The market in about an hour." She shrugged. "And you?"

"I am meeting Marcel at half past, then class."

"Supper will be a little early. Will you be back after five?"

"Maybe."

He stood and leaned to kiss first Fatu then Nadat, who burped as his lips touched her forehead. Then he rose and gathered his keys and a few coins and his prayer book before setting out the door.

The pinched alley outside was a frustration of heat, a near-boil of passing vendors and robed men with heads down. To live in Islamic Cairo had been his choice before he'd even visited. Marcel knew the city and had suggested one of the less-trodden sections, off Muizz Street, and he and Marcel had spent the weeks together visiting assorted apartments and houses within the district. Though he was secretive about the details, Marcel had already been set up with an apartment, his of even sparer décor.

It was a few hundred feet away but required traversing a tangle of thin streets and crooked alleyways, with ancient gutters veined through cobbles and the smell weighty and damp this day. As Fadi walked, a man seemed to rise directly from one of these gutters near Marcel's home, rose from a crouch to stop him, an old man with no visible teeth, holding out some folded piece of cloth and speaking in a tongue beyond decipher, beyond Fadi's growing reach of Arabic. He put his hands up, made the common gesture of respect, and moved down the shadowy lane, cooler now, a gust at his face.

A knock on the wooden door. Marcel appeared. Both men had to duck a bit to clear the doorframes of this old apartment. He invited Fadi in a moment while he gathered his things, a book, some papers, a small change purse.

"You are sweating."

"I am."

By now Fadi had learned the patterns of Old Cairo's streets, could get most places: to the university, the marketplace, a few preferred cafes, Marcel's, knew the general direction to New Cairo, and could certainly make the daily trip to Al-Thaghr. To get there from Marcel's apartment was a short jaunt through zagging back lanes shaded by overhead laundry, then a quick cut down Maizz Street with its mosques and vendors and sandal traffic.

Their building was plain, a smooth white front common to the era of renovation in Islamic Cairo. Made from cool stone, a few wood-slatted doors on the upper levels opened in the evenings to welcome the night air. Georges had put about fifteen-thousand dollars toward its purchase, Ali the same, with the other share being provided by the same elusive donors Marcel alone conversed with. Five men had keys to the place.

Marcel opened the door as a moped buzzed past. The main room was refreshing, the heat and hurry a few degrees cooler than the street outside. The first floor was mostly empty, a few sticks of wood furniture in one large room, a mysterious box of some fifty-odd phonebooks stacked in the far corner. An elaborate mosaic on the far wall, installed by the previous owner, depicted in ocean blue and turquoise and blood-merlot a cartoon view of Mecca from the east as the sun set.

Jesper and Faruz stood smoking in the main room, turned to them, raised a single hand in greeting. Then they all four headed up the stairs, Marcel unlocking the solid door to their regular meeting room. He walked across and unlatched the doors, pulled them open to the din on the street, and Fadi flipped the switch on the ceiling fan. Jesper and Faruz set about arranging the chairs.

Marcel shifted a chair to a place before the window to look out on the street and the vague direction of the river, buzzing and warbled voices below. The other two lit the stove with a match and set the teapot to boil enough water for the remaining four or five. Ali was the next to arrive, heading straight to Marcel without regarding the others, mumbling something to him, then a wide grin before finally acknowledging the rest. The cross breeze wafted his perfume to Fadi, that same piled-on, manufactured scent.

The three Egyptians were next: Mahzar, Omar, and Khalid. Fadi liked these men very much. They were impeccably well mannered, seemed to know the details of every culture in the world, could each recite the Koran from start to finish, and were always showing up with books to recommend, about half of which Fadi could keep up with before they brought new ones. To him, they were like a single being. Each thought and acted in accord with the others, dressed similarly, spoke with the same accent. Mahzar and Khalid were somehow related, and Omar had married into their family at a very young age. All were tied to the university in one way or another. When Fadi and Fatu had first moved to the city, these men made especially sure of their comfort, setting up dates for their wives to meet and walk the marketplace, showing Fatu where to buy cloth and food and cookware and baby needs.

They gathered the stiff chairs in a circle, waited a moment for Marcel to turn his around. His hands wide on his knees. "We have much to discuss today."

Fadi, Mahzar, and Khalid each took out a cigarette.

"We are nearly ready. We have secured passage for our two men to arrive safely in the country, to be met by our four operatives there. Fadi will go over the particulars of money, schedules, and operation of incendiaries. We have delayed far too long on this, are many months behind. It is good to be cautious, but we must balance risk against timing. And to perform this task exactly on this date is absolutely crucial. It *must* be on the fourth. Already we have waited so long as to miss the three major targets. They are no longer at the embassy. We cannot wait any longer. Ali's men will go with Omar by boat, four days from now."

Fadi glanced at Ali to find his face wide with the gloat he'd expected, all chin and smirk. He was so distracted by the anger this brought on that he didn't hear Marcel the first time he called his name.

"Fadi."

"Yes?"

"Could you please take the men through the process?"

"Yes, yes."

Weeks before, Fadi had shown Omar and Ali the exact machinations and signals for the very simple ignitions he'd devised. Omar picked up the workings quickly, though Ali grew frustrated and swore and suggested Fadi had created too complex a system for their needs. And anyway he was much more interested in the explosive power than in the means of the charge. Fadi insisted that each man be able to connect the electrical units to the plastic within thirty seconds, unaided, because they would not be able to take a complete incendiary with them on the boat, but would have to acquire the plastic and assemble the devices once they'd reachedSudan. Ali had pushed for Fadi to join them, after his first attempts to put the units together, though Omar was able to do so after only a few demonstrations.

Why Marcel had immediately rebuked Ali's suggestion Fadi couldn't understand. He was ready to argue a few cases as to why he shouldn't join this mission, but his friend had either sensed his hesitation or else had some of his own motives for keeping him in Cairo while the other two met with their Sudanese brothers and undertook the operation.

Was it because Marcel sensed his disapproval of their chosen target? Fadi had been vocal about other means, other targets, but each time Marcel had offered defenses and logic as to why the embassy in Sudan had been chosen, why it was so perfect.

Today's meeting was short, perhaps due to the heat, or the boredom of topic: a simple outlining by Faruz of the timetables for travel, some financial leftovers. For the first time in many months, Fadi felt as if he were back at the weekly company meetings in Central Square, Yusef listing status items as Marlene took notes to type up and copy. This was the largest target ever chosen by Al-Thaghr, should be the most exciting, the most revolutionary, the most eventful. Yet, here he was, half asleep and daydreaming as the men ticked off items on a checklist, discussed transportation to and from the ports. Passed out phone numbers and addresses.

When the meeting was finished, they rose and folded their chairs, stacked them in the corner. Then each man flapped his rug across the floor, facing the windows. The prayers at first felt hollow to Fadi. The motions that usually calmed him and reminded him of that vocal connection to God felt like motions only, and he wondered if he could sense the same ennui in the others. Not Marcel, of course. His voice was as plaintive as ever, and beautiful as he recited. Fadi opened one eye to study this man as he sang in prayer. "Bismillah, Al Rahman, Al Rahim." *If you doubt what We have revealed to Our servant, produce one chapter comparable to it. Call upon your idols to assist you, if what you say be true. But if you fail (as you are sure to fail) then guard yourselves against the Fire whose fuel is men and stones, prepared for the unbelievers.* Watching him, Fadi could think only of the eight-year-old boy who had traveled from Algeria to Egypt to read from this book by heart, his intonation and tajweed as if from another world, beautiful and begging and from the deep.

CHAPTER 34

"Because I was sick with America. Truly sick. Sick of myself too. And I built walls. We did. I wanted a fresh start for my child."

They sat in classic interrogation position. He was seated in a wheelchair across the table from her, and she was angled with her side to him, one elbow on the table. Bauer had finally put a stop to their strolls in the courtyard, so here they were.

"I felt separate from the people I saw, so different, and I couldn't let my Nadat grow up like that, not even for the first years of her life."

"But Cairo was a dangerous place. You can't deny that. In moving you took your family away from healthcare, away from security, comfort."

"I did."

Fadi's eye shivered back and forth. He reached for the pack of Camels on the table, raised an eyebrow. The guard in the corner flinched.

Emma nodded.

He lit and drew from the cigarette.

"But it was arranged that I teach at the university, a small course load, small pay. Money wasn't even a bit of a thought."

"It still seems a strange choice. I made the opposite one, you know. Ev...Ben was born in Morocco, and my husband found a horrid job back here so we could bring him up in safety. So *he* could bring him up."

"It was a different thing."

"I know."

The fractioned arm raised as he shrugged. "I don't know. I was drawn by how exotic it was. Even though I had just married and found out about my little girl on her way, even with all that my life still felt worthless, without event or marker, or goal. No more football, no more Five Pillars, no more straight A's. Nothing to measure. It was a step. I might not have told myself this at the time, might have said it was for principal, to raise Nadat in an uncluttered place. But it seemed as if doing that would keep me far enough away from temptation."

"What temptation?"

"To be comfortable. To have things be easy. But not just comfort. I saw people striving for things: a toaster, a car, a TV, an educated child. Those goals were so easy, and so attractive. I felt myself becoming too much an individualist, and wanted still to be simply a gear in some greater machine rather than a tiny machine myself. So Egypt."

He was silent and stared forward. Emma saw both eyes, the lights of a person. One of them out for good, the other now joining its partner's gaze, still as crystal, peering either forward or back, or nowhere.

"But it wasn't to teach. You didn't go just to be in Cairo or to teach electrical engineering."

He smiled but not a real one. A drag and a long smoky breath.

"My friends, eh?"

"They brought you there, didn't they?"

"I would not have ended up in Cairo without them. Would not have gotten that job. In fact, I later found out that job was just a front, a hoax, something to explain my presence there, to the US, to Egypt. But I didn't know that at the time." A pause, eyelids snapping shut and then open. "Marcel arranged it all."

Emma's breath stopped. In nearly six months, Fadi had never mentioned Marcel by name. As close as they had grown, never a whisper of it, no more than a shadow cast by his words. Fadi seemed to realize this too, his eye toward the ground.

She let the air settle a moment, unsure of her next word. It struck her how odd this was. In all her years of interrogations, whether in DC's system or the CIA's, she'd always been in complete control of herself, always knew the next move, the next line in the script.

"Do you blame Marcel?"

Smoke crawled upward from his fingers, strong in streaks and then weak and then nothing. He looked sideways, shook his head. Blinked

248

a tear down his cheek. "I don't know." Shook his head again. "I don't know."

"You couldn't have helped their deaths, you know."

A cold gaze.

"There was nothing you could have done."

"I brought them to that place. I took both my little girls away from safety, a place where I could have fed them and protected them. They must have been so scared." A long sniff, exhale, and another drag.

"It was an accident. It wasn't you." She paused. "You were used."

"Bullshit." Shaking his head.

"It's true. You didn't do it, but it was done. There was a reason behind it."

He took a long breath, composed himself. "You know nothing." A grim smile. "You are wrong."

"Why do you protect him? Even after all this time, after all that has happened?"

"You couldn't begin to understand."

"Don't try that shit. Not now. Tell me, what is it that makes you protect a man that has led you here. Look at you. Marcel is free, he's out there, he's planning something else, something you know is going to kill people who don't deserve to die. And yet you sit here, in misery, your entire life stolen from you, and you can't blame the one person who has done this to you. Why the fuck are you doing this?"

His fist pounded the table, and the guard took a step toward them. Emma held up her hand, then whispered, "Why?"

As if from a sudden charge of particles his eye trembled, his jaw trembled, and two tears from separate origin ran earthward. He leaned in. "Because he is a good man."

"He is a murderer."

"He is my *brother*!"

Emma had forgotten the new cigarette between her fingers. She drew one long breath and lit the thing, stood, turned her back to Fadi, and paced.

Fadi studied her, the plain sweatshirt, the exhausted black and gray hair smoothed in a ponytail. Amazing, how he had caved in to her. Still, he didn't know if she was good at her job or simply a kind woman. Or maybe it was that he'd been without true human contact for so long. The cruelty of Mr. England, or the dark silence of Bauer, or the condescending nurses. Woken up to find himself still persisting on this damned planet, alone as ever. Those first, weary months, he had a vague recollection of believing he'd awoken in hell. He'd not been surprised.

But why had he opened to her? Why did he anticipate their visits? Perhaps she could help him. If he just told her that everything he did now was for Nadat. His little being was alive somewhere, and she's been without her papa for two years now and is confused and needs him. She will be disgusted by his appearance at first, but somehow, somehow he will imagine a life for them, one that provides for her, even with one working limb, one working eye to watch her grow into a woman.

She was Marcel's niece, for God's sake. How could he have sent that sewage called Tully to threaten him? He'd given his life for their cause, but God had rejected the offer, sending him back here instead, into this limbo. Here to hash out His insane concept of Right. But Marcel would do it, wouldn't he? His little fig probably living in a tiny room, not eating, not seeing anyone. Without her mom and dad. What lies Marcel could be telling her this very instant.

"Emma."

She did not face him.

"I have something to tell you. Something I have been keeping from you for some time. And I'm ashamed of it."

She turned slowly, arm crossed under her elbow.

"I know I have been in here for a year, cut off from my friends. But there is something I could have told you from the beginning, something that has not changed. It will help you to catch Marcel."

She pulled the chair out and sat, her brow a little less angry, but suspicious.

"I know the date and the target."

Shaking her head. "That would have changed. Unreliable."

"It would not have changed. You see, it is a very special date for Marcel. It is an anniversary. And he is a very special believer in time, in dates. I know the exact day."

"Okay."

"When he was a boy, there was a great event in his life, one that he believes God chose and placed before him. It was a time he was lost, and saw horrific things, had renounced his faith in search of his sisters' attackers. But at his lowest he witnessed a great man, an imam, sweep a tide of people into terrible action. This night was the most important in his life. And it has been nearly twenty years."

She leaned in, put her hand to his hip, and whispered so the guard could not hear. "When?"

"The fifth of March. That is when he will stage the most horrible attack America has ever seen. It will be in D.C., one of three buildings. Those plans were laid out, were supposed to occur before Caldwell. But they are set in stone, and Marcel is a superstitious man, or one who believes in destiny and in dates. This is how you will catch him."

She sat back in her chair, looked down, then at Fadi. "Tell me everything."

The smoke from their two hands mingled and snaked together. Looking at her, at the hot smoke, Fadi still wondered where, exactly, he was.

CHAPTER 35

Ali crouched on his hams in the corner of the small room, crying into his palms and muttering. The rest of the men celebrated. Jesper, Faruz, and the Egyptians embraced yet again and cheered as the English newsman spoke in front of that pile of rubble. Behind him was a charred and crumbled building among a few standing trees, some perfect and green, others decapitated.

They had gathered in their favorite café, which didn't have a name. A small place half a block from the river, with ceiling fans and tea and smoke, and no other visitors on this day. Ali and the others had left Sudan immediately, made it back to Cairo earlier that morning. Though the first news had reached them yesterday, it was not until this very moment that it seemed real, a success, when the men had returned. The Western press was still sorting through the mess, the wounded, the dead, the reasons behind it all. A letter would reach the BBC the next day, one mailed the day of the attack, from Sweden. It would be Al-Thaghr's first introduction to the world at large, and would cite, as a grocery list, the world's ills, the sickness of the West, and the announcement of a new conscience patrolling the non-Muslim world.

Marcel had hugged his friend Georges Fadi, faced him and kissed his cheeks, then put his forehead to Fadi's with closed eyes. He was crying. Fadi could smell the tears, could feel Marcel's body shiver. "We have come a long way, my brother."

"Yes, we have."

He expected his own eyes to tumble with tears any second now, assumed this same mania would wash over him. He was, after all, one of them. And look at Marcel, look at Ali.

Nothing. Save for a bit of relief when the Egyptians had reported how lovely his devices had been. Quicker, smaller, and simpler than anything they had sampled in the past. Simply relief that his part hadn't failed, not joy that the building — the former building — was rendered nothing more than a pair of scorched socks inside shoes. It dawned on him just how adept he had become at his new calling, the innovation equal to that of the elevator system.

Marcel embraced him again, squeezed him tight and jammed his face into Fadi's shoulder, began some muttered prayer and rocked back and forth. Fadi studied the television set. There was conjecture from a few talking heads in the US about its source. Some said Iran, some the Muslim Brotherhood. None could have guessed that one of their own, a home-fed football star, had devised mechanisms to total an American outpost so neatly.

Then back to a recording from the previous day in Khartoum, the Englishman turning to let the camera pan across the damage. News of the event's details had been spotty so far. What little TV reports they could get showed scant footage padded by guesswork. A row of civilians manned a massive hose; some sort of gas fire had apparently just erupted. Dejected men in khakis crouched over rubble and picked through smashed concrete and wood. A stretcher raced by, and Fadi's breath failed a moment before the motionless woman raised an arm, a red and blackened arm, vaguely upward.

Panning farther to the front yard, perfect bushes and pathways, as if nothing had happened. Then the shot honed in on a symmetrical row of white sheets. It seemed impossible that he was looking at this, that anything other than firewood or debris could lie under that bright white. It was too noisy now to hear any comments from the newsman. But Fadi knew. Here his breath stopped, and his shoulders and arms began to shake, which jostled Marcel.

"What is it?"

Marcel traced Fadi's gaze to the TV set, where the camera was still locked on the short row of bodies. The place went silent. It was explained that these were the bodies of five local workers, men and women from the nearby countryside who walked seven miles to work at the embassy as janitors and gardeners. No names disclosed, no faces.

Finally they panned back to the reporter, who clutched a large mic in an obviously shaking hand.

"These are not the only casualties. We can now confirm the deaths of four American citizens in the blast, including two servicemen. The names cannot be released at this point. This is in addition to the nearly two dozen men and women of the United States military and civilians who have been injured by this attack. Several are in critical condition and have been taken to nearby Soba University hospital."

"OKAY!"

It was Ali. He pushed his fist into the air. The Egyptians were silent, but one put a hand to Ali's shoulder with a faint smile on his face. Fadi backed away slowly, fell into a chair, looking toward a place beyond all things. Marcel crouched before him, placed his hand on Fadi's knee.

"I know this is difficult, my brother. But we knew it would be difficult. We know that such atrocities are necessary. Not because of us, but because of *them*. Remember that. Because of the world they have built and continue to build. We will reach a point when death declines, when no more is necessary."

He lowered his head until Fadi's eyes met his.

"This is God's will, my brother. And that will is manifest in our flesh, and we therefore must *act*." When Fadi was quiet he added, "It was like your joining the group in the first place. You remember what you said? Fate. And yes, it was fate, but it was a type of fate that required action. *Our* action."

Staring off across the river. "I don't understand."

"It was me."

Fadi turned to face him, his mouth open.

"What you thought was a mere act of coincidence, or destiny, *was*, in fact, destiny. But it needed orchestration. And it was me who sent Nazim to talk to you, to invite you into our group. Perhaps now I have to show you that not all things will simply happen to you, but that you must move and make certain that God's will is served. And that is precisely what we have done. My friend, you have done the right thing.

You will see, change will happen. Powerful and evil men are cowards when met with such things."

Now Fadi's eyes ran wet. He sniffed, looked about the room, then focused on Marcel. "Like with McHallan?"

Marcel fixed his eyes on Fadi, who felt powerless to look away. And at first Marcel's face was grave, until his eyebrows rose in sympathy. "You are confused, I see that."

Then Fadi said something that had not explicitly crossed his brain before then, but which he knew had been dancing around in his subconscious since the arrival of his daughter. "I fear for my family."

"They are my family as well. Do not forget. That is my sister, my niece. I would never do anything to hurt Nadat."

"With this, we bring ourselves deeper. I'm afraid to lose them." A tear sped down his cheek. "This is too much. I want only to be with my family, to protect them. I have put them in danger. I want to go home. We have gone too far. This is not right."

Marcel was silent, his hand still on Fadi's knee. And now his eyes took on that heavy weight again, starting deep into Fadi, staring *through* him. For the first time Fadi noticed a vacancy he would begin to see more and more in the coming year. It was as if he were just an obstacle, past which this man was gazing. He patted Fadi's leg and then stood.

"We shall correct this, my oldest brother." And then he smiled. "We shall correct this. Do not worry."

He joined the rest of the group, where Ali met him with a cigarette. He held a lighter for him and, while snapping it shut, glanced at Fadi, a slick smile that flashed and disappeared with the flame.

The fans whirred on, cutting and swishing the smoke and heat alike. But the breeze from the river had just changed direction at its usual time in the day. And with it the heavy heat broke into the room. Tears and sweat and thick breathing. Khalid began a song and moved his hand like a conductor. The others joined in one by one, except for Marcel. The chant rose and rose and the place grew hotter.

It went on for several minutes, until a stranger wandered in, followed by another. They were both dark, Arab, but unknown. So they stopped their song, and one of them clicked off the TV while the owner greeted the two newcomers with joined hands.

Fadi sat in his chair, having wiped his face, which was now placid. The others took seats at the table across the room. Ali disappeared. And Marcel swept across the floor toward him. Fadi gazed at his feet, but Marcel raised his chin with one finger until their eyes were locked. His eyes were the same as they had been on that first night at school, sympathetic but penetrating, as if searching for the very core of a person. Marcel put his hand to Fadi's cheek then to the top of his head. Absurd this was the boy he'd met all those years back, absurd the thought of snow falling on this man's shoulder without purpose.

CHAPTER 36

Emma had not been to the grocery store in six months. Since starting her new post, her meals had been a mix of Burger King drive-thru, cruddy 7-Eleven microwaves, Chinese, cereal, and more Chinese. Usually when Evan visited they ate meals out, but for such a long stay she needed real food, and what was more she needed to *pretend* she knew what she was doing in this place.

She pushed the cart as Evan walked alongside, occasionally gripping the bars with his little fingers as he peered at the shelves. They'd started in the produce section, and a panic had seized her. She should know what he eats, what he hates, and what he *should* be eating, what she, as his mother, should force into his tummy. She'd kept her calm, commenting on a few veggies in a light tone, "Oh, carrots. One of my favorites."

As they criss-crossed the aisles, Evan slowly began to volunteer some suggestions – Captain Crunch, Juicy Juice boxes, lime yogurt. This was the first time she'd had to look after him for more than a long weekend. John and that woman were off to Daytona for ten days. Certainly, he'd been hesitant, had probably even voiced his concerns to *her*. When he'd first mentioned it the initial twinge was of excitement, and plans for each night played across her mind, movies, kicking the soccer ball around, watching him play that new Zelda game while she drank a little gin and tonic...no, ice water.

But then all the other ideas came to mind: would he have everything he needed, enough clothes, all his soccer gear, mousse, toothbrush? Suddenly, that room with just the one poster of Cal Ripken seemed inadequate for such a long period of time. And the food…

After a few passes though the cart began to fill up, not with what her father would have called "live" food, but food nonetheless. Emma knew how to cook very little, but had asked Nurse Macnamara, of all people, for a few easy ideas. Mac 'n' Cheese with hotdogs cut up, Hamburger Helper, pizza, burgers, spaghetti.

Evan started to loosen up too, excited by the new snacks his mother was allowing him, the Fruit Roll-Ups and Dunkaroos. And as he became cheerier, his mouth would not stop running. He bounced around, still gripping the side of the cart, going on about how his new friend, a girl named Erin, tried to kiss him on the playground the other day and what the kids were saying.

As they looped down the next aisle, Emma noticed a man coming in the opposite direction. His cart was empty except for a loaf of white bread. He was dark-skinned and wore blue jeans and a white polo, bright white sneakers, his hair combed tight and neat. She stopped her cart, mid-aisle.

When Evan saw this, he said, "We like brown bread, Mom."

She nodded. "Okay."

The man did not look at her but continued down the aisle. One wheel on his cart squealed. Emma went forward, closer and closer, until their carts passed each other. She pretended to be looking at the English muffins behind him, but then their eyes met. His were a deep brown, and she thought she saw the vague makings of some sort of mark or blemish at the center of his forehead.

She pressed onward until she'd reached the end of the aisle. She turned, but the man was gone.

"Mom, brown bread."

"Right, hun. Grab the one you want. Quick, run and let's see how fast you can get it back to me."

He darted down the aisle, jumped up to grab a loaf, and ran it back to their cart. Then they turned into the next lane, which held on either side green and red and yellow cans of tomatoes and vegetables, stacks of dried pasta, and soup of all sorts.

"You like spaghetti, sport?"

He nodded, staring at something on the shelves.

Just then, the same man turned the corner and headed toward them. There was still only the bread in his cart. He pondered some distant jars of tomato sauce, held a few in his hands, but put nothing in his basket. There was a strange, calm gait to him, as if walking through a park in the spring.

Are you going to fucking buy anything?

Closing in on each other again, inching down the aisle.

Then a tug on her shirt. "Mom, this is the kind. This one. And we like the skinny 'sghetti noodles, and we like the shake cheese in the green can."

"Okay, hun."

She put the items into her cart and headed again toward the man. He took a can of black beans from the shelf and set it in his cart. Emma could feel her hands shaking. The man glanced up once and met her gaze, then went back to studying the shelves.

Nice try, my friends, nice try, fucking squirrel.

"Mama, bean with bacon soup too. I get to crumble Ritzes in there, if that's okay."

"Sure, bud."

The distance between them closed until the man was but a few feet in front of her. She nodded at him, but he seemed frozen and could only stare back. She and Evan finished the aisle and at the cross, picked out a few yogurts and a gallon of 2% milk and a roll of cookie dough, which sent Evan over the moon, jumping up and down, and also sent him into a story from school.

They turned down the next aisle, mostly cleansers, paper plates, napkins, in which Evan had no interest. Emma picked out a bottle of dish soap, a pack of sponges, and paper towels. As she loaded the items in her cart, the dark man turned the corner. She stopped and watched, with Evan chattering from below. The man seemed more interested in this aisle, or had likely realized he needed a fuller cart, so he began to load it with packs of toilet paper, plastic forks and knives, a mop, a bucket, some sort of bathroom cleaner. Then once again they began to wheel toward each other.

"Mo-om. Mom, did you hear? Mom?"

"Yes, hun. Of course we can. I'll be goalie."

"No, that's not how you play."

The carts got closer and closer...

You son of bitch. I've got my son with me. My son.

Suddenly, she was emboldened, and as the man grew nearer and nearer, a familiar calm washed over her, the one she felt in all those empty, blank rooms with no windows. As they passed, she said, "Nice day we're having isn't it?" With a huge smile.

The man seemed caught off guard and could only smile and nod and wheel his squeaky cart onward. They did not pass each other in the next aisle, and into the first frozen food section she still did not see him. But in the second set of freezers he again turned the corner, this time his cart brimming with stuff. He seemed more hesitant now, and Emma did her best to remain calm and to pick out the Pizza Rolls that Evan asked for, and the ice cream bars, and also to include a bag of frozen sweet peas and some hash browns. For a moment it struck her how bad a job of shopping she'd done. But the thought was chased away as she and the man once again closed the gap between them, this time her face fixed with a mean glare.

I know, motherfucker. Do I look scared?

As they passed, the man said, with a large smile, "*Very* nice day out, yes." Only the hint of an accent.

After clearing the aisle, Emma headed straight for checkout, and when Evan asked if he could get a Twix she snapped at him. "No!"

He was quiet as the woman loaded paper bags with their hodge-podge of groceries, quiet as they wheeled out of the automatic doors, across the parking lot, and over to her Volvo. She'd just finished loading the back and had shut the door when she noticed him again.

The man came out the front doors, without his cart, and walked at a fast pace toward them.

"Evan. Evan! Get in the car, now, lock the door. Do it, do as I say! Do *not* unlock it."

She reached around her waist as if her weapon would be there, but it was in a locked box in the back, unloaded, now covered by groceries. She flipped the back hatch open and dug through the paper bags, finding the tin box and crushing one of the bags with it as she fumbled with the key.

"Mom!" He was crying.

She unlocked the box just as he reached her.

"Hello," he said, in a cheery voice.

She turned and made a fist as if to punch him, which seemed to confuse the man.

He held his hand out. "My name is Matt."

Emma was still frozen with fear and only lowered her fist.

"What the fuck do you want?"

Now his face fell into complete shock, his eyes wide. "Well, I saw you in the market. We saw each other. 'Nice day we're having?'"

"I remember."

"Well," he said, and quickly reached for his back pocket. As he pulled his hand out, Emma against raised her fist. But he withdrew only a small pad and pencil. He spoke nervously, just that tint of accent. "I was wondering if I might have your telephone number." Before she could say anything he added, "Cute kid."

Her heart was thumping and her breath was fast as she lowered her fist. She turned and locked the box and set it back behind the groceries, then shut the hatch. He was still standing with pencil poised on notepad. She shook her head and walked around to the driver's side.

"Miss?"

She got in the car, closed the door. She was sweating now and her heart still pounded and her chest pulsed with quick breaths. Evan was crying. He sobbed and sucked in wet through his nose.

"Mama, what is it? Who is that man? Mama?"

CHAPTER 37

The first year in Cairo Fadi had neglected to send any word home. The occasional document arrived from Yusef, mostly financial statements or letters that required his signature. But Fadi had been adamant about cutting himself away from that other country. Even Alia. It was sickening at first, to sit and wonder about his little sister, who had filled such a large part of his worry throughout his life. He'd often sit with Fatu and guess about how she was doing, how she was handling their parents, school, a boy perhaps. On a few occasions Fatu had returned to the room with pen and paper. "Write to her then. Put down all these questions on this piece of paper."

"I cannot. This has to be complete. Even the painful parts, I must amputate. Even my dear sister."

"Well, you are a fool then."

It was soon apparent that Yusef had disobeyed his wishes and let their parents get a hold of his mailing address. In October he received a package, which held a three-page letter from his mother and another from Alia. Also included were a dozen pictures, mostly of Yusef and his boys, mouths wide open in smiles. He sat in the main room of their apartment with the fan on and read each letter in succession. His mother's handwriting had always been immaculate, a virtue she'd tried to instill in her kids, failing with all but Yusef. The letter was filled with news and well-wishes and questions about her granddaughter, as if he were right down the street. Yusef and his wife were expecting another, Alia was getting straight A's, Nourredine had quit smoking again. The diner's business — something their family talked about as others might discuss the weather — was given its own paragraph.

Then there was Alia's letter, crowded from edge to edge with messy script and crossed out words.

> You must return home. Dad is sick. He was sick before you left, and mom is now so thin and when I last visited Yusef at his house he drank four glasses of beer and has dark circles under his eyes. You wouldn't recognize our family.
>
> It isn't because of you. Papa is not working anymore, because of daily visits to the hospital, and because he is so weak. The doctors have told us it is a condition of his lungs, but seem to know nothing more than this. He coughs every minute. And I'm ashamed but I find myself unwilling to see him every day because of how he looks, and because of what it has made our mother into. She stands and works without ever stopping. She won't sit. She makes too much food and insists everyone eat, but she won't have even a bite in front of me. She talks about you all the time, asks if I have heard from you.
>
> I know you have reasons, beyond even what you told me when we last saw each other. I know you have been unhappy here, and I hope that you have found happiness in Cairo. But I am confused by your need to cut me off, to cut your family off. I don't know what to do. I can't turn to anyone here anymore. Our family has become sick. Mama is sick because of Papa. And Yusef I think misses you (perhaps more as a business friend than as a brother).
>
> I think I am going to leave school after this semester. I will just take some time off, move back home, look after mom and dad. Once they are better, I'll start back with my own life.
>
> But I beg you to come home, or at the very least write to Mama. Tell her you are well. One sentence would be enough I think to make her well. I don't know when school will be done for you. I know you have responsibilities there, with Fatu, with Nadat. We all long to see our little niece or whatever she is. Even more we long to see you, to have Fatu be a part of our lives.
>
> My biggest fear is that these letters will do nothing more than cause you unneeded worry while you have plenty of your

own over there. That isn't what I want. I hope you know that. Perhaps returning home is not realistic. I know you have always been more grown-up than I have, my big brother. I've thought this through, just so you know. And I am trying to do the adult thing, what you would do. A letter, just a letter from you, might be all it takes. Though Papa won't admit it, and does little more than grumble at your name, he is desperate to know what you are up to.

I really just hope this letter even finds you. Please don't be mad at Yusef. He had no choice. And if you suggest it, I won't bother you again. We all just miss you so much. I miss my big brother. Please tell us what you are doing.

Love,
Alia

ps: I found your old jersey at mom's. It is in good condition. I remember it being so big, like a blanket. I wore it every Saturday I knew you had a game. I am about the same age you were when you wore it. It is still far too big.

CHAPTER 38

In this place, routine was all he had. The simple fulfillment of an ordinal process: he expected this to happen, then it did, and next came this. Daylight shone through the little box window, and then night replaced it, each promising its return to the other. Emma appeared daily with her simple beauty and cigarette smell. Even Bauer and MacNamara, their presence reminded him that life had structure, was reliable.

So when his routine was shaken, when he hadn't seen Bauer or Mac-Namara for several days, longer for Emma, nerves took hold of him. A new orderly still showed up to deliver his meals, but the rest of the day he was left to peer around that same room. The hallway was quiet, no clacking of heels or squeaky rolling. Then one day his breakfast never came.

He sat up in bed. Square sunlight on the floor, so he knew it was well past morning. Then the light went gray. As he sat his mind was flooded with pictures from outside these walls. Little Nadat these last years, so malleable, her mind like drying paint as she grasped the world. "Where is Papa? Who is this man?" Learning for the first time what men were truly like. Every second of this damaged his tiny Nadat, every second he sat in this place, wondering if they would ever catch Marcel, if they would free her before it was too late.

The long lights overhead buzzed and blinked, and the silence grew fat and crowded his ears. Nadat being held up by a stranger, taught Arabic script, her little hands like Mama's hands, her little brain forming its way, the way she would live the rest of her life. *The flames and smoke.* Was this another dream of the inferno his wife met with? No, it was a vision of that day at Caldwell. So rare to recall that day, but once in a while visions of the terrible heat would call out.

Fadi glanced at the tiled floor below his high bed. He rolled onto his side, hesitated a moment, then pushed himself over, trying to brace as much as possible, but the drop was four feet or more, and he hit the floor with a thud, the wind leaving his lungs, his head clanging against the tiles. He lay there a few minutes to catch his breath, let the stars disappear from his vision.

Then he rolled himself over and over, only a few tiles at a time, which quickly exhausted his muscles, but he kept squeezing his core and pushing with his hand, until he'd reached the door. He sat up against the wall, already panting, and raised his hand over his head to grab the doorknob. When it released, his stomach truly sank. He hadn't expected the door to open and was briefly insulted that no one saw the need to lock the door to the room that held the invalid.

He threw the door open, wedged himself in the doorway, just enough to poke his head into the hall. The length of it was empty, same thing the other way. It ran for what seemed a mile in either direction. He rolled out of the doorway, and the door latched shut behind him, sending an echo through the silence. The floor out here was a dingier brown, the ceiling lights that same muted gray, the occasional bulb winking that evil, knowing wink. He'd only ever seen this place partially, during those times when the blindfold came loose, but he had no idea which way was which.

It felt as if they always took him left out of the room, so he faced right and started rolling again. He took long breaths, tucked his arm in, and rolled a dozen times in a row, as quickly as possible, then ducked into a slight alcove to catch his breath. He was amazed at how useless his muscles had become. The hall seemed to have gotten no shorter, and as he sat against the wall, only his panting could be heard, and when he'd caught his breath the silence of the place rang like a great tongueless bell.

Next to him in this slot was a fire extinguisher and a folded wheelchair. This rolling was far too tiring for him to keep up, so he took the chair in his hand and used his forehead to help unfold it. Then he pivoted to the front and tried once to lift himself into its seat, but the chair rolled away and he collapsed to the floor. He locked the wheel and tried again, pulling with all the strength in that one remaining arm, just able to get his ass to the edge of the seat and spin his legs around.

He sat a minute then started rolling the wheel. But twisting only the left wheel caused him to go right, so he had to alternate pushes with the same hand, and even jammed his right nub against the wheel to help it spin. It was even tougher than the rolling at first, but he finally got some momentum and kept a steady pace. He heard a door shut, turned to look down the hallway, no one there. So he picked up speed, shot closer and closer to the end of the hallway, looking back, looking forward. It came to a T. To the left there appeared to be a staircase, to the right a double set of glass doors. So he headed there, opening and squeezing through the first set, then the second, metal clanging sounds filling the hallway, certain someone was right behind him.

Beyond the second doors he rolled onto brown carpet, and the place had a different light, a perfume. It looked like a waiting room, old red-cushioned chairs, an empty coffee table, large windows overlooking the courtyard. He was in the southwest corner then, he knew these windows, little good it did. On the other side of the room was a single metal detector and two metal chairs, which sat empty.

The site of this allowed his exhaustion to catch up with him, and his head went light, his breathing quickened. What was he to do beyond these doors? He, with one limb, orange scrubs, a wheelchair, deep in the Virginia woods, down a deserted lane, first car reporting his odd presence to the cops. Who was he to rescue his daughter? Not a man, no longer a man. No money, no family, that tiny being he'd seen in her first instant balking at the newly introduced world, the same world he'd promised her was actually okay, now surrounded by another sort of men. And here he sat. *Papa, what happened to your legs? Your arm? I thought you were gone, and so I didn't want to stay here anymore, but I wanted to see you and mama.*

He sat and cried. A wailing he had not heard from another soul, a horror unequal even to that which made him want to leave this world, met with a complete and absolute wall. But he couldn't kill himself like a coward. There was no easy way out now, only a knowledge that she was out there, where he would never be.

"What the fuck?"

He looked up, his hazy vision slowly focused to reveal Emma, standing in the metal detector, clutching her bag.

"What the fuck is this?" She pulled out a can of mace, pointed it at him, and crouched slightly.

He laughed and sniffed tears. "Make sure to go for the right eye, please."

She stood there a while, then placed the can in her purse. "Goddamn it, Fadi."

"Yes."

Then she walked toward him. "We've gotta get you back."

"If we must."

And she stood behind him and wheeled him over to the double doors, pushed a button at the side, and they creaked open.

"What the hell did you expect to do?"

"I need to save my daughter."

Emma said nothing.

"She is alive. I know it."

"I don't know if you've looked in the mirror lately, but you have no legs. What the hell were you going to do?"

"They have her."

"You don't have much choice. That's what happens when you blow up a government building. And then lie."

They had turned down the main hallway. "What do you mean?"

She whispered. "You made me look like a fucking idiot, that's what."

Doors passed by on either side, solid things where men had likely stayed, been pressed by the likes of Mr. England or Emma or some other.

"It's my own fault, really, trusting you. You know, back in the day, I never would have done it, never would have told you about my family, about my son, never would have cared a scrap for what you're going through. I've gotten weak, and shitty. And this is what happens. You really did it though. It worked, and it was just enough to throw us off, just enough."

"Why haven't I seen you in so many weeks?"

"Because of your trick. I'm off it now. Don't you see? I'm done. I failed. I kept saying you were different, *give me time with him, he's changed*, he'll help us, he *wants* to help us. But you gave me a date and a place, and that just happened to match another source."

"Ali."

"And that date was perfectly five days too late. Just enough to throw us off, and…fuck. I'm doing it again."

His room would be coming up any moment now, the doors like second markers on a clock, Emma's feet ticking on the tiles.

"I need help."

"Well, you can ask at the next hotel you find yourself in. Fuck me if I'll offer you anything again."

"I know something."

"Oh yeah? Oh shit, great, well I'm all ears then."

"I know what's next."

"Suddenly on my side?"

"My daughter! Don't you see? Nadat."

Emma said nothing.

"She's alive." He tried to turn. "She's still alive. And she needs me. I'll do anything. You know I would do anything for her."

"You know how many people's daughters you just killed?"

"I know she's alive. She is with Marcel. I want him as badly as you do. I'll do anything, and I know something. I want to give you Marcel. I lied, but I want to fucking kill him too."

She stopped at the door, twisted the knob to find it unlocked. "Of course. Those fucking rookie bitches. Give a man more credit." She pushed the door open and shoved Fadi into the room and over to the bed. "I'm sure you can manage."

"Wait, just hear me." As he climbed back into the bed, into the groove in the mattress.

"Go jerk yourself off, lefty." She led the chair into the corner.

"Tully!"

She stopped.

"Tully did it."

Then she turned but didn't say anything.

"You know something, don't you? About him."

"What are you saying?"

"It was Tully. All along, I think. They planted him here, to kill me, originally. Tully is gone, isn't he?"

She collapsed into the chair, nodded.

"You know something. I'm right, aren't I?"

"What did he say?"

"He gave me the date. He gave me everything, told me about Ali. He had been listening to us all along, and he knew I was talking to you. He was in the room with Mr. England, but not when we were outside. He didn't hear what we discussed out there. He's American, but he had help getting into Harrison. He told me that someone made sure he was assigned here. First to kill me, then to simply listen and report. But Nadat is *alive*, Emma. He told me, and I know it's true. He knew things about her. She's with Marcel. We have to get her. She's alive."

"And you obeyed him."

"I had to. They would kill her."

"You could have told me."

"I didn't know how many others were with him. If it had gotten out that I talked, she would be dead." He looked at his hand. "About a year ago, I got my first message, and I didn't know what it meant at the time. It said they would kill her if I talked. And I thought all the while that they meant Alia. But it was Nadat. And you were the first person I trusted, the first person I talked to, even though I knew they'd penetrated this place. But when I heard that my little baby, my daughter…"

"They already did it."

She took a pack of cigarettes from her pocket.

His chest froze full of air. "Did what?"

Removed two, passed one to Fadi, who took it in his lips like a child. She lit his, then hers, sat back in the wheelchair.

"A train. Just north of Manhattan." Crossed an arm under her elbow, held the cigarette in the dim light. "Actually a tad later than they wanted. It was supposed to detonate under Penn Station. Luckily, it only killed about a hundred and eighty people."

CHAPTER 39

As Nadat grew bigger and more mobile, their usual study time began to change shape. Fadi still practiced his script in the living room, though Fatu now rarely had time to do her needlework, instead using the time to play with Nadat.

The family sat close in the main room, Fadi at the great wooden desk with pen in hand while Nadat and Fatu played with a new set of blocks. Today's practice was lost, because with every little tumble or near-question murmured by the little one, his head turned to watch her. He set the pen down.

They had been given an old Egyptian toy by Khalid, who had barely spoken two words about his own family but seemed always to have an inquiry as to the comfort and safety of Fadi's. The blocks were a rather simple game, each face having an Arabic character. The goal was to ultimately build a three-block-high structure with all adjacent characters forming a name or a place from the Koran. Nadat, of course, was too young to fully engage but loved instead to choose the same four blocks and stack and restack them, making the same pillar, then waiting until her dad was watching before smashing the column to the floor and giggling.

Fatu, meanwhile, was obsessed with the game, and while Nadat did her stacking, she engaged in her own complex building, shuffling and resorting the blocks with total concentration.

The day wasn't hot, but the fan was still on, and Fadi watched his girls from the side, the two of them sitting on the floor at the coffee table, flipping and organizing blocks. Fatu held a block before her face, rotated it to inspect each side's letter, and to her right Nadat watched as her mom did this, and so took her own block and mimicked her movements as best she could, and even her brow took on the same crinkled seriousness.

Then Fatu started over, placed that one block on the table, set another flush beside it. And Nadat's little hands worked at the same thing, placing two blocks as best she could snug against one another, looking at mom the whole time, her tiny hands already the same hue as her mother's, the fingers so small to be nearly useless in dealing with the blocks.

Fadi moved over to the couch, sat behind his wife, in the reverse of their usual position, and rubbed her shoulders once. "I got a letter from Alia."

"Lovely. When? How is she?"

"A while ago. She is fine."

"Good."

"My father is sick."

"Gudgy." She rubbed his thigh but did not turn.

"He has been for some time, even when we last saw him."

"But your mother wouldn't say anything."

"No, and she still wouldn't. But Alia…it seems my mother has taken a turn, as well. And Alia is quitting school to look after them. The place is falling apart."

She was quiet and stopped her hands, so Nadat looked up and stopped playing as well. In Arabic, "Go on." Continued with her blocks. "Will you visit them?"

"I think so."

"Will we come too?"

"If you like. Though I would rather not have Nadat make such a long trip."

"She would be good. And she should see her grandparents."

"I would like for her to, and you. I would like for Alia to see her niece. But I don't think it will be a good trip, besides."

"You don't want us to come."

"It might not be a good idea."

"Okay."

He stroked her hair. "I would miss you."

"Me too. How long will you be gone?"

"Two weeks, maybe three. We will arrange for the women to visit often."

"They're bores."

"But just so you are not alone."

She was silent a few moments, then said, "Perhaps I'll travel home while you're away. Maybe that is the best time. Marcel has been insisting on it, though I know he would like for you to come."

"That is a long trip too. In other ways. I would worry about the little mouse here."

"She'll be fine. And anyway my mother will dote on her and I'll likely have more rest."

"I worry about him too," he said, putting his hand on her belly. "Flying might be a bad idea."

She touched his hand, tapped it once. "It is okay this early. It is fine."

"We've never been apart for more than a few hours."

"But you will have your family, and I will have mine. I agree, now, that you should be alone with your father, your mother. They need you. And Alia needs you too. She needs her older brother."

She stacked three blocks then unstacked them, spun the blocks to study their characters. "Do you wish we had not come here?"

"No."

"Your family there is important."

"Are we going to talk about this again? I haven't abandoned them. But they choose to sit in the same place, and what we are doing here is important as well. You are my family. Marcel is my family."

Still looking down at the table, she said, "What about this little bundle?"

Nadat knocked over a stack of blocks and laughed.

"I suppose she is too."

At that, Nadat turned to her father, smiled, then stretched her arm toward the sky, thrusting a block in his general direction, mumbling some word not quite formed enough to hold meaning for anyone but her.

273

CHAPTER 40

"I've been in here a long time. How could I have had a hand in this?"

"You people believe in threes, don't you?"

He was quiet.

"We've known all along the *American Front* would feature a series of three attacks. Too bad we didn't know a little more."

"I had nothing to do with this."

"Your mark is on it. Your signature has become quite famous among the explosives experts. Without you, this would not have happened. And many people would still be walking around, seeing their children, their parents. Because of you they are not. Even if you didn't build it, you helped them. You taught them."

Fadi thought back to every meeting, every plan or strategy men had thrown at the wall. It was amazing, these brilliant minds, what they came up with when exhausted. But Marcel was ferocious with his planning and insisted they form strategies for hours, even after the next few attacks had been decided upon. It took only a few seconds of searching his memory before his mind finally rested on it. One of the new Alexandrians had been an engineer with a German railroad. It was late one night when Fadi suggested a timed charge. He always insisted on simplicity, a small kick in the right place, and the Alexandrian knew the right place to hit on a train. Simple bombs were smaller, easier to place, easier to hide.

She laughed. "Maybe if you had been there to oversee it, the timing would have been perfect, killed more people. Sorry to disappoint you."

Fadi lifted both arms as if to cover his face, but just the one hand did this, over one eye. "He is a monster. My God, he is a monster. But he fits this world so truly. He is what this place is. I am not in hell...I know that now. But I am still in this world. I can feel it. I had no idea. Caldwell. At Caldwell, he was still against it. Killing, I mean. He always told me he regretted Sudan, that women died, that local Muslims died."

She sat back in the chair and looked out the little window. "I must confess something."

He was quiet but turned toward her.

"I have failed. I don't know my job. I don't know you. You see, my only job is to know people, to really *get* them, what makes a man tick. Fuck, I can't keep a man past one date. I don't know what makes me tick, let alone one of you all." She laughed. "Let alone one of them." Nodding toward the outside.

"You did not fail."

"Many people died. The worst attack on US soil in our lifetime. And if we had predicted it...."

"You could not have. He likely kept this secret even from Ali."

"Ali." And she blew smoke, with a cold laugh. "That sick fucker. He was easy. Horrible, but no worse than what I saw in the desert. But he had nothing to give us. You, you were the one I could never figure out."

"I think you figured me just right. I am rotten."

She hesitated. "You are not rotten."

"We talked about many things I thought I'd never discuss again."

"Not everything though."

"We talked about my little one, and about Fatu giving birth, and how I used to play tea with Nadat, and your son and your weekends with him." With a dim smile. "Those two dates of yours."

"But there is a lot we didn't talk about."

Silence, then he coughed from the smoke.

"There are things you didn't tell me. We talked about you as a man, when you were a man like any one of the people outside these rooms. But what did it? You had a child, a wife."

Shaking his head. "I was turned very young, I know that now. Turned sour. Before the Five Pillars. I did McHallan. I did the embassy. But it was earlier. It's when you are a kid, you can be anything, and that's when you start being."

"Those were not Caldwell."

"I knew it was empty."

Though she tried, Emma could not conceal the shock on her face.

"It wasn't supposed to be, but the guard told me. I knew and I went anyway. It was my way out, my release."

She found the words leaving her mouth without thought. "Tell me what did it. Tell me."

His two shortened legs wiggled as he adjusted himself. They wiggled as if no longer connected to his mind. "I thought I knew horror." He looked at her, smiled, then looked away. "I thought I had seen the very bottom. Things done to me, done to my friends. And then the things I had done. Killing, taking lives in Sudan. But that isn't true horror, is it? Because I was still attached to this place. I had my lovely woman at home each night, and this tiny little being with skin so soft...and I had a sweet and innocent part of my life all the time. I knew I still had a corner of this world where I could build a good place, if not for me, then for them." His voice caught, and he lifted his hand to his jaw. "When they were taken from me, my beautiful wife, my little kitty, my life was also taken. I breathed, I ate, I drank water, I remained. But to end my existence, that was all I wanted. I was the target. To me, I was always the target."

"How did you first hear?"

With his face covered. "Marcel." Nodding. "Marcel. He was waiting in my apartment when I returned to Cairo. I can see it clearly even now. The door was unlocked, and I was about to chastise poor Fatu for it, but in the living room sat Marcel. I remember steam coming from the tea pot. He rose. He was so tall, and dark, and he motioned for me to sit down. My mind was blank, and so I let him guide me. I sat and he told me. He just said it. My God, 'Fatu is dead. Nadat is dead. Killed by Americans. I am sorry, my brother.' A huge silence. They were all I had holding me here. 'How?' That was all I asked. And he told me about the raid, how they had been visiting Ali's home south of Cairo. Men with guns. He told me every detail, the shooting, the screaming, the blood. My little, little girl. They had been looking for him. He told me he buried them both. I was not at Fatu's funeral. And I believed it. But all I could see was bright light and horrible, white heat. What my Fatu must have felt."

Then he wiped his eyes, turned to Emma.

"But now I do not know. She is dead, isn't she, my wife? That is the truth."

Emma nodded.

"And how did she die?"

"Our intelligence isn't perfect. We had always believed that both were killed in some sort of firefight or explosion. But records are mostly classified, and there are no death accounts, not of any foreign women. It seems to be true, Fadi."

"Marcel explained it so completely. So calmly. I remember it even now, but at the time it was as if I were being guided. I was like a ghost. I could hear words, and I knew the chair stood beneath me. But I felt nothing. I did not cry, was not angry. I just listened, and Marcel's voice became the only thing. He didn't blame anyone, at first. He simply explained that Fatu and Nadat had been killed, that they had died quickly. Time no longer existed. Marcel must have sat there with me for hours. He offered me tea, but I don't think I had any. Finally, he took the small water pipe that sat on my side table, one I had never used, and he placed some sort of brick onto the bowl, told me to breathe deeply, said it would help me sleep."

The room was quiet. His cigarette ash had grown long and crumbled onto the bed. Emma leaned forward and wiped the sheet.

"When I awoke, he was in the living room, a pot of tea ready." His voice grew slow. "I thought the noises were Fatu. When I awoke I felt the world around me again, though it was hazy. It took seeing Marcel in my home to remind me. And that is when the true pain began. I was paralyzed. I couldn't move from my couch. I could not eat or drink, and I could not think. Marcel was there the whole time, sitting in the room with me, making me drink water, eat a bit of bread. And we prayed, words over and over, for hours. And the smoking too. Whatever was in the sheesha he had brought, it made me go blank, if only for a spell.

And I would sleep a few hours maybe then wake to a flood of hot anger and disbelief. I yelled to him, 'I want to die, let me die, let me be with them.' This went on for days, perhaps a week. It was then that Marcel began to offer me comfort. 'Their deaths will not go without meaning, without punishment. They are my family, they are in heaven, and you will see them again. We will have vengeance, and people will know why.' At first these words meant nothing. There wasn't a single thing on earth, not the cup of tea, not the smoke, not the sun from the window. And not Marcel's anger, or even mine. There was nothing real left for me. Yet Marcel went on. He spoke at length, over and over again, repeating that we would have vengeance, that my family had not died in vain. Over and over. Then I would burst into tears, breathing quickly, until my head was light. Numbing myself, only to wake and find the feeling returned. There was Marcel as I sobbed, repeating, offering the pipe. It took weeks, but he was always there. 'We are your family. Your family is not lost. Your time here on earth is not over. Fatu is in heaven. Nadat is in heaven. Pray with me, my brother. Pray with me.' *Pray with me, pray with me.*"

Fadi took one long draw from the cigarette and did not attend to the single tear that flowed down, but sniffed and took another pull.

"I prayed. I spoke to my daughter. I told her how much I love her and told her to look after Mama. That I was sorry. I prayed to God and submitted myself to Him. For hours I prayed, asking for answers or at least a single voice, for comfort. And then I just prayed to free my mind of all other thought. And I did so for hours at a time, until prayer was all I heard in my head. And God was my friend, and Marcel was, and that was all."

"How long was it before you went back to group? Before you started again?"

"A month, maybe more. But it was different then. I didn't speak. It was Marcel, it was Ali. No one asked for my opinion anymore. Things had changed in the group too. More paranoia, fueled by Ali, thinking we would be discovered any day now. Then they caught Sarhan and his brothers at the airport. That was when we evacuated, went to the coast, to Alexandria. I followed Marcel wherever he went, did whatever he said. We all rode in a van, with Marcel leading prayers all the way. We put what little things we had brought into the small shared rooms. Then Marcel suggested we walk to the shore. So I followed. And looking out at the ocean I could see nothing but space and water. It was as if we'd come to the end of the world, and I remember feeling at that point that he and I had crawled here together, that we had finally lost, and I could feel the pressure at my back, pushing me toward the sea. The sun was going down, the air was neither hot nor cold, and the waves chugged nearer and nearer. It was just the two of us now, the waves, Nothingness lapping right at our feet."

CHAPTER 41

They sat at the dining room table, a place setting neatly arranged for each, with clean glasses and plates and placemats, two candles in candlesticks that were never to be lit. Lara had made a sort of Moroccan chicken she'd attempted only once before, with rosemary and butter and oil, couscous and snappy haricots verts on the side. Alia and the three men sat, at her insistence, as she brought out dish after dish. They assumed it was over after the main course and two sides had arrived — Lara always made exactly one main course and two sides for their Sunday family dinners. But tonight she had slapped Yusef's hand when he reached for the serving spoon. *Wait.* Out she came with a bowl of heaping, chunky mashed potatoes, wooden spoon like a flagpole; in the other hand a spinach salad. Now, finally, Nourredine took the bowl of couscous in his hand, but Lara warned him to sit still, then she went back to the kitchen. This time it was a lentil, lima bean, and red pepper salad, along with a basket of buttered baguette slices.

Nourredine studied her as she finally sat down, although as soon as her butt hit the seat she sprung up and said, "Drinks!"

"We're good, we're good. Sit, darling."

Lara had greeted everyone that night with plates of cheese and crackers, sliced green apples, crostinis with jam, and of course tea service and sparkling cider. They had sat in the dining room only on special occasions, perhaps a dozen times over the course of Georges's childhood. The tablecloth still evoked memories of not being allowed to touch anything, the good silver, the good plates and glasses, things meant to be seen but not used. He remembered the feeling, when he was finally allowed to eat, of not wanting to harm the delicate plates or spill a drop on the beautiful tablecloth.

Lara brought up the weather, the diner, Yusef's kids, light things so as not to tap on the tension around the table. And Nourredine grumbled when asked simple questions, his voice rough when forming whole words.

"So," Alia said, folding her hands together, "when do I see pictures of my niece?"

"I don't have any."

"You didn't bring any with you?"

Georges smiled as he wiped his mouth. "I don't have a camera."

"Oh."

Nourredine began coughing in a slow, tough wave, which went on a while. Then he said, "It would be nice to see pictures of my granddaughter."

The table was quiet after that, save for delicate fork sounds and glasses on the padded table. Georges could feel Yusef looking up at him every so often, as if fighting to hold in something he had to say. Finally, Georges faced him and lifted his brow. "How have things been this year, Yusef? In addition to the grand totals I see on our statements."

"Pretty big news, just a few days ago." Nodding, chewing. He glanced at their father. "We got them." Still nodding, though Georges said nothing. "McConnell, the Hancock. We're in." He laughed. "We got the contract to the mightiest building in Boston, what we've been trying for all these years."

At first Georges's body clenched in a jealous fist, that his little brother had been successful where he had failed for so long. It was as if some ancient speck of his former business self still slumbered deep in there. But his muscles loosened, and a smile spread on his face. "Well done, Yusef. You have done it, finally. I hope you and some of the boys celebrated."

"*We've* done it. It was your car assignment system that really did it. They'll be the first ones to use it."

He shook his head and skewered two green beans. "You've done what I could never do. This is yours. You should be proud."

At this Yusef seemed to slowly deflate, and once again the table was silent. Georges hurried to clean his plate then rose, asked if anyone needed something from the kitchen.

"You're not having any more?" Lara asked, scanning the lavish setup.

"That was delicious, Mom. I can't eat another bite."

"But you saved room for dessert?"

"Of course, yes."

"Good, I figured one of you kids could pick up a few cartons at Weese's."

Alia cut in. "Georges and I can go."

Georges sat at the table a while longer and waited for Alia to finish. She rushed and carried her plate into the kitchen. Then she and Georges put on coats and hats, headed downstairs and into the cold night. On the sidewalk, Georges let out a long puff of breath under the streetlight.

"It's not *that* bad."

The sidewalks were narrowed by snow, and mushy in places, so they walked in the road. Few cars were out, and the short trip to the store took them down lonely streets where most window lights were dim or off by now.

"What is Cairo like?"

"What do you want to know?"

"What you do every day? And Nadat and Fatu. Everything."

"I teach."

"Do you like that? Does that take up much of your time?"

"I like teaching, yes. The kids there are very serious, and it's good when you feel like you're imparting something useful. You can really feel that."

"My teachers are slightly less enthusiastic."

"You've quit school."

"We're talking about *you*. What do you do at night? Is Cairo fascinating?"

"We live in a very humble place. I spend a lot of time with my friends. We talk about where we are in the world, as Muslims, as men. And Fatu and I like to spend quiet nights or mornings together with Nadat." He smiled. "She is walking, has these great little hands and fingers that like to point at things. That's how she asks questions."

"Maybe I could visit."

"That would be nice."

They walked on, salt mincing underfoot, in and out of street light. Snow-clumped cars on either side. At the corner of Willow and Broadway they came to Weese's. The door chimed as they entered, and the new woman at the counter greeted them with a foggy Boston accent. They ordered cookies n crème and a carton of strawberry for their mom. Georges paid and then looped the plastic bag around his forearm and tucked both hands in the pockets of that puffy coat he'd had since college.

They set off down the street, though a different route now, as Georges always insisted on, never the same way back. Alia linked her arm around her brother's. They walked quietly a while. There was the sound of their coats only.

"Why did you come back?"

"Your letter."

"But we never hear from you. I thought I'd never see you again. And now you come back."

"Our family is sick, isn't it?"

"I guess I don't understand, how you can leave us but still care enough to come back."

"I care very much."

"Then why don't you live here? You would live near Mom and Papa, Yusef, me. We'd get to see your family and Mom could watch Nadat sometimes, and I could."

"I moved for a reason."

She looked at her feet. "Why?"

"Because of what it was like to grow up here. And what this place has become to me."

"I was always happy. Weren't you?"

"No." He fought to keep his voice calm and level. "And when I was young I tried to make myself happy. I tried to squeeze in here and change myself to fit. But when I became an adult I realized that's not what you do. You find places that suit you. Not the other way around.

And I want my daughter to grow up in a place that suits her."

"But it's safe here. And you have done so well."

"It's poison. It's a drug here. I finally feel like I am truly living."

"Doing what?"

"It would be tough to describe."

"Thank you."

"Not because of you."

They walked on a few more seconds and passed under a street light that buzzed overhead and then grew quiet at their backs. "You know I have always loved you, very much. You will always be my little sister, no matter how beautiful you become. And I want to make sure things were the best they could be for you."

"I know. You have."

"And when I left, it was hard leaving you. And I want to write, and I want to be a part of our life. I made a very difficult choice, but it was an absolute choice. I want to imagine you growing old and happy and never having to face some things I have had to face. I love you very much."

She squeezed his arm. Alia had never been one to put things into words. Like her mother, she liked to dot the lives of her family with little touches, a grip of the shoulder or kiss on the cheek, wordless but connected through that other way. As they turned the corner to Kidder Ave., she latched his arm tight and set her head on his upper arm.

They arrived back at the house with their noses frozen and red. Georges and Alia stripped off their coats, hung them in the hall closet, and each carried a paper bag up the stairs. The first two steps creaked. Lara always insisted on scooping the gooey ice cream into bowls rather than letting the kids simply dig into the cartons. They sat around the coffee table spooning gobs of strawberry or cookies n crème into their mouths, though Nourredine's bowl, with a single scoop in it, sat untouched.

Afterward, Lara took up the dishes and disappeared into the kitchen. Alia following her a few minutes later. Then Yusef rose, and for some reason dusting his pant legs, announced he needed to go home to the kids. He shook hands with Georges and simply patted his father's shoulder as he left the living room.

Muted soccer players scrambled across the TV screen.

"No ice cream for you, Pop?"

"My stomach doesn't love the stuff anymore."

"Painful?"

He shook his head. "Just a bad idea."

He nodded and looked around the room. No photos, save for a single heavy frame with Lara's parents in front of their old house outside Quebec City, a few pieces of twisted bronze metal their mother had gotten at an alleged Moroccan antiques store. She had opted mostly for the bits of fabric, draped on the mantle, on the side table, or covering most of one wall. These things did not rumble memories of his childhood; only the smell of the place did that.

"You know..." Looking down. "Fatu wanted to come. I thought it better that she not make the long trip."

"I see."

"But then she goes to the coast. Not a short jaunt, itself."

"To see her people."

"She took Nadat with her. I didn't want her to travel though."

Nourredine just nodded, made a sound in his throat.

"Because she is expecting another child."

Here Nourredine took in a long, rattled breath. And his face remained stony a few seconds, before a smile finally pulled up the corners of his mouth, and he turned to face his son. "That is a blessing, my son."

"It is, God willing she is healthy."

Then his eyes widened. "Do you think she is not?"

"No, no. I'm just saying, I worry. I worried with Nadat too."

"She will be fine. How many months?"

"About twelve weeks. She has no belly but will likely be bigger the next time I see her." And here the length of his trip finally fell on him, the nearly three weeks he would be away, not having thought about the little changes his wife or his daughter would go through. And he longed not to be back in Cairo but simply to see the two girls again, to have them suddenly appear in this room. For his beautiful wife to embrace his father. He wished Nourredine could see the way they sat together, could see that he was a man, a husband. Just a flicker of his family life that his father might feel justified in having brought him into existence.

"You aren't here long."

"Eighteen more days."

"Do you have everything you need? Are there things here you cannot get in Cairo?"

"Maybe a thing here or there."

"Perhaps a son this time?"

"That would be nice."

"Though daughters are wonderful when they're little and will love you more as you grow old."

They sat in silence a while, distant, muted clanging from the kitchen. Then nodding from Nourredine. "You remember, when you were just a boy? I showed you a football, an American football."

"I remember."

"It fell to the ground, and it bounced so strangely. I would not let on, but I was also terrified by this new ball, so different from a soccer ball. But not you. I remember your face as your eyes followed it. You had this look, so confused at first, horrified even. But within a few seconds your eyes changed. You kicked it where it settled, watched it flail and skitter. But now your face was different. Within about two seconds you had gone from shock, at what you had been given, to determination. Determination to figure out this new situation, to tame it, control it. And you did. Very well, I would say."

"And you did all this to build that sort of thing in me?"

He laughed. "No. You know why I did it. For money, for college."

Georges smiled, and so did his father. They sat still a few minutes with the two ladies in the next room cleaning plates.

"I look at my son now, soon to be a father twice, blessed as you have always been. I wonder, have you figured out the world you were always so determined to find your place in?"

He paused then shook his head. "I don't know, Pop."

Nourredine stared at the ball of strawberry ice cream in his bowl. It had begun to soften. "The diner will close." He said this as a father might announce the time of a first pitch or perhaps a warm front moving in.

"Why?"

"We cannot afford it. Your mother, me, we cannot work there anymore."

"Pop, Yusef and I have more than enough money to pay for your treatments. You'll never have to worry about any bills."

"That is not all. It isn't money. If we cannot be the ones running it, working each day, assuring quality to all those customers, then the diner cannot continue."

"You need that place. Mom needs it too."

He laughed. "She won't be shedding any tears over this."

"I know for a fact the diner brings in more than enough revenue to stay open. You just need to hire a manager. Hell, promote Hamid. He's more than bright enough to do the books, and he knows the place inside and out. Mom and Alia can show him things too."

He shook his head. "No. If we do not run it, then why would we continue to own it?"

"Because you *built* it, Dad."

"Someone might buy it, maybe keep the name. But it will no longer be ours. That is final. It is decided."

"You can't simply throw away all that hard work. That place has been everything to you. To our family."

Nourredine had been staring resolutely at his ice cream, but now his eyebrows lifted in curiosity, and he turned his head slowly toward his son. "Why does it concern you? You have gone."

His father's eyes held on him a few moments, until he had to look away. The smell of the living room, that old scent of mint and a bit of smoke. Staring at the rug. "I still care very much for my family."

"We will be fine, your mother and I. We will keep our home and our children and grandchildren. We would like to see our little Nadat and her brother." Nourredine drew in a long breath, which rattling on the way in and blew heavy on its way out as if leaving very little behind in its host. "I did not mean to be harsh, Georges. This is a difficult time for us. We could use you here. Of course losing the diner is devastating. It is truly devastating. I realize you do not understand. I was a simple business man. My dream was to own something, to build it and have

287

that feed my family. I know you built something even greater, but it was not what you wanted, as you were able to give it up. To give this up…I do not know what to do now."

"I was always proud of what you built for us here, Pop. You built my business too. Yusef and I, we simply continued what you taught us. I was always very proud."

After a long while Nourredine slapped his thigh. "What the hell." And he leaned forward over the coffee table with a little wheezing, dug his spoon into the mush of strawberry, and shoved a huge chunk into his mouth. Then he sat back and closed his eyes as his cheeks went from full, slowly, slowly, to empty.

CHAPTER 42

*May faith smite our enemies. May His hand at last be made force and might
on this physical earth, and may It guide the righteous and the faithful and
disappear the unbelieving and the wicked and the impure. May the True at
last blanket this physical earth with His word and with His presence and
cast the unfaithful forever into the abyss. God is great, God is great. It is He
who is the Name, and taken from his flesh are we, as it is to us on this physical earth to bid His word and His will. Praise be to God in Heaven and to
those who carry His name. Praise be to God.*

A numbness in both knees, a numbness at his forehead. Heat and
sweat and grains of sand and silence. Then a hand on his shoulder. It
was Marcel. "We must stop, Fadi."

So Fadi paused with his head to the floor and knees purple, and at
last he sat up, then rose with difficulty as his legs had fallen asleep. He
stumbled and fell seated on the concrete. Then Marcel grasped under
his arm to pull him up.

"It is evening. We are going to supper."

"I will have bread at my room."

"Some water would do you good, my brother. Some tea. Come
with us."

Fadi looked about the room: Khalid, Ali, Jesper, and all the
Egyptians, plus the two new members from here in Alexandria. "No. I
am tired. I'll go to my room."

Marcel grabbed Fadi's shoulders and pulled him in for a long and
ill-fitted hug. The others passed in front of him, each making a sign
or touching Fadi's arm. Then the room was empty. Such a small place,

underground, smooth concrete floor and cinderblock walls, the prayers written on cloth hung at the front.

He locked the door and headed down Mansour, away from the ocean. Alexandria was cool this time of year, and the sea had turned violent the past week, waves shouldering past each other to splatter on the sand. A street vendor opened his cart after evening prayer and set out papers and warm bottles of Coke. Fadi climbed the staircase to their shared rooms. Six of them split an apartment, with single beds and a small kitchen, a tiny first room with space for their shoes and little else. The other men tended to gather for tea in Khalid›s room. But Fadi never joined them, nor did he speak with them much, except when Marcel engaged him.

When they had been called to flee Cairo, he could take only a few of his things with him, though he wanted very little. This apartment, these barracks, had been secured by Alexandrian friends of Khalid's, men who now joined their ranks. But Fadi's money had been cut off, impossible to wire and, Marcel advised, dangerous to pursue. So all the men now crowded these small rooms, and they prayed in a stuffy basement, and they lived nearly every hour together as they planned and stewed and waited for secret money to reach them.

He sat on the bed with his bare feet on the floor, gazing at his toes. He wiggled them once and finally lied on his pillow with his feet up. Circulation had returned, and with it pain. Blood brought motion to his legs and to his head and revived feeling there. The room was blank, the ceiling was blank, and his mind now away from prayers and no longer distracted by movement was flooded with pictures, as always happened at night. He painted scenes of his poor little girls burning and wretched with pain and heat and fear. His version always contained prolonged suffering, and screams and reaching for the father's hand, but none came. Never quick, never mercy. His littlest one unknowing, such a new mind as it tried to grasp and order the world, confused by the enormity of the destruction it wielded, waiting for description or meaning, or else waiting, already in her short life, for it to be ended. And every night he saw these figures and never wished them away or sought refuge from their toll but hoped only that he would see an end worse than theirs that he might erase this past. He prayed again, wordless, and sleep came over him to extinguish this place.

CHAPTER 43

"Where is Marcel now? Do you know?"

Emma shook her head.

"Ali. You caught him, he talked."

"Nothing. He told the truth, I know that, but somehow Marcel was tipped off. We staked for days, several places, no sign. Ali gave us a dozen possible targets. By now Marcel's gone. He's in Egypt or some such fucking place. He's jerking off to virgins in heaven, surrounded by mounds of cash, the lousy cunt." She caught Fadi's gaze. "Sorry."

"What will happen to me?"

"I don't know."

"What will happen to you?"

She shrugged. "This is all over. I'll find a new job. Or an old one."

"I'm sorry…for what I did. It was for my daughter. I thought. Now I will never know where she is. I will never see Marcel again, or hear from him." His eyebrows lifted. "What about Tully?"

Emma shrugged, then looked down.

"Then she is lost. I am helpless here, or wherever I end up."

They sat until their cigarettes were done, and she took his and squashed both against the underbelly of the bed, threw the nubs in the garbage.

He shook his head. "We have to catch him."

"We have nothing."

"What did Ali give you?"

"I can't tell you that. Nothing."

"A date, a place?"

She took another cigarette from the pack, put it in her lips, but didn't light it. "What if he gave us a date? So what? Marcel knows who was in here, what they knew, assumes they told."

"But Tully only attended to injured men, right?"

She said nothing.

"Would he have seen Ali? He wouldn't have gotten to him. What Ali has told you could be true."

"He'll hide, run, whatever."

"He won't hide. He won't stop."

"You don't know men like him. When we're at our most alert, they're at their most cowardly."

"I know Marcel."

"Do you?"

"Yes." He nodded.

"And you believe he has Nadat?"

"He does. In my heart I know it."

"Maybe."

At this, Fadi's eyes opened wide, though the dead one a little less.

Emma was silent a few moments, but then a strange sensation came over her, one she'd noticed happening more with Fadi. The usual strategic filter of her words was lifted, and she simply spoke. "Perhaps Marcel planned to kidnap Nadat. He planned to take her all along, and he had her when you were made to think your family was dead. That entire year, as he made more plans to use you. You had lost heart, hadn't you?" She nodded. "Yes, you had. And Marcel can see that a mile away. He's renowned for it. He sensed it in you, his friend, his mentor. It must have crushed him to see you turn from his great cause. So, in one swoop he managed to take away everything you loved, gain the daughter he'd always wanted. And make you into his pretty little bomb. To accomplish that was worth everything to him, even the life of his only friend."

There was not a sound as Fadi's mind traced through all that was just said. Then back to every conversation, every scheme Marcel had collected and molded from the group as if amassing an arsenal. There were so many: cruise ships, skyscrapers, planes, stadiums, a stack of plans that had been germinating in that insane place, that little room in old Cairo.

But something told him this would be the last. Something about Marcel. McHallan was a symbol, and it was American, but no people were inside, and Sudan was an American presence on Muslim soil, but not American enough, not home. Caldwell he'd always seen as a step back, even with an American martyr delivering it, especially when it turned out to be empty. And the train had been a step back too, a failure.

Emma took a breath as if to speak.

He could see Marcel stewing, starving for something bigger. But nothing they'd spoken of in group would do it. The bigger targets would take too long, would be too impossible now that they were on the run, that Fadi was no longer there to invent the incendiary. What was it? More images flashing, Marcel's ghoulish face, the chubby puffs of Nadat's cheeks, Fatu, white heat, such heat, and fear and unknowing. *Your education, your knowledge, will not be a waste. God has always had a plan for you. Just like our meeting, your expertise was formed for a reason.*

"What's the date?"

She rolled her eyes.

"Is it the fourth?"

He watched as she pulled from the cigarette.

"It is. It's the fourth of October. Isn't it?"

She shrugged.

"The Hancock building. Boston."

She looked up at him and moved as if to shake her head.

"He'll use the elevators. My God, he will use my elevators. And it will be during the day, when that building is packed full. The biggest building in Boston. If Khalid and Faruz are still with him, they'll know how to do it."

"Because you showed them."

"We spent a few weeks on a scenario before coming to America. We drew plans, and I showed them exactly how the elevators work, just what would be needed."

"Nothing we have is pointing us to the Hancock."

"Nothing?"

She paused. "Maybe it's been mentioned…why the fuck am I telling you this?"

"All I know is that it's something we've talked about. A long time ago, I explained it to him, that the Hancock was one of the few buildings in Boston we couldn't get into, my old company that is. It's the tallest, and it's not as hidden as one in New York. Taking that down would devastate the skyline, and Boston is much easier to negotiate. And..."

His gaze held fast on the window.

"What is it?"

"It wasn't too long ago that Yusef won the contracts there. So I'd imagine our company still has access to the building's system. You don't think he'd know that, though, do you? That he would go to Yusef, would hurt him?"

"Maybe. I don't know. We don't even know that it's his target. You've been in here a while."

His speech became rapid. "But why not put guards there, or surveillance, or whatever? Isn't it worth it? Isn't it worth saving hundreds of people to have a few men there, watching. Put them there weeks beforehand and even afterward. Put them there ready to spring."

"It's not that easy. There are dozens of potential targets, dates. It's not possible to have men on each for weeks at a time. We have to choose carefully."

"This is our only chance, our only possible link to Marcel."

"*Our* only chance?"

"He has my daughter. Yes, *our* only fucking chance."

She exhaled very faintly, looked at the ground.

"You don't believe that she's alive."

"I have no proof, Georges. I've been trained to always ask who's doing the telling, and what's driving him to say what he's saying. A psychopath told you this, a man who'd been living a false life for over a year, someone trying to mislead you, to get you to do what he wants. Men like that will do whatever they need to. Think about what Tully would try to use. You have nothing else in your life..."

"Thank you."

"To him you have nothing. He wouldn't know to use Alia or your mother or Yusef. He would have invented this, this improbable situation, that Nadat had been kidnapped so many years ago. I'm sorry. I shouldn't have said what I said."

He glared out the window, that little TV set of light all these months, shook his head. Then he dabbed at his eyes, first the living one. "I know this is true. I know that she is still alive. And to catch Marcel is the only way to save her. I have killed many people, and I don't know what is beyond this place, but I will have to answer for it. I already have begun to. But my Nadat is one part of me, the last part, that is still right. And it is unmistakable to me. She is alive." He faced Emma. "We need to catch Marcel, and kill him or bring him in and torture him. Bring Mr. England back here and set him loose on Marcel. I don't care. He is the only way to my Nadat."

CHAPTER 44

The ocean clouds sagged their thunderful jowls, gray gloom shifting ever closer and trumpeting their presence to the city. Bare bulbs hung from the basement ceiling, though darkness was all Fadi knew as he prayed. His eyes were sunken, his forehead prayer worn, and his thin robe hung slack from his bones. *May faith smite our enemies. May his hand at last be made force and might on this physical earth, and may it guide the righteous and the faithful and disappear the unbelieving and the wicked and the impure. May the True at last blanket this physical earth with His word and with His presence and cast the unfaithful forever into the abyss. God is great, God is great. It is He who is the Name, and taken from his flesh are we, as it is to us on this physical earth to bid His word and His will. Praise be to God in Heaven and to those who carry His name. Praise be to God.*

"Come, Fadi." Marcel lifted him by the arm.

As the others closed the place and went for their regular tea, Marcel brought him out into the street. "Why don't we walk?"

Fadi nodded and followed Marcel. Shopfronts were sealed, street-lights floating in the air, rumblings from the sea beyond the buildings. Two cats ran past them, chasing each other.

"We have been here many months."

Fadi nodded.

"Some of the men think we are on the run." He turned and smiled. "Of course, we know that is not the case."

He was silent.

"They will know we are truly not on the run when we show our strength next. And the time to do so is growing near. You understand this?"

"Yes, I do."

"This target will shake America to its core."

"We will show at once that we have the power and conviction to destroy something so secure, so huge." He paused, seemed to consider something. "But there is something missing. There will be something very special about this, my brother, bigger than McHallan, bigger than Sudan. *A symbol*. They have destroyed many Muslim families, *many*." He voice turned to a whisper. "America destroyed *your* family, my brother."

Yes, my family. America.

"Without you, this would not be possible. Your device, the simplicity, the genius. I always told you that God's plan for your education would show itself. And it has."

The wind increased a moment then went soft. A last wink of red sky on the horizon down the street, over the ocean.

"You know, my brother, I owe my life to you."

Fadi made an open gesture with his hands.

"It's true. I was so terribly lost. I had landed in a place unknown to me. If I hadn't met you, my life would have been poisoned, aimless. You were an older brother to me, and you saved my life. I thank God every day for allowing us to meet. For allowing us to have a family in common. My sister loved you dearly as well. My poor sister, who was not meant for this world any longer than God allowed. I know you will see her. You will see her. And you will be a hero in heaven. It will be beautiful."

He faced Marcel, his brow lifted. "And my little Nadat?"

"And our little girl as well."

My God, you are great and merciful and your hand will guide me through all darkness.

"Fadi, Georges. This is the most important time in Muslim history. It is a war, and we have been chosen to fight it. You and I. The others are but sheep. It was obviously the two of us meant to meet all those years ago, to forge a brotherhood, to lead. We are the only two important parts of this weapon. And you know this and have felt it all along. Our journey here on this earth is nearing an end. At last, you will be reunited with Fatu. With Nadat. But our last action on this earth is the mark by

298

which we will be judged in heaven. Yours will be the most monumental of all Arabs, of any man in history."

He turned to Marcel then faced the sidewalk again.

"Yes. The importance of this goal is massive. It will send many messages. That we can destroy such a place, that we are choosing a building from which so many attacks have been designed. But finally, my brother, is the most important piece, the final message we will send, one that will allow us to show we have God on our side, that we do not fear death, to show our confidence in the paradise awaiting us as we take our action. This is done through sacrifice, alone."

Marcel stopped, so Fadi stopped. Marcel turned to him and placed a hand on his arm. He smiled. "I know what life has become for you. I see it daily. Your pain. It is my pain as well. My dear sister, and little Nadat, without a chance to live the pious life of a Muslim woman. And you, my older brother, I know what is in your heart, and I know the dark place this world has become for you."

"I follow you. Now, my life is for God and for you. And nothing more."

"But I have found your future, the only one befitting the man who led me from my own darkness. You will be a symbol, and your grief will be extinguished."

Fadi looked at him.

Nodding. "That is right. I am offering you the highest honor any Muslim can know. Monuments will be built for you. Your action will serve God's greatest purpose." He smiled. "And you will be brought to the very feet of God, where you will see your girls again. You will see your beautiful girls."

My God, my eyes and ears, my heart, guide me.

Tears filled his eyes for the first time in many months. "My God. Thank you. Thank you."

Marcel reached his long arms around him and squeezed. "I love you, my brother. I always have. You will be the messenger and the message, and you will return home. This darkness…" Touching Fadi's chest. "… will be consumed by an eternal light."

Fadi collapsed into tears and clutched the cloth on Marcel's back.

That night outside the library. The flash of white light he had seen all those years ago. Light pure and heavy to erase all sense and encompass all things. Light that was His whisper and His breath. *God, please let me see them again.*

CHAPTER 45

Emma sat with Reg in conference room A, two misty cups of coffee and a cigarette, she in her gray sweatshirt with newly washed hair in a ponytail, Reg in nice shirt and slacks. She caught his glance, lifted her eyebrow as if to suggest she too realized how silly this all was. Reg had made the very diplomatic suggestion of not mentioning anything about Ali's release, knowing it was a point of tension for Alec, Bauer, and most of the department.

Two weeks prior, the CIA had negotiated an extradition of Ali. He was to be handed over to Saudi intelligence. Swiftly, he was. But a few days ago they'd gotten word that Ali had fled custody, or at least never ended up in Saudi Arabia. Most presumed it was his connections with the royal family that got him out, though Faisal and his brother, Turki, head of intelligence, denied this vehemently. To Emma and Reg this meant, simply, that their carefully sealed-in intelligence ring had now been exposed to outside air. Ali had no doubt blabbed, poison to interrogators.

Right on time, Alec Randolph walked in, followed by Bauer, the site of whom surprised Emma as she rose to shake Alec's hand.

"I've asked Agent Bauer to join us." The two men sat across from them. "He's been here quite a while, Emma."

She paused a moment. "Any word on Ali Al-Jeddah?" And smiled.

Both men pretended to ignore her. Randolph had brought with him a manila folder, which he set on the table. He hovered his hands over it, hesitated a moment. "We are very much behind here. I don't know what else to say." He leaned back. "We should have been able to get much more from this group by now. And this...*strike*, that we've been anticipating for so long. It's happening, and soon. Now we've got at least..." Turning to Bauer. "...how many links?"

"Eight."

"Eight men in these walls who have played some role, that have *some* connection to AT. Including two very high-ranking heads. Emma, I know you got a juicy bit of intel from Mr. Al-Jeddah, a few places Karim usually meets him. We were set, we surveilled, we timed, we waited. We got nothing but that low-level grunt. I know that disappointed us all."

She took a long breath.

"And Subdallah. Emma, Mr. Subdallah has been in here for fourteen months." He laughed, crossed his arms. "Agent Bauer, we ever had a visitor here fourteen months?"

"No."

"He wasn't alive for a good half of that."

He put his hands up. "I know, and you weren't here. And you've gotten him talking. About *anything*, that's a huge step, better than anyone else could do. But what have we gotten from him?"

"First, if not for him, we wouldn't have gotten that intel from Al-Jeddah. Plain and simple. It was true, it was useful, and it was what got him talking to us about Karim."

"But what have you gotten from him since? If he's playing ball, why hasn't he been able to provide anything else? Is it because he's been in here so long that he's useless? If that's the case, let's clear him, he's alive again, a civilian, off to some federal prison for the deformed."

"He's still useful."

At this Randolph pounded the manila folder. "He gave false intelligence! *Knowingly*. He could have cost people their lives if we hadn't found out about the Amtrak bombing, what, twelve hours beforehand? He sent us chasing a decoy." He was breathing hard.

Emma let him sit a while, leaned back in her chair. "Why aren't we talking about the goddamn pink elephant getting fucked in the room?" She pointed to the empty corner; Bauer actually turned his head.

"Hassan, Qaras, and Subdallah all had the same date, all came through this place at some point. Why aren't we bringing that up? We all know how they got the same date, don't we? *They* were somehow fed false intel, the same lie."

Randolph fixed her with a stony glare.

"Why don't we bring up that motherfucker, Tully? That faker's been fucking this place in the ass for a year now. How did he get past scrutiny?" She took a long drag, let the smoke seep out a crack in her mouth.

Bauer looked down at the table. Randolph held his gaze on her.

"The squirrel I told you about a month ago." She smiled. "How did he get out?"

"You know that is being investigated."

"I know? He poisoned Subdallah's mind. He threatened him with killing his family probably ten months ago. *Ten months.*" Pointing the cigarette at him. "You know what shit like that does to our efforts?" A thumb to indicate Reg and herself. "First, he thinks he's not safe here, can't trust anyone. Great for an interrogator, by the way. What's more, we've got that dark douche feeding my guys phony intel to then feed us. That's the bed I got into when I came here. So don't throw this on me. How the hell does a squirrel get into such a high-security place?"

He said calmly. "I understand you're frustrated."

"Are we going to catch Tully? Or whatever his name is? Ibn-Isn Al-dickshit?"

Randolph paused as if searching for a word, glanced quickly at Bauer, and faced Emma. "Tully is his real name. That was not some setup. He did not infiltrate us." He shrugged. "He is American. Born in northeast DC. Poor, black, early 70s. Never joined the Panthers or any group that would have red-flagged him, at least not publicly. But like a lot of young, angry black men, he was attracted to the Nation. That we found out."

"You *found out?*"

"It's not something that would have come up during a background sweep. He's an orderly, for Christ's sake. It's not as if he changed his name officially. His name is Tully Corning, finished high school, worked as an orderly at St. Mark's for eighteen years. From all we can tell, he legitimately applied to Harrison. It's a good job. What we don't know is whether Al-Thaghr pushed him here or if he was turned after the fact.

But I'm sure it was not a long job, getting him to join their cause. He has all the hallmarks: anger, alienation, Islam. And he's that sweetest of all things: American."

"Well, from what *I* hear, his paper was put on top of the stack. Someone bought his assignment to Harrison. Someone inside."

"That's a very serious thing to say."

"Well, it's a serious fucking fly in my Vaseline."

Randolph waited a few seconds, let Emma take another drag, which slowed her a bit. Then he placed his hand on the folder again. "We need something."

Reg spoke in a near monotone. "None of the lower grunts know anything. No one we've brought into this place below Jeddah and Subdallah has been able to corroborate. They've never been part of the planning structure. Karim made sure of that. The cells were each their own limb. He passed down instructions when needed, but the grunts never knew anything. Nothing substantial. Jeddah and Fadi are the two keys."

"Fadi?"

"Subdallah."

"Well, we're going to have a bit of a hard time getting anything from Al-Jeddah, aren't we, ten thousand miles away?"

Emma stood, paced to the wall and back, then folded her arm under her elbow. "Subdallah knows something. He just doesn't believe that he does. But the Amtrak thing worked. He thinks it was a success. He didn't know about it, not really, but he couldn't feel guiltier."

Shaking his head, "He's been cut off for too long."

"He and Karim were best friends. Subdallah was like an older brother to him when he first came to America. Karim always thought he had no one. No one, that is, except for Subdallah. This man has information beyond anybody's. It's just locked away. The two of them shared more ideas, more visions, more details." She turned to Randolph. "You remember New York?"

Shaking his head, "No. That's very unlikely. Not after what we found in the parking garage. Thaghr's little rival screwed that up for them. That city is on lock-down."

"That's why it's not New York. It's Boston."

"Very low likelihood."

"Doesn't that make it perfect? Those fuckers hate commerce and… finance whatever else they hate I'm sure is embodied in that building. Huge impact, loss of life, big beautiful American hard-on-looking building gets wiped clean. Aren't many buildings like it in Boston, and there's only one that's the tallest."

"Subdallah said this?"

"He said there was a plan, long time ago, Marcel's baby. And Subdallah came up with the method, using his own baby."

"What's his baby?"

"Elevators. He knows the wiring, knows the mechanics. He taught it to the Egyptians, who we know pretty damn well are still in the country."

"He could never know how large a priority this is, not after all this time. Things change."

"But why not be ready? If they go through with this and we don't anticipate…"

"I know, I know." He leaned forward, flipped the folder open then closed. Tapped the table three times. Then he turned to Reg. "I'm guessing that you two already have a scenario brief."

Reg opened the first of three files. "Weekday. Subject recommends that a charge on every other elevator, five in total, would be sufficient. Forty-five pounders per, sometime between ten and twelve hundred hours, after the morning rush, before lunch. Elevator traffic decreases by about seventy percent by then. He's made a simple override device, very easy to implement. With that in place, you push a few buttons and have control over every elevator, send two to the basement, one to the fourth floor, other two higher up. He admits it might not demolish the thing, but it will essentially wipe it from the map, would kill every living thing in the structure. The staggered approach would block those on the upper floors from getting back down. He's not sure about the strength of the incendiary, that was always a debate. We'd assume the Egyptians would make that call. Maybe more than forty-five-pounders."

Randolph spoke to himself. "We'll need logs of employees, everyone who's started at that place in the last four months, anything funny, any changes."

305

"Wanna know something funny?" She took a drag and turned. "His brother handles all the elevator contracts for the Hancock."

"Whose?"

"Subdallah's. Lives just outside Boston."

Randolph sat up a bit. "Well shit. Did he give you a date?"

"The 4th. October."

"That date's certainly significant."

"But that's something that could change, and we've been banged on the wrong date before. We just have to be ready."

Then Emma sat and put her elbows on the table. "Oh." She smiled downward. "There's one other thing." She shook her head. "Something that lying bitch Tully said to Subdallah." Then she looked up at Randolph, smile fading, paused a few seconds. "He told Subdallah that his daughter is still alive. That Marcel has her."

"I find that hard to believe. She's dead."

"Are you forgetting what Al-Jeddah told us?"

Bauer looked confused, though Randolph's face slowly sank into realization.

"Marcel Karim is rumored to have a daughter. 'He has always wanted a daughter, a clean girl, after what was done to his sisters.' And, I don't know, maybe you *men* can tell me, how exactly does a celibate imam go about having a kid?"

"What are you saying?"

"I'm saying that Marcel Karim kidnapped Fadi's daughter, told him she had been killed. So then he has the daughter he's always wanted— his own niece — and not only that, he's taken every reason Fadi has for wanting to live. An American, a bombmaker *and* a bomb, the best kind of bomb."

Shaking his head. "No. Subdallah was Karim's best friend. He wouldn't sacrifice him."

"He would if Fadi had lost heart."

"Had he? None of the transcripts make it sound that way."

"After Sudan. Fadi went home, he was planning to separate from Al-Thaghr."

Still shaking his head. "Nadat is dead."

"Well, if she isn't, and she's being held, that's an American citizen, isn't it? That's kidnapping, it's international. If we don't act like she's alive we're in a good load of trouble." The smile returning. "I mean, you are."

CHAPTER 46

"Bismillah al-Rahman, al Rahim. Bismillah."

Khalid had the most beautiful voice of them all, but today he just mumbled in song as he stroked the chicken's feathers. Sun shot through the upper window of the barn and onto the hay on the ground. Harold, he had named the chicken. And Harold stood compliant in his master's lap. Khalid soothed the animal and shushed him and mumbled on, more silent with each word, until Fadi could not hear the prayer. And with Harold facing the black-painted mark on the barn wall indicating Qiblah, Khalid pulled the small blade from beneath him, bowed his head a moment, and drew the blade across Harold's neck. He made not a sound, but took several frantic steps away from Khalid before falling to his side. Blood flowed onto the straw, and Khalid bowed again and mumbled onward. "Bismillah."

Then he stood and walked toward the barn door, passing Fadi on his way and smiling. Fadi remained a few seconds after and watched the chicken's body as it trembled and then moved only a few extra spasms and fell still. He wondered if that was all the blood it would produce.

Though he had only watched, afterward he scrubbed his hands and changed clothes, then set off on his regular walk through the grounds. The last weeks had been sunny and hot. There was an arching path Fadi liked to travel through the woods that looped around and returned back to the property from the eastern edge. Marcel described this place as a gift from some Syrian living here in Clifton, Virginia, a man "equal to the cause," who had arranged safe housing for their stay in the US.

But its grandeur still confused Fadi as he strolled through the fields, away from the barn and the main house with its old façade belying all those new fixtures and handsome country furniture, the giant TV and huge garage.

He walked with hands joined at his back and came to the edge of the wood, found the hidden mouth of the path, and was glad to be out of the sun a while and back where not a shred of man's doing could be seen. Through here it was nearly possible to forget any dark fingerprints imposed on the natural way of things, to see that all forces acted only to their true ends and without infringement or transgression on what really should be.

The path was overgrown with nettles and a few thin spruces here and there, and Fadi was tempted to take along the rusty old scythe that sat in the barn but decided before each walk not to do so. For a half mile or so the trail swung in its long arc, the bounds of the place invisible this far in, and he trained his mind to focus only on the trees and the dirt, the dead sticks and cover of leaves. Toward the end, he came upon the ruins of a home from just after the civil war, not much left beyond a brick half-chimney and splattered beams of wood. A few feet after this the main house came back into view, growing larger with each step.

Marcel, Fadi, and Jesper slept in the barn, which was comfortable enough. Borrowed bed sheets spread over hay in the loft, with a breeze from time to time at night, and not a sound from beyond the walls. The men gathered in the garage for each salah, rolled and unrolled their rugs on the empty concrete floor. In the basement of the place they had set up long tables over which they spread schematics and building blueprints, detailed master schedules, and on the far table sat a tangle of wires and assorted transistors and pliers and all the things Fadi and Khalid needed.

As Fadi emerged from the woods, Marcel called his name from the open garage, waving him over. He hurried through the tall grass of the field, sweaty by the time he arrived under the garage doors. All fifteen men had assembled there. Fadi's walk in the woods had taken longer than he knew, and he was late for afternoon prayer. The men squeezed into the place and slid rugs diagonally across the floor. And now Fadi was in a place he relished. Though he still recited the words and the pleading he had learned and he listened to Marcel's lovely chanting voice, this place existed beyond prayer, and that he prayed with other men rendered no added meaning.

They finished and each set back to his task. Some changed into street clothes and packed into the old Volvo in the driveway, while others headed back down to the basement. Khalid went to the barn to get Harold and finish preparations. Fadi lingered, no idea where he needed to go. And Ali approached him and put a hand on his shoulder and patted him, even lifted his lips in an attempted smile. He squeezed Fadi's shoulder and then left Marcel and him alone.

There was very little in the garage, which could suit three cars. A weed wacker, which Fadi had also considered bringing back to his path to do some clearing; a red gasoline tank; oil spots only in one space; and a little pink bike. The windows let in that same light, which filled the place, and the light and any sound bounced through the empty room alike.

Marcel leaned on the table and looked out the window. He had grown thinner in the last month. Fadi guessed it had to do with being on the run, the nerves of having this group's fate in his hands. Fadi too had withered away. The two spindly men stood there tall and spectral in their dangling robes, sunken cheeks, and dark-rimmed eyes.

Marcel pulled at Fadi's beard and asked in French, "Will you miss this?"

"I think it might be refreshing. It's been a while since I was clean. At least the itchiness won't be there. It was pleasant, to grow it out, not worry about grooming or the way I look. I must confess I haven't cared for it in recent years. It made Fatu break out. She would have a rash on her cheeks."

Marcel turned and leaned back on the table, viewed the near-empty garage as if for the first time. "This is where we have ended up. Funny to think, such an opulent place. You know, the owner is not unlike you. He was born here, parents from Syria without a dime. Very smart, came up through the system, did everything perfectly, Harvard, then Wharton. Painfully bright. Very young when he started making money, moved way out to the suburbs here, also had a townhouse in Georgetown. American wife, two children. But he sought me out, or was led to me, and what he told me is that he felt empty. At thirty-five, he felt empty. And it was a chance encounter with an old friend that brought him back to the book, and slowly his path was righted."

"Just like mine."

"Inshallah."

"Do you think so?"

He turned. "I know it."

"I wonder sometimes." He rubbed his beard. "It is impossible for me to understand how these things could have happened. Why."

"It is not always for us to understand. People, we have a way about us. For some reason God has put into us this need to know all things. And even worse, this idea that we *deserve* to know all things. We do not."

Fadi turned to him with a smile. "I just want relief."

"You will find it, my friend. I promise." Marcel put his arm around him. "All of this pain will be over, and the pleasure of the best moment of your life here on earth will be magnified a thousand times."

He walked to the far wall, slowly, with hands at his back. And the robes swished with the movement, just those two bare feet visible to prove he didn't float. Then he set his fingers on the handle grip of the Vespa that sat against the wall. He squeezed the brake once, held his hand clenched.

"I know you worry about your family. But I will always look after them. That I swear. Your mother, even Yusef. And Alia. She will be like my own daughter, and I will make sure she always has enough money, is looked after, even that she finds a suitable husband. She has lost her father, and now she will be without her brother, but I will watch her and raise her. I want you to go to God knowing all this, no second thoughts about what you are leaving behind. In some ways, you are the only family I have, because so much of mine has been perverted."

Fadi stood beside him, moved his fingers across the padded seat. "I know."

The Vespa was skeletal, as if relieved of its flesh by locusts. Its body panels had been removed, along with the exhaust, the gas tank, most of the brake components, even the little two-stroke engine sat now in the basement. It seemed such a weak being, sitting there in the huge garage, rendered nude and shivering, now baring its true worth. Such a pitiful thing. He glanced at Marcel. *God, please let this have the power to take me away from here.*

CHAPTER 47

"Am I wanted for some crime?"

"Yes."

By this time, Yusef was sweating, both at his forehead and in the trough below his nose. He looked back and forth between Emma, who stood with hands on the table, and Reg, who sat with his face directed toward a notebook and a manila folder stuffed with dummy papers. Emma should not have been there, and certainly not Reg. It had taken an extra week of pushing on Alec, insisting. Just as Fadi had been pushing on her to focus on Boston.

So here she was, pressing a domestic subject, just like the old days in DC, following a fresh set of rigid protocol. Yusef had rights, which got in the way.

"Do I need my lawyer?"

She stood straight, and her face went a little softer. Not something any of the Egyptians would have asked.

"Do you?" She shrugged.

"I haven't done anything."

"Good. That's why we didn't make a scene. But you look nervous."

"Of course I am. The CIA pulled me off the street, out of the clear blue sky. Why wouldn't I be?"

"If you haven't done anything."

"I get nervous even when I haven't done anything."

She laughed. "Well, that's a new one to me. I don't even know what to say."

"What is this, profiling?"

"Yes."

His eyes followed her as she paced slowly across the floor, hands at her hips. He glanced once at Reg then seemed to realize something. "It's my brother, isn't it? This has to do with my brother."

Brow lifted in surprise. "The dead one?"

"I'm not like him. You know how many questions I've answered about that man in the last year. It's nearly ended my marriage. I had to take my kids out of school, spray paint on every part of my house and my car, death threats. Death threats to my kids, my wife."

Emma could not hide the shock in her face, so she turned on her heel and faced the wall. She hadn't thought much about Fadi's family, how the worldwide news of his suicide attack would have shaken them. That man she'd been talking to for months, getting closer to, seeing so deeply into, was dead to everyone he loved, and had left a horrible blackness behind.

"It *is* related to your brother."

"So you have seen my record then?"

"Of course." Pointing to Reg, who flinched and began shuffling through the phony papers.

"So you know I've never even had a traffic ticket so long as I've lived, and that I am as American as you or this guy."

"Actually, Reg is Canadian."

"Can we get to the point, please?"

She turned, put her hands back on the table, and leaned in. "Sure. I think you've been contacted by some mean people. Your brother's people. And I think you've told them something, given them something."

He paused, eyes darted away once and fixed back on hers. "Nothing. No. I'm not my brother. I love this country, have built a business here, and a family." Here his voice went cold. "I didn't flee this place, and I don't hate it as he did."

She studied him, held her eyes on him and waited for his nerves to kick in. But his eyes glazed over. Dark circles beneath, as if he hadn't slept in a day. She tapped the table once, then dragged a chair over, set it squarely across from him. "Smoke?"

He shook his head.

"Reg?"

He threw a soft pack of Camels to her, then a book of matches.

"These things'll kill you." She laughed. "I hear that a lot these days. You know, it's the *tar* they're saying now. So I try to get the lights every now and again. But just not the same taste." Waving out the match. "Anyway, I figure that's a ways off, the dying thing. Right now, they make me happy as a clam in shit."

He looked confused.

Why not just tell Yusef everything? Reg, the voice of reason, ever the analyst, straightforward. *Why not tell Yusef his brother is still alive, hell, bring him in? Then tell him Karim has his brother's daughter, his own niece, and we need to catch him. If Thaghr has gotten to Yusef with a threat, this would be more powerful.*

"Tell me about your family, Yusef. Joseph."

"Who, Georges?"

"We know about Georges. Tell me about your wife, your kids."

"You know about them already, don't you?"

"Yes. But tell me."

Yusef's eyes sucked to the tabletop. "They are everything to me. Of course they are. All I think about is what is best for them, to have a better life, to fit in and be happy and not face things we faced growing up. My two beautiful girls have their mother's nose, and my son is tall and handsome like his grandfather. He is the best soccer player, maybe in the whole state. He was. And my wife." He shook his head.

Emma let the silence stand, didn't push him, knew that time and his own thoughts would take hold now. She needed him in this state, thoughts of his family to brittle his defenses.

We can't risk telling him that Fadi is alive, or anything about Marcel or Nadat. A man's family, his real family, is too powerful a thing. I think he'll show allegiance to his wife and children, to their safety. And who knows how he feels about Fadi? Probably hates him.

After a few minutes, Emma leaned and tapped the cigarette over the ashtray. "Your wife."

"My wife." Staring toward the far wall, blank as the table, plenty of space for a man's thoughts to be painted there. His eyes held, he didn't blink, and Reg didn't move a muscle. As Emma stared at Yusef's eyes, they suddenly seemed to tremble. But it wasn't motion; it was that delicate membrane of liquid that had magically formed over his eyeballs and seemed to set them shivering. It was like the glass of a pond top first thing in the morning, the surface just waiting to break. Emma had always gotten a rush from seeing this. The moment when a man was about to break into tears.

He blinked, which sent a surprising amount of teardrops tumbling down. But his face didn't change, nor did he wipe his cheek. "What did I do? I did everything right. I worked hard, was good to my brother, to my family. I was a good American. But I am here. A year nearly tearing us apart, my brother. My dear brother, I pray for him. He is the one who set these men upon us. What have I done?" He did not cry as she had hoped, did not whimper as so many domestic criminals were prone to do.

She said in a cold voice, "Your family will be just fine. We can protect them."

He shook his head. "From what? They are fine."

"Bullshit, Mr. Subdallah. They are not fine. You think you do what these men ask once, they'll just let you go about your life? You know who they are, you'll talk. They can't have that. They have no problem killing women, children. You know what they did in Sudan. What would one more family mean to them?"

"But I am Muslim."

"You're as Muslim as I am."

"Fuck you!" Smashing his fist on the table.

Reg didn't move an inch.

"And fuck *them!*"

"Who?"

"That black motherfucker who sat outside my house. Who had the *balls*...to describe my girls' daily routines. Where they go, what rooms they sleep in, their soccer practice schedule."

Emma nearly let this news break her stony face but instead waited for Yusef to look down, at which time she shot a glance at Reg, lifted her brows. He mouthed, very clearly, *Tully.*

"Um, uh…black motherfucker, you say?"

He nodded.

"What did he call himself?"

Yusef set his elbows on the table, put his head in his hands. "Todd."

A flatulent laugh escaped her lips. "Sorry. *Todd?*"

Yusef peered up at her, a look of disgust on his face, then he turned and faced Reg, who simply buried his eyes in the clump of papers.

"Listen to me, Yusef. *Joseph*. Listen real carefully. We're going to get you out of this. But you've got to be our friend, okay? I'm gonna need you to go ahead and tell us everything Todd has said to you. What he wants, where he's meeting you. When."

She snuffed out her cigarette, leaned way back in her chair, and preceding Yusef's first word by a hair of a second she heard the attentive click of Reg's recorder.

Like a sponge, the little RCA Vocorder RX-1 had sucked in every last drop of Yusef's story, and now Emma and Reg sat as all the little details dripped out for Randolph to hear. At the end of the tape there were only sobs, which Reg mercifully cut off. Randolph was quiet, sat erect in the plastic chair, in the square room plugged deep into one of Boston's concrete buildings in Government Center. Though he was silent, Emma knew what he was now realizing: two positives. An interrogator was used to getting single pieces of intel from one man, one source. Those lone bits so often came to naught or else proved to be lies or the discourse of cowards. But two sources yielding the same info increased its value exponentially. Some of the dumber interrogators called this phenomenon "triangulation."

Randolph looked up. "Okay."

"Okay what?"

"This merits attention. We have nine days."

She sat across the table from him, took a cigarette from the pack, tapped it on the table. Randolph looked at it then at Emma. She didn't light it.

The phrase played in her mind, *I want in. I want in*. But instead she bit her tongue, thought a moment, and said, "This mission requires my attendance."

"No."

"Yes."

Shaking his head. "We've got less than two weeks to make this happen, without scaring away the birds. Needs to be by the book."

"I'm by the book."

"That doesn't even make sense."

"I feel like this is just a redo of our conversation about Maclean Market. Remember that? Domestic experience, better with a firearm than most of your piss-ant feds, and I *know* these guys."

"So you can teach the surveillance team."

"I speak Arabic."

"The men likely involved all know English."

"We don't *know* who's involved. Remember Maclean? If I hadn't been there, we wouldn't be *here*. Who's better at thinking on the spot than an interrogator? We're talking about the possibility that we'll have minutes to orient ourselves once we take a captive. I'm not talking about storming the building either. No civilians around, these guys are never armed. Why *wouldn't* you include me? Aside from you, who's been on this hunt longer than I have? Or more deeply?"

"I'll see what I can do." He started to rise.

"You know what you can do. Make the call here. With all due respect, sir."

"Sir…?"

"You're the one who hunted me down in the bowels of Defense. You brought me along. Now bring me along again."

"*I'm* not even going to be there."

"You're too high-ranking. I'm not."

"Your bullshit is getting riper."

"Ok, that last bit was bullshit, but the rest makes sense, and you know it does. It's the right thing to do. You know I can handle myself and will add layers to this no one else can. Look at Maclean."

"And what about Evan? What do I tell your son if something goes wrong?"

She could sense Reg's head turn toward her.

"I'll tell him everything when he's older. You telling me only bachelors are going to be assigned to this?"

He finally stood, tapped the table with his knuckles. "You can go as an *advisor*. That puts you out of harm's way."

"Absolutely. I'll stay out of harm's way. Nowhere near harm."

Alec rubbed his temples with shut eyes. "I've got to pull these people together. Tonight. We'll reconvene tonight." He took two steps toward the door then stopped and faced Emma. "When we do, please, don't do…" waving his hands to vaguely indicate the recent scene, "*this…* again. Okay?"

"Sure, coach." She could not hide her smile, which Alec caught a glimpse of before leaving the room, and which she then turned on Reg, who absently pressed rewind on the recorder as Emma at last took that lone cigarette from the table and snapped a match to life.

CHAPTER 48

The morning's prayers were exhausting. Marcel's voice had never been more liquid in its tone or more seamless shifting from pitch to pitch. Fadi couldn't help but think of him as an eight-year-old in some grand hall in Egypt at the Koran-recitation competition, having memorized every silky word, bringing grown men to tears. Today, they prayed in the sunlit garage, just as the first hints of summer poured in through the windows and heated the place. These prayers were purposeful, and the air itself seemed to realize this and was made thick with anticipation and heavy with the near future. *Al Rahman, Al Rahim. Bismillah.* The merciful. What will He say to me? Will He be merciful?

The group stood in perfect silence a few moments, and then Khalid stepped next to him, grasped him from beside, and the others joined, all padding him with hugs and kisses on the forehead or the cheek. Mujahedin, they called him. The men had latched onto this word several months ago, and saved it for use on him alone.

Later, Marcel gave him a can of shaving foam and a three-pack of Bic razors, along with some shears.

"I will do this."

So Fadi stood at the bathroom sink, shirtless and perspiring. The house had grown hot, even with every window open. No one dared suggest flipping on the central air system. He regarded himself in the mirror. The close-cropped hair would have even looked military, if not for the few days' growth and sunken cheeks, the eyes rimmed with sleepless black. He'd shaved his ten-year-old beard off last week to pose for his ID pictures.

Marcel stood to his side and ran the razor down his cheek.

In French. "You are fading, my brother."

"No, I am not."

"I can see it. Don't you think I can see it? I have known you a while."

"I am impatient. It has been a long time since Fatu was killed. Since my dear Nadat."

He kept cutting. "It will not be long now. You will see them. The sorrow of this world will seem childish to you. You will know the future. And you will know what our efforts and sacrifice have done for our people."

Staring into his own eyes. "It seems impossible that the pain I feel could ever go away."

Marcel ran the razor under the faucet then shut it off. He pushed his forehead into Fadi's shoulder and held it there. Then he began to cry. Great sobs pushed from his face as if pressurized. Fadi stood and watched him in the mirror. Never had he seen Marcel weep, and never again did he hope to see another man on earth, nor touch another person.

The van ride was quiet as they rolled out of Clifton, past the sweeping farms and large houses. Quiet as they passed through Fairfax toward the beltway. Once they reached it, the prayers began. But the gentle timbre it typically held now sounded droning, and the passion of it had seeped out. Fadi sat in the front seat, and he turned to look at the four men crouching in the back, and beyond them at the flimsy Vespa strapped down and wobbling side to side as the van zoomed along 495 to Arlington.

At Ali's convenience store they pulled into the back lot, not another car in sight. It was here that the others unloaded the bike and Khalid tested its electronics once more. It was then placed in an empty spot, where no one in the group paid it any attention. And in a back room, among columns of boxes, Fadi stripped down to his underwear and caught sight of himself in the mirror, so skinny, his face skeletal and bare as a boy's. He changed into the hot shirt and slacks, cinched his tie, then pulled the jacket on. One more glance into the mirror. *You are Dr. Ross.*

As he emerged from the store and into the sun of the parking lot, the others welcomed him with applause and laughter.

"You look great, my friend." Khalid gave him a kiss on the cheek and a hug.

Ali, too, kissed him and looked upward into his eyes. The darkness there in color and in form. "A perfect American, Dr. Ross."

They readied him on the Vespa, big red helmet firmly on his head. No identification on his body but Doctor Ross's credentials, nothing in his pockets but the secreted dollar bill he would use for a last sip of root beer. And there was the bulky, expensive mobile phone packed into the seat below him, one last call to make before he left this place. He wondered what would happen if his friends found it. Each man patted him and then left his sight, muttering some prayer or word of inspiration, all of which fell flat as unfeathered arrows. He tightened the strap on his helmet and thought a moment about college football games.

Then Marcel, with a smile, tested the ear phones inside the helmet. He spoke into a small microphone, and though he was a foot away his voice boomed and was clear and full of bass.

He nodded.

"Welcome to the Five Pillars Club of UMass."

He smiled, but Fadi could not.

"I confess a jealousy, my one friend. That you are about to meet God. And you will see my dear sister soon as well."

"And my daughter."

"Yes, of course. Your daughter, my niece."

"I have more work yet to do. Two acts of God done through me before I can join you. But you will see me again, my true brother, my mentor. God is beautiful and shines down upon you all His love, which is the greatest thing. You will be stronger than any substance on earth." He faced Fadi. "Are you ready to be with God?"

"I don't know."

Marcel pulled his face back a few inches. "You are ready." He held Fadi's hand in both of his.

"I am ready to die." He clamped the left brake and at the same time twisted the key in the ignition with eyes shut tight.

CHAPTER 49

By the 4th, Boston leaves had begun to sour on the trees. Sunday night the cold was magnified by great gusts swirling around the Hancock. Papers and garbage flew by their position a few times. Then the wind would stop and leave an expectant vacuum behind. The unmarked car reserved for Emma and Agent Hetch sat innocently along Copley Square on Stuart Street. To their right rose the Hancock, Boston's great skyscraper, like a shoe mirror for the gods, to the left the ages-old Trinity Church with its sainted windows and red sandstone trim. As it grew cold, the church steps and its sheltered walkways became a haven for bundled bums and drunks, and tonight the few clumps of heavy blankets gathered out front made Emma nervous, imagining a great firefight at the center of Copley Square, bullets whipping through the air and killing the homeless and wealthy alike.

Though not briefed on all the positions of the feds, she had easily spotted the thick-fingered man at the edge of the square in full track suit, reading a paper at the bus stop. He hadn't gotten on the 502, or the 504b, but just sat there with his nose buried in Friday's *The Globe*. Emma knew the members of Al-Thaghr were historically ill-suited for espionage or more covert operations. They wouldn't notice the guy's brand-new Adidas or tight haircut. Their M.O. was surprise and atrocity. They were used to ramming old Yugos or Vespas into crowds and government buildings, not this cloak-and-dagger bullshit, waiting in cars for hours, posting decoys and watchmen at the perimeter. With surprise there was much less of a need to be paranoid that someone was watching. She just hoped the boys of Al-Thaghr still assumed this was a surprise.

By 2100 hours, they'd already been there four hours, changing vehicles and position once. The wind had picked up as darkness settled in, which seemed to clear the sidewalks of Bostonians, all tucked into their Back Bay or South End row houses by this hour. The bellman at the Fairmont had ducked himself inside the revolving door an hour earlier. Just the church bums, a perpetual bus-bench rider, and your typical 1982 Imperial sitting along the curb with man and woman sitting perfectly still the last few hours.

Hetch said nothing to Emma, not a single word over the course of the evening, except when they'd switched cars. The little walkie coughed and spat numbers and checks from the other positions. She knew there were several agents positioned inside: the elevator engine room at the bottom of shaft eight, maintenance storage at the eastern entrance, two units in tinted sedans to plug up each exit point in the basement garage, a host of blockades ready to seal up a one-block radius at a word.

The plan was simple. The eyes across assorted rooftops would signal when subjects showed themselves, whether by foot or vehicle. Every escape route would be delicately cut off, so as not to alert the targets. The Hancock, itself, would be used as a sort of animal trap. Once all the targets were inside, strategic exits and routes would be blocked off. The point was to capture every single man: the drivers, the Egyptian bomb-makers, the gunmen (on the off-chance that Al-Thaghr had, in the last year, begun to arm itself), or even a senior cell leader, should he have come along for the ride. Estimates, based on Fadi's intelligence and CIA analysts, pointed toward there being between six and eight operatives. Thaghr traveled light in their missions, and quickly.

Entry would almost certainly take place along the western garage access point, using a keycard secreted to the men by Yusef Subdallah. There were regularly four guards on duty, anywhere between eight and ten custodial staff, and a small number of overachieving employees who punched in on weekends. To solve for this, they had sent out a systems outage report to all tenants late on Friday afternoon. It had been a gambit, the risk that someone from AT would catch wind of this and get spooked. But they couldn't risk having some poor shlep from Manheim Insurance absorbing a .22 slug through his weekend polo shirt.

Maintenance staff were trickier. They couldn't all be told to go home for the night, and the CIA (used to the whole espionage thing) were convinced at least one staffer was hooked up to the Al-Thaghr cell. So to keep them clueless, a network of repair notices and maintenance signs had been pasted throughout the building, cutting off safe pockets in which the assorted teams could lie in wait.

That eerie, artificial wind created by the single tall building swooped through the darkness, causing the track suit man's newspaper to flutter and a few plastic bags to gallop across the sidewalk. *Where are all the people?* A voice murmured from the walkie, fuzzy with static. Hetch paused before pushing the button. "Repeat."

The next words were clear. "Visual on targets. Moving north on Trinity Place, white van marked 'Shawmut Cleaners.' Approaching west entrance. Vehicle stopped."

From their post, the van's position was obscured by the Fairmont Copley Hotel, but Emma could now see the track suit man at the bus stop speaking into his wrist as he eyeballed the west entrance.

From the walkie, "Western door opening. Unit four, confirm." A bit more alarm in his voice. "How's that door opening?"

There were seconds of silence, then another voice piped in. "Targets entering garage, proceeding east to level B1. Units four and five are advised. Do *not* engage. West door closing. Unit four confirm visual. How the hell is that door closing?"

"This is unit four. Unknown. Unknown number of targets approaching elevator bank. Vehicle has stopped, engine still on. They're just sitting there. Advise."

Static. "Do not engage. Eagle, can we confirm no other targets accessing location from points Alpha or Fox? We need to make sure no one else is coming. Don't spook them."

"Negative, no visual."

"All positions report. Visual on second target group?"

There was just the sound of wind humming along the backside of the Hancock, then a string of "negative, over" came across the band.

"Subjects exiting vehicle. Vehicle is still on. Repeat, van's engine still running."

"Give us some numbers, unit four."

"Five. No, six total Apaches, at least from what I can see. Six men have exited the vehicle. Subjects walking to rear, opening van doors. *Wait!*" The line went silent. "Someone's coming out of the elevator bank. Unknown subject, unlocking door to the basement elevator lobby, talking to subjects. That's our mole. He's just holding the door for them. Subjects are removing large tool boxes, two each. Shit, they're just walking to the bank. They're not even hurrying. I can confirm, four from the roster, now three unknown. The Egyptians are here. We're going to lose them. Please advise."

"Positions have confirmed. Negative on additional targets. We're clear. Units one and two, take stairwell to basement. All units engage on my signal. Unit three disable elevators. Don't want these boys taking a flight upstairs."

There was once again only silence on the walkie. Emma looked at Agent Hetch, then at track suit man, who was leaning forward now. She could see the pistol in his hand as he held his ear with the other. The quiet went on for another minute, no shots, no status from other positions, just the ghost wind squeezing between the Hancock and Trinity Church.

"What the fuck is taking so long? They're not armed."

"Shh."

The track suit man folded his paper. Emma could sense he was as restless as she was, new sneakers tapping on the sidewalk like heartbeats. He touched his ear again then rose.

Emma said. "This guy's moving in. Why haven't we heard anything?"

"Shut the fuck *up*."

She took a long swallow, watched as the track suit man dropped his paper, now revealing his pistol, though holding it at his waist, aimed at the sidewalk. He moved like a trained man, crossing the street with long steps, then leaning against the corner of the Fairmont with pistol pointed down.

"Why the fuck haven't we heard anything?"

Hetch seemed to know not to shush her again, and he raised the walkie to his ear as if the next orders would come in whispers. There was no sound, and even the wind had settled. No one was out on the streets, no one walked by, only the occasional car could be heard the next block over on Dartmouth. The scene was so still that Emma forgot about the bums huddled at Trinity's steps. When one shifted, it startled both her and Hetch. She watched as he sat up and then stood, blankets still around his shoulders. The two other homeless men regarded him, both looked up from where they lied. The man shrugged his blanket off then headed down the steps and onto the square. He looked once at the track suit man, then put his head down and began to head diagonally across the square, away from the Hancock. Emma studied him, his tattered blue winter hat, old army-green coat, clean work trousers. As his feet worked and got farther away, she noticed his walk. He passed under a lamp, one long step, then sweeping his other foot along the concrete. Step, drag, faster and faster. Brand-new shoes. *Brand new shoes.* Where do I know that walk?

"Tully! You cunt, Tully."

Hetch faced her for the first time in nearly five hours. "What?"

Emma pulled the little snub nose from inside her pocket, pointing it upward. "Tully, *there*." Nodding at the homeless man as he limped away. She opened the door and got out.

"Wait. Do *not* pursue. Shit." Then Hetch opened his door and followed her.

Emma duck-walked across the street, keeping the few trees and benches between her and Tully. She crossed and hid behind a tree then peered around to see him getting farther away, passing now beside a dead fountain. Hetch was crouching behind a parked car. He'd brought the walkie with him and was muttering into it, weapon drawn in his other hand. He caught Emma's glance, pointed emphatically toward her back, then made a swooping motion. She shrugged. He answered with another gesture, banging his two fists together. Emma glanced over her shoulder then bolted next to Hetch behind the car.

"We have to cut him off. The rooftops have an eye on him, but they'll never get down here in time. I'm going around the church, counter-clock. You go the other way. He's going to dart."

"He's not winning any relays, the way he walks. We need this fucker."

Hetch nodded. Emma set out at a crouching run, reaching the northwest corner of the church. On the far side, Boylston Street, there were more cars, a few pedestrians. Tully stuck out with his quick step-and-drag gait. He crossed Boylston at a red light, got a beep as he slid out in front of a bus. Their little flank wouldn't work; he was beyond the church now, headed north toward the river.

Hetch rounded the corner, already panting, having holstered his pistol. He looked up toward the rooftops. "We need to wait for backup."

"Are you kidding? I see him. He'll disappear. We need to get him *now*."

He took a big breath, nodded. "Okay."

"I'll cross to the other side. You go up this way."

Before he could answer, Emma shot across to the east side of Boylston as she plugged her weapon back in her pocket. She stood very tall so she could keep an eye on Tully, who was now a full block ahead and walking more quickly. He turned right onto Newbury Street, so Emma caught Hetch's eye to make sure he'd seen. At a run now, she made it to the corner and stopped. Newbury was more crowded, even on Sunday night, so Emma was able to keep her distance with a few pedestrians between. Tully looked over his shoulder once as she pursued but didn't notice her in her men's white shirt and khakis. From the corner of her eye, Emma could see Hetch on the other side of the street, speed-walking, now overtaking Tully, obviously looking to sweep in front of him and approach from the opposite direction.

They reached Berkeley Street, where Tully had to stop to wait for cars, looking over his shoulder several times. And Hetch stood on the opposite corner, also blocked by traffic. After a minute, Tully went on, dragging that foot behind him but still able to keep a good pace. Hetch sped up. He'd need a good half block on Tully before he could cross the street and close in on him, and Hetch stuck out among the fancy shoppers in his blue cap and navy-blue coat over white dress shirt, missing only the yellow F.B.I. on the breast. So Emma was ready to run after Tully when he got spooked. Surely she could catch that limping bastard.

Almost to Arlington now, Hetch was finally well enough ahead that he crossed the street and began to loop back to their side. He was about a hundred feet in front of Tully, Emma a good fifty feet back, and now they sandwiched in on him. Fewer people on this block but still a few La Chemise shoppers and guests from The Ritz. Emma watched as Hetch closed in, twenty feet, now ten, looking across the street. He let Tully pass him by, then turned on his heel, walked up behind him, grabbed his upper arm, and began to whisper something in Tully's ear. The two men walked and whispered a few seconds, then came to the corner of Arlington and Newbury, with the Common just across the street, Hetch's hand still gripping Tully. They stood and faced forward, neither making a move. A few cars darted south along the one-way street before them. To their left, the doorman helped an older lady and her husband into a livery sedan, which then began to coast toward Hetch's position. Just as the vehicle got within ten feet of them, Tully suddenly squatted, leaned his shoulder into Hetch's rib, and shoved him right into the crosswalk as the car passed. Hetch flew onto the hood of the car and slammed into the windshield, rolling back onto the hood as the car bucked to a halt.

Tully turned back down Newbury and headed right for Emma. She fumbled to get her pistol out, pointing it at him just as he passed her.

"Freeze, you fuck!"

But he was already past, his back now to her as he ran at a surprisingly good clip. He squeezed through two parked cars and was nearly hit by a U-Haul, which honked. Once on the other side of the street, he turned and his white eyes finally met hers and seemed to recognize her. He raced down Newbury, back the way they had come. Emma hesitated a moment, thinking she ought to check on Hetch, but her feet had already begun to move down the sidewalk in a sort of shuffle, and her mind flashed a quick scene of passersby and hotelmen kneeling around Hetch, sending for an ambulance, that balanced against the idea of Tully finally and absolutely blending into the background, hiding, never to be seen again. She had to go after him.

She was darting down the opposite sidewalk, weaving between occasional packs of people, her eyes fixed on that dark shape. She wouldn't cross for a while, but rather use the line of parked cars between them as cover, running at a crouch when possible, gaining on him slowly.

Now back at Clarendon Street, she wondered if her colleagues were having better luck subduing their targets at the Hancock. Tully plowed through a line of college girls at the next intersection. They screamed and caught everyone's attention, including the few shoppers on her side, who now studied Emma as she crouched behind a loading truck.

Now was the time to cross. He was stuck a few moments behind cars at the corner of Dartmouth, so Emma slid between two parked cars, peaked around the corner, and was able to duckwalk low enough as she crossed that Tully couldn't see her. But instead of fully crossing to the far sidewalk, she kept her crouch and moved along the row of cars on his side of the street. Now he was about four cars up and crossing Dartmouth at the intersection, still moving at a good pace. And despite the burning in her lungs, Emma kept up with him and even began to close a little as they neared Exeter. Tully stopped at the intersection, turned around panting, and looked across the street for her. There were two parked cars between them, Tully on the sidewalk, Emma still in the street, going against traffic, locking onto him through the car's windows. Now she crept up one step at a time, her weapon pointed up in the air. People could surely see her, and she could only hope their eyes wouldn't give away her position. He was beneath a lamp, and she had just moved into a dark spot. Now just that one car between them, and his eyes were looking far away for her. This close, she could see the little knife he'd drawn, one of those Leatherman kits with the two-inch blade flipped out. He was breathing very hard, his eyes bulging white and panicked under the light.

There was no closer place to sneak to. If she was going to jump out on him, it would have to be now. An old rich couple passed Tully, and the woman noticed his blade and screamed, which distracted him just enough for Emma to pop out at the car's hood and close to within five feet of him. He turned his head to find the little barrel of her pistol eyeballing him from a foot away.

"Drop that shit, you little bitch."

He froze.

"Or not." Cocking the hammer. "That's just enough to make you shootable."

He put his hands up, though still held the knife.

"That's the opposite of dropping it. You remember me? Hm? From Harrison? I remember you. And maybe you're not as dumb as you played, or maybe you are. Let's see."

Now she could sense the crowd building, at her back, to either side of the street, little mumbles and murmurs. But she didn't budge her eyes or the eye of the pistol from Tully's sweaty face. His hands were still up, and he took one step back.

"Don't move a muscle."

Then another step back.

"Freeze!" Shaking the gun at him.

In a quick motion he turned and darted off down Exeter, moving north toward Comm Ave. Emma tucked her weapon away and ran after him, catching him halfway down the block. She jumped on his back, cinched her legs around his midriff, slipped her left arm around his neck, and with her right, pulled her left forearm into his carotid artery. He staggered and fell back into the steps of a brownstone, falling with Emma hitting the stairs first. But she held on. He stabbed at her leg with the blade, sinking it halfway into her calf once, then digging it all the way in on his second stab. Emma let out a wild, dog-like growl as she pulled the choke tighter. Now Tully began to flail, letting go of the knife and clawing at her arms. But his hands got weaker as the lack of blood shorted his brain, and they swiped at her like a fish dying on the deck, softer and softer, and then his body went limp.

She was half-sitting on the steps with Tully between her legs, so she slipped out from behind his massive weight and inspected her leg. The knife was in there cleanly, and as she pulled the little blade out a good spurt of blood spat onto the stairs. She threw the knife aside and dragged Tully down to the sidewalk. On the far corner the crowd was up to over a dozen people, all watching her as she removed Tully's belt and tied his arms behind his back at the biceps. Then she undid his laces quickly and lashed his ankles together. She waited as she caught her breath and bled onto the cement, hoping the cops wouldn't come yet, or the Feds. *Just give me a minute with him.*

She picked up the knife from the sidewalk and thought maybe

331

a little slice would bring him back to life. So she tried a quick sweep across his belly, which at first didn't do the trick, but then she gave another pass — not too deep — which roused him. He tried to sit up, but was confused by his inability to use his arms or legs. So Emma drew her weapon and shoved it into his neck.

"You're gonna spill your guts, one way or another, you dirty, useless fuck. You hear me?" She still held the knife in her left hand and poked it into the small lacerations she'd made on his stomach. "I have no other reason to keep you alive. I'm not a cop. I'm not a fed. I can do whatever I want."

"Bullshit."

A little more pressure with the knife. "I've already been stabbed, you dumb dick. You get stabbed, you're allowed to start shooting. I'm going to ask this right to your bitchy little face. Where the fuck is Nadat?"

"Who?"

"Fadi's daughter, you know who. You gutless virgin fuckers have kidnapped a five-year-old little girl." She pressed the tip of the blade now against his upper shoulder, poked it in a little, and twisted.

He screamed but said nothing, so she stopped.

"You know where she is. And guess where you're going, Señor Ibn-isn-buttfuck? You're going back to Harrison. And you know who your best friend there will be? It will be me. Except you won't have any dim-witted orderlies to sneak you information. It will just be you. And *this* is the way I do shit." Twisting the blade a little. Then her voice changed to a soft, soothing tone. "So be my friend. Tell me where she is, and you'll be treated nicely. She's a little girl, and I already know where she is. I just need one more person to verify. You're not even hurting your friends, you're just confirming. So...tell me. I know she's still in the States..."

"Freeze! Drop your weapon now!" The voice came from her back.

Without turning. "I'm....F.B.I.!"

"So drop your weapon and move away from him and we'll have a look."

"I need to interview this man."

"Drop your weapon."

She leaned in, the knife in Tully's shoulder, the barrel of the gun poking into his neck. She whispered into his ear, "You ever have one of those chances that you never get back again?"

She threw her gun to the sidewalk, then the knife, her head still right next to Tully. She clung to him, even as two cops tried to pull her off, and she held her ear to his mouth. "Just tell me," she whispered. And a third cop joined and squeezed her wrist to release her grip. Then a whisper came from Tully, right into Emma's ear, two cross streets in Clifton, Virginia. As the cops pulled her off him he didn't move a muscle, but even in the near-dark she could see that beautiful look in his big white eyes, like a crumbling sandcastle. When a man realized you had just beaten him, that what had escaped his lips was not meant to. That sweet thing she knew all too well: the look of the truth.

CHAPTER 50

The new orderly was obviously military, someone with impeccable credentials, no doubt, after Tully. MacDriscoll was his name, and Fadi knew it would take a few days before he warmed up. He seemed above the very menial tasks now required of him. But when Fadi suggested they play a game, the man's chiseled face softened a bit. In lieu of Connect Four, MacDriscoll had suggested Risk. So after several minutes of explaining the rules, they now found themselves deep into a quiet game.

It helped distract his mind. These past weeks had been anguish, long days with no interrogations, no company, no Emma, and all the while hoping for some sort of news from Boston. He knew they would meet with Yusef and hoped Emma would keep her word about not letting his brother know that he still lived, that he was deformed and now nothing more than a criminal and murderer, sentenced to live out his days tethered to a bed in some secure place. *Let me stay dead, please.*

When MacDriscoll had started visiting, at least a few hours of the day could be sped along. But as the game dragged on, some of the empty spaces began to make way for thoughts of Nadat. Scenarios pieced themselves together in his mind, Tully and Ali and Marcel deciding to kill her, or Ali leaving her behind in some basement. Khalid would not abide this, certainly. He would watch after his daughter's life. *She is four...no, five. What year is it?*

The door opened.

Emma stood in the doorway a moment, smiling. She wore a suit, navy blue, with white button-down shirt. Her hair was down and recently cut.

Turning to MacDriscoll. "I got 'em. You're relieved."

He hesitated. "I can stay a while, if you need me to. Just finishing up our game."

Then Fadi said, "I won't touch the board. In fact, if you move the table over there by the wall it will make certain I can't fuck with it."

"Nice language." She limped in. Fadi noticed the wrapping of bandages on her left leg.

MacDriscoll wheeled the table carefully over to the wall, studying it one final moment, picked up his hat, and gave Emma a nod as he left. The door shut.

"New buddy?"

"Bit more of a talker than Tully."

At this her face went serious. She sat.

"You look nice, by the way."

"Fucking monkey suit." Pawing at her collar.

"Been three weeks."

"I'm not supposed to be here. And by that I mean not in the building."

"Couldn't resist me?" Though he tried to say this lightly, it betrayed the worry in his voice.

"I needed to tell you. I don't know why. It can't hurt anything at this point, I suppose."

She patted her coat. "Shit."

"What is it?"

"I won't be back here again. I'm done. We're done."

"What happened in Boston?"

"We talked to your brother, is what happened."

"Did you…"

"No. And he was helpful. He made the right choice. We got a lot from him. But most importantly he agreed to play along."

"Is he okay?"

"He's fine."

"It was four nights ago. Your buddies used him to let them into the Hancock. You were right, they were going to wire the elevators, more or less like you said, but with much bigger stuff. Much bigger. They threatened the shit out of your brother. He was going to do it too. If we hadn't gotten to him, or were ten days earlier or a few days later, it wouldn't have worked. We staked the place out, didn't take much, actually. They didn't suspect anything."

"Who was it? Who was there? Was it Marcel?"

She patted her coat again.

"Who?"

"All your old pals. Even Karim and Ali. They never left the country."

"Are they alive?"

"The Egyptians." Shaking her head. "Those buggers are tough, don't give up. They didn't make it out of the building." Here she smiled. "But Ali, Mr. Al-Jeddah. He was gunned down in a basement, died in an oil patch, face down." Her smile sank. "But they caused enough of a diversion that Karim slipped away."

"But surely he couldn't have gotten out of the city."

"He's a ghost. All that money, the friends. It's been weeks. Some people are beginning to whisper that he doesn't even really exist, that he's just a name…"

"He certainly exists."

"I know he does. And he is still our target. More now than ever. But we stopped what would have been the most devastating terrorist attack on US soil."

"But we lost him. Is Tully alive?"

She smiled. "Yes, and Khalid."

Fadi's mind filled with blood, and though he wanted to speak too many questions lodged in his brain. His breath became quick.

"It's okay. We have every intention of finding out if this rumor about Nadat is true. If it is, she's American. I've made that point very clear to everyone. It's set a fire under everyone where there was none. If those two know anything, believe me, I'll squeeze it from them. Tully will be particularly fun, that masquerading dingleberry." She made a fist and looked at it. "I am going to squeeze the *fuck* out of him. I'll tell you…"

"Thank you. Thanks, Emma."

"Sorry."

"Khalid is a gentle person."

"Gentle enough to blow up a thousand people."

"He will be the most susceptible to emotion. His heart is the key. If he knows Nadat is still alive, it must be killing him. He loves his daughters. He bought mine many gifts. Please use that."

In his mind he saw a shadowy form. It hung outside the window of his mother's home, and likewise just beyond the little window of his room, and it snaked down to some unknown place, a basement, where his daughter sat in a wood chair. He knew that shade would haunt his life, even if news of Marcel's death ever reached him.

He shook his head and gazed toward that tiny window, the light dying now. And he was quiet a while. "How is your son? Have you seen him, amidst all this killing?"

"He is good. He's huge now, like an orangutan, spindly arms flopping all over the place. He's adorable. I'll see him this weekend, doing another Caps game, load him up with Coke and nachos until he's sick." She finally checked her shirt breast pocket and found her cigarettes, took two from the pack.

She put both cigarettes in her mouth, lit them, and passed one to Fadi.

A long drag, his voice in smoke form, "What a lady."

EPILOGUE

The ends of his nubs were sore from the morning's practice, but a terrific soreness he'd not felt in some time. Using the prostheses had at first been like standing an apple on a toothpick, both in balance and tenderness. But by week two the old stability his brain knew had begun to return. He'd not been called upon to balance his body on anything but his back or his ass in over three years, and doing so on stilts seemed ridiculous. He was exhausted too in a way he'd not been since his shoddy escape attempt.

Sitting back in his wheelchair, he rubbed the end of one leg. Through the single, unbarred picture window he looked out on the small yard, wrapped by two layers of razor-wired fence. Though no leaves had fallen over the grass, in the distance the change in their color was unmistakable.

In this room light came with regularity through the large window, something he woke to most mornings and was allowed to watch as it dissipated beyond the wooded hills in the evening. A few of the guards here were decent enough, sharing the occasional game of chess or, at his suggestion, Risk. But he missed Emma, thought often of their walks out in the courtyard, over a year ago.

He'd been allowed a haircut yesterday and wore a crisp, white button-down shirt and khakis with a stiff crease in them, folded nicely below his thighs rather than tied off.

"Well, look at this picturesque, ambulatory shithead, peering out the window."

He didn't turn.

"Sorry, am I disturbing your special Fadi time?"

He pivoted his chair, met her with a cold gaze, which he held a few moments before bursting into a smile. Emma stepped toward him with her own grin and shook his left hand, made a slight stutter at some sort of embrace but thought better of it.

"I hear you're walking."

"Almost. Nearly ready to escape."

"I don't think you're winning any decathlons on those things. Maybe a pirate decathlon."

"Stranger things."

She nodded, dragged a chair across the floor, and sat. "How do I look?"

"As I remember." In fact, her face seemed a few years younger, her hair was a darker and richer color, and her eyes no longer held their dark circles. "How is Evan?"

"He's good."

"Are you seeing him often?"

"The same."

"You look done up."

"Had a date last night, figured I could use a makeover."

"How'd it go?"

She took from her coat a pack of nicotine gum. "About as satisfying as this." She popped one from the pack and shoved it in her cheek then motioned the pack to Fadi.

"No."

Then she took a pack of cigarettes from her breast pocket, made the same offer, to which Fadi simply shook his head. So she slid a stick from the pack and lit it. With a big drag, a long sigh. "Yes, that's the ticket." She turned her chair to look out the window, as did Fadi.

The far hills were streaked with assorted transitional colors, some still a deep green. The occasional cape-style house pocked the landscape.

"What have you been doing all this time?"

"Me? Out of the government business," she said, perhaps cheerfully. "Domestic again. Domestic *intrigue*."

"Do you like that?"

"There are some better things about it. The bad guys tend not to be so ambitious." She folded her hand below her elbow. "Sorry. Didn't mean that."

"How were you able to do this then?"

"Favors, my good man. Favors."

"How long has it been since you left?"

"A few months now. It got pretty slow after the whole thing."

They both faced forward, but Emma could see him nod. Then he was silent, but she knew he was nervous about later this afternoon.

"I don't know," she said. "That's the answer."

"To what?"

"The question you're too much of a pussy to ask. *I don't know.*"

"Does anyone even know what country he's in?"

"We have some guesses. But since I left I hear nothing. There's still an immense amount of power behind Thaghr, and money. This was a setback, but not too serious of one. Things are changing…the world is changing. Seems like now that the Soviets are through, this other sort is taking their place. If only in people's minds. But there's no shortage of volunteers in your business, and no shortage of funds. He'll be fine, if that's what you're worried about."

"That's exactly what I'm worried about."

Emma's grin sank a little, and she shook her head. "Well, don't be. No one will ever find your family. If there's one thing the government does well, it's protecting witnesses. That program is locked tight, no Tullys there. They'll be safe."

"They'll be safe from me."

She was silent then stood and walked to the sink, where she dabbed out the cigarette and spat out the gum. "Awful." Then she stood behind him.

"I know this was difficult to set up."

"It was a cinch."

"I will never forget it."

She laughed.

"Emma, I will never forget what you have done for me."

"This was easy enough."

"Not just this."

She patted his shoulder but could not meet his eyes.

He laughed. "I'm so nervous."

"You'll do fine. I got you something. Come here." She swung his chair around, pushed him over to the sink.

The face he saw in the mirror hadn't gotten much better over the years. Those two polar eyeballs, half his face molded in waxy scars, the fake bright teeth. Emma stood over him, sort of beautiful with her newly colored hair and fresh face.

"Voila." With a flourish she flung a red tie out in front of his face.

"What's this?"

"A tie, dummy. You want to look presentable like."

He laughed. "I haven't worn a tie in years."

"Well, you're wearing one today."

She crouched down in front of him, buttoned his collar, then stood behind him again as she flipped his collar up and set the tie around his neck.

"Funny, I haven't tied a tie in many years myself."

"Me neither."

"Let's see if I can remember." As her hands danced around his neck and shoulders, they confirmed what she'd thought on first seeing him. He'd put on weight, or regained his true flesh. Not the meager bones from before, but a more natural tone and volume. She looped the tie around.

"Emma." Looking at her in the mirror. "Emma."

She stopped, met his eyes in the mirror.

"Thank you."

She paused a moment, shrugged, and set her eyes back to the task of cinching the knot.

"Don't be tempted to squeeze that too tightly."

"I'll resist." A few adjustments, then she folded the collar back down, patted and wiped his shoulders because she'd seen people do that before. "Half bad."

She put both hands on his shoulders, and they both looked in the mirror, not at each other but at the picture framed there. A few more

341

seconds, then Emma patted his arm and bent over to kiss the top of his head. And she walked to the little table by the bed, set the cigarettes there. "For after." She went over to the door and opened it, held it for a moment as she glanced at him. "You'll do fine, Georges."

The door closed behind her and all was silent and still and he gazed at his own face in the mirror and could see himself clearly through the scar tissue and even believed he could see through that false eye. He blinked and shifted the tie with his left hand and checked the clock on the wall. Twenty minutes. He moved the knot on the tie once more and then looked right into his own eyes. *You are a father.*

ACKNOWLEDGEMENTS

This book owes much to my wonderful agent, Marly Rusoff, a brilliant editor and indefatigable source of hope for yours truly. Speaking of great readers, thanks to Laura Chasen for her incredible insight and kindness, along with editor Jason Letts for his five-yard-line magic.

Roland Merullo has been a mentor to me since college and the one ingredient without which the preceding recipe would be impossible. Beyond his writerly guidance, coaching, and bottomless generosity, I thank him here for mentoring me on being a better, kinder, and more gracious human being.

My lovely wife, Erin Palank Davies. Writing is solitary and lonely, but can also be a joy to share with the right partner. Erin is ten times the reader I am, and fifteen times the thoughtful soul. How I got so lucky would prove unbelievable in fiction.